THE SOUTHERNER

SOUTHERN CLASSICS SERIES

John G. Sproat and Mark M. Smith, Series Editors

THE SOUTHERNER

A Novel

WALTER HINES PAGE

NEW INTRODUCTION BY SCOTT ROMINE

THE UNIVERSITY OF SOUTH CAROLINA PRESS

*Published in Cooperation with the Institute for
Southern Studies of the University of South Carolina*

New material © 2008 University of South Carolina

Cloth edition published by Doubleday, Page & Company, 1909
Paperback edition published by the University of South Carolina Press,
Columbia, South Carolina 29208

www.sc.edu/uscpress

Manufactured in the United States of America

17 16 15 14 13 12 11 10 09 08   10 9 8 7 6 5 4 3 2 1

Library of Congress Cataloging-in-Publication Data

Page, Walter Hines, 1855–1918.
  The southerner : a novel / Walter Hines Page ; new introduction by Scott
Romine.
      p. cm. — (Southern Classics series)
    Includes bibliographical references and index.
    ISBN 978-1-57003-729-0 (pbk : alk. paper)
  1. Southern States—Fiction. I. Title.
    PS3531.A24S68 2008
    813'.52—dc22

                                                          2007042743

This book was printed on Glatfelter Natures, a recycled paper with
50 percent postconsumer waste content.

Publication of the Southern Classics series is made possible in part by the
generous support of the Watson-Brown Foundation.

CONTENTS

SERIES EDITORS' PREFACE

"In its thoroughly skeptical engagement with southern specters," writes Scott Romine in his beautifully crafted new introduction, "*The Southerner* is perhaps the most rationalist ghost story ever committed to print." The ghosts in Walter Hines Page's classic novel were the "neighborhood notions" of the past, the hidebound gender relations and religious convictions of the region, and the superstitions and traditions associated with the Lost Cause, specters Page considered thoroughly damaging to the stirrings of a progressive South. Few southern writers wielded as much influence as Page in the early twentieth century. As editor, publisher, and writer, Page functioned as spokesman for, and interpreter of, his region, at once deploring southern backwardness while also showing how the South might exorcise its pernicious ghosts. Entertaining and didactic, *The Southerner* grants modern readers access not only to the mind of a southern ambassador but to a powerful, enduring, and often arresting interpretation concerning the South's failures and potential.

Southern Classics returns to general circulation books of importance dealing with the history and culture of the American South. Sponsored by the Institute for Southern Studies, the series is advised by a board of distinguished scholars who suggest titles and editors of individual volumes to the series editors and help establish priorities in publication.

Chronological age alone does not determine a title's designation as a Southern Classic. The criteria also include significance in contributing to a broad understanding of the region, timeliness in relation to events and moments of peculiar interest to the American South, usefulness in the classroom, and suitability for inclusion in personal and institutional collections on the region.

MARK M. SMITH
JOHN G. SPROAT
Series Editors

INTRODUCTION

As a student at Harvard, Nicholas Worth comes to regret how "we hold to mere neighbourhood notions and superstitions and traditions of a day of blindness as sacred things, and follow now meaningless forms of worship, conceived in a time of scientific darkness; how we wrangle over governmental or social or educational formulas and doctrines 'of the fathers,' instead of banishing disease from the earth and organizing society to train a scientifically high-bred race!"[1] The tone here, as throughout Walter Hines Page's *The Southerner,* is of a rationalist's exasperation. Three decades before William Faulkner identified another southerner at Harvard, Quentin Compson, as a "barracks of ghosts," Page depicts "neighbourhood notions" as the South's ubiquitous phantasms, forever thwarting its social and economic potential. Although the presence of such phantasms had not gone unremarked prior to Page, his view of them was new, decidedly critical, and intrinsically linked to the progressive vision that characterized his engagement with the South throughout a long public career. More than a half century earlier, the South's leading antebellum man of letters, William Gilmore Simms, had offered a different, more conservative view of southern ghosts. The world had become so "monstrously matter-of-fact" that "we can no longer get a ghost story," Simms wrote in 1845, continuing that there is "reason to apprehend that in disturbing our human faith in shadows, we have lost some of those wholesome moral restraints which might have kept many of us virtuous." "It is to be feared," Simms affirmed, "that some of the coarseness of modern taste arises from the too great lack of that veneration which belonged to, and elevated to dignity, even the errors of preceding ages."[2] From the outset Page dispenses with such Burkean logic, calling his reader out from the cave of error and tradition—a single cave, he would emphasize—to see the light of day. In its thoroughly skeptical engagement with southern specters, *The Southerner* is perhaps the most rationalist ghost story ever committed to print.

The sensibility from which Page's sole novel emerged was long in the making. Born in 1855 in what is now Cary, North Carolina, a town later incorporated and named by his father, Page grew up in a prosperous and socially prominent household. The early sections of *The Southerner* closely follow Page's own life. Although Nicholas Worth's father is murdered in a robbery—an event with no parallel in the life of Arthur Page—his Whig politics and Unionist sentiments reflect those of Page's father. Page's grandfather owned a plantation in Wake County that provided a model for the "Old Place" of the novel, and Worth's educational career closely parallels his creator's. By all accounts a bookish youth, Page entered in 1868 the Bingham School in Mebane, North Carolina. Contemporary readers recognized the Graham School in Page's novel as a thinly disguised version of the military academy where Worth, as Page had, suffers the social disadvantage of having a father without a military title. In 1871 Page moved to Durham to attend Trinity College, which would become Duke University but was then a struggling school dominated by orthodox Methodism. Unhappy at Trinity and contemptuous of its academic standards, Page moved in January 1873 to Randolph-Macon College in Ashland, Virginia, where the relatively liberal atmosphere proved more to his liking. Like Worth, Page excelled at oratory, which was considered essential training for public careers in politics, the law, and the ministry. It was the last that apparently attracted the devout Page, who as late as 1874 indicated his plans to become a Methodist minister.

Such, however, was not to be. Although the exact reasons for Page's anticlerical turn remain unclear, an abortive romance and Page's enrollment in Johns Hopkins University contributed to his strong antagonism toward religion. In 1876 Page became romantically involved with Sarah Jasper, his mother's cousin. The romance apparently ended over a disagreement about religion, leading John Milton Cooper Jr., Page's best biographer, to speculate that "this early love must have helped form the pictures that Walter Page carried in his head of southern women as handmaidens of the preachers and the Confederates and thus as retrograde influences on their homeland."[3] Whatever its source, that picture clearly found expression in *The Southerner,* leading one reader to comment sharply that "when a man lays a rough hand on a people's women—we have a few who are wise, as well as good—, a people's religion—I believe there are some good and sincere ministers and laymen—, and a people's dead—they died for what they at least thought was right—, he cannot expect that people to listen kindly and patiently to any message he may bring."[4] Page's religious doubts were confirmed at Johns Hopkins, where he enrolled in 1876 as part of the university's first matriculating class. Although Page would relocate Nicholas Worth's intellectual emancipation to the Northeast and to Harvard University, Johns Hopkins was actually the more modern and forward-looking university at the time. Explicitly modeled on the German graduate university, Johns Hopkins invited the celebrated evolutionist T. H. Huxley to its opening convocation, raising, as Page wrote in a letter to Sarah Jasper, "a very great outcry against the godlessness" of his new school.[5] Although Page briefly attempted to reconcile faith and scientific inquiry, his outlook soon turned decidedly secular and anticlerical. At Harvard, Nicholas Worth remarks on "the freedom that I felt and the rest in having my own religious doubts dispelled" and later writes to a friend that in Cambridge, as in Germany and England, "every really independent mind has long ago thrown away those mediæval dogmas" (96–97). The sentiment, doubtlessly Page's own, marked a sharp contrast between Page and his cohort, even those progressives who shared his views on other matters. As Fred Hobson observes, "Page was one of the very few influential Southerners of his generation to place on religion so much of the blame for Southern shortcomings."[6]

Although Johns Hopkins provided Page with a new orientation toward science and culture, it did not provide him with a career. Trained in classics from a young age, Page considered entering academic life but found the rigorous philology of Basil Gildersleeve, Hopkins's classicist and a former Confederate soldier, dry and wearisome. Page's intellectual interests lay more in the direction of English literature, which he taught briefly at the University of North Carolina after leaving Hopkins in 1878 due to an illness. Searching for a more publicly engaged life than was possible in the ivory towers, Page turned to journalism, moving to Missouri in 1880 to become editor of the *St. Joseph Gazette*. A year later he published in the *Atlantic Monthly* his first important piece of cultural criticism. In "Study of an Old Southern Borough," Page called attention to the stagnation, inertness, and mental torpor of southern culture, themes that would thread their way throughout his later writing. For a "lad from an old borough," Page wrote, the "first dawning of his thought" causes him to "discove[r] for himself the mental stagnation of his surroundings" and to "se[e] the stupid way that is open for him at home." Rebellion means "immediate departure. For, if he begins to deliberate, he is apt to be caught by the spell of inertness, and live out his life and die before he decides whether to go away or not."[7] Although such thoughts presaged Page's eventual course of action, he would return, following a two-year stint at the *New York World*, to Raleigh,

North Carolina, just a few miles from his hometown. What brought him was a plan to found his own newspaper, the *State Chronicle,* which he hoped to use, like Henry Grady's *Atlanta Constitution,* as an organ for New South reform. While in Raleigh, Page joined with a group of like-minded progressives in the Watauga Club (thinly disguised in *The Southerner* as the "Club"), which advocated for industrial education and the creation of a polytechnic institution. Among its members were Charles W. Dabney; Josephus Daniels, who would succeed Page as editor of the *State Chronicle;* and Thomas Dixon Jr., with whom Page would have a long and conflicted relationship.

Despite North Carolina's abundant opportunities for the reform minded, Page stayed in Raleigh for little more than a year, returning to New York in February 1885. Although he would visit the South regularly, he would never again live there. His relationship to his native region would become that of its spokesman, interpreter, and admonisher. In *The Southerner* Page laments, in terms that precisely echo Du Bois's portrayal of African American double consciousness, the North's demand for the "'professional' Southerner" (388)—a demand that creates a "shadow that follows" (389) every southern man. But despite his protestations over this "dead man which every living man of us has to carry"—the "self-conscious 'Southerner' that is thrust upon" men like himself (390)—Page was the eminent professional southerner of his time, a "self-appointed but recognized ambassador from the South to the North," whose opinion, according to Cooper, was sought on any number of issues.[8] Page's arrival in New York coincided with a burst of writing, including articles on the South in the *Atlantic, Harper's,* the *Century,* and the New York–based *Independent.* But Page had hardly forgotten his native audience; he continued to send essays to the *State Chronicle,* culminating in his most celebrated attack on southern backwardness, the "Mummy letters" of early 1886. Responding specifically to North Carolina's refusal to support a state industrial school, the letters show little of the conciliatory, optimistic stance Page had often adopted as the paper's editor. Tar Heel traditionalists, he wrote, "don't want an industrial school. That means a new idea and a new idea is death to the supremacy of the Mummies. Let 'em alone. The world must have some corner in it where men can sleep and sleep and dream and dream, and North Carolina is as good a spot for that as any."[9] Geographically liberated from the inertial spell that he had long claimed threatened the independent thinker, Page caustically denounced southern traditionalism and the men who benefited from it, the "presumptuous powers of ignorance, heredity, decayed respectability and stagnation that control public action and public expression."[10] As in *The Southerner,* Page draws a crucial distinction between public and private speech. "Of the thousands of men who know I am writing the truth," he wrote in 1886, "not one in ten will say so publicly." Similarly Worth calls attention to the men who were "tolerant of all private opinions, privately expressed among men only" (314) but who "ruled by the ghost called Public Opinion" (315), suppressing any heterodox thought voiced publicly.[11] Not surprisingly Page soon became the object of vituperative response, although there was no shortage of southerners who viewed Page's criticisms as words the South needed to hear.

Page's criticisms, however, were tinged with a note of resignation. "We all think when we are young that we can do something with the Mummies," he wrote, "but the Mummy . . . lasts forever."[12] Although the themes of the Mummy letters echo throughout Page's novel, their publication marks a separation between Page's life and Nicholas Worth's: Worth's entrance into public life—first as the school superintendent in "Energetic Edinboro" and later as candidate for state superintendent of schools—has no parallels in the career of his creator. Page saw the Mummy letters as a way of burning his bridges to the South, where, he told his

father in an 1886 letter, there "is no [use] in my trying to do anything . . . any more."[13] For the remainder of his life, he would
remain deeply involved in southern affairs, but always at a distance and always, according to Cooper, slightly embarrassed that
he had not taken a more active role in them. Whatever the merits
of John Donald Wade's uncharitable assessment of Page as someone who sought to "straighten [the South] out by voluminous correspondence," it seems likely that Page used Worth as a way of
imagining what his own public life might have been had he
remained in North Carolina.[14] Certainly in Worth's deference to
the men of action around him—in particular, Professor Billy and
his brother Charles—we may read Page's own ambivalence about
the more passive and distant role he had chosen relative to his
native land.

Even from the North, however, Page's southern engagements
were sustained and productive. What Page's first biographer,
Burton J. Hendrick, calls "the main purpose of his life from earliest days"—"the improvement of American citizenship through
popular education"—led to a close relationship with Charles Duncan McIver, the model for Professor William Malcomb McBain.[15]
Along with Edwin A. Alderman, McIver had traveled throughout
North Carolina during the 1880s and 1890s conducting seminars
for teachers. In 1897 he invited Page to give the first commencement address at the State Normal College for Women, where he
served as president and which he, like Professor Billy in the novel,
was instrumental in founding. Page took the charge seriously,
writing McIver in March 1897 that he hoped to provide "a campaign document that would be serviceable in the great work you
are doing." "I should be prouder," he wrote soon after, "to say
something that would help this fight along than I am of anything
that I have ever done in my life."[16] The resulting speech, the Forgotten Man, struck a chord. According to Hendrick the speech
"immediately passed into the common speech of the South,"

serving as a touchstone for education reformers throughout the region. C. Vann Woodward characterizes the speech as offering a pure formulation of the "philosophy of redemption by philanthropy," while Charles W. Dabney called it "the gospel of the campaign that followed."[17] Vividly rendering the "forgotten man," Page offered a picture of North Carolinian squalor the likes of which had not been seen since William Byrd's depiction of Lubberland. Illiterate, "content to be forgotten"—a dupe and a dead weight—the forgotten man, Page affirmed, did not exist outside the South and existed there only because of its neglect of public education. Nor did Page neglect the "forgotten woman"— "thin and wrinkled in youth," as he described her, "from ill-prepared food, clad without warmth or grace, living in untidy houses, working from daylight till bedtime at the dull round of weary duties, the slaves of men of equal slovenliness, the mothers of joyless children—all uneducated if not illiterate."[18] As an antidote to the forgotten man and woman, Page offered education as a form of attention, of *memory* in a region tyrannized by the dead cult of Lost Cause remembrance.

Cemented by the popularity of the Forgotten Man, Page's reputation as a leading spokesman of educational reform led to his appointment in 1901 to the Southern Education Board. Founded by Edgar Gardner Murphy, an Episcopalian priest in Montgomery, Alabama, and Robert C. Ogden, a New York philanthropist, the Southern Education Board sought to replicate throughout the South McIver's and Alderman's grassroots efforts in North Carolina. Page served as a national spokesman for the group, delivering speeches, writing editorials, and widely publicizing the group's various projects. The board's success in facilitating what Woodward calls the "great educational awakening in the South" can be gauged by the sharp rate of growth in educational spending. Between 1900 and 1913, expenditures more than tripled throughout the South and more than quadrupled in North

Carolina, which, according to Woodward, took the lead in educational reform due in no small measure to the efforts of Page, McIver, Alderman, and Charles B. Aycock.[19]

Page's most important service as southern ambassador—and indeed his most important contribution to American letters—came as editor and publisher. In 1887 Page had joined the *Forum* as its business editor, rising to the position of editor in 1891. Combining investigative journalism, book reviews, current events, and articles tracking the trends of the day, the *Forum* increased its audience as Page helped to reconfigure the American magazine as a middle-class institution. In 1895 he became an assistant editor at the *Atlantic Monthly* and at Houghton, Mifflin and Company, two august New England institutions that had lost market share to New York magazines and publishing houses. In 1896 Page became editor of the *Atlantic,* although he continued to cultivate authors for Houghton, Mifflin. Among the most important of these was Charles W. Chesnutt, who wrote *The Conjure Woman* (1899) in response to a request from Page.[20] At the *Atlantic* Page sought to broaden the magazine's traditional emphasis on literature and culture to include articles on political, social, and economic issues. Despite his success in increasing the magazine's readership, Page left in 1899 and soon after started his own publishing house with Frank N. Doubleday. Due in no small measure to Page's sharp editorial eye and sound business sense, Doubleday, Page and Company soon became one of the nation's foremost publishing houses. Beginning as the American publisher of the British writer Rudyard Kipling, the firm quickly expanded its list to include Ellen Glasgow (whom Page had cultivated at Houghton, Mifflin), Mary Wilkins, and Booker T. Washington. Washington's *Up from Slavery* was written at Page's suggestion—not surprisingly, given Page's deep respect for Washington, the two men's shared sense of the necessity of vocational education, and Page's commercial interest in the autobiographies of important

Americans.[21] Despite a moralistic streak Page was compelled by literary naturalism and its frank examination of working-class life. As editor of the *Atlantic* he had tried to attract Stephen Crane, and among the earliest books in Doubleday, Page's catalog was Frank Norris's masterpiece, *The Octopus.* Page was also instrumental in the publication of Theodore Dreiser's *Sister Carrie,* which Frank Doubleday wanted to refuse on moral grounds despite the support it garnered from his partner and from Norris, who served as the chief reader of manuscripts.

Certainly the firm's most notorious writer was Thomas Dixon Jr., who published four novels with Doubleday, Page that each sold hundreds of thousands of copies. For publishing Dixon—a decision that was largely his, since Norris had urged the rejection of Dixon's first manuscript—Page was privately admonished by Washington and, more harshly, by W. E. B. Du Bois, who refused Page's editorial overtures by writing to Page that he could never publish with "the exploiters of Tom Dixon."[22] Although Page's later derogatory comments toward Dixon suggest that commercial considerations drove his decision, there are curious parallels in the worldviews of the two men. Like Page, Dixon had little patience with Lost Cause remembrance and the mythologies of the Old South. In his first novel, *The Leopard's Spots* (1902), Dixon celebrated the Spanish-American War as part of the "resistless tide of the rising consciousness of Nationality and World-Mission," while Page had vigorously supported the war in the *Atlantic,* celebrating the "management of world-empires" that sprang from "the adventurous spirit of our Anglo-Saxon forefathers"—a race characterized by a "restless energy in colonization, in conquest, in trade, in 'the spread of civilization.'"[23] Sharing Dixon's messianic sense of Anglo-Saxon mission, Page admitted in 1902, in terms that reiterated Dixon's central message, that he had "long doubted whether a democracy could absorb two different races thus living together and yet apart."

Only the "practical results of right training," Page continued, could ameliorate race antagonism.[24]

In "The Rebuilding of Old Commonwealths," the *Atlantic* essay from which these passages are drawn, Page articulated the intersection of the two themes—the need for public education and the "race problem"—that would occupy much of his attention on the Southern Education Board and as editor at Doubleday, Page. As with Houghton, Mifflin and the *Atlantic,* the practice of linking a publishing house with a magazine was common at the time, and Page's new firm soon started a magazine, the *World's Work,* that would claim most of his editorial attention. In many ways the prototype of the modern news magazine, the *World's Work* contained numerous articles on the problems of race and education. As editor, Page devoted far more attention to the South and to African Americans than other magazines of the time.[25] Booker T. Washington, as both author and subject, frequented the magazine's pages, as did the efforts of the Southern Education Board. But despite his numerous publications and position as one of the nation's most influential editors, Page had never authored a book prior to 1902, when *The Rebuilding of Old Commonwealths: Being Essays toward the Training of the Forgotten Man in the Southern States* appeared from Doubleday, Page. Collecting its title essay along with "The Forgotten Man" and "The School That Built a Town," a 1901 speech describing how a public school transformed a backward southern town, *The Rebuilding of Old Commonwealths* was the only book Page would ever publish under his own name. According to William A. Link, "No single document better exemplifies the mood, spirit, and objectives of the Progressive Era in the South" than Page's title essay.[26] Reiterating what had become his standard themes—the need for public education, the stultifying effects of tradition—Page added a new emphasis on slavery as the institution that "deflected" the "Southern people . . . from their natural development." "These old commonwealths," Page wrote, "were arrested in their development by slavery and by war and by the double burden of a sparse population and of an ignorant alien race."[27] Unsubtly echoing the concept of the "white man's burden," Kipling's phrase that Dixon had used in the subtitle of *The Leopard's Spots,* Page signaled his rejection of racial egalitarianism. To be sure, Washington himself had strategically used the concept in his landmark 1895 address at the Cotton States and International Exposition in Atlanta, noting that the South's black population would "contribute one-third to the business and industrial prosperity of the South, or we shall prove a veritable body of death, stagnating, depressing, retarding every effort to advance the body politic."[28] Although Page followed Washington in insisting that vocational training for "the Negro" would relieve the burden he posed, a tendency toward racial stereotyping—including a predilection for speaking of "the Negro"—pervades his writing. In a campaign speech that illustrates the paradox of Page's racial thinking, Nicholas Worth affirms that "the Negro . . . is a burden and a menace unless he is trained. So, too, is the white man. But the Negro is a child in civilization. . . . He is docile, grateful, teachable. He is a man" (251). A *man,* and yet somewhat *less* than a man ("docile, grateful"); *like* the white man and yet *unlike* him a "child in civilization"—such are the contradictions embedded in Page's concept of race, contradictions by no means unique to Page among white southern progressives. McIver and Alderman, for instance, refused to join Page when he dined with Washington in Saratoga Springs, New York, and several members of the Southern Education Board feared that Page's refusal to adhere to southern racial taboos would scandalize the populace they sought to enlist in their campaign for educational progress.[29]

Three years after *The Rebuilding of Old Commonwealths,* Page published anonymously *A Publisher's Confession,* a series of letters on the publishing industry that had appeared in the *Boston*

Transcript. In 1905 he also began, during a period of convalescence following a streetcar accident, what would appear the following year as "The Autobiography of a Southerner since the Civil War." Published serially in the July, August, September, and October 1906 issues of the *Atlantic,* the "Autobiography" appeared under the pseudonym "Nicholas Worth" but otherwise presented itself as a factual record. "I have changed names and places in the story and disguised some incidents," wrote the author, "not essential facts, only because it is unfair to give publicity to some old deeds and opinions of former enemies that we are all willing to forget."[30] From the beginning readers sought to *place* the narrative, to understand the kind of reality claims it made. Proclaiming that "Walter Page is the 'Southerner,'" the *Raleigh News and Observer* applauded the "fresh, vigorous, graphic style" of the work, noting the "peculiar ear-marks that will make it specially interesting to the people of North Carolina."[31] North Carolinians easily recognized Greensboro (Edinboro), Raleigh (Marlborough), and Chapel Hill (Acropolis), as well as McIver (Professor Billy), Senator Matt Ransom (Senator Barker), and Josephus Daniels (the editor of the *White Man*).

Other readers, especially those at a distance, found the story's connections to reality altogether more tenuous. The *Columbia (S.C.) State* called the narrative "a charmingly written story, and an exceedingly plausible one—to that class of people in the North which reads the Atlantic Monthly." "Some of the characters are real ones, with their names changed," the review continues, "but the story as a whole never happened, never could have happened. It was made to fit the New England theory of the South, and it does this admirably."[32] Professor Waldo Adler of the University of the South wrote Bliss Perry, Page's successor at the *Atlantic,* expressing regret that the author had published anonymously. A colleague at Sewanee, Adler explained, had claimed that the author was no southerner and the narrative "merely a clever piece of faking." Seeking to rebut such charges, Adler demanded that Perry "affirm, Sir, upon your personal authority what has been previously stated anonymously and in the advertising pages of your magazine, viz., that the author of these articles was born in the South, of old Southern ancestry, of Southern sympathies, and that the facts stated in 'The Autobiography of a Southerner' are literally true."[33] Far from naive, such reactions respond to the generic ambiguity of the text; with no clues other than those associated with the genre of autobiography, it is no wonder that readers came to radically different conclusions regarding the text's origins, the identity of its author, and the story's relation to the empirical world.

Such questions reappeared when, after revising and expanding the work, Page published in 1909 *The Southerner: A Novel; Being the Autobiography of Nicholas Worth.* As an anonymous review in the *Dial* announced, "When 'The Autobiography of Nicholas Worth' [*sic*] was appearing serially in 'The Atlantic Monthly,' we took it at face value as a truthful record of personal experience. Now, to our considerable surprise, it is called 'The Southerner,' and published as a novel." As the *Sacramento Bee* explained, "Those two words of explanation, 'A Novel,' are all that save the reader from accepting in sober seriousness the genuiness [*sic*] of Nicholas Worth and his autobiography. For the book has all the earmarks of the real autobiography, in its fidelity to the little details and the introduction of that which would seem almost extraneous in a simon-pure work of fiction, but quite belongs to biographical data."[34] In fact this was somewhat less true of *The Southerner* than it was of Page's *Atlantic* version. As Page revised, he sought to employ a less discursive, more scenic and literary style; dissertations on a cotton economy such as open the "Autobiography" are toned down, if not eliminated, in the later version.

Critical comparisons of the two texts have tended to understate their differences. Not only is *The Southerner* nearly twice as long

THE SOUTHERNER

A NOVEL

BEING THE AUTOBIOGRAPHY OF

NICHOLAS WORTH

NEW YORK
DOUBLEDAY, PAGE & COMPANY
1909

The title page of Walter Hines Page's 1909 novel, *The Southerner* as the earlier version, Page changed important plot details and introduced substantial new material. He eliminated a subplot wherein Worth loses a professorship at the state university to a "broken down old Methodist preacher" who teaches "only the Confederate narrative of the Civil War," while greatly expanding the account of Worth's campaign for state superintendent of schools, which serves as the novel's dramatic center.[35] Likewise the character of Professor Billy is greatly enhanced, possibly as a result of Charles McIver's untimely death in 1906: among other things, Page used the novel to memorialize the man he called "the best fellow & the most untiring & patriotic & public spirited citizen of any state."[36] In *The Southerner* Professor Billy shares equal billing with Worth's brother Charles as men who "loved their fellows and found life sweet in toiling for them" (407). In the *Atlantic* version Charles stands alone as the exemplary man of action. "A thousand men such as my brother," Worth writes, "would change the course of history in a generation."[37] (Perhaps as compensation for the slight demotion, Page allows Charles to survive in *The Southerner;* in the earlier version he is killed trying to prevent a lynching.) Nicholas's courtship of Louise Caldwell does not exist in the earlier version, nor does his plan to become a Unitarian minister appear in the later one. Perhaps most important the narrative arc of the two stories differs in structure and tone. In a late chapter entitled "The Shadow Again," Page depicts in the earlier version the rise of racist demagogues who, predicting a "flood of African despotism," are assisted by "popular" novels "describing the crimes and social aspirations of the Negro."[38] In contrast to the demagogic threat lurking ominously at the conclusion of the "Autobiography," *The Southerner* ends on an altogether more optimistic note. Not only are references to the racist novels eliminated—having published the most lurid and popular of these with Dixon's Reconstruction trilogy, Page had perhaps some qualms on the matter—the shadow of racist demagoguery is relocated to the campaign section of the novel, leaving its sunnier conclusion to "The Fruits of Victory" and the marriage of Nicholas and Louise. Indeed the reason Professor Billy does not run for the state superintendent of schools in the "Autobiography" is that he must head the already-established state college for women; in *The Southerner* the founding of the college is deferred until the end of the novel, where it appears as one of victory's sweetest fruits.

Published by Doubleday, Page on September 25, 1909, at a retail price of $1.20, *The Southerner* experienced tepid sales. By February 1, 1910, the novel had sold, according to the publisher's records, only 2,692 copies, netting Page a meager $323.04 in royalties. By August 1 of that year, only 192 additional copies had been sold, and Page's royalties had declined to $23.04. The commercial failure of novel was not due to any lack of support on the part of its publisher. In an undated letter "TO THE TRADE," Doubleday, Page announced to its distributors a special run of a thousand copies to be sent to "one or two of the most influential persons whose names you send us—persons who will read and discuss the book in literary or other clubs, in the pulpit or in the press."[39] In addition, Doubleday, Page sent complimentary copies of the novel to public school superintendents throughout the South, as well as to professors and administrators at colleges (both black and white) throughout the nation. Despite its practical failure, this word-of-mouth campaign left a rich archive of contemporaneous responses to *The Southerner:* along with the novel went a request for informal responses to it, more than two hundred of which survive in the archives of Harvard University's Houghton Library. Some responses were reproduced anonymously in an advertising pamphlet Doubleday, Page distributed proclaiming *The Southerner* to be "THE Novel of the South." "A Professor from the South in a Northern College," for example, is cited as saying, "It makes me wish to go back and work again in the South." (The professor in question was the historian John

Spencer Bassett, whom Page had publicly supported when Bassett, as a professor at Trinity College, had publicly ranked Booker T. Washington alongside Robert E. Lee as great southerners.) But despite the pamphlet's insistence that "critics of all shades of opinion agree that *The Southerner* is a story that will be read for a long time—*not a novel that will pass with the season,*" it was a novel that passed with the season, remaining out of print until now.[40]

The reasons for the novel's poor sales were clear to many of Page's early readers. The New York–based *Editor and Publisher* called *The Southerner* "an extraordinary novel" but suggested that it would "hardly grip the average reader." Observing that "the author frequently editorializes on politico-economic things that are just now salient in the great progressive movement going on in the South," the review concludes that the "present day novel reader does not pardon an editorial in a novel." In *A Publisher's Confession,* Page had written that "the chief reason for the success of a novel is the commonplace one that it contains a story. . . . And the chief reason for failure is the lack of story."[41] Despite his revisions Page was, in the eyes of many readers, unable to take his own advice. Bruce R. Payne of the University of Virginia Summer School called the work "a mixture of essay and novel, more of the former than of the latter," and suggested that "it would probably have been better to have written the volume as essays rather than a novel." (In many ways Page already had.) Lowell M. McAfee, president of Park College in Missouri, wrote, "I take it the plot of the story is of the least consequence, as compared with the desire of the writer to enunciate his theory of the rejuvenation of the South."[42] In a review that supported Page's political message, the *Louisville Courier-Journal* opined that "the book deals too much with the author's theories to be a work of art. . . . It is a novel, but it is a socio-political novel." Even the *Boston Herald* found "too many didactic paragraphs and 'preachy' suggestions." Among less sympathetic reviewers, assessments were harsher. In the *Raleigh*

News and Observer, edited by Page's erstwhile protégé Josephus Daniels, University of North Carolina history professor J. G. de Roulhac Hamilton savaged the novel, writing that the "story drags along, interrupted at intervals by vague soliloquizing and much philosophizing, most of it based on false premises."[43]

Not all reviews, however, found the novel aesthetically unsatisfying. Apparently mistaking the nature of the narrative, the *Tattler* of London wrote that Mr. Nicholas Worth's "autobiographical novel" bears out the claim that "every man could be the author of at least one enthralling story—the story of his own life." "It is all so vividly told," the review continues, "so pathetically and yet at times so humorously expressed, that one reads on and on from page to page as if one were indeed really listening to the stories from the mouths of the chief actors themselves." The *Richmond Times-Dispatch* concurred, writing that "in the narration of events there is a terse vividness rendering them highly dramatic, a play of humor that overlooks no mirth-provoking detail." The novel "pulsates with virile force . . . its utterance is vital, not lifeless, from the beginning." Many readers responded favorably to the novel's realistic style. William Dean Howells, the high priest of American literary realism, wrote Page that he had read *The Southerner* with "great interest and admiration." "I know Southerners only a very little," Howells confessed, "for I have not been south of Williamsburg, but your book bears evidence of . . . the truth which does not need the corroboration of knowledge in the spectator."[44]

The reality effect of Page's novel depends, as the *Sacramento Bee* observed, on its "fidelity to the little details" and its complementary fidelity to the disorganized nature of actual lives. In stark contrast to Dixon's melodramas of white supremacy, *The Southerner* lacks altogether an organized plot of rising action, climax, and denouement. Noting that "readers of Thomas Dixon, Jr.'s hysterical romances of Civil War times may doubt that there is a place for another novel on the Reconstruction period," the *Colorado Springs Gazette* favorably contrasted Page's realistic approach. "The fact is," the *Gazette* continued, "that the first real Reconstruction novel has just appeared. . . . As an antidote for the Dixon stories, 'The Southerner' cannot be too strongly recommended."[45] Although sales figures would suggest the liabilities of Page's style, it is altogether appropriate that, in a work so critical of southern romanticism, Page rejected the conventions of literary romance. More surprising is that Page rejected the satirical approach of Mark Twain, who used bracing ridicule as an antidote to what he diagnosed as the South's "Sir Walter disease." Where Ellen Glasgow countered the South's evasive idealism with "blood and irony," Page countered in a tone of earnest correction, albeit one infused by exasperation and, at times, no small measure of contempt. But whatever its liabilities, commercial or aesthetic, Page's style is particularly suited to Worth's engagement with white southern culture, an engagement marked by careful observation, analysis, and a predilection for puncturing cultural myths. More than education or politics, the novel's primary theme is what constitutes reality in a culture Page depicts as historically averse to it. Put another way, the nature of reality defines the terrain over which the novel's educational and political battles are fought. In the oratorical orbit that the narrative so carefully locates traditional southern education, Worth finds reality to be conspicuously absent. "We thought in rotund, even grandiose, phrases," Worth writes of the "oratorical habit of mind." "Rousing speech came more naturally than accuracy of statement" (93). He observes later, "It became plainer and plainer to me that there is nothing real in the oratorical zone. The real things here are these pines and the sea, these two old men, my brother's work and the cotton fields, Professor Billy and his unwearying plan for a college for girls. The rest is a hollow sham, or sheer inertia" (304).

But one man's hollow sham is another man's tradition, as both Page and his ideological opponents were well aware. What Page critiques as the oratorical zone has been defended as the rhetorical mode by southern conservatives from Allen Tate to Eugene Genovese. Succinctly juxtaposing rhetoric and dialectic, M. E. Bradford defines the former as "reasoning from axiomatic or 'assumed' principles," while the latter is "defined by an interest in first causes and a disposition to seek the truth through refinements of definition or debate." In "Remarks on the Southern Religion," his contribution to the Agrarian manifesto *I'll Take My Stand,* Allen Tate contrasts Thomas Jefferson's rhetorical "reliance on custom, breeding, [and] ingrained moral decision" with John Adams's "'process of moral reasoning,' which forces the individual to think out from abstract principles." According to Eugene Genovese in *The Southern Tradition,* a "world self-consciously experienced" assaults the "deepest feelings" of southern conservatives and "their belief that men ought to take that world, natural and social, as a given."[46] In "The Rebuilding of Old Commonwealths," Page acknowledges the self-evident nature of tradition as viewed from the inside. "These men and women do not feel poor," he writes. "They have a civilization of their own, of which they are very proud. . . . If you propose to change any law or custom, or are suspected of such a wish, or if you come with a new idea, the burden of proving its value is on you. What they are they regard as the normal state of human society."[47] Although (curiously) Page remarks as a curiosity what is surely a universal disposition toward innovation, even an acknowledgment of this kind is absent from *The Southerner,* where, following Worth's initiation into "eager and frank inquiry" (99), tradition appears as nothing more than a set of dead and stultifying formulas.[48] Where once he was blind, now Worth can see, and his anticonversion entails a rejection of religion in all its forms, from the sectarian machinations of the Reverend Doctor Suggs to the cult of the Lost Cause.

That Page houses the latter's relics in St. Peter's Church is no coincidence; nor, one suspects, is his burning the church to the ground.

Although *The Southerner* contained, as Hobson says, Page's harshest criticism of the South since the Mummy letters, the novel surpasses the letters in its attack on southern religion. Page had written to William P. Trent in 1896 that "any discussion of religious influence in the South which does not say strictly, point-blank and with emphasis, that the intellectual life of the people has been hindered unspeakably by the narrowness of religious opinion falls something short of the most important fact that needs to be said about the South."[49] That *The Southerner* said precisely this—more or less strictly, point blank, and with emphasis—was not lost on contemporary readers. E. A. Noble, president of the Woman's College of Baltimore, spoke for many of novel's recipients in writing to Doubleday, Page that "the book does not do justice to formal Christianity, as represented by the Protestant church." Even Bassett conceded that there were at least a few "clear headed preachers in the South." In a bitter review in the *Independent,* Mrs. L. H. Harris wrote that the author of *The Southerner* was unable to write the "spiritual history of the South" because he was "too stupefied by his educational intoxication." Worth thus emerges as "a pedagog who had lost his need of religion by squeezing his soul thru an intellectual sausage grinder at Harvard." More gently the *Mobile Register* called the novel a "sermon worth hearing" but regretted that "the book will probably be withheld from general reading and its value as a text book of the new South lessened by the religious attitude confessed in this autobiography." By dwelling on what "should have been regarded by him as negligible," the review continues, the author "shuts up the text book to thousands who will be forbidden to read it."[50]

Many responses to *The Southerner* followed the *Register*'s strategy, trying to separate the novel's progressive message from its more controversial criticisms. Page's educational and economic themes were received warmly in many quarters, although often viewed as unnecessary in a South that had progressed far beyond the one depicted in the novel. Clarence Poe, editor of Raleigh's *Progressive Farmer,* wrote to Doubleday, Page, "I do not doubt but that the author of 'The Southerner' intended not only to be fair, but wrote with real love for the South; nevertheless I think our section today has progressed immeasurably beyond the weaknesses and backwardness of twenty years ago. As a picture of contemporary Southern life I should say frankly that the story is strongly overdrawn." After all, asked the *Raleigh News and Observer,* hadn't North Carolina spent \$2,863,217.79 on public education for the 1906–7 school year? Less defensively the *Nashville Banner* wrote that the novel "contains enough of the truth to make it in some respects valuable and possibly it may be wholesome for the South to learn some of the lessons it seeks to impress. . . . But to endeavor to separate the South from its attachment to the memories of the past is something aside from such practical undertaking of any form of progress."[51] Such efforts run directly counter to the narrative's strategy of aligning the South's various ghosts as, in effect, a cumulative form of haunting. What amounts to Page's trinitarian doctrine of southern ghosts is suggested by Colonel Stringweather's list as he maneuvers to remove Worth as school superintendent in Edinboro: "*First:* In the Name of Our Holy Religion. . . . *Secondly:* In the Name of our History and our Honoured Dead. . . . *Thirdly:* In the Name of our Anglo-Saxon Civilerzation" (180). As Worth concludes, "Against the Church, and the ex-Confederates and the Pious Lady and our Honoured Dead and Anglo-Saxon 'Civilerzation,' nothing could prevail" (181). In the 1906 version Worth had gone further in collating these "three elemental forces," writing that "the Church, the race question, and the hands of dead men . . . together made the ghost called Public Opinion."[52] For Page, progress required precisely that the South detoxify itself from its cultural addiction to ghosts.

This meant, among other things, that the South acquire a clear sense of its own history. Sharply critiquing the spectral forms of Civil War remembrance, Page spared not even the veterans, writing that "they were dead men, most of them, moving among the living as ghosts; and yet, as ghosts in a play, they held the stage" (46). "The prevalent notion of the Civil War," Worth claims later, "fostered by the Veterans and the Daughters, was erroneous. . . . The people did not know their own story" (150). Embedded in Worth's efforts as historian is a capacious understanding of the cultural role of historiography. New South advocates such as Henry Grady had sought to mobilize a detoxified image of the Old South as a way of creating the New, a common feature, according to Tom Nairn, of nationalist movements generally, which often tell progressive narratives by inventing usable pasts, by "looking inwards, drawing more deeply upon . . . indigenous resources, resurrecting past folk-heroes and myths."[53] Strictly disavowing the supplementary iconographies of the Lost Cause and of antebellum moonlight and magnolias, *The Southerner* tells the story of the South, as Professor Billy puts it, "that nobody knows anything about" (123). Against Colonel Stringweather's inflated rhetoric of an antebellum civilization wherein "illimitable wealth and boundless content were present everywhere" (198)—an image consigned to the "rhetorical orbit" (199)—Worth offers a corrective history in the pamphlet he writes for the schools of Edinboro. In order to "lay the foundations of a new sort of patriotism," he goes "further backward": the people "must get away from thoughts of war. . . . They must know the forgotten story of their grandfathers and of their great-grandfathers, who were men that worked" (149). Because "traditions had long been accepted as facts" (149), facts—such as the "plain, historical fact" (180) that two southern governors threatened to secede from the Confederacy—must be used to puncture traditions. In contrast to Ernest Renan's classic formulation that nationalism depends on forgetting and thus is threatened by professional historiography, Page suggests that an empirical record cleansed of error might serve as the basis of a new patriotism. If, as the *Lexington (Ky.) Leader* claimed, *The Southerner*'s "chief value is historical . . . [as] a sane, honest, impartial and just document for the use of the future historian," its value is not merely archival but also as a meditation on how historiography is used by culture.[54]

This is not to say, of course, the novel lacks archival value. It assuredly has such value, most notably as it intervenes in contemporaneous discourses of race. In his 1903 *Souls of Black Folk,* Du Bois had declared the problem of the twentieth century to be the problem of the color line, and *The Southerner* engages that problem with complexity and, one must add, evasion. Where, on the subject of southern ghosts, Page's strategy is cumulative, his narrative works in the other direction in detaching Progressivism from the white supremacist doctrines to which it was often linked. Although the Club of *The Southerner* works solely for education reform, the Watauga Club on which it was modeled evolved into a seat of white conservative politics. Besides Dixon, among its original members was Josephus Daniels, who had become a leading advocate of white supremacy and a staunch foe of the Republican-Populist coalition that had won important victories in the North Carolina state elections of 1894 and 1896. Dixon had excoriated that alliance in *The Leopard's Spots* as the party of racial mongrelization. While Page hardly endorses its broader political themes in *The Southerner*—indeed Worth's attachment to the Republican-farmer alliance is nearly accidental—the narrative is clearly more hostile toward the racist demagoguery of Democratic Party and its allies in the press, most prominently the *White Man,* modeled on Daniels's *Raleigh News and Observer.*[55] Charles B. Aycock, who had written Page a warm letter in the aftermath of the Mummy letters, won the North Carolina governorship in 1900, two years after the 1898 "Redeemer" election that restored Democrats to power on a platform of reform and white supremacy. Always a strong proponent of public education, Aycock provided a model for Charles Gaston, the hero of *The Leopard's Spots,* who, like Tom Warren in Page's novel, is married on his inauguration day. But while the climax of Dixon's novel consolidates the purity of the white race, Warren's triumph is compromised by the appearance of Uncle Ephraim and the specter of miscegenation. In "The Governor's Inauguration," Page powerfully juxtaposes the voice of white romance—"Such a galaxy of beauty and chivalry, sir, cannot be found in any other capital of the world" (360)—with the black voice that precedes it and, proclaiming that "it gwine ter be bad times some o' dese days fur de col'ed people" (359), still lingers and reverberates.[56] Moreover, in the figure of Julia, the illegitimate daughter of Tom Warren who moves north and passes as white, Page offers one of the few nontragic mulattos in American fiction.[57]

Perhaps most provocatively, Page diagnoses the "Negro-in-America" as a "form of insanity that overtakes white men" (104). Although the immediate occasion for this observation is northern racial insanity, its southern strain is equally in evidence, both collectively, as when "the hidden forces of madness and fear" (265) are unloosed by the racist tactics of the Democratic managers, and individually, as when Captain Bob Logan, the Republican candidate for governor cheated of his office, is committed to the state asylum, where he raves of how the "black brute then choked the sense out of him, left his mind emaciated, with its tongue hanging out, like a dog's—the mind of the whole people with its red tongue hanging out, slobbering lies" (365). Not until Ralph Ellison's *Invisible Man* (1952) and its narrator's visit to the Golden Day would the uncanny capacity of lunatic ravings to expose racial truths be so powerfully explored. Almost literally Captain Bob embodies the reductio ad absurdum of Worth's observation that "we have permitted ourselves in fact to be ruled—in our minds and actions and emotions and character and fears—by the One Subject. We had for three long generations been really ruled by the Negro" (269). But even as he endeavors to speak to "white men" "straight, as God is my witness" (250), Worth consigns the Negro to a passive position. His "definition of the Negro in the United States" as a "person of African blood (much or little) about whom men of English descent . . . easily lose their common sense, their usual good judgment, and even their powers of accurate observation" continues to position the Negro as an object of white subjectivity (104). Complaining that white southerners "become weary of being a problem" (391), Page finds it difficult to think of the Negro as anything but. By offering vocational education as a panacea— as one of his "one-shot remedies to social ills," to use Cooper's language—Page evaded the truly daunting obstacles facing African Americans in the Jim Crow South. As Hobson fairly puts it, Page "did not ever speak boldly, in public address or in print, of the pathos and tragedy of the black American. . . . [He] was one of those Southerners 'ruled' by the Negro, silenced or at least subdued by that 'ghost' of the freedman he himself identified."[58]

In the final analysis the achievement of *The Southerner* lies in its depiction of those other ghosts—the ghosts of the church, the Lost Cause, and "Anglo-Saxon Civilerzation"—as they collectively exerted massive resistance against change. In another context Patricia Yaeger suggests that "the dead—not as the facts but as the 'figures' of history—feed revolutions," their "spectrality" offering the "metaphoric foundations of the new" and providing "the tropes we push off from, or push away from, in order to suggest other, more utopian orders."[59] Page would contest the point. Social progress, he would say, is not achieved through utopian scheming. "When a better social and economic order does come," Worth comes to realize, "it will not come by any 'system' of economics or other doctrine, but by the definite personal work of a long succession of great leaders of the people and by the slow tuition of experience" (406). But in pushing away from what he regarded as the dead specters of the traditional order, Page tried to imagine what a southerner—indeed, what a South—might be in the aftermath of ghosts, systems, and formulas. Had he written the novel he was pondering in 1911—a notebook entry of that year reads "Novel of Present So. Life. Sequel to N. W."—Page might have left a clearer sense of that South.[60] But that novel was never to be written. Page soon found himself embroiled in the world of politics, culminating in his appointment by Woodrow Wilson as ambassador to Great Britain during the Great War. As it was, he left in *The Southerner* a classic document of the Progressive era. Aside from Ellen Glasgow, no southern novelist of the time looked so critically at the cultural myths organizing southern culture; no one, including Glasgow, documented so well how those myths shaped the public terrain on which the work of progress was forced to proceed.

NOTES

1. Walter Hines Page, *The Southerner: A Novel* (Columbia: University of South Carolina Press, 2008), 99 (hereafter cited parenthetically in text). Originally published as *The Southerner: A Novel; Being the Autobiography of Nicholas Worth* (New York: Doubleday, Page, 1909).

2. William Gilmore Simms, "Grayling; or, 'Murder Will Out,'" in *Tales of the South,* ed. Mary Ann Wimsatt (Columbia: University of South Carolina Press, 1996), 80.

3. John Milton Cooper Jr., *Walter Hines Page: The Southerner as American, 1855–1918* (Chapel Hill: University of North Carolina Press, 1977), 29.

4. C. G. Vardell to Doubleday, Page, 13 January 1910, Walter Hines Page Papers, Houghton Library, Cambridge, Mass. All materials from the Walter Hines Page Papers cited in this introduction are found in *The Southerner* file (box 12). I would like to thank Chloe Yellin and the staff of the Houghton Library for their assistance in my research.

5. Walter Hines Page to Sarah Jasper, 15 October 1876, quoted in Burton J. Hendrick, *The Training of an American: The Earlier Life and Letters of Walter H. Page, 1855–1913* (Boston: Houghton Mifflin, 1928), 71.

6. Fred Hobson, *Tell about the South: The Southern Rage to Explain* (Baton Rouge: Louisiana State University Press, 1983), 169.

7. Walter Hines Page, "Study of an Old Southern Borough," *Atlantic Monthly,* May 1881, 654.

8. Cooper, *Walter Hines Page,* 107.

9. Walter Hines Page to the *State Chronicle,* 1 February 1886, in Hendrick, *Training,* 176. The letter was published on February 4.

10. Walter Hines Page to the *State Chronicle,* 8 February 1886, in Hendrick, *Training,* 183. The letter was published on February 11.

11. Walter Hines Page to the *State Chronicle,* 1 February 1886, in Hendrick, *Training,* 181.

12. Walter Hines Page to the *State Chronicle,* 1 February 1886, in Hendrick, *Training,* 176.

13. Walter Hines Page to A. Frank Page, 12 May 1886, quoted in Cooper, *Walter Hines Page,* 80.

14. Cooper, *Walter Hines Page,* 81; John Donald Wade, "Old Wine in New Bottles," in *Selected Essays and Other Writings of John Donald Wade,* ed. Donald Davidson (Athens: University of Georgia Press, 1966), 159. For an account of Page's negative reception among the Nashville Agrarians, see Hobson, *Tell about the South,* 159–60.

15. Hendrick, *Training,* 389.

16. Walter Hines Page to Charles D. McIver, 29–30 March 1897, Charles Duncan McIver Papers, University of North Carolina at Greensboro; Walter Hines Page to Charles D. McIver, 18 April 1897, McIver Papers. I thank the staff of the Special Collections at UNC–Greensboro for their assistance in my research.

17. Burton J. Hendrick, *The Life and Letters of Walter H. Page* (Garden City, N.Y.: Doubleday, Page, 1925), 75; C. Vann Woodward, *Origins of the New South, 1877–1913* (Baton Rouge: Louisiana State University Press, 1951), 397; Charles W. Dabney, quoted in Woodward, *Origins,* 401.

18. Walter Hines Page, "The Forgotten Man," in *The Rebuilding of Old Commonwealths: Being Essays toward the Training of the Forgotten Man in the Southern States* (New York: Doubleday, Page, 1902), 22, 24.

19. Woodward, *Origins,* 400–401. Out of Page's work with the Southern Education Board came his involvement in another philanthropic venture, the

Rockefeller Commission for the Extermination of the Hookworm Disease, which Page was instrumental in founding in 1909.

20. For a balanced account of Page's role in the creation of *The Conjure Woman,* see Richard Brodhead, introduction to *The Conjure Woman and Other Conjure Tales,* by Charles W. Chesnutt (Durham, N.C.: Duke University Press, 1993), 15–21.

21. Doubleday, Page would go on to publish important autobiographical works by Jane Addams, Helen Keller, Andrew Carnegie, and William Howard Taft, among others.

22. W. E. B. Du Bois to Page, n.d., in *The Correspondence of W. E. B. Du Bois,* vol. 1, *Selections, 1877–1934,* ed. Herbert Aptheker (Amherst: University of Massachusetts Press, 1973), 113. I thank John David Smith for calling my attention to this exchange. For Page's exchange with Washington, see Cooper, *Walter Hines Page,* 168–69; apparently the disagreement was not severe enough to damage the professional relationship between the two men. Page compounded his error by advertising *The Leopard's Spots* alongside Washington's *Up from Slavery,* a strategy that may reflect Page's view that Dixon's perspective deserved a public venue. Somewhat disingenuously, he wrote to Du Bois that even Dixon, "who stands for what I regard as my enemies' doctrine," should be allowed "freedom of opinion." See Du Bois, *Correspondence,* 114.

23. Thomas Dixon Jr., *The Leopard's Spots: A Romance of the White Man's Burden, 1865–1900* (New York: Doubleday, Page, 1902), 435; Walter Hines Page, "The War with Spain, and After," *Atlantic Monthly,* June 1898, 725, 727.

24. Walter Hines Page, "The Rebuilding of Old Commonwealths," in *The Rebuilding of Old Commonwealths,* 125.

25. For a statistical overview of the number of articles on the South published in magazines edited by Page, see Charles Grier Sellers Jr., "Walter Hines Page and the Spirit of the New South," *North Carolina Historical Review* 29 (October 1952): 492.

26. William A. Link, preface to *The Rebuilding of Old Commonwealths and Other Documents of Social Reform in the Progressive Era South,* by Walter Hines Page (Boston: Bedford Books, 1996), v.

27. Page, "Rebuilding," 152–53, 139–40.

28. Booker T. Washington, *Up from Slavery,* ed. William L. Andrews (1901; repr., Oxford: Oxford University Press, 1995), 130.

29. See Cooper, *Walter Hines Page,* 146, 211–13.

30. [Walter Hines Page], "The Autobiography of a Southerner since the Civil War," *Atlantic Monthly,* July 1906, 2.

31. "Walter Page Is the 'Southerner,'" *Raleigh News and Observer,* 5 September 1906.

32. Review of "Autobiography," *Columbia (S.C.) State,* undated clipping, Walter Hines Page Papers.

33. Waldo Adler to Bliss Perry, 7 November 1906, Walter Hines Page Papers.

34. Review of *The Southerner, Dial* (Chicago), 16 November 1909; review of *The Southerner, Sacramento Bee,* 13 November 1909.

35. [Page], "Autobiography," 176.

36. Walter Hines Page to Charles D. McIver, 29 September 1903, Charles D. McIver Papers.

37. [Page], "Autobiography," 480.

38. [Page], "Autobiography," 484, 486.

39. Publisher's records, Walter Hines Page Papers; promotional materials, Walter Hines Page Papers.

40. Promotional pamphlet, Walter Hines Page Papers; John Spencer Bassett to Walter Hines Page, 3 October 1909, Walter Hines Page Papers. In the letter from which the blurb is drawn, Bassett, who had moved to Smith College as a professor of history, elaborates that he does not wish to perform "the same kind of work" but rather "to retire on a Carnegie pension and go down there to give all my time to writing about the South, trying to explain the causes of her history."

41. Review of *The Southerner, Editor and Publisher,* 13 August 1910; [Walter Hines Page], *A Publisher's Confession* (New York: Doubleday, Page, 1905), 41.

42. Bruce R. Payne to Doubleday, Page, 23 March 1910, Walter Hines Page Papers; Lowell M. McAfee to Doubleday, Page, 10 January 1910, Walter Hines Page Papers.

43. Review of *The Southerner, Louisville Courier-Journal,* 4 December 1909; review of *The Southerner, Boston Herald,* 13 November 1909; J. G. de Roulhac Hamilton, "'Nicholas Worth' Regards the Confederate Veterans, the Dead and the Church as Obstacles to Southern Progress," *Raleigh News and Observer,* clipping, Walter Hines Page Papers.

44. Review of *The Southerner, Tattler* (London), 2 March 1910; review of *The Southerner, Richmond Times-Dispatch,* 3 January 1910; W. D. Howells to Walter Hines Page, 24 March 1910, Walter Hines Page Papers.

45. Review of *The Southerner, Colorado Springs Gazette,* 21 December 1909. This review mistakenly speculates that Frank Doubleday is the author of the novel.

46. M. E. Bradford, "Where We Were Born and Raised," in *The Reactionary Imperative: Essays Literary and Political* (Peru, Ill.: Sherwood Sugden, 1990), 115; Allen Tate, "Remarks on the Southern Religion," in *I'll Take My Stand: The South and the Agrarian Tradition,* by Twelve Southerners (1930; repr., Baton Rouge: Louisiana State University Press, 1977), 170; Eugene D. Genovese, *The Southern Tradition: The Achievement and Limitations of an American Conservatism* (Cambridge, Mass.: Harvard University Press, 1994), 20.

47. Page, "Rebuilding," 116–18.

48. After reading *The Southerner,* Edgar Gardner Murphy suggested to Page that "in your reaction from formulas you have only exchanged one set for another." Still, Murphy continued, "every man of the South with a deep faith in him ought to *tell* his faith; we need a wholesome self-analysis, from many points of view." Murphy to Walter Hines Page, 16 October 1909, Walter Hines Page Papers.

49. Hobson, *Tell about the South,* 173; Walter Hines Page to William Peterfield Trent, 6 October 1896, quoted in Cooper, *Walter Hines Page,* 145.

50. E. A. Noble to Doubleday, Page, 11 January 1910, Walter Hines Page Papers; Bassett to Walter Hines Page, 3 October 1909, Walter Hines Page Papers; Mrs. L. H. Harris, "A Southern's [*sic*] View of 'The Southerner,'" *Independent,* 11 November 1909; review of *The Southerner, Mobile Register,* 17 October 1909.

51. Clarence Poe to Doubleday, Page, 23 December 1909, Walter Hines Page Papers; "Resurrection of the South, with a Refutation of Some Slanders, and Mention of the Novel, Nicholas Worth," *Raleigh News and Observer,* 3 April 1910; review of *The Southerner, Nashville Banner,* 9 October 1909.

52. [Page], "Autobiography," 163.

53. Tom Nairn, *The Break-up of Britain* (London: New Left, 1977), 348.

54. Review of *The Southerner, Lexington (Ky.) Leader,* 16 November 1909.

55. In "The 'White Man' and the 'Cotton Boll'" and subsequent chapters, Page accurately depicts the role of North Carolina newspapers in cultivating white supremacist feeling. For an account of how white Democratic papers politicized trivial incidents during the 1898 campaign, see Edward L. Ayers, *The Promise of the New South* (New York: Oxford University Press, 1992), 300.

56. Uncle Ephraim's complaint that the new regime "don' give no schools lak dat un I seed, whar de fetch up de young uns to hones' wuk" (359) echoes Page's concern that educational reform in the South had become a strictly segregated affair. In 1910 he wrote, "There is overwhelming testimony that the Negro in some parts of the South—I fear in many parts—does not receive anything like a square deal in the distribution of public school money, particularly in the country." Page to Wickliffe Rose, 24 February 1910, quoted in Cooper, *Walter Hines Page,* 216–17.

57. One review noted disapprovingly that "the author chronicles, without the protest or dissent which a clear visioned man would feel impelled to record, the marriage of an educated octoroon to a white man in the North." Review of *The Southerner,* undated clipping attributed to the *Fort Worth Record,* Walter Hines Page Papers. As Cooper observes, "Page had touched on a subject that almost no white novelists, northern or southern, would confront frankly until 1943, when Lillian Smith published *Strange Fruit.*" Cooper, *Walter Hines Page,* 201. One exception is Dixon's *The Sins of the Father* (1912), which depicts (likely in response to Page's novel) the horrific consequences resulting from a white man's illegitimate child with his African American housekeeper.

58. Cooper, *Walter Hines Page,* 228; Hobson, *Tell about the South,* 179.

59. Patricia Yaeger, "Consuming Trauma; or, The Pleasures of Merely Circulating," *Journal X* 1, no. 2 (1997): 235.

60. Page, notebook entry, quoted in Cooper, *Walter Hines Page,* 204.

THE SOUTHERNER

CHAPTER I

THE FRINGE OF WAR

ONE day when the cotton fields were white and the elm leaves were falling, in the soft autumn of the Southern climate wherein the sky is fathomlessly clear, the locomotive's whistle blew a much longer time than usual as the train approached Millworth. It did not stop at so small a station except when there was somebody to get off or to get on; and so long a blast meant that someone was coming. Sam and I ran down the avenue of elms to see who it was. Sam was my slave, philosopher, and friend. I was ten years old and Sam said that he was fourteen.

There was constant talk about the war. Many men of the neighbourhood had gone away somewhere—that was certain; but Sam and I had a theory that the war was only a story. We had been fooled about old granny Thomas's bringing the baby, and long ago we had been fooled also about Santa Claus. The war might be another such invention, and we sometimes suspected that it was. But we found out the truth that day, and for this reason it is among my clearest early recollections.

For, when the train stopped, they put off a big box and gently laid it in the shade of the fence. The only man at the station was the man who had come to change the mail-bags; and he said that this was Billy Morris's coffin and that he had been killed in a battle. He asked us to stay with it till he could send word to Mr. Morris, who lived two miles away. The man came back presently and leaned against the fence till old Mr. Morris arrived, an hour or more later.

The lint of cotton was on his wagon, for he was hauling his crop to the gin when the sad news reached him; and he came in his shirt sleeves, his wife on the wagon seat with him.

All the neighbourhood gathered at the church, a funeral was preached and there was a long prayer for our success against "the invaders," and Billy Morris was buried. I remember that I wept the more because it now seemed to me that my doubt about the war had somehow done Billy Morris an injustice.

Old Mrs. Gregory wept more loudly than anybody else; and she kept saying, while the service was going on, "It'll be my John next." In a little while, sure enough, John Gregory's coffin was put off the train, as Billy Morris's had been,

and I regarded her as a woman gifted with
prophecy. Other coffins, too, were put off from
time to time. About the war there could no longer
be a doubt. And, a little later, its realities and
horrors came nearer home to us, with swift, deep
experiences.

One day my father took me to the camp and
parade ground ten miles away, near the capital.
The General and the Governor sat on horses
and the soldiers marched by them and the band
played. They were going to "the front." There
surely must be a war at the front, I told Sam that
night.

Still more coffins were brought home, too, as
the months and the years passed; and the women
of the neighbourhood used to come and spend
whole days with my mother, sewing for the soldiers.
So precious became woollen cloth that every rag
was saved and the threads were unravelled to be
spun and woven into new fabrics. And they baked
bread and roasted chickens and sheep and pigs
and made cakes, all to go to the soldiers at the
front.

My father had not gone into the army. He
was a "Union man" and he did not believe in
secession. I remember having heard him once
call it a "foolish enterprise." But he could
not escape the service of the Confederate Government, if he had wished; and, although he opposed

the war, he did not wish to be regarded by his neighbours as a "traitor." The Government needed the whole product of his little cotton mill, and of a thousand more which did not exist. He was, therefore, "detailed" to run the mill at its utmost capacity and to give its product to the Government. He received pay for it, of course, in Confederate money; and, when the war ended, there were thousands of dollars of these bills in the house. My mother made screens of one-hundred-dollar bills for the fireplaces in summer.

I once asked her, years afterwards, why my father did not buy something that was imperishable with all this money, while it had a certain value — land, for instance.

"Your father would have regarded it as dishonourable to use money in this way which he knew would lose its value; for this would have been taking advantage of the delusion of his neighbours."

Thus the thread that the little mill spun went to the making of clothes for soldiers and bandages for the wounded — mitigated human suffering somewhat, it is now pleasant to think; and thus it happened that my father was at home when the noise of cannon came. It was in the first soft days of spring. There was a battle at Marlborough, they said. Would they fight here, too? The slaves were terror-stricken. What was going to happen to them? Would they be carried off and shot? Old Aunt Maria, the cook, shouted throughout the day:

"Dey say dat de niggers'll be free. I ain't gwine ter have none o' deir freedom, I ain't. May de good Lord carry me erway in er chariut o' fire."

Officers in gray came to the house all day and all night and all the next day. Their horses pawed the lawn and ate the bark from the mimosa trees. Coming and going, asking for food and drink, all talked loudly, their swords clanking, and big pistols hung from their saddles.

Colonel Caldwell, my father's old friend, was one of these officers; and he and my father sat by the fire a long time that night talking in sad excitement. My mother in after years recalled their conversation to me.

My father said that the war ought immediately to be ended, that our army ought to give up, that there was no chance of success, and that no more men ought to be killed.

"True, true," said Colonel Caldwell, "but they are invading our homes. They are despoiling and starving the innocent. Shall we tamely submit? Shall we be cowards? Your own home, Worth, may be plundered before another night."

"As for me," he went on, "even if I were relieved of my command on this line of retreat, I should not dare be found at home when they come. That would mean death or capture. God knows what will become of my family. My wife expects me to call at home to-morrow to tell her what to do. I can but ride by and go on."

"Sacrificing more men," said my father, "every cruel day."

"Men!" exclaimed the Colonel. "What of it? So long as the conflict goes on, we cannot regard the life of a soldier. Its very cheapness is the basis of all war. We have become used to death. It is better than to go to starve in prison. If I must die, let me die fighting."

"But, after that, what?" my father asked. "Even if we could win, the country is dead. That is the thought that troubles me—the coming anarchy."

Then the roll of musketry was heard down the road.

"God save you, Caldwell"; and the Colonel and his companions rushed to their waiting horses and rode away in the moonlight.

We now all lived in my mother's room. I remember that my father sat by the fire with his face buried in his hands. The bed had been taken from the bedstead and put on the floor, because the floor, being below the windows, was a safer place from bullets. I was lying on it, my brother Charles beside me, and my mother held the baby in her arms.

I had feverishly heard all that had been said; and it seemed to me that the end of the world was about to come. The earth rolled toward me. In a moment it would crush us all. Then, as I held my breath, the great globe became light as air and floated away. The feverish dream came again and I cried out. My mother caressed me. Then she took the baby again and sat at the fire by my father, with one hand on his knee.

And soon after daylight the blue-coated cavalry of the "Yankees" came down the road. They had a little cannon on a horse and they put it on the high ground behind our garden and shot a ball clean through John Root's shanty, far down the road. John's old mother believed the rest of her days that when it struck the house she was killed and went to heaven. She met her husband there, and he told her that they had plenty of rations in the army of the Lord and that they slept in houses with gold window sashes. He had been a carpenter.

And that night the Union officers occupied my father's house. A colonel made his headquarters in the parlor, and he appropriated two bedrooms upstairs. But a good deal of work had to be done during the afternoon to make them comfortable for him; for, before he came, looting cavalrymen of his regiment had run their swords through the beds, looking for hidden silver; and the hearth had been torn up on the same quest. I saw one soldier who had three silver pitchers hanging from his saddle.

Old George, a lame slave, a simple old man, hovered during the day about the back porch, to be near the white people, and a Union soldier thrust a pistol in his face.

"Say, old man, tell it quick or I'll blow your head off—where is everything hidden here?"

Old George fell on his knees.

" 'Fore God, Marster, don' shoot a poo' old nigger—your 'umble sarvant"; and, in an ashamed, frightened way, he led the "bummer" up the back stairs to the place in the ceiled wall through which many things had been put into the garret of the "ell." The soldiers broke into this hiding place and found food, and little else. In their chagrin they brought out sacks of flour, cut the bags and emptied it on the floor through the bedrooms and down the stairs. Thus the Colonel walked to his bayonetted bed up a stairway strewn and packed with flour, and slept in a room where the bricks that had been torn from the hearth were piled to right and left.

I slept that night on a trundle bed by my mother's, for her room was the only room left for the family, and we had all lived there since the day before. The dining room and the kitchen were now superfluous, because there was nothing more to cook or to eat.

An army corps built its camp-fires under the great oaks and cut their emblems on their trunks, where you may see them to this day; and, while they were there, the news came one day that Lincoln had been killed. I heard my father and the Union General talking about it; and, so solemn was their manner, I remember it clearly. The news that somebody had been killed had become so common that more than the usual solemnity was required to impress any particular death on the mind.

A week or more after the army corps had gone, I drove with my father to the capital one day, and almost every mile of the journey we saw a blue coat or a gray coat lying by the road, with bones or hair protruding—the unburied and forgotten of either army.

Thus I had come to know what war was, and death by violence was among the first deep impressions made on my mind. My emotions must have been violently dealt with and my sensibilities blunted—or sharpened? Who shall say? The wounded and the starved straggled home from hospitals and from prisons. There was old Mr. Sanford, the shoemaker, come back again, with a body so thin and a step so uncertain that I expected to see him fall to pieces. Mr.

Larkin and Joe Tatum went on crutches; and I saw a man at the post-office one day whose cheek and ear had been torn away by a shell. Even when Sam and I sat on the river-bank fishing, and ought to have been silent lest the fish swim away, we told over in low tones the stories that we had heard of wounds and of deaths and of battles.

But there was the cheerful gentleness of my mother to draw my thoughts to different things. I can even now recall many special little plans that she made to keep my mind from battles. She hid the military cap that I had worn. She bought from me my military buttons and put them away. She would call me in and tell me pleasant stories of her own childhood. She would put down her work to make puzzles with me, and she read gentle books to me and kept away from me all the stories of the war and of death that she could. Whatever hardships befell her (and they must have been many) she kept a tender manner of resignation and of cheerful patience. There was a time—how long I do not know—while Aunt Maria was wandering about looking for the "freedom" for which she had said she did not care, when my mother did the cooking for the family; and I remember to have seen her many times in the wash-house scrubbing our clothes.

I have often wondered, and no doubt you have,

too, at the deficiencies of the narratives that we
call history; for, although they tell of what men did
with governments and with armies, they forget the
pathetic lack of tender experiences that has ever
fallen to war-shortened childhood, and the child-
lessness of women who never had mates because
the men who would have wed them fell in battle
in their youth. In histories of this very war I have
read boasts about the number of men who per-
ished from a single State!

After a while the neighbourhood came to life
again. There were more widows, more sonless
mothers, more empty sleeves and wooden legs than
anybody there had ever seen before. But the
mimosa bloomed, the cotton was planted again,
and the peach trees blossomed; and the barnyard
and the stable again became full of life. For,
when the army marched away, they, too, were as
silent as an old battlefield. The last hen had
been caught under the corn-crib by a "Yankee"
soldier, who had torn his coat in this brave raid.
Aunt Maria told Sam that all Yankees were
chicken thieves whether they "brung freedom
or no."

The little cotton mill was again started, for I
must tell you, in the very beginning, that the
river ever ran and the mill kept turning; and I
should be ungrateful if I allowed you to forget
that on every year, whose events will be told

in this book, the cotton bloomed and ripened and opened white to the sun; for the ripening of the cotton and the running of the river and the turning of the mills make the thread not of my story only but of the story of our Southern land—of its institutions, of its misfortunes and of its place in the economy of the world; and they will make the main threads of its story, I am sure, so long as the sun shines on our white fields and the rivers run—a story that is now rushing swiftly into a happier narrative of a broader day.

The same women who had guided the spindles in war-time were again at their tasks—they at least were left; but the machinery was now old and worked ill. Negro men, who had wandered a while looking for an invisible "freedom," came back and went to work on the farm from force of habit. They now received wages and bought their own food. That was the only apparent difference that freedom had brought them.

My Aunt Katharine came from the city for a visit, my Cousin Margaret with her. Through the orchard, out into the newly ploughed ground beyond, back over the lawn which was itself bravely repairing the hurt done by horses' hoofs and tent-poles, and under the oaks, which bore the scars of camp-fires, we two romped and played gentler games than camp and battle. One afternoon, as our mothers sat on the piazza and saw us come loaded with apple-blossoms, they said something (so I afterward learned) about the eternal blooming of childhood and of nature—how sweet the early summer was in spite of the harrying of the land by war; for our gorgeous pageant of the seasons came on as if the earth had been the home of unbroken peace.

CHAPTER II

A MEMORY OF EBENEZER

AND soon a school opened its doors at Millworth. There were twenty pupils, I suppose, some of whom walked a long way, to sit all day on benches that were high and stiff and hard. A young lady from the Female Seminary, whom my Aunt Katharine had commended, taught it, I have no doubt, with as great patience as inefficiency.

The school was a very solemn thing, since it naturally leaned heavily on religious instruction; and Miss Cic'ly Wyatt had a strong faith in Sacred History, for which, I dare say, the Seminary was to be blamed or commended, as you will. One of the text-books, as I yet vividly recall, was a Sacred Geography, which took much of our time. Palestine was "bounded" day after day, and the height of Mt. Pisgah was recited over and over again. Where was the grave of Moses? Into what does the River Jordan run?

When I asked Sam this question, he replied: "She run into de ocean, some'hers."

"No."

"Don't she run into de ocean nowhar't all?"

"No."

"Den it's one er dem mericles."

If the truth were told, our own little river was far more interesting than the Jordan, for it had fish in it and there were two boats on the pond; but the school, like the war and the church, was an institution; and I learned, even at this early age, that nobody tells the whole truth about institutions. They prefer to accept traditions and to repeat respectful formulas. Miss Cic'ly herself was interesting when she went fishing or rowing, but at school she was professional.

Yet the school was frivolity itself beside the religious "revivals" which were held in country churches with especial violence in the late summers of those years. As the war strain on the emotions was relaxed, religious excitement was, I suppose, the most natural exercise for country people who had no sports.

The cotton had been hoed for the last time, and the "protracted meetin'" was begun at Ebenezer church, two miles from home.

The Reverend Abner D. Babb, who "rode the circuit" that year, had made the announcement the month before that "a meetin' would be held, to call for an outpourin' of the Holy Speerit, to the conviction of sinners, the reclaimin' of backsliders and the sancterfication of the chillun of God."

All the neighbourhood gathered that Sunday,
and in every buggy and wagon there was a bountiful dinner. The horses were unhitched and tied
to the trees. The women went into the church
and all sat on one side of the house. The men
gathered in groups outside and exchanged neighbourhood news till Lewis Sorrell's voice was heard:

> "Am I — a sol — jer of — the cross,
> A fol — wer of — the lamb ?"

Then the men solemnly marched in. By the
time the hymn was sung, the congregation was
seated. Mr. Babb's bald head rose out of the
old box-pulpit and he read another hymn. After
that had been sung, he read an awful passage from
Revelation about the Last Day.

Still another hymn was sung and the terrifying
tones of old Lewis's voice, as he shut his eyes and
bawled along the corduroy tune, were enough to
frighten the most hardened sinner. He saw a
vision of the wicked burning in Hell and he
rejoiced, and he quickened his pace somewhat,
for he had intimations of the ecstasy that was to
overcome him an hour later.

The Reverend Mr. Babb selected as his text a
sulphurous sentence, and he preached and spat
himself into a spasm.

"Amen!" groaned old Lewis at proper intervals; and Miss Anna Baucomb, the mute of the
neighbourhood, swayed to and fro.

"We invite all those who wish to flee the wrath to come to kneel at the front seats while the congregation sings."

Little Tillie Downie, a ten-year-old, boo-hoo'd in her intense conviction of sin and ran to the front bench.

"Come, my sister, seek peace in the Lord — the first sinner to seek forgiveness." The singing of the hymn went on. Other children wept and rushed forward.

"There are older and more hardened sinners in thy presence, O Lord. Smite 'em with a conviction of sin, as with a red-hot iron. Come down, Holy Speerit and move 'em!"

This was too much for Bill Jenkins, the wickedest boy in the neighbourhood. Bill "perfessed" at every revival, for he became a backslider in good time to pile up a fresh load of sins for the next awakening. He knelt and Mr. Babb kindly laid his hand on his head. Bill blew his nose and sobbed. The hymn dragged on wearily.

Then the congregation was dismissed for dinner. The religious excitement did not weaken appetite. Every housewife had her best food —Mrs. Person her famous pickles and jellies, Mrs. Thomas her best spiced and iced cakes, and Mrs. Ellis her boiled ham. From buggy to buggy and from wagon to wagon calls were made and returned, and at every one good cooking was praised and famous recipes were swapped. A well-fed content with life and a natural cheerfulness would soon have come over the company, as at a picnic, if old Lewis's voice had not broken forth again:

"Je — sus, lov — er — of my soul —"

The dishes and the baskets were hastily put away, and the company marched again into the church as to a funeral procession, all the men on one side, all the women on the other. Refreshed, the Rev. Mr. Babb roared more loudly:

"Havin' purtaken of nourishment for the physical man, we will ask the Speerit of the Mos' High to descen' like a dove an' feed us manna for our souls." And the rafters rang with his prayer. "Bless God, there's grace strong enough to move mountains — to save us in battle, to sway cannon-balls from their courses, and to save sinners, even the wust sinners in all this worl'."

The allusion to cannon-balls frightened old Jonas Good'in, who had been a deserter in war-time. He had stood in particular dread of cannon-balls. He argued now that, if God had turned one from its course and saved him, it was time that he made acknowledgment of his obligation. When the prayer was ended old Jonas, hairy and heavy, arose; he put his quid from his mouth, he wiped his beard on his sleeve, and, with a shame-faced motion, he went forward to the mourners' bench.

"The wust sinner can be saved!" shouted old Lewis, before he began the next tune; and, while the singing went on, the preacher flung forth exhortations in a triumphant tone, as much as to say, "In the very beginning of the meetin', we've bagged the biggest game in the wilderness."

I remember the hint of a smile that I am sure played over my father's face when old Jonas walked to the mourners' bench with the manner of a captive.

While the battle against sinners had been waged inside the church, Sam had fallen asleep in the wagon, guarding the dishes and thinking of what he should do when the " 'vival season" came at the Negro church and Aunt Maria should fall to shouting.

When I woke him up, he asked:

"Did he git you?"

"Who?"

"Mars' Jesus at de mou'ners' bench."

There was an indescribable terror in this violent religion for me, and (I suspect) for my mother, too. The preacher came home with us, for he was in some way remotely akin to us — or his wife was. He was bald and forbidding. He called me "sonny," and he spoke of God as if he managed the world for Him. He held family prayers, and he prayed so loud that old Aunt Maria, who knelt in the hall just outside the parlour door, began to shout. Sam sneaked away to the kitchen in terror. I felt more fright than I had felt on the night when the "Yankees" came; and I asked my mother if I should go to the mourners' bench the next day.

"Do you want to go, Nick?"

"No, mother."

"Well, you stay at home, then."

But my brother Charlie was sick and gave us much concern, and the preacher had prayed so long and so loud for his recovery, that I had said to God:

"God, if you will cure my brother Charlie, I'll go to the mourners' bench and be snatched from the burning."

It lay heavily on my mind, whether I ought not to trust God sufficiently to fulfil my part of the bargain first. But, when the next day came, I was glad to shift the responsibility to my mother, and to stay at home. Yet the terror and the gloom of that week, as I heard reports from the meeting, I can recall now. I had an impulse to run from home till it should end, for there was no school while the meeting lasted; and the next week even the solemn dullness of Miss Cic'ly's routine was a relief.

But you would fall into error if you supposed that even the terrifying preacher permanently darkened the cheerful spirit of my boyhood any more than it permanently frightened old Jonas out of his cowardice and away from his bottle. For I had a joyful and mellow place to visit, a place that was a sort of shrine, which happily was not associated in my mind with the horrors either of war or of religion. It was my grandfather's plantation, which we called the Old Place.

CHAPTER III

NOW, if you would clearly understand the story that I am to tell, and the confused vision and the groping through the mist (for this was a dark time of our country for youth to find its way) you must know the background of my life. What a medley of experiences go to the making of a man! Therefore, I say that, if you wish to get the key to my story, you must remember that an autobiography is like a gentleman in this — that it begins with a grandfather. And, as for me, it is surely true that my grandfather was the beginning of me.

He was Nicholas Worth, for whom first my father was named, and then I. He was yet hale at a very old age. He lived at the Old Place a few miles from the state capital (the capital city, we called it), and he had lived there all his long life, in the very house where he was born. It had received additions first on one side, then on another, and a "new house," itself now fifty years old, had been built and the two houses were connected by a porch. The Old Place and the

old man antedated the State and, of course, the
capital itself.

The story was untrue that he had been a
drummer-boy in the Revolutionary war, for he
was not born in time. But his father served under
General Washington; and, after the war, he came
from an older colonial settlement into this wilderness, as it was then, where good land could be
had for the taking; and thus the Old Place came
to be built by Revolutionary hands.

And it was a real piece of the past. Later
wars, even this most desperate latest war between
the states, had seemed to touch it only lightly.
True, two sons of the house had been killed; but
even this ghastly experience had not changed
the historic relations of the place nor of the man.
They seemed to belong to the century before. The
Old Place was the oldest house in the region, the
old man was the ruling patriarch, and the traditions and the flavour and the manner of the old times
clung so firmly to both that intervening events,
even tragedies, were easily forgotten. Besides,
every family had lost sons in this war, and the
loss of sons conferred no special distinction.

And the old man had done his thinking before
the period of secession. He used both idioms
and premises that had long gone out of fashion.
He regarded the war as an error. He had lived
through it as a good sailor goes through a storm.

However strong the wind may blow, he knows that, when it passes, the sea will be calm again. The old man was too old, as I was too young, to take part in the thought or in the fighting of the time. We, at least, had been saved from danger to body and from the worst distortions of mind. If his thought had for a time been interrupted, he had taken it up where he had left it off, as a man becomes himself again after a bad dream.

As every lucky child has a Great Place to go to, the Old Place served this gracious use for me. It was ten miles away from my father's home, and the drives between them had been my chief journeyings. The Old Place was the background of my life, therefore, a sort of home back of my own home. The visits that I had made there were the happiest times of my childhood, for I felt that all things were stable there. The mellowness of the place, the ripened wisdom of the old man, the cool quiet of the library were parts of the foundation of things; the garden with box-hedges and beds of sage and thyme and a row of fig trees by the fence — the odours of these have made my memory of the place savoury and pleasing through whatever barren stretches I have traveled in any period of my life. Plenty and Welcome, too, had their abode there, even during the days of severest privation.

The slave quarters were still kept, most of them, by the same families of Negroes that had lived there in bondage. My grandfather's especial servant, Uncle Ephraim, had not been away in search of freedom at all, for no one could think of the old master without Ephraim, nor of Ephraim without his old master. They had for a long generation been the embodied wisdom for big house and quarters. Each had the habit of talking to the other even when the other was out of hearing. When my grandfather would rouse himself from a nap on the piazza, he would ask, "What d'you think of that, Ephraim?" even if Ephraim were a mile away; and Ephraim used to mutter to himself, as he walked alone to the stable or to his cabin, "Yes, old marster, I 'grees wid yer."

It was our habit to visit the old man before any important enterprise was undertaken; and now the time was come when I was to go to the famous Graham boarding-school, and I went to bid him good-bye.

This was the school where the sons of generals and of colonels and of other gentlemen were trained under military discipline, made severer now by the grim memory of Stonewall Jackson, under whom Colonel Graham had served and whose spirit he revered as his knights their lord, King Arthur.

I found my grandfather eager to discover my expectations and ambitions, and he asked me many questions, making smiling test of my readiness to answer difficult ones.

For the saddest and vividest of reasons, even the little incidents of that particular day, stay in my memory yet. I recall my grandfather's manner when he asked:

"My son, do you write a fair script?"

I sat down at his secretary and wrote a line for him that I recalled from a copy-book and I wrote my name under it — "Nich's Worth III."

"Not that way," said he, and he took his quill and wrote "Nicholas Worth."

"Spell it out." His "script" was like George Washington's, now become a little tremulous, but still strong and clear.

Write fair script, sit your horse erect, do not pull the trigger till your aim is clear — these were maxims that fixed themselves in my mind that day. For he had me mount my horse and ride for him; and, when one of my cousins and I shot at a target behind the garden, he walked there to see how well we did it.

After an early supper I bade my grandfather "far'well" (he always said far'well); and he reminded me that some day I should be the head of the family.

"Dat's so," said Uncle Ephraim, "for Mars'

Nick, he is de ol'est, and Mars' Littlenick is de ol'est in de line."

"Far'well, my son; I shall hear good reports of you — be sure. Far'well."

"Mars' Littlenick gwine t' sen' good 'ports, you be boun', ol' Marster. He's de smartest of 'em all. He ain't done name' fur you and Mars' Nick bof, fur nothin'."

My aunt Eliza, who had been the mistress of the Old Place since my grandmother's death, wished me a safe ride home, and Uncle Ephraim assured me that the moon would not go down till midnight. "Mighty good night for 'possums," he remarked; and I rode home in the cool of the evening. Most of the road lay through woodland. The cabins that stood here and there were lighted chiefly by pine knots, which gave a cheerful glow, and a fice now and then ran out and barked till I was beyond its hearing. Now and then, too, a hog would run from a fence corner with a sudden grunt which startled me to tighten my grip on the reins.

It was a beautiful night with moonlight shadows of the pines across the road and with dense, dark places here and there through which I galloped. It is just as well to pass deep shadows as fast as you can — not from fear, of course, but because we are children of light.

The night and the earth and the pine forest —

when you come in direct contact with all these at once, you feel yourself akin to fundamental things, especially if you are a boy and your alert imagination is quickened by every sound and perfume. And you will carry the odour of the earth and of the trees in your memory at whatever distance you may live from them and however many years thereafter. Go into the woods at night now, if you are old, and you will be likely to recall a road and a wood that gave forth the same odours half a century ago; and you may even conjure up some particular night and recall with distinctness all that happened then. You may call back old friends that you had half forgotten; for the memory of those whose childhood was spent on the soil likes to make its return circuit on the ground.

And so I rode on, over the bridge beside which the mill-dam roared, then up the steep hill, and at last I came into the main road. I quickened my pace for fear my mother might be uneasy about me, and in a little while I was near the public well by old Jonas Good'in's. As I galloped around the short turn in the road there, my horse snorted and stopped and began to rear. In front of me was a company of horsemen in white, with white cloths over their horses — a little army of them, it seemed to me. I coaxed my horse nearer.

"Ku-Klux," said I to myself. Although my pulse beat somewhat more quickly, I knew that they would do no harm to me if I rode on. Besides, why should I run?

A deep-voiced member of the clan dismounted and said:

"Your horse don't like us, young fellow. Has he been doin' any deviltry?" And he led him along by the bridle.

There was a Negro man drawing water at the well with all his might, and a group of white, masked figures stood about him.

"I want a hundred more gallons to fill me up," said one of them. "It was hot in hell to-day and I got thirsty. Hurry up, old man."

"Say, young fellow, do you know of any niggers that need attention?" another gruff voice asked. My horse by this time had passed the group and ran as if the whole clan were chasing us.

I fear to omit this unexciting single experience of my life with the Ku-Klux Klan; for my whole story might be discredited if I had no encounter with them at all. And many a time these many years I have had occasion to think of the romances and the political tracts and the political speeches that abler men than I would have made out of even this encounter. But a truthful record like this can make nothing more of the incident than the report, which was spread the next day, that

they flogged an old Negro in the neighbourhood
whom they frightened into a confession of having
stolen a pig.   I can only express regret that it was
not at least a mule that he had stolen, so that my
own adventure with them might thereby have
a greater dignity.

It would be a glorious thing to go to the Graham
School, for the sons of the best families for a
hundred years had gone there.   I had not supposed that there was any other school for boys in
the world that could be compared to it.   But
some doubt crept into my mind during the next
few days; for Dick Caldwell came to our house
and he was going to England to school.   We
talked over letters that his father had written
about this English school; and I wondered whether
he were the luckiest boy in the world, as I had
hitherto thought that I was.

He was going to England because his father
was now in the Khedive's army in Egypt, and Mrs.
Caldwell would be sick all her life, they said, and
must stay where the doctors could see her every
day.   The children had lived with their aunt since
the father had been gone; and now, when my father
had at last found someone to buy Colonel Caldwell's
home, the money was to be used — or as much
of it as was necessary — to send Dick and Louise
to him.   Dick was in high glee.

He was somewhat younger than I, but even Sam confessed that he knew many things of which we were ignorant. His sister, Louise, was too young to take part in our gravest discussion of schools and such things, but she was excited about the ocean voyage. "And the ship will go on and go on and go on, and there'll be no land."

None of us had ever seen a ship, but Sam's imagination seized on the ark:

"Does a turkle-dove fly out and fin' de lan' and come back an' tell 'em which er way to go? An' how do de dove know?"

My father went to the city to make arrangements for their journey. He had received the money, he had their railroad tickets to the big city where the ship was loaded with cotton — how we talked over every detail of these preparations later! They would start the next day; and, since we must have an early breakfast to be ready when the train came, we were sent to bed early.

My father said to my mother that night that, if he could sell the farm and the mill, he would think of going away himself; for life was not yet safe even on the highways. These were the turbulent after-years of the war. And the camp-followers of two armies and many other low adventurers from all parts of the United States were in the towns, preying on the silly freedman and robbing whom they could.

After the moon had gone down — it was one o'clock — there was a violent rapping at the front door. My father got up and, walking into the hall, asked who was there. The answer was not clear; but presently, after a smothered conversation between men on the outside, one said that he was an officer of the law who had come from the city in search of a criminal, and that he had ridden far and was tired and could not go back to the city that night — would he be permitted to stay till morning?

When this unsatisfactory explanation was repeated in a confused and contradictory way, my father had decided not to go to the door.

He had by this time with some difficulty found in the dark the shot-gun that Dick Caldwell and I had shot rabbits with on the day before.

After another and now more violent demand, he refused to admit them. It was a thin double door, one part of it opening from the middle on either side, and it could be easily broken down. There was a transom of glass above it and one on either side.

"Break it down, then," said a voice on the outside; and a heavy foot kicked one of the light panels and it flew open. The man who kicked it stood behind the other panel — that was certain; and my father shot through this closed thin panel.

This surprised the obtruders; but they, in turn,

shot back into the hall. A great scar in the wood of the staircase remained for years which a bullet from a carbine made.

They ran off a little distance and shot back at the house several times. Meantime the door was open and my father stood in the hall with one charge yet in the little double-barrel gun. At last he crept toward the door on his way to a closet in the front of the hall where there was more ammunition. To prevent being seen, he closed the door that had been kicked open. Instantly there was a volley fired from the yard.

My father fired the other barrel of his gun through the glass and the men on the outside, evidently concluding that there was a strong battery within, ran away and fired no more. But, just as my father fired his last charge, a ball struck his gun and, glancing, entered his head. He died instantly.

There he lay with the gun beside him. My mother, with my little sister in her arms and Louise Caldwell clinging to her, sat on the floor by his body till it seemed safe for me to go, by the back door, to the cabins where I found the Negroes in terror. They did not know what had happened, but Sam had already armed himself with an axe. By this time two men, having heard the shooting, had come from the mill settlement by the river.

The slow breaking of the daylight that morning is the loneliest memory of my life.

My father had outlived the war and a settled difference of opinion with most of his friends — he had no enemies — to die by the shot of a burglar who had that day seen him in the city receive a roll of money for the journey of the children of his friend.

I did not at once go to the Graham school; but half a year later, my mother having herself taken the management of the little mill, said in her sad, determined way, that my father's plan for me must be carried out.   It was her plan, too.

And fortunately the ripening of the cotton and the running of the river which turned the mill made my going away to school possible, as they have shaped most greater events that have come in our Southern life since the cotton plant found its best home here.

CHAPTER IV

THE FLOWER OF THE SOUTH

THE son of a general, if he were at all a decent fellow, had, of course, a higher social rank among the boys at the Graham school than the son of a colonel. There was some difficulty in deciding the exact rank of a judge or of a governor, as a father; but the son of a preacher had a fair chance of a good social rating, especially of an Episcopalian clergyman. A Presbyterian preacher came next in rank.

I was at first at a social disadvantage. My father had been a Methodist — that was bad enough; but he had had no military title at all. If it had become known among the boys that he had been a "Union man"— I used to shudder at the suspicion in which I should be held. And the fact that my father had had no military title did at last become known; and one day Tom Warren, a boy from the "capital city," twitted me with this unpleasing fact. In a moment or two, we were clinched in a hand-to-hand fight. Of course a crowd gathered, and presently Colonel Graham himself appeared.

"Stand back and see it done fairly," said he, and the boys made the circle wider.

"What is it about?"

"He called me a liar, sir," said Tom.

"Well, no gentleman will take that," said the Colonel.

"I didn't call him a liar, but I do now, and I'll choke him, too," and I made a grasp at Tom's throat; and we were again a whirling mass of swinging arms and dodging heads.

"Halt!" Instantly we stood and saluted. My collar was torn and my face was bleeding from Tom's scratches. But we stood erect in silence.

"Sir," said I.

"Speak."

"He cast reflections on my family, sir."

"What have you to say, Tom?"

"I said, sir, that his father was not in the war."

"He said my father was a coward, sir."

Some boy in the crowd cried out, "I'd fight at that."

"Halt!" cried the Colonel, and we kept from clinching again, and again we stood erect, each quivering with anger.

"I see you'll have to fight it out," said the Colonel in a moment, "before you feel better. Square off. Give them room."

Then the fight began again. After we had scratched and pounded one another and torn one another's clothes, I at last threw Tom, and the Colonel called out, "Halt!"

We were on our feet in a second. Each saluted. We were commanded to shake hands. The Colonel explained to the crowd in a sort of oratorical fashion that he had known Mr. Worth, that he had given his time and fortune to his country, and that there was no better man in any part of the Government's service. The incident was over. The crowd of boys went away. The Colonel went back to his office smiling. I was unspeakably grateful to him.

At his office, which was a wooden shanty at one end of the barracks, the Colonel renewed his conversation with a gentleman who had come to plead for his son's reinstatement in the school.

"I cannot tell you, sir," he said, "how deeply I am grieved. But I cannot argue the subject. I fact, I have no power to reinstate your son. I could not keep the honour of the school—I could not even keep the boys, if he were to return. They would appeal to their parents and most of them would be called home. They are the flower of the South, sir."

This boy had cheated on an examination and had been sent home by the first train after his conviction.

That night, a half hour before taps, when my three room-mates were absent, one of my best friends came into my room.

"Worth," he asked, "wasn't your father a colonel?"

"No, but he was in the service of the Confederate Government and he wasn't a coward."

"I didn't mean that he was a coward. But I want to tell you something," and he went on in the sad tone in which we speak of great misfortunes. "You won't tell anybody, Worth, will you? My father — my father isn't a colonel nor nothin'. But I swear he isn't a coward. I saw him whip a man once. Worth, don't you ever tell anybody — he's a good father to me"; and the boy had a sob in his voice. When another fellow came into the room, he warmly shook my hand — since, as he saw it, we had a common misfortune — and he went away.

The rough beds were turned down from their edges whereon they rested all day against the wall of the log room, the poles were drawn that held the blankets and the mattresses in place; and we four room-mates went to bed. Taps were sounded; all lights were out; and the day of my first fight with Tom Warren was done.

The boys said that I had shown my mettle; among my friends I had a day or two of some little glory; and at the beginning of my second year I was made an officer of the battalion, and only "brave" boys were chosen as officers.

Lest you should imagine (and thereby, too,

fall into a grave error) that fighting was the only manly art cultivated at the Graham school, you must be informed that, between military exercises, successful onslaughts were made on Latin and mathematics. The master's educational code contained three laws:

A boy must have a sound body, and the more roughly you use him the sounder his body will become and the greater his physical bravery.

A boy must know Latin or he cannot be a gentleman.

A boy must know mathematics or his mind will not be trained.

And the years swiftly passed at these barracked labours, as the years pass swiftly elsewhere at that time of life. Our forced growth — for we had reached the emotional level of manhood while we were yet boys — gave us rapid development.

One high day of school life every year was the parade-day of the battalion at the State Fair. The cadets wore their new gray uniforms of the same colour as the tattered coats in which their fathers and kinsmen had fought on Virginian battlefields. And, on this particular year, the second year of my cadetship, it was a greater day than usual, for a bust of Stonewall Jackson was to be presented to Colonel Graham. Colonel Flint, a veteran of great oratorical power, who also had served under General Jackson, was to make the presentation address; and all the Confederate veterans within reach had been invited. They came from every part of the land, many with armless sleeves, many on crutches, most of them in well-worn, and many in ragged, gray uniforms, in battered hats and caps, and some with remnants of flags. They were the saddest relics of a brave army, I imagine, that were ever seen; for most of them were now but wrecks of men. Years of exposure, of ill-fed fighting, for some of them years of prison life, and years of neglected wounds and injuries since, years of poverty, too, and years of political oppression — these men had borne the physical scourging of the nation for its error of slavery.

They had borne it innocently, too, for they were plain countrymen who were blameless victims of our sectional wrath. But they had borne it also recklessly. They had looked on death — had lived with it, indeed; and they had miraculously survived and crawled to barren homes from the clash and slaughter and from starvation and such deadly vain endeavour as no other men had ever known and lived; and now a brief period was left them to muse on their great adventure, which so filled their minds that thought on other things was impossible.

The little bust was covered and placed on a pedestal which stood on a platform under the trees in the fairground this beautiful October day; and the battalion of cadets stood as a guard of honour about it, in their shining new uniforms.

A bugle was sounded and a drum was heard, and the veterans formed in line at a distance, to march to the benches that had been reserved for them next the standing cadets. A vast crowd filled the few seats farther away and stood all round about.

When the bugle sounded, a mighty shout went up. It was a yell that became a roar, and the crowd took it up, yell after yell, and then the band struck up "Dixie." Every voice in that vast crowd sang. The veterans were by this time in line, limping and leaping rather than marching, coming with more eagerness than precision to the place left for them.

As they came within sight of the crowd every man and woman arose. Hats and handkerchiefs were thrown into the air. They shouted, they clapped, they yelled. The old soldiers bared their heads and limped and leaped along, barely hearing the military commands of their leaders. At last they reached their places; quiet came; and after a long prayer the orator was introduced.

As soon as he stood up every old soldier arose and yell after yell was given in his honour.

"Come down, we want to hug you, Colonel," one man, with stubs of arms, cried out.

But at last the orator began.   Even if he did speak almost two hours, nobody in the audience, except the babies, became weary, not even the hundreds of men who stood on the outskirts of the crowd.   He was talking about the Lost Cause and Stonewall Jackson, and many of his hearers would have sat till they had dropped asleep from exhaustion, hearing this great adventure praised. It was meat and drink and rest to them.

The climax of Colonel Flint's long speech was the unveiling of the bust.   It was covered with a cloth and a cadet stood at either side, who, when the orator gave the cue, was to pull the cords which would remove the covering.

I was one of these.   At last Colonel Flint stepped to the very edge of the platform, gave the signal to uncover the bust, and, lifting his great voice to its utmost, said:

"Soldiers, Comrades, Heroes!   Behold our immortal commander!"

The band played Dixie again, but nobody now heard it.   The old soldiers yelled — yelled — yelled — yell on yell, great folds of shrieking applause; and the crowd echoed every burst of it.   The veterans swayed forward.

"God bless old Stonewall!"

"There he is!"

"Get out of my way, boy."

"The immortal leader!"

The cadets presented bayonets to keep them back. Old soldiers snatched the guns from the boys' hands and, yelling, broke their line. Some were stuck by the bayonets. But no accident nor incident stopped them. The officers who sat on the platform motioned them back. But, with "God bless old Stonewall," on they rushed.

Before anybody knew how the feat was done, one veteran snatched the little bust from its pedestal and, holding it high, kissed it. Another took it and embraced it. It was passed back through the struggling throng. Old men, one after another, grasped the orator by the neck and everybody seemed to be embracing somebody else. As Colonel Graham cried orders to his cadets to re-form their line at the side of the stand, his order was cut short by the shouts of a group who gathered about him and threw their hands wildly in the air.

In a dazed state, I was standing at one side with the cord still in my hand.

"You showed him to us," shouted a gigantic mountaineer, and he seized me and handed me to his neighbour. Thus I was passed from man to man far out into the crowd, my cap lost and my coat torn, before I could reach the ground.

I saw my cousin Margaret in the crowd near where I reached the ground. She had been weeping as everybody else wept from such an emotional strain. But she laughed at my plight and waved her hand at me.

After the long railroad ride back to the school that night, I had just life enough left in me, when I pulled my bunk down and recalled the wild scene of the day, to remember that my father had once spoken of the Confederacy as "a foolish enterprise," and I fell asleep wondering if he had been mistaken.

I have since sometimes thought that many of the men who survived that unnatural war unwittingly did us a greater hurt than the war itself. It gave every one of them the intensest experience of his life, and ever afterwards he referred every other experience to this. Thus it stopped the thought of most of them as an earthquake stops a clock. The fierce blow of battle paralyzed the mind. Their speech was in a vocabulary of war; their loyalties were loyalties, not to living ideas or duties, but to old commanders and to distorted traditions. They were dead men, most of them, moving among the living as ghosts; and yet, as ghosts in a play, they held the stage.

Revered, unreasoning, ever-present, some of them became our masters, others became beggars — some masters and beggars, too. We did them honour and we doled them alms, and for years they frightened us into actions that we did not approve, for we feared to offend them.   But now, forgetfulness and peace — peace and forgiveness — they are almost all gone; we honour them while we pity them; they were our fathers and they were brave; but we did not become ourselves till they were buried, if indeed we are become ourselves yet; for this was not merely a fierce war — it was a fierce civil war.

CHAPTER V

ON A certain summer morning during one of my vacations my Aunt Eliza spent a precious hour or more in writing this letter, about which, of course, I knew nothing till many years later. But, when I found it, I easily recalled the day. I think I told you that my Aunt Eliza was the youngest of my grandfather's children, and that she had been the mistress of the Old Place since my grandmother fell dead when they brought one of my uncles home from the war to be buried beyond the garden. She had never married. She was a war-spinster — one of that large company whose mates wedded death on Virginian battlefields.

Her letter, written in her neat handwriting in her diary, ran in this way; for I now copy it just as she left it when (not long ago) she died at a ripe old age, having lived at once maid, wife, and widow, a life of radiant resignation:

"*My Beloved Captain:* Again our wedding day! Here where I wait it is a day of a perfect

48

sky, as it ought to be. I am as happy in your love as this sky is clear and deep. It is as refreshing as the breeze that blows into my window from the garden. We would walk there now if you were with me and the old-fashioned odours would make us glad. You liked them, I remember, and I have kept the garden as you knew it.

"Every year my love grows. This you know, for I have every year told you, and telling makes me content. Every year, my beloved Captain, I come nearer to you. Your absence is shorter now than it has ever before been. I thank heaven that *you* cannot suffer impatience, although at times I almost wish you did.

"I am waiting, not wearily any longer. For we can wait patiently for what is certain to come.

"I shall be happy all this our wedding day — happy even if I turn aside now and then and weep a moment. Forgive me that, for the happiness that you taught me and that we shall always have will outlive all weeping and all waiting.

"I cannot write 'good-bye' because you are always with me, O brave Captain of my life."

The date in the diary where this is written is the anniversary of the battle in which her betrothed Captain fell. She kept the anniversary year after year in a bridal spirit. After the news of his death came, for the rest of her patient life she wore white, and moved among us as a gentle and almost silent presence, consenting from sheer goodness to take part in whatever concerned us. But her own self lived in another world, into which at times we had glimpses. It was a world of radiant expectation, even of ultimate sweet certainties to her. Habitually she spoke of the Captain as if she had seen him yesterday, and in a tone which meant that she might see him to-morrow.

There was, then, nothing unnatural in her greeting of my Aunt Katharine Benson who had driven from the city to see "Eliza, poor soul, who lives too much alone:"

"I am glad to see you, Katharine; for it is my wedding day. I have written to the Captain, and now the day is ours."

My cousin Margaret came to the Old Place that day with her mother; and she and I made a very glad time of it, as I easily recall we made of many days there. We romped about the grove, we rode horses down the long, lone road, and we talked with Uncle Ephraim. We tried to push around the long arms of the old cotton-press, as old in its pattern as Pharaoh, but it was still in use every fall making insecure bales of the precious crop. We walked about the old slave-quarters — rows of log houses they were, very like the barracks at the

Graham school. Some of them were yet occupied by the Negroes that worked on the farm.

When Uncle Ephraim, giving full range to his imagination, had told stories of the slaves and of the slave-quarters and of the revelries there that he remembered, the quarters had seemed to me miles long. Their spacious fire-places had seemed almost as large as the cabins themselves were. He carried in his memory a larger scale of measurement than the huts now gave hint of.

"I wonder, Cousin," I said to Margaret, "if the old times were really as 'gret' as Uncle Ephraim (and other historians) think?"

By this time we were come to a double cabin in which the hand-looms still stood, upon which my grandmother's slave-women had, under her direction, woven much of the cloth that was used in cabin and in "big house." There they were, now become only so much lumber; and the spinning wheels seemed likely to fall to pieces in the dry dust that heavily covered them.

Although these things were supposed to symbolize a great, dead, happy era, and in spite of Margaret's mood of defence of Uncle Ephraim's large measured imagination, cabins and looms and spinning wheels and the ginnery and the cotton-press all seemed out of repair, out of use, old, as depressing a part of the past as the two old men were cheerful parts of it. After we had gone by the spring, we walked up the cedar lane in silence to the house.

After dinner we went into the library where lately a number of old books and documents, which had been rescued from a garret, had been put in a high book-case. This was the work of Aunt Eliza, upon whom the habit had come of putting everything in order in anticipation of the final leave-taking both of my grandfather and of herself.

We sat in the cool, high old room and fell to talking of the family stories that Uncle Ephraim had told us. The old man passed through and said:

"Dem was gret times," and he winked and chuckled — "gret times when yo' gran'pa sont me wid his complimen's to de young leddy twenty mile er way."

"Was that grandmother, Uncle Ephraim?"

"Sho' it was. Who you spec' it was?"

"They *were* great times, Nick," my pretty cousin said. "For, if any young 'gem'man' were to send his 'complimen's' twenty miles to me, I'd like it. They don't do such things these days. They did have good times," she rattled on.

"Why, mother herself told me that Aunt Phœbe — your own blessed grandmother — wore a pink belt at a great ball where your grandfather danced with her and said something that pleased her;

and she didn't wear that pink belt again till old Uncle Nicholas married her. That's what I call being in love."

"Rather silly, don't you think?"

"No, I don't. She was in love, Nick. Don't you know what being in love is and how they act? And that's a true story about old Uncle Nicholas sending Uncle Ephraim twenty miles every day or two to carry a note or something."

"Why didn't he go himself?"

"Why, he did go, of course. But he couldn't go every day; and he sent his servant on the days when he couldn't go himself. Old Uncle Ephraim says, 'Dey co'ted fas' and fu'ous in dem days.'"

"Here's a funny book," she said presently. She had taken down an old account book, written with the most precise penmanship.

One entry was: *"Nicholas Worth"* across the top of the page.

Then came: *"One slave Pompey, $800."*

Farther down: *"One barrel of whiskey."*

It was not plain whether the whiskey and the slave were bought or sold or swapped.

"That sounds sober," said I. "That dear old man sitting in the piazza now, do you suppose, cousin, that he recalls these things?"

"Go ask him, Nick."

"Not for a thousand dollars."

"I couldn't think of the same man 'co'tin' dear

Aunt Phœbe 'fas' and fu'ous' and then selling or buying 'one slave Pompey' and 'one barrel of whiskey.' Do you suppose they really loved one another?"

"Just as we do now, coz."

"But you never sent me your 'complimen's' twenty miles. To say this at short range costs nothing. 'Dem sho'ly was gret times,' and the sons are not worthy of their grandfathers."

"Well," said I, "you wait and see."

"I'll never love you, Nick, if you're a Methodist. Mamma says that the only Methodist that ever went to heaven was Aunt Phœbe, and the only other one that will ever go is your mother. *You* can't go to heaven as a Methodist. Aunt Phœbe bequeathed to every one of you her big nose and her Methodist religion. You've got the nose."

In the afternoon when Aunt Katharine and Margaret had gone, my grandfather came into the house and sat in his deep leather-bottomed chair; he rearranged the fire, as was his wont, for it had become slightly cool, and he rang his bell for Ephraim and said:

"Margaret is a likely child, Ephraim."

"Yes, ol' Marster, a mighty purty young miss, sho'. She 'kin to Miss Anne and Mars' Littlenick, you know."

"Call Nicholas to me."

When I had sat down beside him, he asked:

"How old are you, Nicholas? Yes, yes," he said, when I had told him; and then he began to talk, looking into the fire:

"I had a mind for public life myself when I was young, but the plantation needed management, and I was married early and then — well then, I reckon Ephraim needed management — you remember your grandmother, son?"

"Yes, grandfather. I remember I saw her many times when I was little."

"Well, she came here then, and I gave my time to other things. You will marry, too, Nicholas — not now, son, but some time." Uncle Ephraim smiled and touched my elbow. "But are you going into public life when you are a man? I hope you will, for you will be the head of the family one of these days, and it is time we were in public life again. My grandfather was an important man in the government of the colony. Every family must serve the country by its best men. It was so in the old time."

"Grandfather, you were a Justice of the Peace?"

"And I sat in the General Assembly for many years. Then," he went on as if he were talking to a memory of something long past, "we made plans for the development of the State which would have made it long ago one of the richest and most powerful commonwealths in the Union.

The State had the money, and the chance was ours. Great men and great States are builders. We ought to have built great public works. But the public mind was soon drawn from all practical things. Talk with your mother, son, and tell her that I wish you to become Governor, and build public works."

When I told my mother the next day, she simply said: "Dear old grandpa, he doesn't know what 'public life,' as he calls it, means these days; and she went on with her preparations for us to return to Graham's, I for my last year and my brother Charles for his second year. For she was managing the mill in her quiet, thankful way with success. The price of cotton and of its products during those years was high, as doubtless you will recall.

A few nights later we were turning down the beds from the walls in our room in the barracks; and I always thought of my cousin Margaret as we put down our work for the night; and now every colonel's son of us was again playing the game of Latin, Mathematics, and the Honour of a Gentleman —not a bad game for youth whether in that cloistered school or in the world.

My hardy Colonel, it was a narrow segment of life that you moved in and marched us over in those years of guns and drums and paradigms and Presbyterianism. I recall with a smile and yet with affection your amusing pomp and your martial precision. But you stood erect; and that is a pleasant memory in a world where I have since seen many men cringe.

CHAPTER VI

THE EFFERVESCENCE OF THE SPIRIT

ARE you a new student?"

An ecclesiastical fellow flung this question in my face in a kindly, abrupt way, when I got off the train and found myself standing in the rain at the darkly lighted station at Clayborn.

"Yes."

"I'll show you to the college office and help you. Know any old students?"

No, I knew nobody. I had a letter from Colonel Graham saying that I had finished my course at his school "with distinction." That was my only introduction.

We went to a dingy office, where a fat man in clerical clothes wrote down my name, asked me the same questions again, and called out:

"Powhatan Row, number 10."

My friend of the rainy darkness went with me to this place, which I found to be a plain square room with two windows, a fire-place, a bed, two hard chairs, a washstand, no carpet — well, it was a room and it was dry. He lighted a lamp; we kindled a fire; he told me that I could get meals at any one of a dozen boarding-houses in the village and he invited me to supper with him.

A cheerless beginning, surely, of that period of adolescence of the spirit during which youth finds itself and establishes its relations to the universe!

Again I wished most fervently that I could have gone to the University where I should have been in my own State and had companions from Graham's and had common traditions with those about me.

But the University was closed, because, in the political convulsion of the time, the "Carpet-bag" Legislature, seeing that the Kingdom's come, all men are free and a new era is at hand, had opened it alike to white and coloured students. No coloured students came, I think, but no white students remained; and the Legislature withheld its appropriation till the "proud whites" should relent. During this deadlock, I came of college age. This church college, therefore, although it had the disadvantage of being in another State, was regarded as the best one for me to attend, partly because it was a church college and partly because a great orator and preacher was then its president.

I may undertake in this chronicle to explain why a man came to love one woman rather than another; why a whole people lost their minds on one subject; and why men who seemed vapid and commonplace became powerful, popular leaders; for even subtle tasks like these any man may try without fear of utter failure. But I shall not try to tell what happened to me, or what happens to any youth at college.

I know that the years of *our* life there opened a new era, but I cannot yet understand why there are men who really think the same thing about the commonplace years of *their* lives there. These years were years of an expanding horizon. Even now I can summon the mood of perpetual youth, recall the keenest joys of comradeship, and feel the effervescence of the soul — slide a door of the mind and shut out the things that are and leave with my true self only the things that then were — that then were and, therefore, are perpetual, because they never were. It was life under a sort of dome that reflected and magnified self-consciousness; but it opened a vista to the stars or to man's highest endeavour or into the great processes of nature, and thus trained the eye to see vistas forever. To miss this is to miss the divine ferment of youth and to fail of a secret that cannot be imparted.

As I wished and started to say when the effervescent mood cut me off, in due time I found myself and my companions; for this is the aim of the whole experience, along with the incidental aim, while the spirit is expanding, of furnishing the mind also with mathematics and the classics; and in the course of time I left Powhatan Row for other lost newcomers piloted by kind "theologs."

During the years that counted for something, I lived in Greenwood Cottage, a little building that stood by itself in the corner of the yard; and my companions there were John Cary and Preston Harvey. However little you may know of these deep things of the spirit, you must permit me to write here that, wherever they or I have been since those years, in heights or depths, we have known and understood one another; and, wherever we may henceforth be in the great spaces of the universe, I think we shall know and understand one another — with a large charity and a complete sympathy — till the lights of our knowing go out.

We came from three different States — one's State was then one's very mother. A man who lived in South Carolina was for that reason a different man from a man who lived in Georgia. They had different allegiances, different heroes, different traditions. But we were all "Southern," and that was a strong common bond. The flame of patriotism burned bright in us, a strong light with a mellow religious tinge. Whatever else we might fail in, we should never fail in our patriotic duty to our States and to the

South. Our aims differed in other ways, but not in this way.

Only one student in college had ever been "to the North." Half a dozen, perhaps, had been to Washington, and none of the others had seen a city so large except two students from New Orleans. Yet we came from eight or ten Southern States. But, if our horizon was small, the heavens were near; and we were not aware that we lived in a corner of the world. Unless you know the universe, you are pardonable for thinking that the centre of it is where you stand. "The South" was ours — that we all had in common wherever we lived, and "the South" surely was no mean country.

We had the deep seriousness as well as the blythe spirit of youth. One night we sat talking of patriotism, as we talked many nights, and of our duty to our country. True, we did not know the political events of that year, nor even of that decade. We lived far from the world where stirring things were going on. But we did know that the South was a discredited province of the Union, that its voice was not now heard, that its influence was gone and that we were disinherited children of the Republic which our fathers had framed. We were reading Jefferson and Madison as a diversion— the kind of diversion that is one's main matter of life. There were now no Southern men of corresponding influence. But there *should* be more such, and the old land should know that it had not become barren!

On this particular night, we drew the curtains, locked the doors and knelt before the fire. All serious actions were begun with prayer, and all resolves took the form of oaths. John prayed aloud:

"Great God of our Fathers: Help us keep the oath that we are about to take, and consecrate us to the highest and most honourable service of our stricken and beloved country. She *shall* rise again to claim her own right influence in the world. Keep us strong and resolute, for Christ's sake."

Before we rose we clasped hands and John swore this oath aloud:

"Before God and these witnesses, I swear to be loyal and true to my country and to let no selfish motive move me from this resolve."

Then I swore the same oath and then Preston.

We arose, a glow of ambition warming our souls. We sat in silence for a time and then we grasped each other's hands again and went to bed.

Any man who knows no better may, if he choose, laugh at this juvenile solemnity. But in that college to this day there are three youths every year who swear this oath — three selected by their predecessors; and they read over with pride the names and the careers of all who have sworn it before them; and there is not one who has not kept it by his conscience.

Thus the State became, especially during that particular year, our love, our mistress, our religion; and we read the political fathers and made patriotic orations.

Our loyalty to one another and our intimacy were complete. We even told our love stories to one another. My cousin Margaret's photograph hung in my room and there was never a day I did not look at it and feel the thrill that her beautiful face gave me.

Preston Harvey, who was already thinking of becoming a preacher, had, I recall, a pretty ceremony. Before he went to bed he lighted a candle in front of the pictures of his beloved and of his mother, while he said his prayers, for religion and the love of women were ever near neighbours.

John was madly in love with a young lady in the college village, a girl of a pious mind, who, knowing that John's father was a preacher of great renown, had made up her mind to turn him also to the pulpit before accepting him; and she had at times an exasperating way of giving him sermons in return for his love-making — at times, for at other times she showed that she knew the language that John spoke.

One night he came home and threw his hat down in despair.

"It's all off. Damned if I'll have any more damned sermons from Grace Makepeace. She may keep 'em for some soft-palated 'theolog.' Beggin' your pardon, Preston, I'm not that kind of a rooster. I'm done — I am. Just because the old man is a big preacher, I've got to preach! I've told everybody I wouldn't, except mother; and now Grace Makepeace thinks she can 'snatch me from the burning.' I'll burn a little longer."

"It seems to me you *are* pretty warm," said Preston.

"Hot as hell! Forgive me, old man. But nobody has a right — have they? — to *drive* a fellow to preach — much less a girl. But, by Jupiter, she's a nice one when she's right. But she's all off to-night.

"Beg pardon again, old boy. I meant to do all my swearing before I got home — damn it!"

But reverent in spirit we surely were, John as well as Preston and I. Every act of our lives, from sitting at table three times a day to going to bed at night, was preceded with a prayer. It was not respectful to eat without "grace," and it was a part of the making of one's toilet to say one's prayers before going to bed. Prayer was woven into the very respectability of life. It seemed ill-bred not to pray. But John was becoming somewhat weary of it. He had done praying enough already, it occurred to him, to last an ordinary lifetime; and he woke up to the conclusion that so much praying was absurd, was wrong indeed, because it was perfunctory. It was not sincere, not praying at all, but mere mummery. Yet he was afraid suddenly and wholly to leave it off.

He took vehemently to the study of religion. He conceived a suspicion, which soon became a conviction, that the Greek gods might possibly have been as efficacious and helpful as the Hebrew Jehovah; and that they were all philosophical speculations. Why not pray to Zeus? And he framed him a prayer to each of the more important Greek deities. He wrestled with this subject long and hard, as Sam and I had wrestled with the question of the reality of the war. He considered the evidence of the inspiration of the Scriptures, the evidence of the miracles and all the rest. And lo! there was no evidence. There were declarations and traditions. There were arguments by analogy. There was a colossal structure of argument and appeal built up on a mere supposition; and a supposition very like it, we found out, had underlain every religion. This was one year's work for us. And we had opened a chasm indeed — a great yawning before us.

"It is all a vast humbug and delusion," said

John; "a cruel thing." But we found no rest in that conclusion or in that feeling. We were yet in a state of dire disturbance, and where could we get help?

On any other subject we should have found some-one to talk with. Yet here was the most important subject of all, and we were practically forbidden to express a doubt, on pain of the severest social punishment. If we had frankly told our fellows of our state of mind, we should have been regarded as worse than heathen, as a sort of outcasts, unbe-lievers, revilers (except by Preston, who of course, kept our secret, was true to us, and prayed for us).

Yet to keep silent was to live a sort of hypocrisy. To be frank and honest — that was next to impossible.

In a desperate frame of mind, John sought the President one Sunday afternoon and tried to tell him of the doubts that blocked our way. The President was accustomed to hear the doubts of those who were professionally known as "sinners"; and John soon saw that he was not making his own case very clear to him — he was hearing it with professional ears, and he spoke in a professional tone.

"Why, my son," said he, "if you go far enough in that direction, you would come to doubt the very inspiration of the Scriptures. Think of that! You cannot conceive of yourself as an unbeliever,

with your father's faith and your mother's prayers.
Turn back. We all go through these periods of
doubt. Seek help in prayer."

The doctrine of the inspiration of the Scriptures!
That was the very thing that John had gone to
talk with him about; and he, good man, had
thrown a fence about it so completely as to forbid
approach to it. There was no help in that direction. If John had told him what he really thought,
he was afraid that he would regard him as a public
enemy, and a fear arose even of expulsion from
college — certainly of sorrowful letters to and from
his father.

Then by agreement with John I took up the
quest. I made a sort of parallel between some
phase of Greek theology and Christianity and
went to talk with our gentle Greek master, Professor Randall.

"*That* was the religion of beauty," said he,
using another formula, "whereas ours is the
religion of conduct." And thus he closed all
approach to the real subject.

And so it was all around the horizon. There
was no answer to our inquiries except answers by
the old formulas; and no discussion seemed possible except at the risk of excommunication from
respectability. Formulas so took the place of
thought as to forbid inquiry. We must keep a
hypocritical place or invite fatal consequences.

Very youthful all this, to look back at, from our present time of day. But what a cruel organization of society that was! Education? When the most important subject that may concern a soul — its relation to the universe — may not be inquired into at all. The whole organization of life took for granted the rigid maintenance of the prevailing orthodoxy.

And all the while John's mother wrote him of her prayers that he might follow the career of his father.

Small, then, as our world was, it was large enough to present to us some of the gravest problems of life.

Our teacher of Greek would, I dare say, now cut a poor figure among more modern philological scholars; for he was a man of the most delicate and sincere cultivation, and he regarded Greek literature as literature, to be read for its form and its beauty, and to be read in great stretches.

He must have got this notion in England, for he was pursuing his studies there when the war began. He had an adventure that stirred our blood and he told it in a sort of Homeric way. He came home on a ship that ran the Union blockade, with several narrow escapes. He immediately went into the Confederate army as a private and served for four years, and the story used to be told that a pocket copy of Homer saved his life, when he was wounded, by deflecting the ball. It is certain that he had a copy of Homer that had been shot, for I saw that with my own eyes.

At any rate his patriotism and a love of Greek literature were so linked together in his mind that he would never believe that any "Northern" scholar really knew his Greek. The war ended and his little fortune gone, he turned to his classics, and our college had been lucky enough to engage him. He took a born teacher's profound joy in such of his pupils as cultivated him and his subject.

There were four or five of us whom he won and who would have gone to war for him, if need be. He had won us by his simple, superb enthusiasm. He conducted his class wholly with reference to us four or five. I think that he was often unaware of the existence of the others. We who loved him spent much time at his simple table and in his library. We read the Greek orations with him in this way and the great tragedies. Thus it happened that we had a great teacher, a rare spirit, and a man of ennobling culture, a gentleman, moreover, if the round earth held one.

Among other adventures that we had were high adventures in oratory; for the college was, especially in those years, a place of orators. Had our fathers, in State and in Church, not practised oratory for half a century, to the exclusion of the other arts? And should we fall below them? Besides, youth becomes what it sees and hears and feels, and the President of the college was a great orator. He could throw his audience into the heroic mood and play upon us as a master on the keys of his instrument. There was no depth nor height of emotional adventure to which he did not lead us.

The two great debating clubs were both the social and intellectual bodies of our world. They combined sport and toil and gave exercise and glory, and such of us as aspired to leadership worked in them diligently. The really great event of Commencement week was the Furman Oratorical Contest; and, when my last year at college was closing, I was chosen by my Society as a contestant for it.

There were four to speak for it and the winner became the hero of the year. Nothing was too good to predict for him, no compliment too high to pay him. For two months I pondered my patriotic subject, read about it, hammered out my periods, found my illustrations. On long walks I would declaim passages to hear the rhythmic swing of the best phrases.

At last the great evening came. The hall was brilliantly lighted and decorated and packed to the doors. All the young women of all the young men came. My cousin Margaret had written to me that she and her mother were coming, "For we both know that you'll be sure to win; and I want to see you, cousin, in your hour of triumph." My mother was too ill to take the rather long journey.

Surely it was a little world that we lived in where an oratorical contest by youth, who did not even know the history of their own country, was taken as seriously as the contests that Pindar celebrated. The crowds that now throng to see a foot-ball game are larger and noisier; but they have only one emotion — the sensation of sport. This oratorical game was both sport and real achievement — a serious part of the business of life, as people of all ages regarded it. Very few men and no women doubted that the winner was sure of great honours thereafter. Indeed, the winning of the prize itself was a great honour, for oratory was yet the greatest of the arts.

The President of the college presided and explained the prize. He called the names of all its winners. He magnified the art of oratory — how his resonant praise of it runs yet through the memory of the youthful mood that was quickened by it! He raised the audience to a plane of tense expectancy. Then he introduced each young man, as if he should say, "My noble youth, the prize awaits you."

The partisans of each speaker heartily applauded. As every one delivered his oration, he sank back into the long sofa exhausted, hardly conscious of his identity; for it was the highest tension in all his life.

My turn came third of the four. The President was now introducing me. He was saying pleasant things about my personal bearing and good scholarship and again a word of gratification that the best students cultivated the art of expressing themselves.

With a sort of pleasant surprise that I knew my own name when he called it and with still greater surprise that I knew my speech, I arose. I caught my cousin Margaret's eye instantly. I had not before seen her in the audience. The resolution came strong in me that she should be pleased at my effort whether I won or not.

When the emotions are at their tensest, as a man plunges onward into the making of a speech, every sense is quickened. He can see a hundred faces at once and recall his relations to each of these people. He can, at the same time, think over long past events connected in his mind with them. The orator, the young orator, surely, has two consciousnesses. One is fixed on his oration. The other runs along beside it, or makes excursions ahead of it, or wanders over the argument, or fixes itself on an important phrase that is yet to come, or roams around the audience, or comes to his support if he lags and says, "Rouse you now!"

Poor is the man who has not felt this deep pulsation of high effort to win an audience!

When I saw Margaret, my sentences were flowing without hesitation, my mind was true to the order in which they should come, and yet I felt anew, How beautiful she is! And this thought came to me again as I approached the most stirring patriotic climax in the oration; for, of course, it was a patriotic speech — on "The Disinherited South."

The applause of my friends was loud; and I saw my cousin rise to her full height and beam approval, while she clapped her hands.

I sat down, feeling a sort of numb contentment, and I lived through the speech of the last contestant without distinctly hearing it.

Then the President asked the judges to retire and to make their decision. There arose three men — a lawyer, a preacher, and an editor — three men of great influence. Everybody seemed content that they were the judges, and a ripple of applause spread over the audience as they went to the reception room behind the platform.

They were merciful, and they were not gone long. The lawyer came forward and with a grave dignity (he was a famous orator himself, for his oration on Poe was regarded as a piece of literature as great as anything that Poe himself had written) — with great dignity he picked the huge medal from the desk and awarded it to me.

Then there was pandemonium. The President congratulated me. So did my competitors. The audience applauded; and in a jiffy my associates in my Society lifted me to their shoulders; and, while the President tried to dismiss the audience they marched with me up and down the aisle. When they put me down at the rostrum, the crowd repeated its applause, and the President said graciously, "And the world is yours to conquer."

In spite of the amazing grandiloquence of all this, I fear that I regard it now more seriously than I have regarded many serious things since then; for we were and are "disinherited"— we who had no more to do with the Civil War than with the Punic Wars and no more to do with slavery than with the Inquisition, and yet we suffer the consequences of both slavery and the war. I spoke the truth, however high-flown the speech; and every man and woman who heard it answered in spirit to the hope that we may come into our own again.

When the crowd had somewhat dispersed and all my friends had shaken my hand, I was able at last to make my way to my aunt and my cousin, for they had kept their seats, awaiting me. My aunt kissed me and whispered, "An omen of many honours to come."

Margaret kissed me, too — a cousin's modest right.

"I knew you would win," she said, "and, before we came to the hall, I wrote to your mother that you had won. Here is the letter, sealed and stamped. Send it to the post-office for to-night's mail. She will receive it before she gets the morning paper. My dear cousin, we are so proud of you"; and she patted my arm with her hand.

When we were alone, after the reception in the Society Halls, "Dear cousin," she said, still aglow, "and we do all love our country. It was a noble speech."

And, when the company broke up and Professor Thomas, at whose house they were staying, walked home down the long yard with my aunt, I walked behind with Margaret. As we passed under the long arch of lights, it seemed to me she had become more beautiful since she sat in the audience. She wore a sort of radiance of pride in me.

I looked into her eyes and I saw there a light that is like the rosy imminence of dawn. At Professor Thomas's house I kissed her good-night. She gave a shiver of surprise, for I had never before kissed her in private — it was a personal, not a cousinly kiss. But she smiled and we said:

"Good-night," and

"Good-night," and

"Good-night."

The dazed happiness of the last two hours (had it been only two hours?) ran higher, as a great tide runs in, to my complete immersion in a sea of emotion that swept me back across the yard. The lights were now even more fairy-like, and there were so many of them! I was going to the President's house where the contestants, all former contestants and the presidents of the two debating societies, were always asked at that time to a sort of Order of Orators, a round table of them that speak. A simple supper was ready in the library — sandwiches and tea and an ice.

The little company sat down in good humour. The losers had received at least the congratulations of their friends, and they were now eligible to this company by reason of their effort.

The talk was first of reminiscences of previous contests. Some humorous stories were told. Other winners were recalled. The careers of some were spoken of with pride.

Then the conversation came round to the President's recent journey to Philadelphia. He had never been to Philadelphia before. No other one in the company had ever been "North." It was as if a traveller had now come back from a great city at the other side of the world.

He had gone as a "fraternal delegate" from the Southern church to the Northern church, which had just held a great meeting in Philadelphia. These two branches of a common faith had become separate organizations because of the sectional bitterness that preceded the Civil War. And now the two bodies had paid each other the courtesy to send "fraternal delegates" to convey messages of good-will.

"I had no idea of the riches of the North," the good man said, over his tea. "Prosperity abounds everywhere. Everywhere are evidences of accumulated wealth. In the home where I was entertained, there was the most lavish display of wealth that I have ever seen.

"My dear doctor," he said, "turning to a former medal winner, who was now a preacher in a nearby town, "they pay their preachers four times as large salaries as the Governor of our Commonwealth receives."

After he had answered many questions, he was moved to tell what he had not meant to tell — how on the evening set for the great meeting to hear the delegates from the Southern church, the presiding Bishop had called on him to speak, after which much business was on the programme. He arose, and the scene of splendour about him fired his imagination. He contrasted it with the poverty of his own church and people; he expressed the brotherly sentiments which the Southern church held for all mankind, those of their own spiritual kindred in particular; and, if God would show a way in which all memory of all past differences could be obliterated, he and those for whom he spoke would welcome it as a new evidence of the spirit of Christ.

That is what he said he told them. But, when he had delivered his message (with his marvellous voice and with all his own emotions tuned high), the meeting broke up. There was a rush to the platform to shake his hand. Men gathered in little groups to talk about him and what he had said.

"A message for a new era," they said.

"A most remarkable address."

"God will find a way."

Some one began to sing the doxology, the rest of the programme was forgotten and the audience went home under the spell of this unexpected experience. They were unwilling to hear anything else that evening.

By this time, tears came into the President's eyes, and he was attuned to another thought than that which he had expressed in Philadelphia — the complement to it — the pathos of the South's poverty.

"And the next day they offered me churches in New York and Chicago and a salary of $6,000 a year and a house. This will show you the unimagined scale of magnificence that they have in those great cities. They told me how I could preach there with effect the message of restored national brotherhood and help to bind up our country's wounds.

" 'No,' said I, 'my own poor country needs me. We must train men. We that are left owe it to the sons of those that fell to see that they are not neglected. God has called me to our own field, where our own people are dear to me.'

"My friends, I wept for our old Commonwealth. She needs men with all the training they can have, with all their inspiration. With the intimate intonations of the great dead, a patriotic past calls us to make the future patriotic also. My young friend stirred a great depth of loyalty to-night. Let us live for our people — live for the State, which in her poverty calls on every man for his highest endeavour. He that hesitates to respond is unworthy to lie in her sacred soil, where our fathers rest and where their deeds light the path to the highest duty."

Every man at the table had moist eyes and a quickened pulse; and presently the little company dissolved.

When I shook hands with the President, he said: "My son, the future calls you."

I walked again across the yard, past Professor Thomas's. There was a light in only one window. Is it hers? I wondered, as I went to Greenwood Cottage for my last night there.

I knelt, as I said with fervour, "O God, I thank Thee for my country and — for her."

CHAPTER VII

THE BURIAL OF AN EPOCH

IT WAS my grandfather's ninety-fifth birthday and we were gathered to celebrate it at the Old Place.

"Yes, he's becoming feeble," said my Aunt Eliza, when I arrived that morning. "He eats less. He sleeps more. During the last year he has become more and more silent. He wishes us to talk, but he says little himself."

"Does he like you to read to him?"

"No, but he has been reading a little himself lately. His sight is wonderful, shrunken as his eyes are. But he is apparently idle as well as silent most of the day. It is amusing and pathetic to see him sitting quiet and Uncle Ephraim nearby fallen asleep.

"He had us ransack the garret not long ago to find pamphlets and speeches published before the war. He lives more and more in the old times.

"He sent for Judge Bartholomew, who is almost as feeble as father himself. But he came and they talked about the politics and the public plans of their young days; and each paid to the other a hundred times, 'What excellent good judgment!' Your grandfather had Judge Bartholomew go over his will, but he has not told me why."

When I went into the sitting room, the old man arose, with Ephraim's help.

"God bless you, my son. I am glad you've come." His small, sunken eyes seemed as clear as ever.

He walked out to his accustomed seat on the piazza, and, when he had adjusted himself to his chair and given his cane to Uncle Ephraim, he made a surprising speech to me.

"Nicholas, my son, I have wished to see your mother. Has she not come? No?

"Well, she must come. I wish to confer with her, for I wish you to go to Harvard College."

("Whar's dat, ol' Marster?")

"To look at our country's problems from another view — from a distance. We have had a distracting period here since you were born. In the North I hear they have done some works that we have too long deferred — some public works that we should have constructed if — (and he seemed to fall into a sort of reverie) — if Judge Bartholomew had won the day — of most excellent judgment."

Looking up at me again, "It is well to travel.

You have, I hear, done well at college. You must go and see what works have been done." He stopped a moment, as if to recover breath, before he went on.

"Yes, grandfather."

"I will confer with your mother about the share of the plantation that will go to your father's estate, to pay your expenses. Perhaps it might be sold now——"

("Sell de lan', ol' Marster?")

"After a year or two you will have time enough to settle down and ——"

("Dere'll be less lan' a'ter some on it's sol'.")

He dropped his turkey-wing fan over the banister and Ephraim went to pick it up, saying to himself:

"Don' lak dat sellin' ob de lan'."

"When Mr. Clay was here ——" my grandfather said, but Ephraim interrupted him:

"Is he libin' yit?"

"His spirit still lives, Ephraim."

("Speerits o' jus' men made parfec'.")

"Our public improvements ——"

("He must be a mighty ol' man — Mars' Henry Clay — by dis time.")

"I have conferred with Judge Bartholomew, of excellent judgment, and we thought Harvard College, in Massachusetts, a proper place to learn of the works that have been done. They had men of excellent judgment in Massachusetts in the old days. Our works must be constructed."

("Glad Mars' Littlenick gwine whar he wan' to go, but I don' lak dat sellin' ob de lan'.")

Other members of the family had now come.

"I am pleased to see you, my children"— that was his precise formula, as everyone greeted him.

There was one great-grandchild, a baby; and the old man asked its name three or four times before it seemed to stay in his memory. Then he'd say, "A likely child."

But that day did not have the jovial spirit that we had meant it to have, chiefly because of my grandfather's silence. We had expected his old-time volleys of questions, serious and playful, whereby he used to make us tell all our adventures and opinions. Even dinner passed without much talk, and we felt constrained. A change had surely come over him.

He slept much of the afternoon, and Aunt Eliza explained to us the plans that he and Uncle Ephraim had made even within the last year to build a new ginnery and to cut a new road out to the main road and thus make "the avenue" longer — "in spite of the fact," said she pathetically, "that he hasn't a dollar in the world to pay for building anything."

But the impulse to build was waning now and the "instinct of death" was coming, as gently and naturally as our instinct for sleep when the day's work is done.

Early in the evening, Uncle Ephraim announced that my grandfather was in bed "kivvered up jes' lak a chile." He had recently ceased to have supper with the family, but took his toast alone.

Aunt Eliza went to his bedroom, as was her custom, and we all followed her. We gathered about the high four-post bed.

"We have come to tell you good-night, grandfather."

There, framed by the pillow and the linen, was the strong, wrinkled, but serene old face smiling and saying:

"God bless you, my children, to the second and the third and the fourth generations."

As we gathered again in the sitting room one after another wiped away a tear — of joy, perhaps, that we had all seen him again, or perhaps of fear; for he had changed, and the Great Day would not be long in coming.

It was not ten days later, when a messenger came, saying that he was dead. Let Uncle Ephraim tell the story:

"I come out 'n de li'l room into de big room whar he sleep, same as I does ev'r mornin'; and I buil' a li'l fire in de fire-place an' I whets de razzor an' gits de warm water ready. Den I look 'roun' at de big bed and ol' Marster lay dere jes' as still as a chile. 'Mighty quare,' seys I to myse'f. 'He don' usual sleep dat er way dis time er de mornin'.' Den I stole ter de bed, and 'for' God! what did I see?

"Miss 'Liza, she knock sof' on de doo' 'bout dat time, and she say, 'Unc' Ephum, is father still 'sleep?'

"When she see me lookin' at him in de bed, den she say, 'Father!'

"But ol' Marster never answer.

"'Father!' she say ag'in.

"But ol' Marster never answer.

"Den she say:

"'Daid!— Ephum, he's daid!'

"'Ol' Marster done gone home,' I says; 'done gone home, sleepin' jes' lak a chile in de big bed, an' lef' his ol' sarvan' behin'. Did'n' say nothin' —jes' gon' 'sleep lak a li'l chile.'"

It seemed to me that the history of the world fell into two periods — one that had gone before, and the other that now began; for, when we buried him, we seemed to be burying a standard of judgment, a social order, an epoch.

The mill not only ran, but by this time it had, under my brother's good management, been enlarged. I could go to Harvard College without my grandfather's aid. In fact I did not receive his aid because, for one reason, the old plantation could not now have been sold to advantage. He had left a part of it in his will to Ephraim, "my faithful servant and wise companion for more than sixty years." The whole place, therefore, was put under Ephraim's management. Old as he was, he was yet vigorous.

"It's the only thing to do," said my brother; "for old Ephraim belongs there as long as he shall be able to get about and he can do more with the place than anybody else."

But my grandfather's suggestion took deep root in my mind, and it was decided that I should go to Harvard. He hit upon Harvard chiefly because Judge Bartholomew knew something about it; and they both reached such a judgment by their large intuition, for their minds moved in a big orbit. My grandfather did not even know the bitterness and the sectional feeling that the Civil War had aroused.

There was some criticism of the plan among my acquaintances. My mother herself had a silent misgiving because it seemed so far from home and from all our friends — from "our people." To others it seemed a wild plan, tinged with a sort of treason. Tom Warren, for instance, said when I next saw him:

"Heavens, Worth! to the bitterest part of the

North, the home of the old abolitionism and hatred of the South!"

I knew little about it myself, but the plan appealed strongly to my sense of intellectual adventure.

And Margaret was yet very young.

CHAPTER VIII

PERHAPS it was too late to make more ultimate intimacies in college, but the fellow who lived across the hall from me, in Harvard, became my good friend — not, I confess, precipitately. But what our friendship lacked in haste it has made up in endurance.

Everybody with whom I had to do was polite — it seemed to me studiously and conscientiously polite; but my speech was noticeably Southern. Perhaps that was a barrier. Naturally shy, too, I was not tactful, I dare say, in making advances. Whatever was the matter, I encountered a reserve such as I had not before seen in youth or in men. I had not known reserved persons. Even my neighbour Cooley's somewhat formal interest in me, therefore, was very welcome.

I discovered later that there was at first a tinge of suspicion even in his attitude toward me   He had known but one Southerner before, a fellow who came to college the year when he entered, a dandy, who wore conspicuous clothes, and owed his tailor, and owed him yet; who brought letters to the Holworths, made love at the same time to four young girls in their set, borrowed money from his room-mate, knocked down a coloured student, and ran away and wrote fierce letters from Alabama.

"Seceded," I remarked, when Cooley told me about him.

Cooley's mind moved cautiously and always in a straight line, but his curiosity about many Southern subjects hastened his approaches in spite of his reserve.

One day he asked me if the whites were not permitted to attend the schools that the Northern missionary societies had established in the South for the Negroes.

After I tried to explain the relation of the races, he asked: "Well, then, how will the Crackers — the poor whites — ever learn good English?"

Another day he wished to know my opinion whether there would be a race war if the Federal troops should be withdrawn from the South.

No, I thought not.

"Well, in case there should be, do you think the mulattoes would take the side of their white fathers or of their black mothers?"

Cooley's logical simplicity gave me many things to write to my mother and to Margaret — his mind was so orderly!

But we each gradually solved the riddle of the

other. He used to twit me with carrying my "immortal soul" on my sleeve.

"Why, Worth," he'd say, "you tell me things as a matter of course that no other man I ever knew would disclose under torture."

But my "immortal soul" was a very simple thing and there was no mystery about it. I had grown up in an atmosphere (a raw atmosphere, no doubt,) wherein we permitted our emotions to have free play, till in many cases they had been mistaken for thought, I dare say — a raw, rural society where there was a suppression of thought but never a natural reserve. He had grown up in an atmosphere in which it was not good form to let one's self go.

My cousin, Margaret, and his sister, Adelaide Cooley, illustrated this difference. If you had never seen Margaret nor heard of her and if she were merely to flit by a door where you got only the swiftest glimpse of her, that glimpse would reveal a beautiful girl. Her motion and the liquefaction of her clothes would tell you as much. But you might spend a month with Adelaide Cooley and then find yourself asking whether or not she were beautiful. You were not sure. She had no "motion," and her clothes suggested petrifaction. Yet, after all these years to think the subject over, I assure you that she was probably as beautiful as Margaret. But being beautiful was not the business of her life. She was athletic. She rowed, she skated, she belonged to a walking club and walked ten miles at a time. She was strong rather than graceful. Yet she had a superb fulness of life and rich-flowing blood. My cousin and she were both young women; but that is all that they seemed to have in common. Margaret moved softly, spoke slowly, was restful in motion and in tone and in spirit — the perfection of womanhood for a young fellow to love, surely. Adelaide Cooley was good for the outdoors, and for an almost masculine companionship. To talk love to Margaret was inevitable; for one thing, there was little else to talk about. But the young man did not live, I was sure, who had or who easily could mention that subject to Adelaide at that time at least. Books, art, music, sport — she suggested everything that went on in the world of exercise, physical or mental. She had tastes, she had preferences, she had a most orderly mind, but emotions — except enthusiasm for sport and for knowledge — she did not seem to have.

So much did I yet have to learn, in spite of my intellectual emancipation that was already giving me great joy.

There was no real reason for surprise in Cooley's first attitude to me nor in the attitude of other men whom I met; for the Southern youth of that time in particular had what I shall call the oratorical habit of mind. We thought in rotund, even grandiose, phrases. Rousing speech came more naturally than accuracy of statement. A somewhat exaggerated manner and a tendency to sweeping generalizations were easy to us. You can yet trace this quality in the minds and the speech of the great majority of Southern men of my generation, especially men in public life. It came from an undue development of their emotional nature and a lack of exact training — the result of a system of life and of study that was mediæval.

The furnishing of our minds was of a corresponding grandiose and general quality. I had not read a dozen books of American literature. Poe was the only one of our poets who was regarded seriously in my circle of acquaintances. I had read widely and loosely in English literature, and I knew the Greek writers better than I knew any American writers. If I had come out of a monastery I should hardly have been more of a stranger to the great economic world, the practical world about me, or to American life, than I was the day I went to Harvard.

One day, in my absence, among the men at the table where I ate, the conversation turned on me. Somebody recalled the bombastic young fellow who had brought all Southerners under suspicion, and somebody else maintained that Southerners were all alike. I was a quieter sort of fellow — but wait and see. I'd make a fool of myself yet.

Then Cooley came to my rescue. "I tell you, boys, he's the real thing — genuine. You do the man an injustice. He's a nice fellow. He speaks his Southern lingo, but he's square."

Having defended me he now came nearer and by his good offices I became acquainted with other men under favourable conditions.

He implanted in the minds of his mother and sister (they lived in Boston) a curiosity about me some time before I knew them. He used to quote to them what he regarded as my unusual sayings, so that they knew much about my grandfather and Uncle Ephraim and Colonel Graham and Professor Randall before I was invited to dine with them.

Inevitably at dinner the talk turned on the Southern subjects. A story that I had told them of the excessive religious life of the country people startled Mrs. Cooley into saying:

"I didn't know the poor country people in the South had churches of their own or religion of any sort. We are always sending money there for missions."

"Why mother!" exclaimed Adelaide.

A young lady at the table, a friend of Adelaide's, asked me to explain the "Cult of Uncle Remus." It is but fair to her to say that everybody in the world had not then read Uncle Remus. He was new and he spoke an unknown tongue to this group of people.

"The Cult of Uncle Remus," I repeated, pondering the impulse to which I at last yielded. "Yes, that is the Cult of the Hare. There was a powerful African tribe who had this religion; and a slave-dealer long, long ago, from Bristol, Rhode Island, captured the crown prince of the tribe and he was sold in the slave-market at Charleston, South Carolina. But, through all the horrors of slavery, he kept his ancestral religious cult and handed it down to his oldest son, and he to his oldest son.

"Uncle Remus —'uncle' really meaning priest — is the direct descendant of this prince; and he is now the head of the Cult."

I expected my yarn to be broken off before I had unwound even this much. But the young lady asked:

"Do they really worship the rabbit?"

"Well, the degradation of slavery, you know, caused all the African religions to be corrupted and the Uncle Remus of our day has a corrupted version of these religious tales and ceremonies."

"Something like Voodoo?"

"No, not cruel. On the contrary, the Cult of the Hare is a very gentle thing. They tell it to little white boys. Every neighbourhood — almost every family — has an 'uncle' who keeps these traditions alive, and he is a gentle old man."

Nobody had smiled yet.

"And do they admit white persons to their ceremonies?" asked Adelaide.

"And mulattoes?" asked her friend. "Is Joel Chandler Harris a very black man?"

"As black as night," said I.

"And does he believe in this cult or has he written out these stories as a contribution to comparative religions?"

"I do not know. Mr. Harris is a very reticent man."

Mrs. Cooley confirmed my story by saying that there are now families in Bristol whose fortune was laid by the slave-trade and that they had never, even to this day, quite recovered from the moral taint of their ancestors.

If the humorous sense of the Cooleys seemed to me a little sluggish on that particular day, it is only fair to remember that we had lived in such different worlds that we hardly spoke the same language — on that group of subjects.

But what an emancipation I owed to that candid and straight habit of thought and life which has no social or intellectual punishment for those who differed from it, at least on the subjects about which I was then especially concerned!

I even now recall with gratitude the freedom

that I felt and the rest in having my own religious doubts dispelled.   It was like the tingle of the New England air in the early spring.   But my mother? And Margaret?   Dear little Margaret would not even understand why there had been any doubts in the first place.   I wrote nothing of these things to them.

But I did write to John Cary:

"It is as we suspected.   In Germany, in England, and here, every really independent mind has long ago thrown away those mediæval dogmas. The histories and biographies and recollections and traditions that make up the Bible were gathered from many sources.   Critical scholarship has now traced them all, or nearly all, to their authors or to the places and times of their origin; and many of them were written by other men than the men whose names they bear.

"Of course, too, the doctrine, that your conduct will depend on your faith in these books, is false. People talk about these things here with perfect freedom.   I'll send you a number of books if you have time and a mind to read them that will clear up the old difficulty."

I soon received this answer:

"It was very good of you to have my soul's salvation at heart in the new world that you're gone to conquer.   Thank you, thank you, very much; and what you say is reassuring.

"But I've ceased to trouble myself about the matter. Father and mother had, of course, to give up their plan of my going into the pulpit; and, as soon as they abandoned that, I ceased to bother myself. I don't believe the old stuff, of course. I never did. But they do! And I can't discuss the subject with them or with anybody here. I simply go on in silence. I'm in business now, you know — building a railroad; and, so long as I go to church, say nothing about religious doctrine, and vote the Democratic ticket, I'm all right. And I'm going to keep up a show of acquiescence in the old order of things as long as the old folks live. I wouldn't give them pain for the world. It would simply kill my mother to read this letter, and as for father — he'd go to the lunatic asylum — or send me there.

"I will keep the peace; and, since I am kept busy at practical affairs, it's all right.

"Thank you, old man. Don't send any books. I must live with the dear old folks, and I wouldn't have such books as you'd send in the house. We'll talk over these things some day, I hope. Great success to you!"

John Cary is yet an interesting man to those who knew him when he was young. But his suppression made him a cynic, and very greatly embittered his life. He himself has said: "I had to live a lie too long."

My old blind speculations and wonderings and gropings and fears and hopes about science now gave way to a revel of freedom and to eager and frank inquiry. There must be youth who come every year upon that tingling surprise of first finding out what science teaches about the universe — or do they now acquire it in childhood as a matter of course?

For the first time I got a conception of its orderliness, its immensity, its continuity, its fruitfulness, the place that man holds in it; how our "cooling cinder" is a negligible part of a small solar system, which is itself a negligible and transitory part of the universe; how man came up — a sane theory at least, in place of a fable that told nothing — how by slow steps he has organized society; how even yet we have close kin-creatures in the jungle; how we hinder our rational organization and our conquest over Nature by wasting time in wars with guns and wars with words; how we hold to mere neighbourhood notions and superstitions and traditions of a day of blindness as sacred things, and follow now meaningless forms of worship, conceived in a time of scientific darkness; how we wrangle over governmental or social or educational formulas and doctrines "of the fathers," instead of banishing disease from the earth and organizing society to train a scientifically high-bred race!

The sweeping generalizations and possibilities

both of the physical and of the historical sciences, most of which are now nursery commonplaces, were then first receiving formulation for laymen; and my reading and my talks with men of the same eagerness of mind brought an intellectual exaltation. While I missed my old Southern companions, I feared that they would be companions no more.

But, if I could not write to Margaret of these things, I could tell her of the music, which I now heard for the first time, of the audiences, of the splendour of the women on gala occasions, and a few great paintings that I had seen. I had before seen nothing better than family portraits, most of which were very badly done.

And my mother — I could explain to her the Cooley home, where there was an orderliness of a different sort from my mother's orderliness. It was more elaborate. The Cooleys had many more things in their house than I had ever seen in a house before, and yet every thing had its place.

"Such orderliness leaves nothing to the imagination," I said to myself when I first saw it. But I soon came to thank heaven that it left the imagination for other and higher uses. I fancy that Southern housewives of the old time spent more energy in directing and doing over the work of slaves than will be required to conduct the whole domestic economy of the millennium. I was reminded of the famous talker of our little capital who had recently died and of whom Dr. Benson had said truly, "He spent more intellectual energy and wit in entertaining loafers at the hotel than any man in town spent on his profession." So our Southern women of social importance spent more energy in managing slaves and in fussing with them than the women of Boston spent in acquiring a knowledge of literature and the arts.

There were several Southern coloured students in college. I came to know one of them because he and I exchanged confidences about the extreme Bostonian intonations and inflections of the lecturer under whom we sat. Coming out of the classroom, this coloured lad would amuse us by mimicking him and then by translating parts of the lecture into good "nigger" English, which only he and I of the company could understand.

He amused other students by exaggerating our Southern drawl and inflections.

Another coloured student came into much notoriety for a time by an accident that made him a hero.

He had his room in a private house and somebody hired the house who objected to his presence because he was a Negro. This as once raised a storm of protest. It was the first display that I had seen of that sentimentality toward black persons which makes them pets — and victims — of a determined and ostentatious display of "justice."

Nobody had hitherto paid any especial attention to this fellow till it appeared that he was
persecuted. Instantly the "New England conscience" became active and showed its morbidity.
Everybody seemed bent on doing what nobody
would naturally and normally have done before.
A dozen men offered to take him as their room-
mate. It should never be said of them that they
had suffered a man to be unjustly dealt with because
of the colour of his skin. One of these generous
volunteers was Cooley. He'd take him as a room-
mate at once.

"I suppose you'd regard it as a degradation,
Worth, but I can't see that man hounded because
he is black."

It was a fine spirit. But Cooley was too late in
his good impulse. Another man had anticipated
him. A man named Foster, who had an hereditary
claim to abolitionist sensitiveness, had helped the
Negro move his books and belongings into his
own rooms; and for the rest of that year they
lived together.

The way of the saints who fail to take every-day
facts into account is still a hard way. Foster was
years later black-balled in a social club in a
Western (not a Southern) city, by peculiar persons
to whom this generous conduct made him objection
able, for their zeal had a different tangent.

This foolish incident gave me much to think

about. I had known before that we had a grave "Southern problem," which included white people and Negroes too. It was now that I first found out that we had also a "Negro problem." For two years the Negro student had been there and no white lad had invited him to share his room. When the new tenants of the house objected to him, I could not see why it did not occur to his friends to help him find another room for himself. That is what would have happened if he had been a white boy — if anything would have happened. But, since he was black, that was not enough. Dozen of men who had not even been his friends — had not known him — felt impelled to take him into intimacy. Impelled by what? I had only a psychological interest in the incident. But that interest was, I confess, great. I asked Cooley, but he could not explain this to me very satisfactorily.

"Cooley," said I, "suppose the boy had been a German boy, and the people in the house had said that they objected to a German, would you have asked him to room with you?"

"Certainly not. Why should I?"

"If he had been a Roman Catholic, or a Jew, and objection had been raised to his religion or to his race, would you have come to his rescue?"

"Certainly not. Why should I?"

"Why, then, merely because he is a Negro?

Wouldn't the German or the Roman Catholic or the Jew also be victims of 'persecution'?"

"No."

"It becomes 'persecution,' then, only when the victim is black?"

It was many years afterward that I ventured this definition of the Negro in the United States:

"A person of African blood (much or little) about whom men of English descent tell only half the truth and because of whom they do not act with frankness and sanity either toward the Negro or to one another — in a word, about whom they easily lose their common sense, their usual good judgment, and even their powers of accurate observation. The Negro-in-America, therefore, is a form of insanity that overtakes white men."

This definition may have ethnological defects, but psychologically and historically much can be said in its favour.

The vacation months of that year I spent in Europe with a little group of Harvard men, and thus I was away from home for two years.

During my second year, being now at ease and having got my bearings, I worked in a new field of intellectual labour with zest and happiness — taking time now and then to wonder whether Adelaide Cooley, since I had come to know her better, were really less beautiful than Margaret.

I had not seen my cousin for so long a time that this question was hard to answer. I had it, therefore, for consideration whenever I chose, during that whole year. The marvels of the universe excited me less violently, my old religious tortures were happily ended, and I gave my full working power to my historical and economic studies.

I did a task of research, an honest if poor thing, in a field that was new to my instructors — to wit, an inquiry to show the good start in varied industries that my native State had made while it was a colony, how, indeed, it had outstripped the colony of Massachusetts Bay; and I made an effort to show what would have been the results, in the history of our country, if slavery had been prevented and such "works" as my grandfather used to speak of had been done. The novelty of the subject, at that time and in that place, and the earnestness that my work showed won me the applause of my Department.

In the midst of this inquiry, when my mind was full of the facts that I was finding out and of nothing else, an affectionate letter came from Professor Randall, my old teacher of Greek. He had found an error — a very little error (but all scholastic errors are of the same size) — in a technical paper by the Professor of Greek at Harvard — an error in a reference to the use of the preposition with the infinitive in a certian passage of Aristophanes.

Since it would be unseemly in him to correct a Northern scholar in a Northern journal (there was no Southern philological journal), I might use the information, if I would. "Use it gently," he adjured me.

I still thank heaven for such a gentleman as that! What a long-lost world this letter brought back to me! For I did not even know the Professor of Greek at Harvard, and I had not (the greater my shame) opened a Greek text since I had come there. How far we travel sometimes on a little journey!

My thesis in economics brought me my degree and — to my surprise — an offer of an instructor's position in the college for the next year. I suppose that I now pronounced our mother tongue without the most noticeable Southern intonations and elisions. At any rate I now escaped being often reminded by look or word that I was a Southerner.

I was pleased by this offer, but — well, I had had no other thought than to go home. But what should I do when I went South?

I was now at home at Harvard; free, too, as I had not before been. Could I ever be free in the South?

But I seemed to hear the flow of the river where it ever turned the little mill; I thought of my mother and of her heroic endurance for me, of my sister, Barbara, now a girl quite grown, of my cousin, Margaret, the restful softness of her speech and ways — expecting me — and of the grave of the old man to whose large intuition I owed these expanding years. I thought of my own people — the openness of their lives, their humour, the glow of their unrepressed kindliness, their closeness to the soil, of the pathos of their lives, too, and of their ancient misfortunes, of their barren inheritance and of their hard problems, and these drew me. I recalled our Southern spring with its perfumed and brilliant woodland, and the smell of ploughed ground and the soft, cool nights; and sweet orchards, with bees, and the roses running on garden fences; the green choir of the pines, the flickering brown carpet of their sanctuary and the fathomless blue dome above them. I thought of the ripe, deep summer now coming on — a mellow land — and of the white fields opening their fleece to the sun.

All these meant home, a home that pathetically called to all its sons to build on the old foundations, laid before the Great Shadow crept over the land.

CHAPTER IX

AS SOON as I crossed the Potomac on my journey homeward, I was aware that I was coming into another world. A feeling of homelessness came over me and I felt a doubt whether I really knew either of these worlds. I recalled the remark of a Professor of History at Harvard, that these two peoples were radically different, that the folk of New England and the folk of the South would never wholly understand one another and would never be really one people. I had laughed at this remark. But had I not laughed ignorantly?

I had forgotten even how sparsely the country was settled through which I was going. I had forgotten the neglected homes visible from the cars, the cabins about which half-naked Negro children played and from which ragged men and women, drunk with idleness, stared at the train, the ill-kept railway stations where crowds of loafers stood with their hands in their pockets and spat at cracks in the platform, unkempt countrymen, heavy with dyspepsia and malaria, idle Negroes, and village loafers. There had been a heavy rain and the roads, where I caught glimpses of them, were long mudholes. It occurred to me for the first time that this region is yet a frontier — a new land untouched except by pioneers, pioneers who had merely lingered till they had thought the land worn out and who thought that their old order of life — now destroyed by Time's pressure of which war was the instrument — had been the crown of civilization. Here was poverty — a depressed population, the idle squalor of the Negro now that slavery was relaxed, and the hopeless inertia of the white man who had been deadened by an old economic error.

Was it my home and my land, where there were no neat villages and well-kept lawns and painted fences as in New England? Would I — would any man who had seen the green hills of New York and of Pennsylvania or who knew about the rich prairies of Ohio and Illinois — ever come to live here because the land or the life drew him? If those that I loved did not live here, would I ever dream of coming back?

The journey stretched itself through the long hot day, and time and chance came for many moods.

The loafing Negroes were so good-natured that I began to see many things to laugh at. They were an elemental part of the landscape, belonged to it as elephants or monkeys belonged to Africa.

The earth itself seemed to revolve slowly. It *was* another country from the country whence I had come. It must be accepted as it is, I reflected, and judged by its own standard.

We passed an excursion train of Negroes, which was standing on a side-track. Women with red head-kerchiefs leaned far out the windows and called loudly to acquaintances a hundred yards away; and men crowded the platform and hung on the steps — all hot, all happy, all vociferous.

One old man called to a boy: "Whar yo gwine, Jonas?"

"Aint gwine no whar. Done bin whar I'z gwine."

At last I slipped back into my former self, and the stations and the long stretches of country became familiar to me as we came nearer to Marlborough; and I began to feel at home again, or nervously eager to be at home. I recalled my own impassioned description of the old red hills and of the pine barrens. "They once bred men; they shall breed men again." And at last a sort of patient pride swelled up in me that I, too, was a part of this land, had roots deep in it, felt it, knew it, understood it, believed in it as men who had come into life elsewhere could not.

I approached the little capital city with eager excitement. Of course the dusty train was several hours late, but it came bravely, with a great blowing of the whistle and much ringing of the bell, into the same dirty "shed"; there were the same noisy Negro hackmen, shouting as if the travellers were a mile away, and pointing with their whips to the same ramshackle carriages that I had seen in my boyhood; the same black and yellow women held apparently the same fried chicken and hard-boiled eggs up to the car windows, insisting on their freshness; and the same Negro boys offered red apples at a profitless low price. The noise was out of proportion to the six or eight passengers who, in dirty linen "dusters," had at last reached the end of their belated journey. You might have thought from the number of carriages and coachmen that the whole population of "the city" had been "to the North" and was expected home on that train.

It was very hot. The afternoon air danced before your eyes as you looked up the dusty road toward the town. That day's train to Millworth had already gone, and I must "lay over" till to-morrow, or go the hot twelve miles, over an almost impassable country road, the memory of which now came to me with dread.

At the hotel, there seemed to be three or four Negro porters for every guest, and the clerk adjusted his necktie and put on an air of momentary energy as he turned the book to the newcomers.

He bowed and gave a pen to the first of the four, and for everyone in turn he had a remark:

"Pretty warm, Major."

"A little late to-day."

"Rather dusty up the road."

With such phrases he raised expectations of coolness and promptness and cleanliness that you afterward looked for in vain. The big, square, bare, dirty room, the chipped pitcher on the washstand, the broken bricks above the fireplace, against which the feet of last winter's statesmen had pressed too often and too hard, the split-bottom chairs whose seats had sagged with the long-borne weight of heavy, lazy men, the soiled and torn window shades and the dirty windows (was nothing ever mended or washed?) — as I looked out to the court-house across the street, I saw a Negro boy spinning a top and five white men standing about him, resting heavily on their own trousers' pockets; and the whole unchanged and unchangeable scene and surroundings amused me in spite of my depression. Surely I had seen all these things before in some previous embodiment. For I was two men — one who knew this scene and contentedly took it for granted, and another to whom it now came as a revelation of despair.

As I walked toward the State House, the treeless street seemed absurdly wide, making the business buildings on either side ludicrously squatty; for, since I had been gone, the Board of Trade, wishing to give the business part of the town a metropolitan appearance, had induced the aldermen to cut down the elms which fifty years had made beautiful. Broadway, in New York, they said, had no trees on it.

But the oaks in the capitol square yet stood, and the dignified little granite State House was impressive, its deeply worn stone steps suggesting antiquity. It was cool and shady there; and the squirrels ran over the grass and scampered up the trees, showing far more energy than any other creatures I had yet seen. The wide avenue that led to the left to Dr. Benson's — there, too, the old elms still stood. What a beautiful village street it was, leading past the churches, and the deep-shaded girls' seminary with its ivy-covered stone buildings, on by modest, shaded old homes from whose yards the heavy odour of magnolias came! This at last was what I had come to, and it was worth coming to. I met nobody on the street that knew me; but I recognized the old man who kept the drugstore, whose white hair was always oiled and carefully brushed high above his kindly face. He bowed as we met; for men did not then pass even strangers on the street without greeting. And I met an old Negro man who pulled off his hat to me.

Aunt Katharine herself met me at the Benson door, become more beautiful, I thought, with the deeper gray (almost whiteness now) that these two years had added to her hair. After a glad greeting — her eyes moist from the joy of the surprise — she called "Margaret — come; guess who's here. Hurry, child."

They would have me stand up with my back against the door to measure my height — six feet, and a bare inch more. Of course I had not grown taller, but a little side-beard (the fashion, then, among young collegians) gave me a somewhat strange, a sort of foreign appearance. Margaret took me first by one arm and turned me about, gazing at me playfully, then by the other arm, and looking up said with mockery, "A great, big man-cousin, from a foreign country, and he talks a foreign language too!"

There was no doubt now which was the more beautiful. The liquefaction of her voice as well as of her clothes surpassed even my loneliest recollection of their soft sound and motion.

It was the tender welcome of the old years. A cool cleanliness covered everything as a garment. The plainness and the coolness and the old fashion and the neatness of the house, the speech and the intonations and the smiles of my kinswomen were grateful. The very furniture seemed to greet me affectionately.

Good Doctor Benson came in from his office and his dignified gaiety and his heartiness as he stood before me with both hands on my shoulders showed the kindliness which is the first quality of a gentleman.

The frolicsome girlishness of my cousin's manner reminded me of the day in the garret at the Old Place. Yet she was a grown woman now, and presently I felt a certain new dignity in her tone as the conversation turned to family subjects. She answered questions about my mother and Barbara in a manner that said, "I am now among the grown-ups."

"The Old Place is just as it was, they say. I have not seen it, but they tell me that Uncle Ephraim is a good master and manager."

As supper-time came the rector of St. Peter's came in, the Reverend Donald Yarborough, whom I had known at the Graham school, where he was an upper-classman when I entered. Very clerical he was, and his intonations were the droopings and the dronings of the service. He had a solemnity of manner that somewhat checked our gaiety; and he spoke of our school-days with condescension — surely an unreal note. We were obliged to talk of church news and church plans, in which I observed that my aunt and cousin played even a more important part than they had played in former years.

I felt a renewed wish to go home that night, and I hired a horse at the hotel. The road was as bad as it had been years before. There were deep gulleys in which bushes had been thrown and a little earth put over them, and the earth had been worn away and the brushes cracked under the horses' steps. At other places paths had been cut through the woods around holes, too deep to fill up, but I rode on eagerly. I passed the old campground, now a waste space grown up in broom sage, ghostly and desolate in the moonlight. Old Jonas Good'in's house had a dim light in it; and I wondered whether this were the bottle-period or the "converted" period of the old fellow's year.

Just as my brother was about to shut the house for the night, I arrived. Although a moment before the day had been done for them, for us all it now began again. At last I was at home, and the old feeling of fathomless gratitude surged over me. We asked questions, jumping from this subject to that. We wandered over the whole house — I must see every little change that had been made or look at certain rooms because no change had been made. Mother prepared a late supper with her own hands, almost forbidding even my sister to help.

I recall my mother's restless happiness because I had come, and all her three children were again

with her. While we sat at the table, she would rise
and touch each of us — a hand on this one's
head, a kiss on this one's cheek, a stroke on this
one's hand.

Late as it was when I went to bed in my old
room, I did not soon fall asleep.

I lay and let the years pass in procession before
me. It was the old home. Was it I that had
changed? The room seemed at times like one
that I had once seen somewhere in a dimly remembered house, or had read about in a half-forgotten
book. The red clay hearth, the high mantelpiece
with the odd little clock and the blue jar on it, the
bare, shining, clean walls, the plain curtains —
these all grasped my remembrance and my
affections. But were they mine?

The door opened softly and I saw my mother
come in. I kept silent and she came and looked
down at me:

"I thought you might be awake. Your coming
has given me happiness instead of sleep," and she
bent over and kissed my forehead.

Seated on the side of my bed, she talked — of
what I should not now tell you if I could; but
her presence I recall as one recalls a gentle melody
or a pleasant odour years afterward. Little
nothings, pleasantries or recollections, incidents
of family life, jokes about Barbara and Charles,
an allusion to my father — she was near me and

that was her happiness; and full hearts tell the deepest emotions by talk of most trivial things.

"You know, I think Charlie's really in love with Alice Maynard.   What if it should happen?

"Yes, Barbara has finished the Seminary course.

"I have nothing on earth to do.   Charlie manages the mill and sometimes almost refuses to tell me about it.

"Yes, your Aunt Eliza is just the same.   Didn't you think her remarkably cheerful to-night?

"Are you sure you are comfortable and will not be too warm with the bed so far from the window?"

At last she stood at the foot of the bed and laughed at our spending the night in so foolish a fashion "as if all the days to come would not be ours to talk over everything."

"Good-night, dear boy.   You are sure you are comfortable?"

I could hear the flow of the river.   In the morning I should see the little mill.   And the fields must now be white and red with the blooms of the cotton.

CHAPTER X

I SEE GREAT FORCES RANGE THEMSELVES

IT TAKES some time to recover from collegiate astigmatism; and it is doubtful whether my cousin Margaret helped me toward recovery. But there was no doubt about her beauty nor about the grace of her movements. What a variety of simple, light summer gowns she had! Although our Southern summers are long, I did not decide that whole summer which colour became her best. Such a question has often taxed wiser men than I for a longer time, I dare say. But this I know — all her frocks yielded to her graceful ways, as gowns ought to yield to supple motions in languid summers; and the days passed in unhurrying wonder how I should serve my country.

One chance indeed seemed likely to be thrust upon me, only to be snatched away.

I had made up my mind to write a history of the Commonwealth, as what youth has not during his first summer out of a university? Thus I came to discover the old State Library. Very few persons knew that it existed. You wound your way up a spiral staircase in the State House till you came to a dingy room at the base of the dome. The librarian was there — an old placard on the door informed you — between three o'clock and five on Mondays, Wednesdays, and Fridays during the sessions of the Legislature, "unless a notice to the contrary was posted beforehand"; but any member of the Legislature (they alone were supposed to use it) could get the key at any time from the office of the State Treasurer on the first floor.   I often went up there early in the day — nobody else came — and ransacked the dusty piles of miscellaneous things — old public account books, flags and government reports, which lay on the floor obstructing your way to the book-cases.

Somebody was kind enough to propose, since I had found the library, that I become a candidate for State Librarian.   The office was filled by the Governor's appointment; and the next Governor doubtless would appoint me if I secured sufficiently strong endorsements.   The duties were light and the salary was $200 a year — that much money just picked up.

As soon as this suggestion was noised about, old Mr. Birdcastle, the librarian, who had once been foreman in the newspaper office and had lost one eye and went on crutches from rheumatism (he was, moreover, an old soldier of honourable record) became excited.   He approached me one afternoon:

"Mr. Worth, haven't I allers treated you fair?"

"Certainly, Mr. Birdcastle."

"I've allers thought you a fair man."

"I hope you do yet, Mr. Birdcastle."

"Well, from what I hear, I have sometimes thought maybe you wasn't. You see, you're a young man with a good eddication, and you've got some property and you can do what you've a mind to do. I don' see, then, whaffore you want to dispersess a poo' man an' a ol' soldier like me of this poo' livin' outer this libery. 'Tain't much. But it ain't confinin', especially in summer, and my health ain't good enough for much else."

I assured him that I had no thought of making such an effort. Then he proposed to have a duplicate key made for me so that I needn't take the trouble to go to the Treasurer's office; "for many a time, as you know, atter the Legislatur' adj'ines, there ain't nobody in the Treasurer's office more'n half the time."

Marlborough did not seem to me a part of the real world, and I am not sure that it seems so yet. It had no fixed relation to time or space. It was remote and indefinite. One year's calendar was as good as another year's there. It was, I suppose, the dullest settlement of English-speaking folk in the whole world.

A visiting wag declared that, if it were bodily taken up and moved to New York and exhibited under a huge circus tent — everybody leading his life without change or knowledge that the town was on show — the admission fees would build the Soldiers' Monument.

The busiest men in the town were the preachers and the physicians. The preachers not only preached twice on Sundays, but they held prayer-meetings on Wednesday nights and other meetings on Friday nights for missions and such. For this reason on Wednesday nights no session of the Legislature nor any important meetings were held even in winter, to say nothing of summer. Of course it was permissible to play poker as on any other night, for that was a private indulgence and not a public disrespect to religion. The doctors dosed everybody. The city "enjoyed its proverbial good health"; but everybody had some trifling ailment, perhaps the result of the physic. Thus life ran its circle in Marlborough from ailment around to ailment again.

If you were to go there even now, you would soon lose your reckonings. The sense of responsibility would slip from you. The days would come and go, every one like every other one. You would hear the same remarks made at the same time of the day that were made there at that time of the day in the years of your grandfathers. Your own emotions and sensations would become illusive and uncertain, and life an intangible continuity

of a vacuous monotony. While he lives, a man
may there study himself, dead — touch his own
corpse and commune with his own suspended intelligence.

Of all strange places in the world, therefore,
to find an energetic man, surely old Birdcastle's
dingy eyrie was the strangest. But that's what
happened. I went up there one day and the
library door was open.

"Well, Mr. Birdcastle, I've caught you at last."

"It's a bird of another feather," said a pleasant
voice from near the floor; and there knelt, over a
pile of old newspapers, a big, hot, ruddy countryman. He looked up and said:

"And you're a ghost. Nobody else would
come here. How are you? Let's shake hands
on this singular experience — the only two men
that ever met here. My name's Bain."

"And my name's Worth."

"I reckon we know one another. Are you
writing a history of the state, too?"

"Yes, are you?"

"I've found out just enough to know that
nobody knows anything about it. It is the clearest case of arrested development to be found in
human annals."

"Strong men came here," he presently rambled
on. "They worked; then they bought slaves
and stopped working; then they wrangled; then

they fought; then they were oppressed; and they were on the defensive from the time slavery came. They are side-tracked now, and are just about to find out that the track they are on leads nowhere. Is that good history?"

There he stood with his coat off, telling a century of a people's story in a sentence.

Thus I first saw Professor William Malcolm Bain; and he explained to me as we came down the stairs that he was an instructor at the University and that he had, at his own request, been sent to visit the country schools of the State — "to hold teachers' institutes"— for two years. He was now holding meetings in this neighbourhood; and in the fall he would go back to the University and teach there.

"That's the real service to our country in our generation — the school-master's," he said. "That's my historical conclusion."

So he ran on. I felt at the end of half an hour that I had always known him. When we had come down into the capitol yard, he ran away from me, a sentence unfinished, to give the squirrels peanuts.

He had a benignant, round, ruddy face, which showed innumerable freckles when he became warm, and he looked at you out of very large, round eyes. He had a big body and wide square shoulders, but he moved with quickness. Yet his infinite good nature and mildness concealed his strength, or caused you to think of it as held in check; for so gentle was he that he seemed often either to be unaware of his power or himself to be laughing at it. As he went down the street, almost everybody greeted him familiarly. Some called him "Professor," others "Professor Billy." For everybody knew him.

His next meeting of teachers was at Millworth. My brother, I discovered, knew him and called him Professor Billy. The teachers of half the county gathered in the school-house, about twenty young women and one young man. I asked if I might attend.

"Surely," said he, "and help us."

He shook hands with them all. He had each one fill out a card and thus write down a condensed autobiography. He sat down and explained his business — to lecture about teaching.

"But we won't call it that. We'll simply talk about how to interest the children."

"Miss Thomas, what most interests the children in your school?"

Miss Thomas wasn't sure. She'd have to think.

"Miss Lloyd, do you ever have the children in your school tell you stories?"

"No, sir."

"We'll try that to-morrow. When we meet I shall ask one or two of you to tell us stories — no matter what, something you've read, something you've seen, anything that you think will interest us." A smile of astonishment went around the room.

"You see," and he arose and began to lecture — "you see anybody can hammer the multiplication table and a few rules of grammar into a child's head, if you take time enough. That's necessary. You all have regular lessons in arithmetic, in spelling, in reading, in writing, and in geography. I'll conduct a lesson in each of these subjects before I go with the children of this school; and then I'll ask some of you to conduct a lesson or two — after the children have heard you tell stories for an hour. For the main thing that I've come to tell you is that you must manage first to get all the children interested."

These teachers had come to the "institute" to hear formal lectures on "The Theory and the Art of Teaching"; and their surprise grew as this big, ruddy, jocular fellow alternately sat down and stood up, lectured and asked questions. But one thing was certain — *they* were interested. By the time they might think that at last he was fully launched on a formal lecture, he would pull from his pocket a copy of "The Vicar of Wakefield," and ask one of the teachers to read a page aloud.

He invited them to ask questions, most of which were very formal and very silly. Quite an animated controversy sprang up between two of the young women, whether it were better to teach spelling orally or by writing out the words. One stated her case with earnestness. The other stated her case with quite as great earnestness; and he asked each of them many questions. When there was the greatest eagerness to hear his decision, he said:

"Well, now, I'll tell you. Uncle Eben had a pig. He sold it to a white man who lived two miles down the road. The next day the pig came back to Uncle Eben's. Then he sold it to another white man who lived two miles up the road. While the second white man was on his way home with the pig, he met the first white man.

" 'See here', said the first white man. 'That's my pig. I bought it from an old nigger yesterday for two dollars.'

" 'No,' said the other, 'I've just bought it from an old nigger for two dollars and a half, and I'm taking it home.'

"After quarreling awhile they agreed to go back to Uncle Eben's and call him to account.

"The old Negro came out of his cabin, and the two men angrily confronted him.

" 'I paid you two dollars for the pig.'

" 'And I paid you two dollars and a half for the same pig.'

" 'Now, boss,' said Uncle Eben humbly, 'I

ain' niver yit mixed up in no white folks's quarrels, an' I ain' gwine ter mix up in 'em now. I leaves yer ter settle yer own diffunces.'

"Now, I have never yet mixed up in controversies between ladies," said Professor Billy, "and I leave you to settle your own differences."

The next morning he was going through the mill with my brother, asking questions about everything that seemed to work with precision — every interesting process. In the afternoon he was in a cotton-field, talking with a Negro about the distance between the cotton plants. At some time during his stay of three days he learned that Mr. Markham, the carpenter, was an unusually skilful man with tools; and he asked him to show him how he used a certain plane.

"Mr. Markham, how could you teach all the carpenters in the county to do their work as well as you?"

"They could larn theirselves."

"Yes, but they don't. How could you show 'em?"

"Dinged if I know," said Mr. Markham.

The last night of Professor Billy's visit to Millworth, he made a speech in the school-house to everybody who would go to hear him. He told what a country school ought to be, and he asked half a dozen persons in the audience, by name, how often they went to the school-house.

That night he and Charles and I talked long about his notions of a school; and as he went on I saw the people of a rural commonwealth doing their work in ineffective, hereditary ways, half starving on a fertile soil, wasting more than they garnered, the victims of isolation and stability, sprawling in poverty. Teachers, preachers, politicians praised them, cajoled them, fed on them, and left them as they found them. A thousand years of these same influences would leave them as they were. There was a lot of formulas that were called Education; there was another lot of formulas that were called Religion; and there was another lot of formulas that were called Politics. So, too, there was a lot of formulas that were called Cooking, another lot that were called Farming, and so on. And nothing changed.

But here was a man who knew that a change could be brought about. He believed in these people as no other man I had ever seen believed in them; and he thought he saw a way to wake them up. The school must teach them to do their every-day tasks well instead of ill. The school must mean something different to them from what it now meant, and it must reach adults as well as children. It must teach any man and any woman how to do his job better. That was the beginning of constructive statesmanship.

He went away on a train at midnight. As I

walked back home from the station, I thought
I saw a vision of what might be done — in a
hundred years.

"He has more life and spring in him," said my
brother, "than any other man in the State. The
political bosses regard him as a school-teacher.
They'll find out at some time that he is constructing
a revolution.   Then something will happen."

In a little while the dullness of the monotonous
summer was broken in Marlborough; for the town
was getting ready for a great meeting of the Daughters of the Confederacy, which was both a patriotic
and social event out of the common.   Preparations
were made in all the best households to receive the
visiting ladies.   It would be a notable company
of young women, and the vocabulary of oratory
and of gallantry must be polished up.   The
Governor, of course, was to make a speech, and
most of the preachers would have a chance to
pray at their meetings; and there would, during
the week, be other oratorical occasions, to say
nothing of the grand reception at the Governor's
mansion.

The day came.   After the Governor had made
his gallant and patriotic address of welcome,
Colonel Stringweather was introduced amid great
applause.   He had been a hero at the battle of
Malvern Hill, and there was no patriotic occasion,

during these years of which I now write, that Colonel Stringweather did not grace.

He praised the women of the Confederacy in resonant periods, and he praised their daughters. It is cold and meagre — this mere telling about it — and unfair to Colonel Stringweather.

"As God is in heaven," said he in a pious ejaculation, "the sun never shone on a sight so fair or on an enterprise so worthy as this gathering of the beauty and the devotion of the old State, and every fold in her blood-stained flag kisses the wind of heaven as a benediction on you."

There were tears on the cheeks of the women; and Colonel Stringweather's voice wept, too, as he went on, to a climax that likened the meeting to heaven and the Daughters to angels.

The particular purpose of the meeting was to decide whether the Daughters should build a monument to the women of the Confederacy. But the Colonel did not think to mention the business of the day.   He was like many men who write about "literature"— he forgot to mention the subject.

At another meeting Professor Billy made a speech. The Daughters had not yet acquired the art of speaking themselves, and they seemed content to be spoken to.

Professor Billy, too, had a compliment for them and a story.   But he remembered their eagerness to do some service to the commonwealth — especially for the women. Then he told how many illiterate women there were — how they were rearing illiterate children. "And they cannot be taught for lack of teachers." He unfolded a plan to build a State·school to train teachers and prayed them to let that be a monument to the women of the Confederacy.

A few hours later at the hotel Professor Billy was telling a story to the company — Colonel Stringweather among the rest — about an educated pig that he had seen in a circus. The Colonel told a story of an educated horse. Presently in that company of story-tellers all the domestic animals were educated.

"We'll educate folks after a while — don't you think so, Colonel?"

"I was just countin' the schools in this city to-day," replied Colonel Stringweather, "and it seems to me that every old lady and every second young lady has a select school for chillern, and I hear of three more that will start in the fall. Then there's the Female Seminary and Miss Green's School for Young Ladies and three schools for boys, the Masonic Orphan Asylum, the college for niggers, and the free school to boot. What's lackin' in education, Professor? There's a school under the auspices of every church in town."

"Did you ever notice," Professor Billy asked,

"how there is always a school under every 'auspices'— except now and then you find a Sunday-school picnic or a church fair under one?"

"I noticed," he went on, "that the best educated man in Sylvanus County keeps a thoroughbred bull, and has a good road across his land, and he has more sheep than dogs. Wouldn't it be a good plan to have a Professor of Roads, and a Professor of Sheep added to the faculty of the University, to travel about, and to teach the people?"

The Colonel laughed immoderately at such an absurd notion.

Then, in a more select company at the dinner table, the Colonel berated Professor Billy on his "infernal educational scheme." "Don't you know, Professor, that we have this meetin' of the Daughters here now to warm up the women to the old soldiers? A political campaign's comin' on before mighty long, and the ladies must help in their own sweet ways, God bless 'em. Give 'em a rest on your educational scheme. They don't want to think. We want to work up sentiment."

Ah!

There was still another public session of the Daughters and the preachers lectured the ladies on the Christian Aspects of Patriotism. Patriotism meant good homes. Good homes meant good Christian influences. So spoke the Reverend Doctor Babb. And similarly the Reverend Doctor

Suggs spoke on "The Virtue of the Love of Country, a Proper Element of Womanly Character."

After these reverend gentlemen sat down, Colonel Stringweather ventured to make a few additional remarks, in offering a series of resolutions which he had been asked to read.

He declared himself the most steadfast friend, throughout his life, of education, as everybody knew; and he thanked heaven for the unsurpassed educational advantages that our beloved State enjoyed.   Since this was so, then, he did venture to believe, with all respect to learned gentlemen who might hold a contrary opinion, that the fair Daughters of the Confederacy hardly wished to become an eleemosynary institution or to engage in the charitable work of helping the free schools. That was for others to do.   Then he read a resolution in favour of an enduring monument in brass or marble to the heroic women of the Confederacy.

Out of the shimmering blank monotony of life in Marlborough, there thus began to come into clear view the pious force that kept things as they were, and the resolute patient force that must at last change them.   The town did not seem quite so dull as it had been.

And the glow of patriotism became my Cousin Margaret well; for she had thrown her whole enthusiasm into the crusade of the Daughters. Colonel Stringweather was her hero. "What a beautiful oration he made, cousin!"

"Gallant and pious nonsense," said I; and she was ready to cry because of my sacrilege.

She put her hand on my arm and said sweetly (it was a pink gown of lightest texture that she wore that day): "Dear cousin, you have lived away from us so long that you may forget our own people. You won't, will you?"

CHAPTER XI

MY CAREER BEGINS

THE town of Edinboro, having outgrown its former limits and its old-time ways, had taken on an energetic mood. Its cotton mills, its lumber mills and its stores that supplied the country merchants over a wide area had brought a new spirit of commercial activity; and this activity had attracted ambitious country youths who were making the town grow very fast both by their work and by their talk. Many of them wore badges that bore a double E, which stood for Energetic Edinboro. Especially when they made visits to the neighbouring towns it was a point of loyalty to wear these badges. The Edinboro *Torch* printed "Energetic Edinboro" at the top of its first page, and every week the leading editorial was in praise of the town. One week its readers found this piece of news for their encouragement:

"AGAIN THE BEST THERE IS

"The new graded school will be finished next week — the finest public school-building in the State. The finest building — next, the finest school. That's coming, too. The Board has, with customary energy, engaged as superintendent Professor Nicholas Worth, a scion of one of our old families, and a man who has studied at a Northern university, and is thoroughly acquainted with all the latest and most progressive methods. We welcome the learned Professor. The best is none too good for Edinboro."

This hopeful and interesting career was opened for me by the activity of Professor Billy, for already he was consulted by everybody who was in earnest about school work.

"Young Worth is personally all right, I suppose," said Colonel Stringweather (for Edinboro had the distinction of being the home of this distinguished citizen); "but" he asked at the meeting of the school-board when I was elected, "wouldn't it have been as well to get some man who was educated in our midst and has no new-fangled foreign ideas?"

"We want the newest methods, Colonel," a commercial member had said. "We want the most advanced things."

"Oh, well, it's only the free school, anyhow," said the Colonel. "Every gentleman sends his chillern to a private school."

The people received me pleasantly and I caught the energy of their mood.

But the school-houses were, of course, very bare; and I sent for some cheap prints for the walls — portraits of famous men and pictures of great sculptures and of historic buildings; and I explained them to the children until the teachers could repeat my explanations. I bought a little flag for every child — two flags in fact, one of the State and one of the United States. They had no sports. I made the yards attractive as playgrounds and tried to teach them new games. The school soon began to be interesting to them, and the teachers became very engines of enthusiasm. Instead of a long drawn hymn when the school-day began, the children sang a patriotic song. I took a class in geography a mile or two up the river and showed them how the stream had worn its way between the banks. Such simple devices came as revelations to both children and teachers. They thought that I had invented all these things. I fitted up a rough workshop in the shed. The boys soon made crude tables and book-racks and shelves, for the tools were new and sharp and it was easy to work with them. A teacher gave the girls lessons in sewing. Once a week a meeting of all the teachers was held and they went over the list of the children and explained to each other how everyone was doing. And they asked one another, "What do you know about the home life of this child?"

It soon became impossible for the teachers to do this pastoral sort of duty. I, therefore, proposed to several ladies of the town that they take the school records of all the children and visit their homes and report what they discovered. These became "the Ladies' Public School Club." Miss Stringweather, the Colonel's daughter, found an outlet in this work for her energy. The club took a rough school census of the town. Hardly more than half the children of school age were in any school at all. Some of them, it is true, worked in the mills; but there were many who neither worked nor went to school. But within a few months, by the activity of the club, the public school attendance was almost doubled. I did not wait until "commencement" to invite the people to visit the school. I went one day to a meeting of the Board of Trade and invited every member to come the next the day at noon. I showed them how the children marched. They heard them sing. They saw the boys in the workshop. They saw the simple decorations of the rooms.

"Gentlemen," said I, "I want a small engine and a lathe or two in the shop. The school board has no money that it can spend for such a purpose. Can I not depend on energetic Edinboro for these things?"

"You bet your life, Professor," said one of the

young merchants; and, to everybody's amazement, the money was collected and the workshop
was fitted up. "The Professor is a hustler," said
the *Torch* the next week.

There was a public school on the outskirts
of the town for Negro children. When I first
visited it, I came away almost hopeless. The
stupidity of the one teacher and the rag-and-tag
quality of the pupils and the neglected and forlorn
appearance of everything were discouraging.
Either there must be no school or a better school.
I hardly knew how to begin. It I should recom-
mend the dismissal of this teacher, where could I
get a better one?

There was in Malborough a college for Negroes
that was maintained by the mission society of
one of the Northern churches; but I knew as
little about it as any other white man in the
capital. But the next time I went home I went
to see it, hoping to find a capable Negro teacher.
The Principal of the Institute, as it was called,
was the Reverend Doctor Snodder. He had a
meek, hang-dog manner, as if to say; "I am
called to be a teacher of the oppressed." He
regarded himself as a martyr and in martyrdom
he found such joy as he got out of a solemn,
poor life. He had been, I afterward found out,
an unsuccessful preacher at home, and he was
permitted to "take up work in the South." He

spent half his time at the school and half in New England, telling his story of his difficulties, which were real enough, and collecting money to carry his work on.

A vigorous man could long ago have made himself known and liked in the community. But he generally kept within the bounds of the school property, and, since nobody asked him to go anywhere, he was seldom seen by the towns-people. He cut himself off still more because of the encouragement that his wife gave him to martyrdom. She was a vigorous and ambitious woman; but, when she first came to her field of work, she had no opportunity to make even the slightest acquaintance with any of the ladies of the town. Then she withdrew within herself and became bitter. A few of the white women of the country on the neglected side of the city beyond the school, who brought garden products to Mrs. Snodder, became the typical white women of the State in the stories that she told her friends at home — except of course the few "proud, fine ladies of the city," about whom she had an exaggerated and wholly erroneous notion.

The Snodders were neglected and tactless foreigners in a strange land; and they grovelled in martyrdom and made it their chief stock in trade both in misshaping the temper of the students and in keeping up the subscriptions from the North.

I once asked Uncle Ephraim what he knew about the Institute, for the Negroes have underground channels of information that white men lack.

"Don' set no sto' by it, Mars' Littlenick. Dey has dere, 'cordin' to what I hears, de stuck-up young niggers what 'brudder yer dis' and 'brudder yer dat' — preacher niggers what ain't got no ol'-fashion' 'ligion. Dey don' think much on 'em 'bout here."

I shared Uncle Ephraim's opinion after I had made a visit to the Institute. The courses of study led chiefly to the classics and to theology. Snodder himself taught "Christian Ethics."

I told him my errand, but I did not find such a teacher as I wanted for the little black ragamuffins of energetic Edinboro.

But the next summer I went to Hampton, Virginia, where I had heard of a school for coloured people that had been worked out by a man of genius for such a task. Professor Billy went with me. I recall that we thought it prudent not to permit the newspapers to know where we were going.

After a day there, we spent the night talking over what we had seen. "Not a white woman in our State can get such instruction as these Negroes have"; and he sat long in thought, looking out the window on Hampton Roads. Presently he roused himself.

"There was a great naval battle fought out
there — wasn't there? And it changed the whole
business of fighting on water for all time to come.
Our people fought well. Isn't fighting pretty
hard work, Worth — don't you suppose? Why,
then, don't the same people who fought so hard
work hard also? I know a widow of one of the
heroes of the Confederate Ironclad. She is as help-
less as a child. She can do nothing. She 'presides'
over a little school for girls, and somebody else
has to do her work. The other people, in fact,
treat her as a guest and wait upon her."

The next morning was Sunday and we heard
five hundred voices at Hampton Institute sing
Negro melodies as we had never heard them
sung before.

"I wish Uncle Ephraim could hear these," I
said; and Professor Billy remarked that no
white congregation sang so well.

I engaged a teacher to go to Edinboro, and
his name was — John Marshall.

In a little while "Professor" Marshall had
the children come to school in whole garments and
with clean bodies. He taught them to march, to
sing, to sew, to make things with jackknives;
they painted the school house; they mended the
benches; they kept the floor clean and the yard,
too. And the attendance at the Negro school
increased beyond the capacity of the house, so

that he taught one school-roomful of children in the forenoon and another roomful in the afternoon. He taught on Saturdays also.

The fame of the Edinboro public schools was spread by the energetic men of the town. Margaret wrote: "I think, dear cousin, you are doing the noblest work in the world — teaching the children of the poor and making their schools attractive. It's as good as being a missionary."

But Captain Bob Logan said: "You're going too fast, Worth." "Cap'n Bob," as almost everybody in the town called him, was the town wag and philosopher. He was a politician — he chose to call himself a lawyer, but he gave slight attention to his profession, and spent his time in reading and talking. He was supposed to have inherited a small fortune from a distant kinsman. At any rate, he frequently went North and that meant at least money enough to travel. He was a friend of the President of the United States, and he made visits to Washington, as became a Southern Republican boss of that time. His friends accused him of accepting Republicanism for professional reasons. Indeed, few persons gave this interesting and eccentric man credit for sincerity in anything, for nothing was sacred from his wit. Yet he was much liked by his neighbours — "personally, not politically."

"You're going too fast, Worth. The town can't stand the gait. Some young fellows here encourage you to think that we are really an energetic people. Don't you make the mistake to think so. It's a passing mood. We're born under a long sun. Your ladies' school committees will get tired. Your little niggers will go back to their rags. Go slow."

Strangely enough the first protest came from the Negroes. Professor Marshall had taught the children to plant cotton in the proper way, and this agricultural knowledge gave offence. One day a committee of Negro men and women came to see me.

"Yes, suh," said the preacher, who was the spokesman, "we don' lak to make no complaint; but he's wastin' o' de chillern's time, larnin' 'em to plant cotton, when dey oughter be larnin' outen a book. Ev'y collurd pusson, sartainly in dis country, know how to plant a cotton seed. Do'n know whar he been ef he don'. Jes' wastin' de chillern's time — dat, too, when dere so meny on 'em dey can't git in de school-house 'ceptin' half de time. We lays dese 'monstrances 'fore you."

I took the "'monstrances" seriously, and I had Professor Marshall get lantern slides of good cotton and of poor cotton, of the proper way to plant it and of the wrong way, and of the difference in yield. He invited the parents of all the Negro children to come to the school-house on a certain night, and he delivered an illustrated lecture on planting cotton. I also made them a speech.

"What do you want your boys to do — to hang around town and carry satchels and shine shoes and to become loafers? Or do you want them to become independent men, to own farms, to grow cotton and to grow it right?" The tide of Negro opinion was thus easily turned. It is a docile race.

But this incident set another tide flowing. Colonel Stringweather was heard to remark that "Young Worth and his smart school nigger will turn the heads of all the nigger boys in town, holdin' meetin's and forbiddin' 'em to carry a white man's satchel or to shine a white man's shoes, or to hol' a white man's horse, or to wait on white folks. I don't know 'bout havin' a nigger school 't all if such infernal doctrine as this is set up."

The Colonel even remarked to me one day, in a condescending tone, "Young Worth, don't go too far with your little niggers. Nigger education is a ticklish bus'ness. You know your job and I don't; and you mean the right thing, I am sure. But, remember, this is a ticklish bus'ness. The nigger mus' keep his place in our civilerzation."

I found that the text-books of history used in

the school contained practically nothing about the history of the State. I compiled a simple narrative and had it printed, as a pamphlet, at the *Torch* office. That paper, therefore, spoke in the most flattering adjectives about the little book and its author. The book contained only a few pages about the Civil War but it declared that there was such dissatisfaction with Jefferson Davis's conduct of the war that two States threatened to secede from the Confederacy — a plain historical fact. When Captain Bob Logan had read it, he came to see me.

"Why, man, there are some things you can't say. All history is a perversion or a suppression of some facts — generally of the main facts; and the only history of themselves that these people will accept must conform to their pet perversions and suppressions. Nobody may happen to notice this sentence, for nobody but the children will read the book — or any book. But, if he hears of it, old Stringweather will snort and raise hell.

"I say, by the way, I told the ladies some time ago that they'd better put up in the school-house portraits of Jeff Davis, of General Lee and Stonewall Jackson and Edgar Allen Poe and William Gilmore Simms, if you can get them. The Apollos and the Madonnas and the Tennysons and the rest that the cheap-print fellow had in his catalogue are all right; but, when you put up pictures of great men or angels or of spirits or of what not, don't you forget the patron saints of the region where you live. Are these pictures on the walls yet?

"You're brewing a storm, Worth, and I don't believe you know it. Old Nixon, who goes about in his ancient plug hat and faded gloves reciting lines from Vergil to himself — he'll have no boys to teach at his academy if you make the public schools much better. Nothing but a life-insurance agency will await him. He's beginning to see this, and he's capable of raising a perfect tornado. The mill men are complaining, too, that they can't get children enough for the mills.

"Where do you live that you don't hear all these things? We are born and baptised and grow up and live and eat and think and vote and swear and drink and go to hell — all by formulas. You've got to keep to the right formula."

I laughed, but I saw that portraits of General Lee and General Stonewall Jackson and the rest were put up. They had been omitted only because they were not in the catalogue of cheap prints by which the other portraits had been bought, and it took some trouble to find them.

I compiled, too, a primer of "Our Industries,"

in which agriculture and lumber-cutting and furniture-making and cotton-spinning and such things were explained; and the *Torch* (at whose office it was printed) praised this also. It was given to the children, free; and I observed that nearly twice as many copies were asked for by the Negroes as by the whites.

Thus, in spite of Captain Bob Logan's rhetorical fears for me (the Captain's business was to have fears), my work went well; and Professor Billy's philosophy was sound: the school-master — a new sort of school-master — must lay the foundations of a new sort of patriotism, must even prepare the way for a new view of life. Now an important part of this new school-master's task is to have the people, the young people in particular, rightly to understand our own history. They must get away from thoughts of war. They must go further backward. They must know the forgotten story of their grandfathers and of their great-grandfathers, who were men that worked. I must, therefore, expand my successful primers into a history of our own people, in dead earnest; and I spent such time as I could spare from my school work in getting my materials. I had by this time found out that I knew nothing about the history of the State, and that nobody else knew more than I knew. Traditions had long been accepted as facts. Society "before the war" was thought, even by men whose lives ran back into that period, to be very different from what it really was. A few phrases about "cavaliers" and "great planters" had made a picture in the popular mind that, so far as our State was concerned, was wholly untrue. The prevalent notion of the Civil War, fostered by the Veterans and the Daughters, was erroneous. The real character even of General Lee was misunderstood. His name was worshipped, but his real opinions were unknown and had been curiously distorted. It was as if the past, except the war-period, had been eclipsed. The people did not know their own story.

And now there came a week that I meant to give wholly to writing and I determined to make a journey to the Old Place and work without interruption. Besides I could stop in Marlborough and see Margaret.

CHAPTER XII

THE Old Place had ceased to be a place of interest to most of the family. Uncle Ephraim and his wife, Aunt Martha, lived in the old "big" house, now sadly gone to decay, and they kept the new part of the house for the white folks if they should ever come to use it. With them lived a very light mulatto girl, Lissa, who was a sort of adopted daughter of Aunt Martha, and whose baby Aunt Martha was helping to rear. The other Negroes on the place lived as they had lived in my grandfather's life-time — in the cabins. Uncle Ephraim, old as he was, had shown a masterful spirit. The place had lost a white master but it had gained a black one. The Negroes worked parts of the old plantation "on shares," and they found Ephraim a hard task-master. The old man was thrifty — they called him stingy. The neighbourhood decayed. It seemed as if my grandfather had been the only prop to its falling value for years.

Aunt Martha met me at the gate.

"Where's Uncle Ephraim?"

"De ol' man done tuck ter his bed ag'in — mighty poo'ly sense de fros' fetch de rheumatiz."

"You're not here alone with him?"

"Yes, Mars' Littlenick; but he don' want much. Nur he ain' gwine ter want dat long. He done see speerits, and he's gettin' ready fer ter go — so I 'specs."

I sent for Dr. Benson, who found nothing to warrant Aunt Martha's fears. The old man had indigestion, but he seemed sound yet. I sent then for the best of the young coloured physicians in town, to come and stay with him until he should get up again. Uncle Ephraim had never before seen a Negro physician.

"See here. I don' wan' no nigger a-doctorin' o' me. I'se good enough to have white doctors when I'se sick. I'se allers had 'em, same as ol' Marster had afore me. I wishes to speak to Mars' Littlenick 'bout dis nigger doctorin' o' me."

"He's a trained nurse, Uncle Ephraim," I explained. "He's been taught by white doctors. He knows just when you need the medicine that Dr. Benson left for you. He'll do the right thing. Let him stay in here with you. I sent for him."

"A kin' o' owl nigger what don' need no sleep? Ef you says it's all right, Mars' Littlenick, den it's all right."

Old Ephraim was old Ephraim still. So I

went across the porch to the "new house" and sat by the fire to work at my task.

But the thing happened that always happens when an awkward craftsman who ought to ply a humbler trade makes elaborate preparations to write. I filled one sheet and tore it up. I filled another with the dullest stuff that ever soiled good paper. I moved the writing table to the other side of the fire-place. Presently I moved it back again. Then I found the secret of my bad start, for I had tried to begin the most difficult chapter of all. How foolish! I began an easier chapter, and I filled two sheets. The fire had now burned low and I stopped to rebuild it. I saw the moonlight between the cedars out the window. Perhaps if I walked I should then write more easily. I ran over what I had written — dull nonsense! My mind would fix itself on anything but on this task.

I went around the house. "I'll see how the old man is," I said to myself, and I entered the side door to the "old house." There was a noise of voices in Uncle Ephraim's room. He sat erect in the bed. Aunt Martha was kneeling at the foot hysterical in prayer. Dr. Dixon was trying to soothe the patient.

"I know's he was dar. I seed him and he says, 'Dar my ol' Ephum, done come, too.' And I says, 'How dy' ol' Marster?'

"Dar he is now — see him — dar! Yes, ol' Marster. What is yer want ter say to Ephum?

"He lif' his han' and look lak to gwine ter say som'in.' Yes, ol' Marster, I'se here, suh ——

"Dar Mars' Littlenick, too. Mars' Littlenick, what did ol' Marster say? And whar he gone to? I seed him standin' dar and I didn't ketch de words when he lif' his han'. Whar he gone, Mars' Littlenick? And what he say?"

Then he fell back exhausted in his delirium.

"Ol' Marster com' back to him," said Aunt Martha. "Dat's a sho' sign he call him ter de odder sho'." But Dr. Dixon assured us that his delirium was not so bad an omen; and, since he slept soundly in a little while, I went back to my History.

I built up the log fire again in my room — "And my marriage would bind me still more firmly to the State, to its traditions, to its conservative character," I found myself saying to myself. "A married man, I suppose, must have patience." And I smiled. Was marriage a necessary preliminary to a writing mood? I thought of myself in a quiet house — in Edinboro, perhaps in Marlborough; should I have to give up my school work? Oh, no. Still she'd prefer to live in the capital where she had always lived. She had developed a sort of mastery of her own world. It was good for her — activity and effectiveness added to her soft beauty.   And beautiful she surely was.

I should then surely finish my History of the State.   A man must ripen toward the writing of a great book.   He can't do such a task offhand. Why try to hurry the processes of Nature or of historical composition?

Before going to bed I wandered into the garden. I stood a moment by the grave of my grandfather. The cool moonlight fell softly on the earth, and a gust of wind rustled through the branches of the cedars.   Yes, he lived his life, and I must live mine.   We fulfil our destiny by falling into the endless line that Nature devises.   If Margaret had really known the old man as I had known him, she would the better understand me now.   Did she really understand?   Well, she loved me — she would love me.   Was that not woman's whole duty — or the greater part of it?   Was not that the old man's own philosophy?   The soft and tender home-maker — that was his ideal for a woman, not a political organizer. Loyalty to her husband was a woman's first duty.

By that measurement was not Aunt Martha a model of womanhood?   "These be very deep, if very rambling thoughts," said I.   "But, seriously, how well *does* she know me?—the man I am now become?   That's my sweet privilege to find out.   I'll see.   I'll see to-morrow."

After all, could I do better than to balance my judgment by the old man's standard? Here I belong. I am a part of Nature *here*. She is, too. We spring from the same influences. Dear, dear cousin, I come back — back to the fundamentals of life — back to you.

What kind of woman was my grandmother? I mused. Really, I never knew her. And grandfather seldom spoke of her. She had a vigorous wooing, if Ephraim can be believed. But after that? The Old Man in the days when I came close to him, gave all his thought to the State. "Serve your country," said he, over and over again. And, "Widen your horizon," he always advised.

As I went to bed, I threw away all thought of writing more. To-morrow I would go to Marlborough.

I rode into town, on that resolute day, which I now easily recall, saying that, after all, it was best to fix my life to the life about me, to adopt its traditions, to identify myself with the past, the conservative, the organized. Otherwise I was likely to be wholly misunderstood, to drift or to be driven away from the real moorings of my life. I surely was not an enemy of my own people.

As I rode through the crisp air, my purpose became stronger — became a sweet eagerness.

She was beautiful. She was restful. She was "our people." She would bring me content, and I shall settle down in line with life about me.

At the hotel, which was the gathering place of all important loafers, there was an unusual company of colonels and majors and captains. I had forgotten that there was a great meeting of the Confederate Veterans coming on.

"Here's Professor Worth," said one of them. "Worth, you are just in time. You know there's to be a volcanic occasion in this town. We all bury our hatchets — all become good Indians and George Washingtons to boot, and help the ladies out with their old soldier racket. God bless the old soldiers — I'm one myself, so that I can talk as I please. And — with all respect to all concerned — a bigger humbug never was hatched than these meetin's. Now, the real old soldier — he's all right. But the men who do most of this big-meetin' business are the women — God bless 'em. An' it costs money to feed a lot of ol' fellows that the railroads bring for nothin'. It's worse than war."

"Hold on, Colonel," said another, "don't be hard on us, who really were soldiers."

"I'm talking for private consumption. Just as long as there's an election to be won, I'm for the tattered veteran, to the last man. If one party did not have the ol' Confed', and if the other didn't have the nigger, dinged if I know what we'd do — we who have to save the country. What shall it be, Major — rock and rye? or rye, and trust the rockin' and the rollin' to Providence?"

"Let Worth deliver an oration on Jeff Davis. He's a scholar and an orator. Worth, we are veterans and we've all spoke out — said our little pieces; and we ought, for decency's sake, to keep our oratorical mouths shut."

"Jeff Davis — it's him that the ladies — God bless 'em — are now praisin' to the skies. Durned queer to me; for I'm old enough to remember what a failure old Jeff made of it; and he didn't get credit then even for what he deserved. Why on earth they have taken up old Jeff, I can't tell. My wife thinks that he was as great a man as Lee; and I couldn't convince her if I tried a month."

"Colonel," said another major, "this has puzzled me, too. You will recall that during the last days of the Confederacy, there was a well-matured plan to depose old Jeff, and to make General Lee dictator. It failed only because the patriots or conspirators (as you choose to call 'em) knew, when they came to the point, that General Lee would never accept such a proposal.

"Why, North Carolina and Georgia were at one time about to secede from the Confederacy.

Both Governor Vance and Governor Brown reached a point beyond which they would not endure President Davis's methods."

About the Confederacy and the war I cared not a rap. They were brave men who fought in it — I was willing to honour them for their bravery. That was easy. But — that was not all. If I should address such an audience on such an occasion that would mean my identification with all that stood in the way of the people's rise. The line of cleavage ran there — precisely there. The line between honesty and humbug ran there. No, I could not disguise that fact.

I made my escape and passed, in the best way I could, the few hours before I should go in the afternoon to see Margaret. But the thought would recur to me — "to fall in line with the life about me," does it mean falling in line with these colonels and their activities?

Professor Billy was in town. Wherever two or three were gathered together, he was there. He came to my room, ruddy and jolly. But, after a jocular greeting, he sat down and said half seriously:

"Worth, you ought to save your pretty kinswoman, Miss Benson, from all this veteran flubdub. Maybe you are doing that very thing, you rogue. This Veterans' and Daughters' craze has struck the land hard. It was a pretty idea, a very pretty idea, at first. And I suppose, we mustn't take it too seriously now; for the young women of society must have something to engage their time. But the colonels have captured them all, your cousin among them; and the old fellows are using these young ladies as their strongest and perhaps their last defence. Their old breast-works have been battered pretty badly. They may lose leadership and have at last to confess that they were whipped in war and that other men ought now to lead. They have used the churches, and this fortification is yet strong, but there are gaps in it. One church hates another, and they sometimes forget the common enemy. But, with the women organized to praise them, these wonderful military relics may still longer suppress free thought and free action. It is the shrewdest move that they have made. I am often impressed with their ability in their decrepitude.

"You remember how the old cock scratched and clucked when he thought Uncle Reuben might be coming to catch him, and his cluck brought all the hens about him; and they made so much noise that Uncle Reuben admired him and was discouraged."

It was strange how on that day, in spite of my own determined silence, everybody spoke to me about Margaret. When I picked up the after-noon paper, I saw portraits of Jefferson Davis, of the best-known generals, of the war governor, decorated with the stars and bars; and below these were portraits of the officers of the Capitol Chapter of the "Fair Daughters of the Con-federacy," Margaret's in the centre of them all. Not one of these fair daughters was out of her cradle and most of them had not been born when the Confederacy was launched. But "chivalry," "beauty," "heroism," "the sacred dead," "loyalty to the Southland" were the A-B-C of the fulsome vocabulary of this after-noon newspaper. The feeling crept over me that Margaret was become a sort of public personage and must be saved from this shame. I wondered how good Dr. Benson and my aunt felt about this. I mused on this as I walked to the Benson house. I'd soon find out. I'd soon find out — more than that!

I heard a buzzing voice inside, and the maid whispered to me as she came forward:

"De Col'nel makin' a speech to de ladies"; and she pointed to the big reception room. "Will you go in?"

I recognized the voice of — Colonel String-weather. He was narrating to a gathering of young women his own experience in "the heroic withdrawal" of the President (Davis) after the

fall of Richmond. I heard that phrase —
"heroic withdrawal after the fall of the capital";
and here was a roomful of young women, eagerly
listening to this interpretation of history as one
of the very heroes of it unfolded it.

"No," I said. "Tell Miss Margaret that
I will call after supper."

CHAPTER XIII

THE RELICS AT ST. PETER'S

THERE were in Marlborough two noble monuments of the early days of the Commonwealth, of the days when men built institutions and houses with dignity. One was the granite capitol, its floors deeply worn, its rooms without conveniences, and the whole building far too small even for the small business that was done there. The place had, from my childhood, stirred my patriotic emotions. I think I never walked through its cool halls — they were thoroughfares east and west and north and south and were as much used by pedestrians as any street in the town — without taking off my hat. And this was the custom of many men, especially of men of that old generation of fine manners who always bowed to a stranger in the street.

The other memorial of the time of the builders was St. Peter's. Its stone walls were like the walls of a fortress. Its great doors hung on wrought hinges. Its beams were held together by wrought bolts and wrought nails held its well-worn floor.

Its silver service was a present from a colonial
governor. It was the most venerated building
in the region, and most others seemed commonplace
or frivolous by comparison. And it had served
the highest social as well as religious uses for two
hundred years. Patriotism clung to its history as
the ivy to its walls. The boards in the floor
were deeply worn by innumerable feet of wor-
shippers and of those that had been wedded and
of those that had brought children to be christened
or the dead to be buried.

There was one pillar that was historic. A
musket ball had imbedded itself in it, after coming
through the mantle of the Virgin in the window —
a musket ball that had been shot by the enemy
during the little skirmish that the retreating
Confederates had with the advancing Yankees.
It was thought to be typical of their vandalism
that the ball should hit the mantle of the Virgin;
and the round hole was so patched as forever
to show the sacredness of the Lost Cause and
the sacrilegious nature of the invaders. The
bullet had been taken from the pillar and was
preserved in a little walnut box that hung under
the window, to show to visitors. Rolled in a
case and hanging under the bullet-box, was a
Confederate flag, which had been thrown over
the coffin of the rector who died in wartime as
chaplain of a Marlborough regiment. The pew

was marked in which General Washington and General Lafayette and General Andrew Jackson and Henry Clay and Jefferson Davis had sat.

The best social life of the town was yet, as it had always been, sustained by the women who worshipped at St. Peter's. The Baptists and the Methodists had each built a costlier house of worship. They were more numerous, too. Their churches had even, each in its own circle, aspired to be regarded as the home of the fashion of the city. But in its historical consciousness and most ancient respectability, St. Peter's yet had social as well as historical preëminence. Especially was it identified with the Confederate leaders. There worshipped old Colonel Gaunt every Sunday that his crutches could carry him so far — the historian of the State's troops in the war. There worshipped the old State treasurer, whose father had been treasurer in the old time — before the carpet-bag régime. There worshipped now most of the devoted widows and fatherless daughters of the brave men of the city who fell on Virginian battlefields.

The Bensons, of course, worshipped at St. Peter's. The good doctor was a vestryman, my aunt one of the most pious of women in her quiet attention to her religious duties, and my cousin Margaret had become a leader in church activities.

After an early supper at the hotel, I walked through the capitol — it fitted my mood (for I was bent on an absorbing errand and consequently my thoughts wandered) — east and west and then north and south. As I sauntered, I read on one door in faded gilt letters, "The Governor." The man who now sat there had done most valiant service in praising the Veterans — had outdone all his competitors and got his reward. On another door was "State Treasurer." There, I reflected, since the Legislature was not in session, I might, perhaps, if the Treasurer were in, find old Birdcastle's key to the library.

I have been told that, as a man marches into battle for the first time, his mind runs over his whole life and lights on this unimportant remembrance or on that, and will not stay by the deadly matter before him. So, too, when a man goes to make love with deliberate intention. I would not go straight to Dr. Benson's. Far from the State House I walked, led by some impulse of hesitancy (perhaps of trepidation) down the street that led by old Judge Bartholomew's. Might I not step in a moment and pay my respects? But when I reached the gate I smiled at my cowardly mood and passed, although I saw the old man with a shawl over his shoulders walking in the garden in the cool of the early evening.

But I did stop a moment at St. Peter's. The door was open, for men had been at work making repairs and they were now gathering up their tools. I walked half-way down the aisle. We should, of course, be married here.

Then my thought did come to the business before me. Yes, I had thrown away hesitancy. But should I find that Margaret had? I wondered if she really loved me. Had we not always loved one another? We had not formally said so. Perhaps I was to blame for so long a delay. Had I possibly caused her suffering? Or perhaps —perhaps — she had ceased to care. More likely she, too, had been waiting for my road to become straight. And now I had a career before me. Why did I not hurry on?

At last I was at the door. But it was yet so early I would not go in — they were still at supper, I saw through the window. Yes, I had taken supper very early surely, and they doubtless were late because of the meeting there in the afternoon.

I walked by and wandered farther than I had meant to go — out by the grounds of the Young Ladies' Seminary where she had been educated. They did teach young women pretty manners at least. But what else? I wondered. What had Margaret studied? What had she read? I had not thought of that before.

But it was getting late — later than I meant it should be when I called. I hurried back. I had been walking almost an hour.

I heard the fire bell ring — wasn't it the fire bell? And I hurried. A crowd was following the slow little fire-engine that started from this end of the town, and the word came back that St. Peter's was burning. How St. Peter's could burn was a mystery. Its stone walls could withstand a siege with cannon. But, by the time I came near the church, the cry was that the roof was afire and would surely fall in. The crowd in front suddenly divided itself, and some-one was coming bearing the body of another.

It was Dr. Benson. Good man, he was always prompt wherever he could relieve suffering. Why did they permit him to carry the woman alone? Why did not some one help? I bounded forward.

"Let me help you, Doctor."

"Margaret," he called, as he looked down on the form in his arms.

"Is it Margaret?"

Together we bore the limp form through the way promptly made by the crowd, and before another word was spoken — in a few minutes — we were in his house.

We bore her to the big lounge in his office, and he began to examine her, Aunt Katharine helping on the other side of the lounge. Margaret presently opened her eyes, and the doctor's efforts to revive her began to be successful.

"Did I save them?"

She had held in her hand the little box that contained the bullet, but the case with the flag she had evidently dropped. She had risked her life by running through a suffocating smoke to make sure that these sacred things should be saved.

After a while the doctor declared her free from danger he thought — "No worse harm than a severe shock."

The good doctor never chided anybody, and I noticed that even Aunt Katharine did not express surprise that Margaret had made so dangerous and (as I thought) foolhardy an effort.

Many a man, as you may have been told, has made love to a woman because of the curve of her cheek or of the shape of a curl on her temple or of the movement of her chin when she smiled. Nature tricks us with little things. So, too, I suppose, many a man before me had suffered postponements because of incidents or accidents quite as little as these; for, beyond a certain distance, which we fancy we travel by our own will, any little wind or wave may beat us back or carry us on or drive us to one side and delay our journey, light sailors as we are on this capricious sea where we have our brief adventures.

CHAPTER XIV

ON THE ALTAR OF A COLONEL

IF THE reader be weary of my interrupted wooing, I shall not pretend to any sympathy with him, for was I not even more weary?

Margaret was commanded to keep her room for a few days at least, to make sure of her recovery from the shock, and I was not in a mood to hear the great speeches of the congregated colonels. Therefore I went to Millworth — also to recover.

Barbara was loquacious and excited beyond her quiet wont.

"I'll tell him myself," she said almost as soon as she greeted me, seating herself between mother and me. "Mother was going to write to you to-day and so was I."

"About the burning of St. Peter's and Margaret?" I asked.

"Heavens! Is Margaret burned up?"

"No, no, but you had heard that St. Peter's was burned last night?"

"And what happened to Margaret?"

"She was shocked and choked with smoke. You hadn't heard? She foolishly ran into the burning building for the old Confederate flag and fainted there. She will be all right in a little while."

"No," Barbara ran on, "it wasn't that."

"Cooley's coming?"

"No — mother was going to write you, Brother Nick, that I'm en—engaged. Weren't you, mother? To Tom Warren. You knew it was going to happen, didn't you?"

And she kissed me and ran out of the room.

Knew it would happen? I had never thought of such a thing.

"Too young, mother; too young," I said.

She had crept back into the room in time to hear me.

"Too young!" she cried out at me; and, curtseying low to mother, she asked, "And how old were you, madam, when you were married? A whole year younger than I am! Too young! (To me.) You old, old thing you, yourself!"

The day was almost gone before I had a chance to talk with mother seriously about it.

"And what do you think, Nicholas?"

I did not answer directly because I did not know what I thought. Tom Warren was well born — a gentleman. He was fast succeeding to his father's law practice. He was well thought-of, and an honourable and reasonably prosperous career seemed to await him. And he was an attractive fellow, with dash and some audacity. But he had seemed to me likely never to see beyond the county line. He was content with things as they were — content with anything that was. He did not lack courage except the courage of a new idea. He would perpetuate the old order of things because it was some trouble to bring a new order; and he did not like to take trouble of this sort. For my part, I could like him more easily than I could respect him. He would never stand for what I most prized.

I told this to my brother more plainly than I could express it to my mother.

"Yes," said he, "but, Nick, very few men ever have a new idea. And those that carry such a thing find it troublesome baggage. If he's square, had we not better be content?"

My own wooing ardour was somewhat cooled for a time — shall I confess it? — by this most serious consideration of another couple and the possible hazard of the matter. If Tom Warren would be slow to catch a new idea of life, would Margaret be quick?

But I felt two days later that I ought to return to Marlborough and get news of her. Moreover, I had promised Professor Billy to go over with him his plan of campaign for a practical school for girls which the State must establish.

I found him busy among the Veterans. They

were encouraging the young women everywhere to organize Chapters of the Daughters, and the aim that they set before their tea-parties and sewing-clubs was still to finish the monument to the women of the Confederacy.

"Why not deflect this purpose to a better one," Professor Billy was asking them, "and build a great State school for the neglected young women of the country?"

"If," said he to me, "I can commit the Veterans and the Daughters to it, I shall have made a good start."

When I had run away from the chance to deliver an oration on President Davis, Professor Billy received the invitation. But the oration that he delivered was a plea for the education by the State of neglected country girls. He had someone find a plea for education that Mr. Davis had made in some conventional public address in early life, and he took this as his text. You might have thought that the particular labour of Jefferson Davis's whole life was the education of women. But the Veterans cheered his name and the speech was regarded as a success.

When, however, it became known that a resolution would be offered in their meeting the next day to approve this plan, the managers became serious. Colonel Stringweather called a group of leading spirits together and made them an oration on the danger of permitting the organization of Veterans to endorse any eleemosynary plan or institution. Only Captain Bob Logan saw the humour of that. The Veterans themselves got only the notion that the plan for a girls' school was an eely, slippery scheme which it was their duty by all the memories of Appomattox to disown.

On this particular errand, therefore, Professor Billy was unsuccessful, as I think he expected to be. But he took a cheerful, long look ahead. His hopefulness was of such a quality that what happened now was of little account. What happened even in one generation made no great matter. Did he expect to live forever that he could be so patient about results? He had, in a way, already put himself in the attitude of an immortal, for he thought in terms of the only immortal personage that we know in our democracy, namely, the people; and these dying survivors of a past epoch were only an incident to him, unless he could use them as an instrument.

But my cousin Margaret scored a success out of her misfortune. At the last session of the Veterans' Encampment, she was thanked by a resolution for risking her life to preserve the flag. The orators and the newspapers sounded her praise in exalted phrases, and she was the heroine of the whole Great Occasion. When

I called to ask about her she bore her honours
so sweetly as she reclined on a sofa that it were
almost worth while, it seemed to me, to create
a false world and a false atmosphere to give so
graceful a creature a pretty place to show her
charms of spirit and of manner. She spoke
with great reverence of the old heroes, of the
sacred relics, and even of the eloquent prayer
which the Reverend Donald Yarborough had
offered at the closing session.

"Cousin, if I had called a little earlier that
evening you would not have been hurt. I came
here first in the afternoon but you had a meeting
and Colonel Stringweather was making a speech;
and I was on my way to see you when the fire
bell rang that evening. I wish I had been sooner,
for I might have saved you from that rush to St.
Peter's."

"You mean, you'd have stopped me? or gone
yourself? I'd have gone, too. Nothing could
have stopped me. Cousin, it was a patriotic
impulse. You approve of that?"

"I should like to have kept you from that
danger and from all this folderoll since — kept
you, my sweet cousin, in the old, soft, pretty
ways and in the quiet of home. Have I not
always loved you in quiet, rather than in the
glare? Dear Margaret —— "

She lifted herself bolt upright and her pink gown

swept against me — perfect in its soft folds and
in its colour-harmony with all about it. I touched
the hem of it as it lay on the lounge, and "My
cousin —— "

"Mr. Nicholas Worth, you don't approve of
me — you don't, you don't! You don't like
my saving the flag. You've gone away from
our people. You've got your Yankee notions."
She was sitting up declaiming at me, somewhat
jocularly, still in good humour, but also with
some seriousness.

"You wouldn't deliver the oration on President
Davis. You do not admire him. You do not
really care for what our fathers fought for. You
are not Southern. You are not patriotic. Now
be a good cousin — as you were long ago —
and don't drift away from our people."

I could not go on then. It takes two to quarrel
and — to make love. I should have to wait
till another time.

I said good-bye in a little while and went
back to Edinboro, my week gone and not a line
of the History written.

Although the success of the "graded" schools
was great, as the *Torch* boasted and as the
energetic commercial men of the town thought,
a surprising thing happened the next summer.
My brother wished to buy machinery to enlarge

the mill, and he and I made a visit to New England. My going back to Harvard was the subject of a fulsome paragraph in the *Torch*.

"The learned superintendent of our schools seeks the shrine of his Alma Mater to get new inspiration." That was an innocent announcement surely. But it happened that a Negro student from the State was that year one of the orators of the graduating class at Harvard; and by mid-summer a paragraph about him worked its way down into our local newspapers.

On the same day that Colonel Stringweather happened to read this paragraph, he called to a Negro boy as he drove up to the postoffice and commanded him to hold his horse.

"Please 'scuse me, boss, I ain't got no time, suh. De perfesser is a-waitin' fer me. I try to holler fer a boy fer ye"; and he ran, yelling:

"Come here, somebody, and hol' Co'nel Stringweather's hoss," and he disappeared in the direction of the Negro school.

"Damned if this hasn't gone far enough," snorted the Colonel, after he had waited for some time for another boy. "A nigger graduates at Harvard; a Harvard man has our niggers taught not to hold a white man's horse — the bottom rail's gettin' on top, by Gawdamighty, too fast."

His anger boiled, and forgetfulness was not

one of his qualities. He wrote to the President of Harvard College and asked if a dinner was served after the Commencement exercises and if coloured graduates were admitted to the dinner. The answer he received informed him that "no distinction is made at Harvard College between students on account of race."

At the next meeting of the school board the Colonel was still excited; and he surprised the meeting by saying first that he was not thoroughly convinced that there was a clear constitutional warrant for free schools anyhow, since they seemed necessarily to involve the education of Negroes, which was surely a performance not contemplated by the framers of the Constitution and was subversive of society in its effects.

He then moved that the board elect a superintendent for the coming year, and he put in nomination a broken-down old preacher who delivered lectures on "Christian Literature," and "Education without Christ a Sacrilege," at church fairs and such places. This summer he had made a new lecture on "To Educate the Negro is to Bring him into Competition with the White Man: Is our Civilization to be Anglo-Saxon or African?"

Most members of the board were astounded. Was Mr. Worth not a satisfactory superintendent? They had heard nothing but praise of him. It was supposed, of course, that he would continue his work. Had he not gone away expecting to return? Was it fair to bring up the subject in his absence?

All this the Colonel heard in silence and with patience. After every man whom he suspected of friendliness to me had spoken, he arose:

"I will briefly explain my motion."

He first explained that the superintendent was elected year by year for only one year, by the law; and he expressed great personal regard for me and the profoundest admiration for my "learning and zeal." (You would have thought him my beloved guardian.) But a sacred duty to our firesides, aye, to our very religion, to the sanctity of our homes, and to the purity of our faith and of our race, and to our reverence for our brave and noble heroes — to these, he said, he owed a sacred duty.

He was loth to criticize a young man of learning and zeal — and of good family, too; and he had hoped that his motion would prevail without discussion. It ought to be a quiet proceeding — "among ourselves." Some of the gentlemen surely knew the grave reason for his action. He would make no public charges and he insisted that what he said should not be repeated. Then he arraigned me "not in anger, but in deep sorrow."

"*First:* In the Name of Our Holy Religion. He is not a communicant of any church, and on one occasion he expressed, in the presence of a pious lady, doubt about the divinity of our Blessed Lord.

"*Secondly:* In the Name of our History and our Honoured Dead. He wrote in a book, which was put into the hands of the children, sentiments disrespectful to the Confederacy, for which so many gave their lives." (The sentence that he referred to was one that explained the threat of two Governors to secede from the Confederacy — a plain, historical fact.)

"*Thirdly:* In the Name of our Anglo-Saxon Civilerzation. He would teach the nigger just as well as he would teach the white child. He had held public meetings of niggers and promised as much — had promised more school-houses and more money. He had been taught in a Northern college where (I have taken the trouble to ascertain) nigger students and white students are on an equality; and he has imbibed ideas subversive of our civilerzation. I could overlook other mistakes and indiscretions — in fact, I had overlooked them. But at the graduating exercises at Harvard this year, Professor Worth actually ate with niggers." (He read the letter that he had received from the President of the College.) "A nigger from this State was awarded honours

and was at the Commencement dinner, which
Professor Worth attended. That can not be
overlooked."

Against the Church, and the ex-Confederates
and the Pious Lady and our Honoured Dead
and Anglo-Saxon "Civilerzation," nothing could
prevail. My defenders gave up when the letter
was read from the President of Harvard College.
I was dismissed, for a failure to reëlect me was,
of course, a dismissal; and I had no appeal.

Many a man during these years had his career
cut short by the simple process of invoking these
forces against him. You will find them in
almost every Northern and Western State in the
Union — men with the same burning patriotism
that we bound ourselves to at college, now
winning success at every calling and hoping
in quiet hours of self-communion that a chance
may yet come for them to show the genuineness
of their boyhood's ambition. The backwardness
of the Southern people is to a great degree the
result of this forced emigration of many of its
young men who would have been the leaders
of the people and builders of a broader sentiment.

My dismissal was not published in the newspapers. To withhold news about public business
was often done at the request of the dominant
colonels. But I could not help wondering, as soon
as I heard of it, what Margaret would think.

CHAPTER XV

THE HARBOUR OF ACROPOLIS

WISE men have ever consoled themselves for the slings of Fortune by laughing at Fortune's pranks in her absurd humours. And this consolation was ours. What, for instance, could be more comical than the beggarly Confederate Veterans' wildly voting down a resolution in favour of a State college for women because they did not wish the schools to become an eleemosynary institution? Or what more ludicrous than Colonel Stringweather's church maintaining two missionaries on the Congo?

But something even more comical than these things now happened. The members of the Edinboro school board who acquiesced in my dismissal but who regretted it, though they did not dare oppose it, wrote me a fulsome letter of approval and sent me a gold-headed cane "as a small token" of their "great esteem." Any donkey could then put on a lion's skin and label it "Nigger Equality" and bray us into a panic, and only Captain Bob Logan and Professor Billy Bain and the gods would have laughed.

They laughed immoderately at half the public acts done in the Commonwealth. But their sense of humour had different effects on them. Captain Bob laughed and became melancholy. Such folly oppressed him and made him cynical. He disrespectfully ridiculed the community, and the community of course resented his ridicule.

Professor Billy, the wiser man, laughed even more heartily, but he could not be cynical. He showed us the absurdity of much solemn nonsense, but he made the humour of it enliven life.

Fortunately I, too, was able to see the comical aspects of my dismissal; for the same mail that brought me news of it from Captain Bob (I was never officially informed of it) brought news also of my appointment for one year as Professor of History at the State University. The old Professor had died during the summer and I was appointed *ad interim* by a committee of the Faculty till the Board of Trustees should meet again the next spring.

Colonel Stringweather was an influential member of the Board of Trustees — a fact that Captain Bob did not forget; and presently he wrote me:

"Old Stringweather, you know, is a member of the University Board. Wondering how he would regard your appointment, I asked him if he approved it.

"'Yes,' he said. 'That'll save him, and he's

a fine young man except for his damned foreign notions. There ain't no niggers at the University and he can do no harm. I'm glad he's got a good place. I simply didn't want no nigger-business 'round me.'

"In God's name, was there ever such a human comedy?"

There was still another little solemn farce before my appointment was confirmed. The Reverend Doctor Suggs, the editor of the Baptist paper, having heard of Colonel Stringweather's indictment of me for unbelief, published a protest against so ungodly an appointment. But my old friend, the Reverend Doctor Babb, now editor of the Methodist paper, made amends for the fright he had given me in childhood by asking the next week if Brother Suggs regarded Colonel Stringweather as an eminent authority on orthodoxy. Then he published a long and fulsome eulogy of my father and of my family. In the choice of professors at the University the religious sects each insisted upon representation; and it so happened that now a representative of a Methodist family was required to maintain the equilibrium. Else it might have happened that the Reverend Doctor Babb should have pressed home the Reverend Doctor Suggs's inquiry, and they could have defeated my confirmation.

Doctor Suggs had also alluded to my supposed

belief in Evolution.   And Doctor Babb answered
him in this happy fashion:

"Even if the learned young Professor has
read the treatises of these modern heretics, Darwin,
Huxley and the rest, a man of his intellectual
power would instantly detect their fallacies."

Professor Billy amused us by calling me the
great champion of Methodism and anti-Evolution.
I think that no human creature got more joy
from life than he, for every event fed his joc-
ularity.   In a previous embodiment he had surely
been Balzac (whom in this life, however, he had
not read).   But his cheerfulness was serious,
too.   "We've begun to laugh both at the colonels
and at the preachers," he exclaimed; "and, when
the public sees the fun, their day will be done."

Then he made a fable: "There was a time
when the Mule was a Beast of Dignity.   But
one day he Backed when he should have gone
Forward and gave vent to his Feelings and thus
betrayed his unfortunate Voice.   The White Man
thereupon laughed at the foolish Mule, and gave
him to a Negro.   Forever thereafter the Mule,
stripped of Influence and Dignity, became the Companion of the Servile and the Butt of Ridicule."

Thus there ran through those sombre years
— if they were sombre — a strong note of enjoy-
ment;   and the reader who should think the

struggle was a joyless one or that our life was sad would make the same grave error that many visiting commentators and many noisy statesmen made, who gave us their pity and their sympathy and got our smiles for their pains. One of the grimmest jokes that Time and Fate have played on us, who have been the very butt of Time and Fate, is this — that those who assailed us during those dark gray years and those who defended us, those who came to write about us and those who rose up among us to describe us — all, by some malign trick of the gods, seem to lack the humour that makes life and writing tolerable.

The very solemnest stupidities of a half-century of discussion — alike of attack and of defence — were spent on the South. Pity and sympathy and reproach and praise and encouragement were all dull — without one gleam of the humour that was necessary to bring it home to us — to us who even in our gloomiest moods laugh at the absurd trimmings on the skirts of Despair and often drive her away. I think we hate with a necessary and ineradicable hatred only those who have no humour and therefore credit us with none. Colonel Stringweather and the Reverend Doctor Suggs and William Lloyd Garrison and Jefferson Davis are for this reason without monuments in the Commonwealth to this day, whereas we love Captain Bob Logan and Professor Billy and Abraham Lincoln and Uncle Ephraim. It occurs to me now that I was not wholly pleased by Barbara's engagement to Tom Warren for this same reason : Tom was not quick enough to see the absurdities of the ludicrous life all about him. It shows a bad perspective to take one's self too sombrely in a world so full of bright colours. If we must perform pilgrimages let's do them in Chaucer's mood.

From our mountains to our sea — what colour and motion and riot of growth — stream and sun and wind — Nature has for all time had joy here. Her solemn moods, of course, she has, as in our monotony of pines. But even there wild flowers laugh up at you through the brown carpet. And the men and the women who came here from merry England were none of your oppressed emigrants, for they wore bright clothes. They were resolute conquerors of a wilderness but they laughed and made love and were merry.

True, some came from a neighbouring colony (as my historical researches have shown me) who had been taken from the debtors' prison in England. But *they* surely did not take life very solemnly, for their descendants to this day do not pay their debts with a conscience-driven haste.

And the Negro, the innocent cause of our

woes, is the least solemn of human creatures, whose very countenance God made to grin and who loves barbaric colours and finds joy in his melodies. The solemnity of the Southern people, therefore, is not fundamental nor characteristic. It has been imposed by their misfortunes and by the literature of their misfortunes.

Therefore, as I was going on to say when you interrupted me and, much to the delay of my story, we fell to talking about our natural cheerfulness, life now had a fair outlook, since I could laugh at Colonel Stringweather's impeachment of me. My mother kissed me, when I told her of my promotion to a more dignified position, and called me "Professor Worth," and she asked if this were what I should like to do for a career. There had not gone wholly out of her mind, I fancy, the pious ambition that she had first cherished for me, nor perhaps, next to that, the ambition that my grandfather had held up. Either of these, I think, appealed to her more strongly even than the teaching of history to young men.

But it would be a useful and surely honourable task to teach the youth at the University something of our own story as well as the usual chronicle of wars and kings in other lands. If I could make it clear to them that their grandfathers both laughed and worked — were happy men

as well as earnest — that would be much, linking
the old time to the present and forgetting the
obtrusive Era of Error, with its solemnities and
discussions and gloom and war.

And there was at the University a pleasant
small company. What a quaint, remote village
it was in those days! The railway which should
have run by it was purposely deflected a dozen
miles or more lest it should corrupt youth; and
you were obliged to ride these dozen miles in a
stage coach that was proper penance for more
sins than youth had been saved from.

There were the benignant President of the
University, Judge Bevan, a man of the old time
who had retired from the bench to this quiet,
academic post, and his wife and daughter, to whom,
by the way, Professor Billy Bain was soon to
be married, the lucky dog! For the course of
his love ran smoothly. The way it came about
was too funny to omit. The tale got out somehow
and I had as well set it down here.

He had been a more or less frequent visitor
to the Judge's; but he was a frequent visitor
to almost every house in the village, and that
meant nothing to the gossips. But one night,
when he was telling stories to Miss Jennie, he
stopped a moment. Then he changed his tone
wholly.

He looked straight at her out of his mild,

childlike eyes — looked long — and said suddenly, with the slight lisp that you would sometimes notice in his talk when he was unduly excited:

"Miss Jennie, we ought to get married now."

"Why, Mr. Bain!"

"Ye-th; it will be well. That is what I wi-withed to say. It is time now. Don't you think so?

"Ye-th," he went on without stopping, "we will get married now, if you will only say so, Jennie," and, giving her no time to protest or to coquette or to enjoy the sport — it was a cruel, straight onrush of a strong purpose that saw no difficulties, playful or real. "It is time"; and he had each of her hands in his and was swinging them back and forth.

"Mr. Bain!"

"I wi-th you would call me William, and, if you say so, it is time," and his great arms enfolded her.

She had said nothing yet. But she could not get away.

"If you say so," he presently went on, "we will tell the Judge now"; and he led her — almost dragged her — into the President's library.

"May we come in?" asked Professor Billy.

"Judge, it is time we were getting married — if you say so."

"Bless my life! Bless my life!" said the President, looking over his glasses.

Mrs. Bevan must have guessed that something out of the common was happening; for she came in the door just as the President was trying to recover from his surprise.

"Y-eth, Madam, it is time we were getting married, if you say so"; and Professor Billy, having released Miss Jennie, now grasped both Mrs. Bevans's hands and began to swing them.

"Well, Jennie," asked her mother, "what do you say?"

Miss Jennie had yet had no chance to say anything.   But she put her head in utter confusion on her mother's shoulder. Then Professor Billy drove the matter home by embracing them both.

In a little while the couple went back to their conversation about — the procession of the seasons, I suppose — and so the story ran. He had done another great deed without knowing that some men find it a difficult task and that most men, from necessity or from choice, make it a somewhat lingering task.

When I heard this story, I said to myself, "Courage, man; courage!"

Louise and Richard Caldwell also were of the group at Acropolis.   They had spent their boyhood and girlhood in England while their

father was in the military service of the Khedive,
during the troublesome years that followed our
Civil War. When he died, they came home and
took up life at Acropolis where he had left it off.

Richard was elected to his father's place in
the Faculty. Louise was — her friends and
neighbours sometimes said — "different," whereby
they meant, perhaps, that her speech had memories of English intonations or perhaps they
meant that till she was aroused she seemed
somewhat sad. Certainly there was a deep
seriousness in her nature, whether it were sadness
or not; and the gossipers of the village sometimes
connected it with the overwhelmingly sad event
in her family. But gossipers may guess wrong —
they have been famous for it in the little circles
of life that I have known. You, no doubt,
have had similar experiences and even been driven
by gossip to try to find out what the truth is.

Then, of course, there were others in Acropolis.
Most important and most interesting of all, there
was the company of raw but eager youth who
had been badly taught but whose joy in life
(the quality that makes youth youth in all lands)
meant more than learning.

There were men, of course, who talked of
the waste of time and sometimes of the danger
to character in that little university life, and
others of the danger of receding from the practical

which they supposed a college experience caused. But there was ever going on in the life of these youths, as of others elsewhere, that fine tempering of the spirit which is the eternal gain that may not be translated into common speech. I have sometimes thought that a college is the only place where large bodies of men have the ultimate honesty, and there is no such comradeship as theirs.

Our life at the University was enriched, too, by the visits of my old Harvard friend, Cooley. On the first visit he made me, he discovered the unusual qualities (as I think) of my brother as a man-of-affairs, and he invested much of his own fortune and his mother's in the mills at Millworth — profitably, too; and thus he had to bear the reproaches of some of his friends for becoming "an ardent Southerner." Cooley still lacked humour — at least he did not suffer violently from it; and he accepted many Southern sophistries as true. It was fine sport to hear him, at the Caldwells' table, who were our most frequent hosts, defend the South against Professor Billy's criticisms, made for the occasion.

We had all worked with Professor Billy on his plan for a College of Housewifery and of Teaching, as we had now come to call it — a State school for the neglected country girls. We had even gone further in our plan-making, for we had sketched also a School of Cotton Crafts, from farming to weaving and selling — how many crafts there are that have to do with cotton! But the College of Housewifery was the first thing to demand.

A total defeat of this plan in two Legislatures — defeat by utter indifference and neglect — had not shaken Professor Billy's purpose. For, if those whose duty it was to vote the money to build it were slow to act, that was their misfortune not his fault. But he did not for a moment doubt their ultimate action. He had since the last Legislature organized a club of about a dozen active men who saw the need of better training for all the people; and he made them, in a way, spokesmen for his plan. By this College of Housewifery, we should make a beginning of a revolt from the old stupid, formal, exclusive teaching of the favoured few.

And now another Legislature had assembled. He was ready with his bill and with a petition signed by his allies of the Club. It had got so far as to have a hearing set before the Committee on Education. The first speaker before the Committee was the Reverend Doctor Suggs. He had held a caucus of the Baptist members of the Legislature at his office, and it had been decided to oppose the bill. Doctor Suggs, therefore, informed the Committee that "the proposed measure to appropriate moneys from the Literary Fund to a college for women deserves prayerful attention for several reasons:

"*First:* Would such a school be under godly conduct? Would it train *Christian* womanhood? There are no better women in the world than our country women. If some of them are lacking in the higher accomplishments, they do not lack in Christian character. The State school for men (the University), to which much of the public moneys are given every year, is not an institution noted for its encouragement of a holy life. The most brilliant young man in this city drank himself into a drunkard's grave after he had graduated with honour there.

"*Secondly:* Since we, of our church, tax ourselves already to maintain our own most excellent Seminary for Young Ladies, it behooves us to consider whether we should justly be called on to pay a double tax — our contribution to our own school, where the daughters of our own people are educated, and a public tax in addition, to educate other men's daughters at a State institution.

"*Thirdly:* If the proposed institution should be established, who shall conduct it and who shall be its teachers?"

Then a new enemy came forward — Major Thorne, the editor of the *Globe*, who was reputed to be a great constitutional scholar. He arose, he said, "simply to inquire whether the true spirit of the Constitution of the Fathers permitted the expenditure of the public revenues for a *class* of the community, as distinguished from the whole. Lovely and estimable as this class was — God bless all our women! — they are not voters. I merely think it proper to inquire whether the Fathers had not meant primarily to shape the school system, maintained by the public revenues, with chief reference to the public service, as the militia is maintained. Is manhood education not implied rather than the education of women — a special class? I am not myself wholly clear as to this constitutional point; I simply throw it out for the consideration of the learned committee on the Literary Fund."

The Episcopal bishop nodded and said half aloud to the learned editor that it was an ingenious presentation of the subject to say the least.

"Gentlemen, are you all done with your doubts and questions?" asked Professor Billy, when he arose with the air of a Covenanter. He was the very impersonation of cheerful combat. He stepped forward with a gait that said, "Come after me who will; I am ready." First he told a barnyard story that caused the committee to laugh at the learned lawyer's constitutional argument.

Then he swelled up and spoke in earnest. "I have travelled from one end of this State to the other. I have met the country women. I know them. I know how narrow a life they have. I know how they would profit by such a school, if it were theirs — were the people's — were free to them. In all our rural counties there are young women of the same good English and Scotch stock that you belong to. They come of a class of our people that we always praise. Many of them are ignorant. Thousands of them are even illiterate. The only chance under heaven that will be given to them and to their children will be given by trained women who shall go out into our country places as teachers; and this school will train such teachers. We have none now. The State makes provision for the education of its sons. Any energetic boy may get at least the rudiments of an education. Moreover, he can go away from home. He can walk. He can work. The doors of opportunity are not closed to him. Not so with our girls. There is no way open for them. This is the supreme failure and ghastly tragedy of our civilization."

But the Church and the State were both hostile — "We are the happiest people on God's footstool" — and the committee did not even report the bill to the House.

For the great event of the session that winter was the proposal to pension Confederate veterans. Such a pension would increase the taxes, it was feared; and to increase taxes was, of course, unthinkable. Still something must be done for our heroes who were wounded or who are destitute. There was no difference of opinion about granting the pensions, but the debate was: How great shall they be? And that consumed the whole session. Almost every member delivered a long speech on the bill. Oratorical narratives of the whole war and the most profuse praise of our heroes were delivered, day after day, till the bill itself was forgotten. The talk was only about the relative merits of this orator and of that. Colonel Stringweather's description of the battle of Malvern Hill was thought by most persons to be the finest oratorical effort that had ever been heard in the State House perhaps the greatest speech ever delivered in our language. It was "destined to become classic," and give him rank with Burke and Calhoun and Yancey and Toombs. It contained this passage descriptive of the Southern civilization for which these veterans had fought:

"Illimitable wealth and boundless content were present everywhere. Her civilization was, in all that makes up the real blessings of civilization, the purest and loftiest time has ever yet known. Her people stood apart among the nations of the world. Their bosoms were the home of the most exalted honour. Whatever was mean, or low, or sordid, fled scorned from her borders. Majestic truth, imperial conscience, Olympian power, toned by the very courtesy of the gods, lifted its noble men and its glorious women far, far up, above the levels of other civilizations. Content, happy, prosperous, moved always to splendid action by the highest ideals, if some god descending from superior worlds, in quest of the race most akin to his own, had swept with his vision the land of the South in '60, he would have claimed us as his offspring and here made his home."

And so the years seemed likely to pass in this rhetorical orbit; but even orbits sometimes suffer change.

CHAPTER XVI

THE "WHITE MAN" AND THE "COTTON BOLL"

YOU might ride all day along sandy paths through the forest of primeval long-leaf pines, hearing their moan at the slightest touch of wind, and you would see nothing to break the monotony of the way. The same high, green, singing trees, the same sandy level, the same sparse undergrowth, the same floor of brown needles, even if you rode for many days. The little unpainted houses that you would pass are of the same pattern, a little porch, two rooms, an "ell," and a hot space under the roof, and a yard with no green thing growing in it — sand everywhere. The Negro cabins, too, are all alike. The absence of paint and the absence of green would soon depress you.

If you turned your way toward the river, you would come at last to the swamps of huckleberry, magnolia, and cypress, with weird "knees" sticking up like deformities. Here you would find impenetrable places unless you knew your way by long habit of going. It is a monotonous and almost uninhabited land.

Near the county-town on the river you might meet a countryman on the road in the spring and if you asked him what he had in his wagon he would say:

"Fruit and lumber, God bless you," by which he would mean huckleberries and poles to make barrel-hoops; for "fruit" grew wild in the swamps and the making of rosin barrels was the chief craft of the region.

Even the lumberman had not yet come here except along the river; and the "turpentine-getter" was the master of industrial life. You knew his presence by the sepulchral appearance of miles and miles of pines which he had "boxed," and the exuding turpentine painted a tombstone on every tree.

The turpentine-worker is a nomad. He makes a trail further and further into the forest, and the Negroes whose craft is the boxing of the trees and the gathering of the turpentine are wandering labourers. Nomadic, too, are many of the Negro workers in the lumber camps on the river.

The simple, sparse, backward agricultural population of the region were in the main the neglected, untrained, home-keeping, poor country folk, who toiled in slovenly ways and to little purpose — the pathetic by-products of slavery. Upon them were thrust the lumber and turpentine workers, rougher by far, and lawless when pay-day and grog-time came.

At the county-seat of this somewhat lawless, lone region of poor white men and migratory black men, there had long been published a commonplace weekly paper that had been like hundreds of others in inanity. But an energetic youth was now become its editor and he found excitement in describing all the disorders of the lumber and turpentine camps. Sometimes one drunken Negro stabbed another; that event was worth mention. But sometimes a Negro stabbed a white man, and that event was more serious. Once in a while a drunken row ended in murder. Between serious crimes there were always the thefts of hogs and chickens.

And once there was a particularly wicked crime committed within the county-town itself; and the drunken Negro was quickly swung to a tree. In the excitement that followed, the editor took the phrase that was on everybody's lips as the motto of his paper; and in large type he declared, "This is a white man's country."

There was such a response to this original observation that he changed the name of his paper from *The Examiner*, which meant nothing, to *The White Man*, which meant much; and *The White Man* every week published under its large-typed motto an account of some crime by a Negro. If no crime were conveniently committed in the neighbourhood, he copied from some other paper the report of one that had been committed at a distance. *The White Man* thus became a repository in general of reports of crimes committed by black men.

In the inane politics of the region, the editor of *The White Man* found it easy to be elected to the Legislature, where also he became the best authority on Negro criminality. For several terms he was endured with silence and was regarded as a nuisance. There seemed no imminent danger that the country would be overwhelmed with crime because of occasional crimes by drunken Negroes in lumber camps.

During these same years, if you had ridden over another part of the State, you would have seen endless miles of cotton-farms, whereon men toiled at the primary industry of the region — toiled in the old wasteful way of slavery, and mortgaged the poor yield of ill-tilled acres for bacon and guano, before the cotton bolls opened — a population in poverty on a land of unsurpassed fertility, and the only land in the world that has a practical monopoly of a great staple crop.

A leader arose here, too — a harebrained, energetic, oratorical man of long whiskers and a long tongue, who rightly saw that the farmers were in the bondage of the cotton-merchants; and he organized a revolt. His paper, *The Cotton Boll*, demanded this and demanded that; but most of all he preached organization. And, since these farmers had plenty of time, they heard his speeches and organized lodges. Thus *The Cotton Boll* and *The White Man* became powers in the land, one crying for the disfranchisement of the Negro, the other for the building by the Government of warehouses where cotton might be stored and money advanced on it.

Another campaign for the governorship would come on after a while. For years Senator Barker and his subordinates had found nothing else necessary to keep his party in easy control than praise of the old soldiers and more recently of the fair Daughters. "The platform," said Captain Bob Logan, "has been, 'We hold on,' and the battle-signal is the waving of the Confederate flag."

But now a new cry must be found. The Veterans were pensioned and the war was further and further behind us. *The Cotton Boll* had made an organization of agricultural discontent such as the political leaders had never before faced. Moreover, there was now an almost open rebellion against the further rule of the "generals and colonels."

The manager of State politics was Colonel Stringweather, and his vane turned on an easy pivot.

And everybody now began to be aware that the campaign was coming on. One man would say to another in the street, "The Colonel will soon start the ball rollin'." We had an instinct for campaigns. The Marlborough *Globe*, which had been as dull as the town, began to publish little remarks about the Colonel. You could read one day that this, that, or the other prominent gentleman had conferred with him; another day that he would soon have an announcement to make; another day that he had almost perfected the plans for the convention. In this way, the capital city and the whole State became aware afresh of Colonel Stringweather, for he had gone to Marlborough and made his headquarters at the hotel. When he walked down the street everybody spoke to him with much greater consideration than they had usually shown. Colonel Stringweather was on the horizon; the political game was about to begin; and the town would be filled with people when that noteworthy week came. The boarding-houses were cleaned; the platform of the town-hall was mended; and the hackmen rubbed the mud from their vehicles.

The course of coming events was as clear in Colonel Stringweather's mind as the campaign against France was in Von Moltke's. But like a good strategist he let it out gradually. It was an interesting thing to watch — the waking-up of the whole community when he gave the signal.

"General," said he to Senator Barker, "I reckon we've done our duty to the old soldier, and I reckon he's done about all he can do for us. We'll not forget him, God bless him, but we have now turned him over to the tender care of the ladies. This nigger business is gittin' serious. See the list of race crimes in this one issue of *The White Man?*"

The next political battle-cry was thus decided on — especially since other Southern States, far blacker in population than ours, had shown the way to make successful anti-Negro campaigns.

But Senator Barker knew the absurdity of demanding Government warehouses and Government payments on cotton. "We'll hold the farmers on the white man's rallying-cry," said he. He would use *The White Man* to keep *The Cotton Boll* within bounds.

This cry for the disfranchisement of the Negro, moreover, made within limits its appeal to reason and even to righteousness. We had year after year had a ballot based on corruption and fraud in the Negro counties. Men who regarded themselves as good men and noble citizens preferred to see the Negro cheated at an election to risking a return of the debauchery of the Reconstruction period. Yet it was more and more demoralizing to have the ballot fraudulent. Not only were men's consciences blunted but their practices became more and more immoral. White men cheated white men. The foundations of political morality were undermined.

Were it not better, even the best men asked themselves, openly and by the forms of law to disfranchise the mass of the Negroes?

The church papers took this view; and Colonel Stringweather knew that he could reckon on the support of the Reverend Doctors Suggs and Babb and make a moral appeal to the civic conscience of the best citizens.

Just before the Democratic convention, *The White Man* gave all its space in one issue to a recapitulation of the crimes of Negroes against white men in our State and in adjacent States, and all the other papers discussed the startling list — this, of course, at Colonel Stringweather's suggestion.

The farmers, too, were becoming conscious — in the mass — that something was wrong. The waters of their long patience were stirring. And there was grave danger in the people's weariness of barren legislation — danger to their political masters. And we now had further lessons in that most fascinating of all studies — the study of the rising up of a people — how it is and why and when a mass of men will move or be moved, and in what direction, and by what impulse; and what are the ways whereby their motion may be directed to their upbuilding or deflected to their confusion.

We of the Club, whose ideas were now beginning to become clear, welcomed the rising tide of rural discontent, and it gave us courage to prepare a plan to direct it. We wrote a little statement:

"That it is an economic necessity to build and maintain schools at the public expense to teach farming and hand-work (as well as book-work) — one for white boys and one for Negroes; and

"That to divide the public-school money between the races in proportion to the taxes paid by each race is fallacious and dangerous to our economic welfare; for the basis on which universal public education rests is the economic value to the State of trained men over untrained men.

"That limitations of the suffrage ought to apply alike to each race."

Every member of the Club (there were now but seven) signed it; and I presented it to Colonel Stringweather. (We had, of course, never quarrelled and had silently forgiven one another, as good Christians should.) Would he not use his influence ("using influence" was the current euphemism) to have this put in the Democratic platform?

"I'll be damned if I do, Professor," was the quick answer that he gave. "We're taxed too much now and to be taxed for nigger education — why, there are three niggers in that woodpile you've got there : a school to teach niggers farming (a mule and a plow is the school they need); next, white men's taxes (not niggers' taxes) to pay for nigger education; third, to make an ignorant nigger as good as an old soldier. Too much nigger — nigger — nigger. This is a regular Radical platform. Go over to the nigger party or burn it up. It's a crazy business, just when the niggers' day is about to end for good."

But the suggested plank was published in *The Cotton Boll*. A few days later I met Colonel Stringweather on the train.

"Building a fire behind me, eh? That's your game, is it, Worth?" The Colonel then showed me letters from several committeemen ridiculing our suggestion; from others meekly asking him what attitude they should take toward it; none favouring it.

"Your game won't work — you fellers have gone clean crazy about education, particularly of niggers"; and the Colonel took a fresh chew of tobacco.

The Democratic Convention met; and all the political colonels with broad hats and chin-whiskers came to the capital. There was the usual gossip the night before at the hotel and the usual caucusing. For Governor — since a young man must be put up, to meet the criticism that the Generals and the Colonels had held power too long — Tom Warren seemed clearly to have the lead. Most men who are spoken of for high office fancy that such talk springs up because of their conspicuous fitness; and Tom was very like other such men.

Among the delegates little was heard about our proposed plank in the platform. There would be a committee on platform; and what do conventions have committees on platforms for if not to bring in the usual ringing empty periods? Had any platform ever been discussed in convention?

When the convention assembled, the usual things were done. The roof echoed applause to the presiding officer's speech. He "castigated" the National Republican party and congratulated the people of the Commonwealth on having the best State Government under heaven, where the white man's supremacy was preserved; and "heaven itself, when we shall all reach the golden shore, will have few surprises for us because it can offer few felicities that we have not already enjoyed." Everybody applauded this happy climax.

The platform reported by the committee contained not even an allusion to our proposed plank. One delegate arose and proposed it as an addition to the platform. The chairman facetiously explained that it would "teach a nigger to read and spoil a good plow-han', and put the bottom rail on top and perch a nigger woman on the fence."

"A coloured lady from a college," added Colonel Stringweather in derision, and the convention laughed as it yelled, "No—o, No—o."

The platform that was adopted was *The White Man's* platform — to divide the school money between the races according to the amount of taxes paid by each; and to exclude illiterate Negroes from the polls but not illiterate white men who had served in the war or whose fathers had so served. It boasted of the sums spent for education; and then followed the usual "castigation" of the enemies of the public welfare. The platform was read by a man with a voice that filled the hall; and at the conclusion of his reading a little dramatic scene was acted that Colonel Stringweather had arranged. He leaped to the front of the platform, waving his hat in one hand and a tattered Confederate flag in the other, and cried: "The Ladies—God bless 'em—and the Old Soldiers, now and forever!"

A group of young women rose from the front

seats in the gallery and waved Confederate flags. Men threw their hats high toward the ceiling and yelled themselves hoarse. They forgot the order of the proceedings; and, when the confusion had gone beyond the hope of restoring order, the chairman declared the convention in recess till two o'clock.

I sat in the gallery and I saw my cousin Margaret among the flag-wavers. With her sat the Reverend Donald Yarborough.

The Club, of course, had as its only purpose the training of the neglected youth of the State to useful occupations, to make work again seem worthy, as it had seemed before the blight of slavery. We had no other purpose. But the colonels had so directed the convention and so shaped public discussion that every proposition of the Club had been turned into an apparent defence of the Negro. Nor had we thought or said any criticism of the Confederate veterans. But the game had been so skilfully played that the Club had been made to appear as hostile to the veterans, to the Confederacy, to "our heroes," to the history and traditions of the State — made to appear as a conspiracy of traitors, and even as insulters of "the ladies, God bless 'em."

And when Tom Warren was nominated next

day, with a great shout, much was made of his youth and, therefore, of the great chance that all young men have.

I congratulated Tom on his nomination; but I remarked, "I wish you had put up a better man for Superintendent of Public Schools."

"Don't you like to see the Baptists recognized?" Tom asked, with a smile; for the convention had nominated Dr. Craybill, a broken-down preacher who had as the "financial agent" of the Baptist college made many speeches about "Christian Education"; and he had lately written much in the newspapers about the necessity of regularly reading the Bible in the common schools. Captain Bob Logan amused himself by writing a letter to the Edinboro *Torch* saying that nobody had ever objected to the regular reading of the Bible in the common schools and that the controversy, therefore, was one in every way worthy of the powers of the reverend gentleman.

"If," he went on, "there are possibly a few schools wherein the Bible is not read, the failure is due not to a lack of Christian character but only to the inability of the teachers to read."

Thus "Christian Education" also was most heartily endorsed by the Democratic Convention.

And my fight with Colonel Stringweather was not yet ended — nor with Tom Warren.

CHAPTER XVII

AN EXILE FROM HAPPINESS

THIS swift succession of political events into
which I found myself drawn, because of
the forced activity of our Club and without the
slightest intention on my part (for I was now
really about to begin the writing of my History
of the State, having gathered much material
and got my work at the University fairly a-going)
— these events have forced me forward in this
chronicle so rapidly that I must now go back
and pick up my story.

Barbara for a time was very happy in her
engagement to Tom, as earnest young natures
are wont to be under such interesting experiences;
and we looked forward to their marriage in
due time.

But she happened to make a visit to the Old
Place, where she took much interest in the baby
of Aunt Martha's ward — a "cunning" child
that enlivened the somewhat dreary household of
Uncle Ephraim.

She came home saying nothing about this to
anybody — except to Aunt Eliza. But she shut

herself in her room for days, and a strange melancholy seized her. All that the household knew was her announcement one day, in a casual tone, as if she were speaking of something that had happened long ago — that her engagement with Tom Warren was broken.

She gave herself still more devotedly to her religious and school work in the mill village. She was a very angel to every sick person there and to everyone who had suffered a sorrow, till at last she announced one day (again through Aunt Eliza) that she was going as a missionary to China. It was on the very day when the Democratic Convention nominated the Hon. Thomas Gaston Warren for Governor, that Barbara held the last meeting of her Mothers' Club in the little Methodist Church at Millworth. She told them that she should not meet them again — certainly not for a long time, perhaps never in this life; for she had now made arrangements to carry out the plan that God had plainly showed as her duty.

The factory women who heard her burst into tears, some audibly. Nobody spoke for some time but the sobs became louder; and presently by a common impulse they all knelt to pray. In a trembling voice, Mrs. Vawter expressed in her homely way what they all felt:

"Our Heavenly Father, we part with our

best frien', the sister who Thou callest to a holier
work in a furren lan'. Go with her, Heavenly
Father; lead her by the han' in rough places.
Bless her sweet young life to the conversion of
the heathen. O Father, keep her in health,
save her on the sea, preserve her from sickness
and bring her back safe to us who need her and
love her — with sheaves of glory. An' if we
meet no mo', O Heavenly Father, gather us
all round the great white throne whar thar'll
be no heathen and no partin'. For Christ's
sake, Amen."

They arose hesitantly and clumsily, bowed
with a deep grief; and they sat sobbing for a
long time. Barbara could not speak for her
emotion. Presently she went to the little organ
and began to play the tune that they usually
sang to the hymn:

> From Greenland's icy mountain,
> From India's coral strand.

"I came," she then said, "just to say good-
bye. I shall go away the day after to-morrow.
Everything is ready. It is hard to part, but
I shall be happy doing God's will; and I want
you to remember me in your prayers — always.
Let us look on the cheerful side of it — I'll
come back again; and I shall hope to find
you all alive and full of the love of our dear
Saviour."

They pressed her hand; some of them threw their arms about her; and one good old woman knelt and kissed her gown, the tears running down her face in a stream.

Barbara wished that she were to take the train that very minute, as she came out of the little church and locked the door. Was it wise to go, after all? "God calls," she muttered, and she clenched her hands in resolution. She was impatient to reach her room where she could pray alone; and she dreaded to see her brothers or anybody else, for the very sight of them might pull her back. It *was* hard to go — she had not known how hard.

The train from Marlborough stopped just as she came by the station and I got off. I saw her and waited for her; and we walked together to the house. Except a bare greeting neither spoke for a minute or two. Presently I said:

"Have you heard the news from Marlborough?"

"No."

"The Convention nominated Tom Warren for Governor to-day."

"That is what was expected, wasn't it?"

"Yes."

Another silence followed; and soon we were at the house. She put her arm on mine, before we ascended the steps and said:

"Brother Nicholas, you must not talk to me

— any of you — about my going away. Please tell them all" —and she fell heavily on my shoulder — "all — all — that they must talk about something else. I wish I did not have to go."

It was a very difficult supper to sit through that night. I told Charles about the convention. At one time, I became really interested in what I was saying, when I explained with indignation how the managers had pretended to do everything that the people needed but had dexterously avoided doing anything — how they had nominated Tom Warren to draw the young men's vote and old Craybill, the Baptist "financial agent," for Superintendent of Schools — to draw the Baptist vote, and how they had caught the old soldier vote — and Colonel Stringweather's open hypocrisy about the whole game.

But again a silence fell on the company. As Barbara put her arm about Charles's baby's neck to adjust its napkin, she drew the little thing close to her.

"You precious child," she said; and she kissed her and called her "little Barbara, my little Barbara — you'll grow and grow — you are little Barbara now."

We had finished supper — or had we? Never mind; she went around the table silently kissing every one of us. Then she went to her own room, taking the baby with her.

Charles and I sat for some time on the piazza. In silence I arose and walked to and fro for a while.

"By heavens, Charles, it all comes over me now as a sea of humiliation. I haven't done my duty. If I had stayed here she might have been spared this morbid experience. I ought to have paid Barbara more attention — got her interested in something else. I could have taken her to Acropolis to live with me, or, if I had known in time, I could have travelled with her, perhaps, and devoted myself to her in some way and have prevented this turn of her mind. We ought not to have permitted this religious mania to prey on her disappointed affections."

"You couldn't have done it, not to save your life you couldn't. After Bishop Jarrett came here from China and made his missionary speeches, nothing could have stopped her. If you had had her where she could never have heard of him, perhaps she wouldn't have gone; but it's only a 'perhaps.' For Barbara has been excessively religious from her childhood; and this missionary purpose was in her mind and make-up from the beginning. It is the logically noble thing to do from her point of view. If you are going into church work at all, go into the hardest, most glorious part of it. It is the same impulse in her that has moved you in your work — to do the best thing in sight."

Aunt Eliza came out and spoke in low tones of our martyr.

"You ought both to feel proud of Barbara. She's giving you both up. She's giving up everything she loves here — to obey the highest call of duty. She's the crown of the whole family, the blessed girl. If I had had her opportunity and her call after the Captain died — I wish I could go with her now."

She went back into the house.

"Don't you see, Nick, how she looks at it?" said my brother. "Almost everybody but you and me looks at it in that way. They glorify her. They envy her. The preachers and the bishops praise her. It's all in the point of view. She's got to work out her life herself as we work out ours ourselves."

Next morning Barbara was unnaturally cheerful. She spoke of her journey as one would speak who was going on a pleasure trip. She spoke of the arrangements that had been made. She and her old school-mate, Grace Etheridge, were to meet Bishop and Mrs. Jarrett in Baltimore. She had just heard from them. There would be a party of seven in all; and the journey would be full of new experiences. She should have many things to write about even before she reached China.

When a thing once becomes inevitable, we

are so made that we accept it and in a little while regard it as a part of Nature herself in her unquestioned workings.

The young missionaries went away and added one more to our smothered tragedies.

The one thing in our lives that the Old Shadow did not fall on was the mill by the river. The water flowed ever, the spindles turned, the looms were busy. Human bodies somewhere in the world were clad with the unfailing woof of the sunbeams on our fields.

CHAPTER XVIII

THE REVOLT

THE Club promptly met after the Democratic Convention, and somebody said: "We will fight now, if we have any courage in us."

"Yes," said all the rest.

Time for discussion had passed. We had made a programme for better public schools, for schools to teach trades, to teach agriculture, to train teachers. We had not been, and we did not now wish to be, a political club. But, as soon as we had tried to do a task that was worth while, we were ridiculed and opposed by the most powerful organization in the State.

"There's only one way to do," we agreed. "We'll tell the people the truth about the schools and about politics; and we'll call a convention and nominate a State Superintendent of Schools on our platform."

Bolt?

Yes, bolt. We'll take a stand for independent action and be beaten if we must. It is time men were saying what they think in this State.

This was the platform and the "call" that we drew up:

"*To the Voters of the Commonwealth:* —This is a political platform in which you will find no evasions. If you wish to face the truth, you will read it. If you wish to make the State a better place to live in, you will act on it.

"One-fourth the adults in our State are illiterate. This is almost the very worst condition in any of the States.

"Yet the men who settled our colony were as sturdy men as ever came from England and Scotland. They were men who worked. They cleared and plowed the earth. They manufactured things, too. There was a time when our population and wealth gave us a high place among the States. Our grandfathers and their fathers were not only industrious, they were trained men. They regarded it as honourable to work with their hands. If you will look back into your family history, you will probably find that your grandfather or your great-grandfather was a wheelwright, or a blacksmith, or a carpenter, as well as a farmer. They made iron that was sold in Massachusetts. They made the steel from which the guns used in the Revolutionary War were forged. Our great-grandmothers spun the cloth that they wore. We had a prosperous State — one of the first in the Union.

"Then slavery came. Instead of growing everything that was good and useful, people now began to neglect other crops and to grow cotton only. The slaves worked the cotton. A few men came to own great plantations which slaves worked for them.

"A great change thus came. But it came so gradually that no one generation saw how great it was. After a while, it had become the fashion to have slaves do all the work. Men who owned slaves ceased to do work with their own hands. Work with the hands came to be considered somewhat disgraceful — the mark of a poor man; and 'hands' came to mean other men's hands, for why should a man work with his hands if he could own slaves?

"Thus it gradually came about that nobody worked with his hands but slaves and poor white men; and a white man who worked with his hands showed thereby that he was a poor man, doing a slave's work. In this way the white man ceased to love to work. Slavery killed his working habits.

"Slavery thus kept the poor man poor and made him poorer. It denied him as good a chance to be respectable, to be educated, and to educate his children as his grandfather had had.

"Yet slavery became the fixed doctrine and habit. The public men defended it. The preachers said that the Bible sanctioned it. Thus religion and politics championed slavery and made life harder and harder for the poor man.

"At last we had a war, and slavery was abolished. Everything had gone from bad to worse by that time. The Negroes were even set to rule over us for a period. Such a state of things, of course, could not last long. It is passed now. We can rule ourselves as we wish. But many of the old habits of slavery continue. Very few white men know how to work skilfully with their hands. Still fewer Negroes now know; for there has been nobody to teach them since slavery.

"The result is, we have become poorer and poorer. We do not make enough things. We do not cultivate our farms well enough. Too many men yet look down upon work. We buy everything from the North — even our axe-handles and our plows and our buckets and our harness. We even buy our bacon. The way to get out of these habits and out of this poverty is to start again just where our ancestors were when slavery began to destroy their habits of work.

"Now let us see how we can do it.

"We propose to have schools for boys, where they can learn to farm better. In the Western States men make twice as much from an acre of ground as we make. We want schools to teach trades, too. The people need these schools and we mean that they shall have them. There must also be a good common school within the reasonable reach of every child in the State. There must be the same sort of schools for the Negroes, too. The only way to make them better is to train them — to teach them trades, to teach them the honour and the necessity of work. The Negro menace is Negro ignorance. We must do this not only for their own sake, but also for our protection.

"Does all this not seem reasonable? We think that it is both reasonable and necessary. Therefore, we drew up a petition and presented it to the Democratic Convention, asking that these things be put in the platform. Then the Legislature would vote money for them. Otherwise it will not.

"But they refused to hear us; and we now propose to demand these things ourselves.

"These are our purposes; and we have no political purpose. Training is more important than parties or politics; and we should not favour independent political action if the Democratic leaders had favoured these measures.

"We do, however, think it wise to limit the voters; but it must be fairly done. A man who cannot read and who will not pay a poll-tax of two dollars does not deserve to vote. But white men and black men ought to be treated alike. To permit an old soldier to vote who cannot read and will not pay a poll-tax — merely because he was a soldier — and to forbid a Negro to vote who cannot read and will not pay a poll-tax, is to give the Negro an incentive denied to the soldier; for it gives the Negro a reason to learn to read, and it gives the old soldier content with his ignorance.

"Most of the talk about the old soldiers is humbug; and you know it. Any man who served in the war — if he be a man — asks no favours because he was a soldier. If he asks special favours now, he was probably an unworthy soldier. Most of the talk about the Negro also is humbug. If we limit the suffrage, and deal fairly and enforce the laws, and train the ignorant to industry, we shall have no Negro problem.

"The truth is, men of the Commonwealth, this kind of humbug in politics is keeping us back, keeping us poor, keeping our children ignorant. And the insincere men who are our leaders are driving many young men away from home. Young men leave our State by thousands for freer chances elsewhere. They go where work is better paid for, where there are better schools, where men may think and speak with freedom.

"We propose, then, to nominate an Independent State Superintendent of Public Instruction who thinks as we think; and we ask you to send delegates to a convention for that purpose that will meet in Marlborough on August 1st. And we ask you to make your candidates for the Legislature pledge themselves to these plans. If they do not, nominate Independent men who will. We do not propose a new party. We have nothing to do with national politics. But we do mean to build up our State and our people. We are tired of humbug and insincerity."

We sent a copy to every newspaper in the State, and to every man who we thought might help us. We sent speakers to as many county-seats as we could, to stir up the people to send delegates to the convention.

"Since we wouldn't take 'em in," said Colonel Stringweather, "the boys will be a ten-cent sideshow to the Radical Republicans. They are welcome to all they can get out of the combination."

But Major Thorne thought it worth while to discuss the Address seriously in *The Globe*, as well as to ridicule it:

"They demand more schools, they say. We have spent millions on schools — such a record, in proportion to our wealth, as few countries can show." (This lie had been repeated till it was believed.)

"They demand schools for teaching agriculture and the trades. Any boy can now learn to farm — by farming; or to be a carpenter — by going to work with a carpenter. The real gist of this demand comes out in the Negro clause. The whole plan

is to educate the Negro into competition with the
white man — or rather to catch the Negro vote.
For, whenever the Negro is educated into competition with the white man, we shall have a
race war.

"The Party of Seven insults our able educational
authorities. It does worse than insult the old
soldier — it heaps abuse upon him. The day
will never come in this State when the public
will approve of abuse of the men who offered their
lives in a war of defence.

"It reviles even Christian education, by opposing
the Democratic candidate, who distinctly and pecu-
liarly stands for the use of the Bible and the teaching of piety to the poor in the common schools.
The good people of the State will never sanc-
tion a godless education."

There was no more danger to the supremacy
of the white race than to the supremacy of the sun
over the moon; and nobody supposed that there
was any such danger. But, if you praise a man
who is worthless for some quality that seems to
put him in the company of good men — seems
to give him a standing that he had before lacked
— you please him beyond calculation. When it
is made a political distinction to be a white
man, that white man who is most in need of
distinction responds with the greatest readiness.
There was, therefore, political shrewdness in

emphasizing this obvious proposition as if it were a new discovery.

There was at once a heavy handicap on the new movement; for it was "irregular." Every man who hoped for political preferment at any time in the future hesitated to ally himself with any irregular party or plan. Orthodoxy in politics was even stronger than in the church.

To the gratification and even to the surprise of the "Seven Foolish Virgins," as the orators had begun to call us, four good men were found who could go forth to persuade the people to send delegates to our convention. I went, too; and the hot four weeks of midsummer I gave to this work. In twenty days I made speeches at twenty-five places.

One of these was at the mountain court-house of Funnel Rock. Caldwell was spending his summer there, making surveys for mountain roads. He had built him a bungalow, and what prospects he was making accessible!

When I arose to speak at the small meeting in the court-house, I saw Louise sitting with her brother. They had come in just as the meeting was beginning. There were not more than forty men present — half of them, perhaps, residents, the other half summer visitors. There were a dozen curious boys and no women but Louise. Women then did not go to the political meetings.

My speech was an elaboration of the Address to the People. At intervals Caldwell applauded, and the crowd tamely followed his example. But it was a stolid audience. They did not seem clearly to understand even as simple a proposition as I made. Individually, perhaps, they could have understood it, but they seemed incapable of a collective understanding.

They had so long associated all political action with the formulas and the machinery of the two regular parties that a suggestion of independent political action dazed them. They regarded it as a suggestion of some sort of revolution — an irregular proceeding that must be long discussed and pondered over. Captain Bob Logan once said that our people would rather be damned "regular" than saved as "independents." They would not act then; but, when the meeting had adjourned, one man said that he thought a delegate could be found who would go, if his fare were paid. Nobody in the county could afford to go to Marlborough at his own expense on this sort of business.

Caldwell congratulated me with gusto. "It it glorious. It is a righteous crusade. We may not win this time nor the next, but we shall win!"

I spent the night with the Caldwells, and Louise and I rode the next morning to the great cliff to see the sun rise. It was a perfect atmosphere — so perfect that merely to exist in it gave a thrill. As we approached the Rock from which the whole world seemed spread out below us, her horse sniffed the clear air. It was a beautiful creature, fit for so good a rider; for her motion was a swift grace of Nature. Her riding skirt draped her form, quivering in the wind; strands of her hair flew across her face as she turned to look back at me; and a soft gray hat sat well on her.

"Hurry," she said, "the gleam is spreading"; and she galloped across the level mountain-top to the very edge of the precipice. Far eastward the valley stretched to the next range, which was lower than our plateau. From peak to peak shone streaks of light with great crimson spaces between; and the shadow of the mountains receded down the valley.

She sat erect, gazing silently; and I saw her clear-cut profile against the brilliant banks of sunrise. Her chin was firm, her forehead high, her hair made blacker by the light gray of her hat. She breathed quickly, her erect form rising and sinking with deep inhalations, her cheeks as ruddy as the light on the mountain. Her hand hung gracefully at full length, and her superb neck — I think I had not before noticed its graceful poise. As she sat silently there for a moment, I forgot the sunrise — gazing at her, as at the centrepiece of the great spectacle.

There was no suggestion of softness about her, not even of rest, but only of graceful action — health with the joy of motion. Repose? Vision rather, and rapture, more like the wind than like the rose — fitted to high altitudes, moved by quick pulse-beats, herself a superb piece of high nature.

"So will the great movement light the valley of the people," she cried; "for the morning is coming."

We sat our horses a little while and watched the growing area of colour and its spread in the valley; and then we rode back as from a baptism of splendour.

At breakfast, she sat in a soft gown, but almost masculine in her energy, and all the talk turned quickly on the campaign.

"I have made up my mind," she said; "I did that last night. I am going into the campaign. If I may not speak, I can at least write. I shall write letters to all the men I know and to many women whom I do not know; I shall write for the newspapers. Here's a cause at last worth working for with all one's might and all one's enthusiasm.

"This is a crusade; and I, who was born to fight, have for the first time found something to fight for. We must win"; and she stood up waving the sugar tongs at her audience of two. As she sat down she added in a lower tone: "Forgive me, gentlemen, I am but your housewife for the moment; but I dedicate myself to this emancipation. Now, what may I do for it?" And she turned to me as if she expected me to put on her the warrior garments of Joan of Arc.

Well, the day of the little convention came. We tried to have it called the Educational Convention, but the wags among our enemies got the better of us. We were referred to as the "Seven Foolish Virgins."

But ridicule was less difficult to meet than the dumb wonder of a large part of the people. Many of them feared that we might have lost our minds. More schools? In heaven's name, if we had enough of anything, surely we had enough schools. School-teachers couldn't make a decent living now, there were so many of them. And higher taxes? No sane man could surely seriously propose raising taxes and expect the people's approval. Let men who were so eager to educate their children pay for it themselves. This inertia was worse than opposition.

Nevertheless the convention met. It was neither a noisy nor a large crowd. A few of the most earnest and one or two of the most eminent

men in the State came, and among the delegates
— who were all practically self-appointed (for
they represented no organized body of men) —
were agitators for the farmers' organizations.
Of course, most of the discontented and unsuccessful "orators" of unpopular "causes" came.

The "Seven Virgins" had a platform and "a
slate" prepared. Professor Caldwell, of the University, presided; the usual routine of conventions was followed; the platform was adopted,
after ineffectual efforts of several economic reformers to engraft a demand for free cotton-warehouses
and loans of Government money, and such like;
and then the question arose who should be
nominated for Superintendent of Schools.

The Club had discussed this for a month.
Professor Billy was far-and-away the best man.
As Caldwell once said of him, he could put the
wisdom of the ages into a barnyard story which
any rustic could understand and on which no
philosopher could make an improvement. But
he insisted that he could do more good in the ranks.

The decision reached by the Club at last was
that I should be nominated. I shrank from it,
as I thought of thus becoming a public agitator,
for the influence of a public agitator is short, very
short. Doubtless the chance for me ever to
build up an influence of any sort would pass if I
should be defeated. I should be in politics an

"irregular," which meant political death; in education, I should be a "crank" — a fanatic, the *Globe* had already called me.

But this cause was eternally right. If I had any courage, now was the chance to show it. For once the hesitancy about method and about occasion, which has ever been my weakness, was overcome.

"Yes," said I, "put my name up, if you think best."

My name was presented. So was the name of some other unknown man; and the convention took a recess.

When the ballot was taken, I was nominated.

The cause was a high cause. It was right. It was fair. It was honest. It meant going forward — throwing off the rule of the dead — no matter what fate awaited any individual who took part in it. Now, at last, I could at least try to serve my country.

"With all my heart I congratulate you and the State," Louise telegraphed me as soon as she had heard of my nomination. "Fight it out. We are sure to win, for we believe in the people."

The next day Captain Bob Logan came to see me. He was excited, eloquent, and profane — in a mood of exaltation.

"The lowgrounds are gettin' broke up," he said. "The kingdom is at hand, Worth. I'm going to

be the next Governor of this grand old Commonwealth as sure as there is a God in heaven.   We've
got 'em on the run — the whole drove; and you
kid-glove academic fellers have scared the life out
of 'em.   The combination of hayseed and school-
books unsettles the old donkey's stomach.

"Now, I've come to see that you win.   There's
only one way to do it.   Runnin' on a side-track
you'll get nowhere.   But you fellers have stirred
up the country folks.   Our crowd has 'em stirred
up a good deal more.   We're going' to make
a combine.   The Populists mean business.   They
want their warehouses as the niggers wanted forty
acres and a mule.   I'm willin' they should get 'em
— get anything — if they'll make me Governor
and give me a chance to down that old gang.

"We've come to an agreement.   The regular
Republicans are to have the Governor, and the
Populists the rest of the offices.   That's our slate.
We've fought it all out, and we'll put through the
deal.

"Now old Craybill was put up by Stringweather's gang to get the Baptist vote.   He'll
get it, too.   We've got to go for the Methodists.
We'll make you out a hell-of-a-Methodist before
the campaign's over; and I propose that our convention endorse your nomination.   I think I can
put that through, only you must play the game."

"What is the game?"

"You must run on the main line, not on a side-track."

"But we're not mixed up in the party fight."

"The hell you're not! You straddled the nigger-vote business; you are Mr. Facin'-both-ways; you can jump on either side of the fence that has the softer place to light on. But you can't straddle and win."

Captain Bob was not only ambitious to become Governor, but his rebellious spirit sought revenge on the crowd that had long insulted him.

It was hard to make him understand our sincerity. His conception of politics excluded sincerity, although it did not exclude energy and desperation.

The Republican Convention the next week carried out his programme. He was nominated for Governor; the other nominees were all Populists except me — for they "endorsed" the nominee of the "Educational Convention."

I did not formally accept that endorsement. I remained a wholly independent candidate for an office that had nothing to do with political party doctrine. I stood for a clear-cut plan of building up our people and I should be glad to receive the votes of men of any party. Nevertheless I was regarded as the candidate of the "Scrubs" and of the Republicans.

I had put myself outside good political society

and the Colonels and the Daughters were confirmed in their opinion that I was a "traitor to
our people." My political conduct, they said,
justified my dismissal from the Edinboro schools.
I had, of course, resigned my professorship. I
had thrown away all my chances in the future,
academic or political, many of my friends said.

My brother's comment was: "You will start
a great movement that will succeed a long time
hence; but you will be beaten."

When I tried to explain the whole situation to
Margaret, I felt that I made little headway.
Her manner and her tone were "cousinly," but
she could not understand how any good could
possibly be done by acting as "a traitor." She
seemed to hold fast to the conviction that I would
see the crime I was committing and throw up the
nomination.

"You will not really desert us, will you, cousin?"

CHAPTER XIX

A GENTLEMAN FIGHTS FAIR

IN A little while the usual grand Democratic ratification meeting was held at the capital. As I walked to the hall I vowed that we should have a campaign without bitterness, if I could make it so — on my side a purely educational campaign. I should direct it wholly to the building of up the schools, and I should not be diverted to any merely partisan discussion. The campaign, whether we won or lost, should be worthy of our high aims.

When I came into the hall, Senator Barker was speaking. I had never seen him so wrought up. "We are about to be engulfed in a flood of African despotism," he said. "Our liberties are in peril; our very blood will be polluted; dark night will close over us — us degenerate sons of glorious sires — if we do not rise in righteous might and stem this flood of barbaric darkness."

I saw how race hatred was to be made the staple of the campaign. All the speakers who followed him took his inflammatory cue. A state of society was pictured which every man who heard it knew, when he was in his senses, to be a horrid lie. Yet for the moment they believed it. For men are easily frightened if you lead them to the edge of this dark and unfathomable abyss — this difference of race. Look into it and you cannot say surely what you see. What may the future contain? A race that is only a few generations from savagery — is the savage extinct? Can you be sure of that? Men's fears rise as children's in the dark. It is not what they know that frightens them. It is what they do not know.

The plain fact was, of course (as every man would have acknowledged six months before), that the Negro did not threaten the white man. Life was going as peacefully as at any time in the history of the State. The Negroes did not take a very active part in politics; and, when they had, they had been defeated by fair means or foul; and they had lost interest in this form of activity. So, in truth, had many of the whites, too; for politics had become a small section of life. We had begun to have larger tasks in hand. But the cry was now raised that something must be done unless Anglo-Saxon civilization was to be abandoned and our homes ruined. The Negro was a savage, a brute, a constant menace. Educate him? Then you only make him more cunning for evil. He must be put down.

The newspapers and the whole community took the cue. Men whose faithful Negro servants had shined their shoes in the morning and cooked their breakfasts and dressed their children and groomed their horses, and had driven them to their offices and were constant attendants on their families — such men spent the day declaring the imminent danger of Negro "equality" and "domination." "We must put them out of politics once and forever." This was an election that must be won. The governorship and a senatorship were at stake.

During the early days of the campaign, my audiences were Negroes. I was regarded by them as the nominee of their party; and the Democratic leaders had sent out instructions to discourage the whites from hearing me. "Let him train with Radicals and niggers — that's where he belongs."

I was waited upon by Negro delegations and asked what I proposed to do "for the race."

Now I had no false sentiment about the Negro. I am sure of that. It seemed to me that the "problem" was far less difficult than it had been represented. Here was a mass of ignorant folk. Their unwilling coming was the cause of all our woes. It was the one structural error made by the Fathers when they built the wide arches of our freedom. But our duty seemed to me plain. They are here. They must be trained to usefulness. I made this speech to them:

"Men, I come to tell you the truth. The white man and the Negro live here together. They will always live here together. The way to live together in peace and to help one another is plain.

"First, we must get rid of certain false notions and certain lies, and certain bad practices. We must be honest with one another, as I am now honest with you.

"I tell you these truths, then. The white man is not going to have what is called 'social equality' with the Negro. The white man is not going to eat with the Negro; the white man is not going to invite the Negro into his parlour; the white man is not going to marry the Negro woman. The two races must live socially apart, yet side by side, and they must work together.

"And the white man has got to treat the Negro fairly. He's got to treat him as a free man, not as a slave. He's got to pay him fairly. He's got to give him a chance to work, to buy land, to build a home, to raise his children decently.

"The white man has got to do more than this. He has got to train the Negro. He's got to give him good schools. The Negro must help pay for this. But he's got to have good schools — as good as there are in the world — schools that will teach his children to work, and show them how to work, that will train them to make honest livings and to lead decent lives, and to be good citizens — schools to teach the children not only to read but to use tools and to farm right. There must be schools for the best boys and girls when they get older, where they can learn to build houses and to make furniture and harness, to make butter, to plant cotton right, and to make twice as much corn as they now make, to raise chickens and sheep (these are better than dogs) — and the girls to sew, to keep clean houses, to cook good food. Everyone who has any brains must know how to make his living.

"The Negro has got to have his fair share of school money to make his schools as good as possible, and to keep them open as long as possible."

("Dat ain't so, *now*, boss.")

"I know it isn't so. But it's got to be so. We have got to quit lying to one another.

"And there is one other thing that I tell you men: The white men have got to let your women alone; and you have got to bring up your daughters virtuously. And you've got to let your own women alone — let them grow up to be clean and honest wives."

("Dat's sho'ly God's truth.")

"If we can do all these things, we shall live together peacefully and as happily as men live together anywhere."

("Dat gits my vote.")

"You may vote for me or not, as you please. If I am elected Superintendent of Schools, I shall try my best to do what I have said ought to be done. At best it can be done slowly. Even the white man is yet untrained. Both races must have such schools as I have described."

("What about de offices?")

"Nothing. No man ought to have any office that he can't fill well, and no man who can't earn a good living at his own business ought to have any office. Running for office has ruined many a white man. It would be still surer to ruin a Negro. You know very well that the white men of either party are going to give Negroes very few offices, if any. They lie to you about this. If I am elected, I shall have many offices to fill, the best offices there are; and I shall wish to fill them well. If I can get money enough, I shall want a thousand of the best Negroes in the State — the very best — to fill these offices."

("Now, yer talkin'.")

"These offices are — school-teachers — honest men and women who will teach your children not only to read and to write, but to grow up to be good and decent men and women. Am I talkin' now?"

("Yes, boss — dat's it.")

("Which party does yer b'long to, boss — 'Publican?'")

"The party that believes in making good and decent and honest men and women of your children — the party that tells you no lies. You would be better off if you had never heard of the Republican or of the Democratic party. My party is the School-House party — a school-house within the reach of every child, white or black, a school-house where no lies are taught. That is my party."

After several weeks of public speaking, to audiences made up chiefly of Negroes, I came home to sleep. I was tired in body and mind. But I could not rest. The impossibility of the task — why, many men who held my faith and had talked with me freely a month ago about building up the people would not now even go and hear me speak, so strong was the old party tyranny. There seemed no way to reach the people.

The whole commonwealth lay neglected, its people's development arrested. Other parts of the Union were becoming prosperous; men elsewhere were growing in riches, in intelligence,

in freedom.   Here was stagnation.   Thought and
well-being moved forward hardly an inch.   And
yet I, for trying to move them, was accused
of treason!   Most of the well-to-do had now
become my open opponents.   They were persuaded, or they pretended to be persuaded,
that I stood for a sort of anarchy.   They were
ruled by dead men's hands.   My instruments
must be the humbler, the ignorant, perhaps
only the Negroes.   Nor did *they* understand.
They knew only that I stood for revolt.   Our
constructive purpose they could not see.

One night, thinking of this bondage of men's
opinions, I walked to and fro in the old avenue
of elms, in the yard.   The early autumnal air
was refreshing.   The gentle wind shook the
leaves down the long row of trees and the moonlight
flickered on the walk.

"If men were free!" I said to myself.

The odour of ripe fruit came from the orchard.
Silence everywhere.   It was a beautiful world;
bountiful the earth; pleasant the night air —
"if only men were free, what land so desirable
to live in!"

To-morrow I should continue the campaign.
The "issues" of the contest — the political principles — they were as nothing.   The hollowness
of the political phrases irritated me.   They were
all mere formulas.   Men said them as monks

count their beads, mere incantations, meaningless words, rallying cries.

I never saw more clearly than at that moment the profound meaning of our action — its necessity, its positively holy nature.

"There is no other way out."

Up and down I strode, muttering a sentence now and then to myself — now walking rapidly, then recovering my self-consciousness and slackening my pace.

I heard someone come through the gate — there were a number of men — more and more. They came with hardly a sound. My impulse was to sit on a seat behind the shrubbery and let them pass, so that I might hear them and see who they were. "Cowardly," I said, and checked myself. I walked out to the middle of the drive-way and faced them with a "Good-evening, gentlemen. Were you coming to see me?"

Then I saw that it was a group of Negroes. Joe Goode was the leader.

"Yes, suh," said Joe, "we'se come ter confer wid you, suh, 'bout a promus what was made, if we'se in de order for a confearance."

"Well, what is it, Joe?"

"Yes, suh, we 'lowed how as you might be — if you was dissuaded by de plaus'bleness of some what does not know de 'pinions of de leaders, suh. It is 'bout dat 'ar promus' ter de Bishop of de Mefodis'."

"What promise?"

"'Bout dat ar school 'p'intment. Dey said dat you was ter giv' dat ter Bishop Wood. Maybe 'tain't fer us to say; but dere's a heap mo' Baptistes 'mong de colo'd folks dan dey is Mefidises. Yes, suh, 'twas dis wot we done come ter 'spress a 'monstrance."

"Who said that I had promised any office to anybody?"

A Negro far back in the group spoke up: "Dat's what I ax de brudder 'Who says so?' I says. ''Spose dere's nothin' in it. Den we done made fools er ourse'v's.' *Didn't* I say dat, men, when we come along?"

"You sho'ly did," said another.

"Let me give you men a piece of advice. When *I* say something about an office, and you hear me say it, then it will be time enough to talk about it. Don't let your people believe every silly thing they hear."

Then the whole company laughed at Joe.

"Done mak' a fool er yerse'f and o' us, too. De boss — *he* ain't got no offices. Didn't I tell you dat?"

"Well, so long Mr. Worth. We'se wid you ennyhow — all 'cept dis fool Joe, an' he ain't got sense enough to be wid nobody." And they went away muttering at Joe.

"O God, if we would be frank, we should become free."

And the odorous, cool night enfolded me. I walked back to the house and — poor duped devils — I fell asleep, to the sound of the river which turned the spindles and the looms; and it was pleasant to think that unnumbered millions of persons would be clad by the fleece of our fields, unintelligently as they were tilled.

The next morning I saw the humour as well as the pathos of it, and I wrote to Louise Caldwell a note about my political callers of the night: "What an exhilarating intellectual level the campaign takes! How it calls for one's profoundest thought! What exercise of the highest faculties!"

Well, why not *make* it appeal to the highest character?

And when I began making speeches again more and more white men came to hear me; and I did speak to them straight, as God is my witness. I said:

"White men, let us get rid of all lies and face the truth. That is the mark of brave men.

"And, since no other subject can be discussed than the Negro, what is the truth about the Negro?

"The framers of our Government did not, in the beginning, make slavery impossible. That

was their monumental error, and we yet —
even we — pay the penalty.

"The Negro was brought here. He will stay
here. We must make the most of him. He
is a burden and a menace unless he is trained.
So, too, is the white man. But the Negro is a
child in civilization. Let us train him. That
is our economic duty, our economic necessity.
Let us teach him how to do productive work,
teach him to be a help, to support himself, to
do useful things, to be a man, to build up his
family life. Let his women alone. Help him.
He is docile, grateful, teachable. He is a man.
Our civilization menaced by·the Negro? That's
a lie, and you know it. The only way in which
the Negro can be a menace to our civilization
is by his ignorance. The State must train him.
We must have schools to teach every Negro
child to work — that's what a school's for. And
we must have schools to train every white child
to work, too."

And they cheered. The country folk saw
the truth of this; and, when I described a school
that taught everybody in the neighbourhood, they
wanted such a school.

That programme would at last surely win.
Else there was no hope in right reason, nor in
the sanity of the plain people, nor in universal
manhood suffrage.

But patience, sweet Heaven, infinite is the patience called for. For we were yet "apart,' oratorical, emotional, "peculiar," in spite of the distance that separated us from slavery and the war. Patience is the word, a long, long patience. Changes have come and are coming. The people will rise; our lands will become richer; our vision wider; our temper more tolerant. The South is not a "problem." It is a social and industrial condition. You cannot solve a condition. You can only gradually improve it. And no social condition is either as bad or as good as any one man or class of men may guess by the small section of it that they see. Great results are visible only generation by generation.

So that I at times felt most hopeless and at other times most hopeful. I could not get away from my love of the land and of the people. Those that work only for themselves seem to miss the larger inspiration of our democracy; and I did get — certainly I got at times — the triumphant sense of trying a hard task, hard enough to be worthy of the most heroic ambition. And so I went on betwixt high hope and heavy weariness, as I dare say earnest men have gone on since human society began.

And week by week more and more the white country people came to hear me; and the enemy became alarmed. Training all the children in good schools was a popular proposal, as soon as they understood it.

The people's thought, then, must be kept from this proposal by the wheel-horse colonels, or they would surely lose the election. The Democratic press and the Democratic speakers, therefore, let loose a flood of personal abuse. "The nigger Professor" they called me, "with a plan to educate the blacks and to put them above the whites"; "to put the bottom rail on top"; "to subvert Anglo-Saxon civilization." One caricature represented me teaching history to a class of Negro boys. It was labelled, "What our University would Become." Another represented me as building a fence. I had put down as the bottom rail a white man — a one-armed Confederate veteran — and the top rail was a grinning Negro. Ever since I had attended Harvard College, I had been "tainted" with a wrong view of the Negro. One paper published this inquiry addressed to me "in sorrowful emphasis": "Would you marry your daughter to a nigger?" And it added: "Until the gentleman answers that test question, we need not pay more attention to what he says."

The hard-pressed political machine was willing to loose even volcanic fires if it could thereby save itself. The menace of the Negro must ever be kept in sight. Men who had seemed hitherto to be commonplace lawyers without clients, editors of newspapers that did not yield a profit, hangers-on to legitimate industry, who had not been burdened with convictions, suddenly assured us that they were civilization's most zealous guardians; and they came forth with social and political convictions for which they would stand to the death!

A large part of the Southern people were thus persuaded that the Negro must be kept to a level reminiscent of slavery, forgetting that on this level he can be only a burden. Thus they held down all the people in economic ways. Nor was this the worst result — they hindered the free play of thought.

Even the young were fired with this mania. It became a part of the general notion, a kind of creed, that the Negro was likely to efface the white man, if he were not repressed. Men wrote about it in the newspapers; preachers preached about it; young women chose it as the subject of their essays. Sensational novels appeared describing the crimes and social aspirations of the Negro, and they became popular; a code of personal conduct toward the Negro was set up even for Northern men to which they must conform. And so the hot battle raged; and one day there appeared this inquiry in *The White Man* in the form of a letter from a distant town:

"To the Editor of *The White Man*: There is a rumour here that one of the nigger-loving candidates for high office has put into practice already his social equality creed. Give us the facts."

The Editor published the note under this headline:

"TO WHOM DOES THIS REFER?"

The letter and the headline were copied the next day in the *Globe* and were re-published without comment for three or four successive days.

Then an editorial appeared in the *Globe* saying that the inquiry ought to be followed further. That was all.

But by this time all the Democratic papers in the State had published paragraphs about it, and gossip had been very active. Almost every man in the State now knew the story which had been set going by word of mouth from the Democratic headquarters.

Colonel Stringweather had said this in his drawling way to his fellows:

"Gentle-*men:* We've got to look after this young Worth — Niggerlass Worth. Old Craybill, whom we are running against him, is more'n half fool an' he ain't holdin' up his en' o' the campaign. Reckon it's about time we were fixin' young Niggerlass."

"What can we do?" they asked.

"I haven't spent much thought on it," said the Colonel. "But I'll throw out an idea and see if you catch it.

"His grandfather's old place, you know, is just out of town here a few miles. Now they tell me that there's a mighty likely yaller woman there who has a still yallerer baby; and young Niggerlass has been known to spend the night there — the night there in the house with niggers, mind you. An', if you want to work up the public feelin' a little more, you can get some tassels to the story. My authority for this story is Pompey, the barber. Pompey says that this is what the niggers in Egypt say."

"Oh, Colonel," protested a member of the committee, "I don't think we want to bring the campaign down to this level. Do spare us this."

"And get beat?" replied the Colonel. "What are we here for, to conduct a ladylike campaign or to win?"

The committee discouraged it. But the Colonel became more and more alarmed; and mysterious letters of inquiry about the candidate who had the habit of spending nights in Negro houses appeared more often in the newspapers.

At last the Colonel gave the word. He had a long conference with Major Thorne, the editor of *The Globe*. The story was to be written as hearsay. I was not to be directly accused, but I was to be called on to explain the rumour.

The editor and the Colonel worked on the story for a day or two, and at last they had it in proof-sheets to their satisfaction. "It'll put all the women ag'inst him, God bless 'em," said the Colonel; "and no man can win in the State with that handicap."

Proof-sheets of the broadside were to be submitted to the committee, and one of them, of course, was Tom Warren. It reached him two days before the day set for publication. He was a day's journey from the capital, making campaign speeches. The mail came just before he was going up to bed. The boy at the hotel handed him the envelope. He opened it and retired to his room.

"Send no names up to me to-night," he said to the clerk. "I am going at once to bed." Tom sat a while with this proof-sheet on the table before him.

"My God! Shall I never get rid of it? Will it follow me through all eternity?"

A scene came up in his memory that had often haunted him, but it had never before risen with such distinctness. The vision he saw was this through the haze of memory:

He was shooting rabbits at the Old Place and he had left the fields and was wandering alone back toward the house through a stretch of woodland. He had come to a path and he sat on a log for a moment idly holding his gun. A stream at the foot of the hill kept up a soothing murmur as it fell over the stones. Now and then a bird flitted through the branches. Once he thought he saw a squirrel. And now he was sure he heard a noise behind him; and when he turned he saw a girl in the path.

"You scair'd me mos' ter death," she said. "Don' shoot; 'taint nobody but me — Lissa. I'se jes' gwine over to Aunt 'Cindy's to tell her Miss Stone wants her to do some washin' ter-morrow. Don' shoot me — 'tain't nobody but me. I am jus' gwine thro'. It's nearer dan roun' de road. I ain't no rabbit."

"Come along, I won't shoot."

"When I fust seed you, I run back a little. Den I says to myself, 'It's jes' one er dem young men what shoots rabbits f'um de ol' Worth place'; and I comes 'long back ag'in, sayin' to myse'f, 'He ain't gwine to shoot you — go 'long.' He! he! hee!"

"Well, come along, then."

"Yes, I'se gwine," and she drew nearer, with a grin; "but dere ain't no need to run, fer de washin' ain't got to be done till ter-morrow."

There was a saucy smile on her face, as if she had caught him half-ashamed, resting while he pretended to hunt.

"Is yer by yourself?"

She was now near him. She put her foot on the end of the log on which he sat. "Is dat gun loaded?"

She was a wild thing of Nature, supple, graceful, with loose-swinging garments, and a soft light lemon complexion. "Lemme see if dat gun is loaded?"

"What did you say?"

She was now standing by him. His quick pulse answered the wild nature in this primitive, soft creature. The rush of blood gave him the sensation of worlds whirling about him, and his tongue was dry as in a fever. He arose and touched her shoulder. It seemed softer than silk under the coarse garment. They were two young creatures in a wood, and it seemed a thousand years ago when worlds whirled through his hot brain.

Such was the memory that Tom Warren saw, with stinging vividness; and he hit the table with his fist and said aloud:

"I will not profit by such a lie. I will not be a party to such a lie! By God! I will not."

A man in the next room of the hotel said to his companion:

"The candidate for Governor seems to be giv'n' it to 'em in his sleep."

"To appear Friday," Tom read across the top of the proof-sheet. "This is Wednesday night. It shall not appear Friday nor any other day."

He rushed out the door and asked the night clerk of the hotel if he could arouse the telegraph operator; for the office in the little town was closed early.

At the telegraph office he sent this message to Major Thorne:

"Proof-sheet received. I know the whole story to be false. I forbid its publication. I will not conduct a campaign on such a level. If the article is published I shall resign the nomination. I shall take the morning train for Marlborough."

"Lacks grit in his craw," said Colonel Stringweather when Major Thorne showed him this telegram the next day. "We can't win campaigns on squeamish platforms in ticklish times like these. That's what we get for putting up a sentimental young fellow for Governor — no stomach. Will resign, eh? I guess we'll see about that. Of course, Major, you're going to publish it, as we agreed?"

"I've no doubt we'll publish it, Colonel, but little will be lost if we postpone it a day; and we ought to hear what he has to say. He has thrown up engagements to come here, and he will arrive to-night. Be at my office at nine o'clock. We'll hear what he has to say. No doubt we'll put it to press on schedule time."

Tom went straight from the train to Major Thorne's office. There, as he expected, the Colonel and the Major were waiting for him.

"You received my telegram, of course?"

"We did, sir," said the Colonel, "with some amazement and, I may add, some amusement."

"You understand that I forbid the publication of the article."

"By what authority, sir?"

"Have I not at least some authority in this campaign? Am I to play the part of a dummy? I am afraid you chose the wrong man."

"I fear we did," growled the Colonel, "for we need a candidate that has some sand in his craw. This article will win the election. It will instantly put every woman and practically every white man in the state on our side. It draws the colour-line sharp."

"But it's a lie."

"Who says it's a lie?" roared Major Thorne.

"I say so."

"What do you know about the case?"

"I know it's a lie. I know that Worth is not the father of that child."

"Damn the facts," roared old Stringweather.

"Every young fellow is likely to get into such a scrape. I don't bear young Worth any malice whatever in the matter. We simply mean to show him that he can't go about and preach his 'poor nigger' doctrine in this country. The article doesn't say that the child is his — it's only an inference. If he's innocent, he can defend himself. It simply shows that he loves niggers in general — spends his nights with 'em. He preaches social equality: we'll give him a dose of his doctrine — that's all."

"Colonel Stringweather," said Tom, rising and declaiming at him, "you have heard what I have said. I have known Nicholas Worth since he was a boy. He has his fantastic doctrines. He's gone wild about education. He's suffered Northern influences to warp him. But he fights fair. He is a gentleman, and I am a gentleman; and no gentleman will take such an advantage as this of another. I would not have an election won in this way.

"My understanding is that I am the Democratic nominee for Governor. I am not a scandal-monger. I will not profit by such a campaign. That is my ultimatum."

Colonel Stringweather and Major Thorne went out of the room. When they came back, the Colonel said, in a tone of authority:

"Warren, we respect your delicate feelings

toward the enemy. They do your heart credit. You are sentimental and youthful, and that is not the way to win campaigns. We have the responsibility of conducting this, not for personal pleasure, but to win. Major Thorne will publish the article as intended. We have decided, with all respect to you, that we cannot be responsible for losing the election for any such squeamish reasons. You will soon see the matter as we see it, when you have had time to confer with your friends and when you see the effect that the article will have. I do not think we need say more."

"I have an addendum, then, which also you will publish," said Tom. "I will write it in a moment."

Presently he handed this to the editor:

"I disapprove of this article for two reasons: (1) It is an ungentlemanly way to fight a man, who, whatever his faults or doctrines, is a gentleman. (2) I am myself the father of the child spoken of in the article. I had rather publicly confess an error of youth than to do another man injustice.

"I, therefore, hereby resign the nomination of the Democratic Convention for Governor, and leave the Executive Committee free to choose another candidate.

"THOMAS CARTER WARREN."

"I ask you to publish that with the article. If you decline, I shall give it publicity elsewhere at once. I need not say more. Good night, gentlemen."

"Major, we'll lose this election," said Colonel Stringweather, and he put on his hat and went away.

CHAPTER XX

ALL the hidden forces of madness and fear had been unloosed. Not a day passed but unexpected things happened, things that the day before had seemed incredible, till now nothing was incredible or unexpected. Everybody lived in dread. A mob might anywhere bring a race war.

Nobody had dreamed that public feeling could be wrought up to such a pitch. We of the Club had surely never expected such a "roaring hell" as Captain Bob Logan called it.

What had we done? We had only emphasized the need of training the people, of quickening their ambition, of hastening the building of school-houses. If the Democratic managers had not insulted us we should never have thought of holding a convention. We had no idea "of going into politics." Certainly we had not meant to engage in civil war.

It was rung into my ears, day in and day out, that I was inciting the Negroes to crime and provoking exasperated white men to revenge —

a lie that would have been ludicrous if it had not been so ghastly.

The newspapers, many of them at least, had become active incentives to violence. Every little disorder, not to say every crime, was reported with lurid details. Even hearsay made as good matter for headlines as real events, and the newspaper readers were kept excited by rumours of more trouble than came. I did not know till now the hidden fury that lay in race-hatred. Race-difference, which may be ever so friendly in the even course of events, seems to hold a latent quality that may on occasion flare into the fiercest hate. It is something akin to the fury of Asiatics, as in the Sepoy rebellion, or the bloody fanaticism of Mussulmans. And yet it all seemed manufactured.

There was no more likelihood of the white race's losing its dominance than there was likelihood of a river's running up hill. Nor had there been any event to change the old time friendly relation of the races — no event but this campaign. This fanaticism seemed to be something that had simply been talked into activity. But, if it could be thus talked into activity, it must have lain in men's hearts dormant all the while; and it must be there at all times, ready to be talked into activity when needed.

But, as I frankly tell you, I do not understand

it. Here was the spectacle of a good-humoured,
kindly people, lately at peace with the Negroes.
They had cheated them at the ballot-box, but
there had seldom been bloodshed; for ours
was not one of the Southern States in which
men's lives had been most lightly held. Three
months ago we were "the most happy and contented people on God's green footstool." Certainly we were at peace. Now the hard pressed
old party machine found *The White Man's*
crusade a convenient tool to keep alive a waning
loyalty; and *The White Man's* cry was repeated
by most of the other newspapers. If a Negro
in the next county was reported to have stolen
a pig, lo! there was danger to our white civilization.

Shall I guess at an explanation?

Fifty or sixty years ago our grandfathers (not
the Old Man who lies beyond the box-hedge in
the garden of the Old Place; and herein may be
the explanation of my failure to understand how
close barbarism lies to the surface of our kindly
nature) — fifty or sixty years ago our grandfathers began a long wrangle about slavery
and it waxed in violence until they thought and
talked and wrote of few other subjects. Their
opponents in the controversy had many other
subjects to think and to talk and to write about
— trade and the building of cities and the opening

of new lands and the development of the people in many ways.

Then the controversy came to the violence of war. It was the same old controversy, about the same subject. And then came defeat. Whatever else defeat meant, it still meant the concentration of thought on the Negro. Nor after he became free did he disappear from our father's minds as the chief subject of thought and of talk. From the minds of their opponents he was well-nigh gone. He did not live with them. They had not suffered defeat. More energetically than ever they were building cities and settling new lands and driving trade and finding a healthful variety of occupations.

But now more than ever the Negro was the One Subject of our fathers' thought and speech; for during the time of Reconstruction he was set in authority over his master.

And so for fifty or sixty years, the full working life-time of three generations of men, we had had but one main subject of thought and of talk; and that was the subject which was linked with defeat and humiliation and the passing of the old order of things. It did not matter that through most of this long period of the monopoly of our thought and speech, the Negro himself had been passive; for even most of his crimes of the Reconstruction time were not primarily his crimes but the crimes of his leaders and new political masters, in whose hands he was a tool.

Now, if three generations of men think and wrangle and talk and write and fight (and how many died!) and suffer humiliation about One Subject — this One Subject only engaging them — may it not happen that the mind of a whole people may be deflected by such an experience and that they may come to think awry about it and to feel unnatural emotions and to fear impossible things and to believe the incredible and to act without reason — on this One Subject?

If this be so, then we have permitted ourselves in fact to be ruled — in our minds and actions and emotions and character and fears — by the One Subject. We had for three long generations been really ruled by the Negro.

And the old One Subject was uppermost to-day; so that men who would have heard our plea for training were hearing and would hear only the old Negro controversy in a new form; for the Negro yet dominated men's thoughts. He ruled us yet.

There was no reason to be surprised, therefore, shocking as it was, to read one day in the great headlines of the newspapers that the distinguished Colonel Stringweather had been killed by a Negro and that there was a race riot in Edinboro.

It was early in the day when I received a

telegram from Captain Bob Logan asking me to come as quickly as possible. "You may save life," was the last phrase in his telegram.

Colonel Stringweather had been murdered one afternoon. It was the next night when I arrived at Edinboro — just when men were going home to supper.

Captain Bob met me at the station.

"Hell's broke loose!" he said. "Come over to my office and tell me something. You can help; but not a word as we go along. The town's in a dangerous mood."

We shut ourselves in after he had ordered a drink to steady his nerves; and then in his wild way he began to laugh aloud. There was something demoniacal in his manner.

"Worth," he burst out in a wild tone, "I've had the most interesting speculation all day — an absorbing problem in morals. While I've been sitting on the edge of this volcano, the most interesting problem in morals has come up that you can find in all philosophy; and there isn't a man here I could mention it to — not a man."

"But about the volcano?"

"The volcano'll wait. I reckon it'll wait a few minutes; or, even if it goes off, let's first decide the question of morals. Won't you have a drink?

"No? Well, *I* will. The question of morals is this——"

"Stop and tell me about Colonel Stringweather's murder. Anything more than what appeared in the paper?"

"We'll come to that in this question of morals. Sit down." He stood up and took an oratorical attitude.

"The question is, whether the murder of old Stringweather was a harm or a help to civilization. Consider:

"*First:* If he were alive he'd be bawling, 'Down with the nigger.' Yet his murder by a nigger will give his side more help on election day than anything he could have done alive. He helped *his* cause, then, by being killed. That is the same as to say he is doing more harm dead than he could do alive. Therefore, it's unfortunate that he is dead. That's clear — isn't it?

"*Secondly:* The sooner an old firebrand such as he was is taken away from any community the better for the community on general principles. Therefore, it is equally clear that it is well he is dead.

"*Thirdly:* As to the manner of his dying: If he had died a natural death, it would have been wholly good for the community. If he had been killed by a white man, while his absence would have been a blessing, the community would have been the worse off for having had a murder. (Don't get impatient. I'm coming to the nub of the whole matter.) But, since he was killed by a nigger and the nigger will be lynched — probably the wrong nigger at that — old Stringweather himself is accessory to a murder or two, even after his death; for he would have done as much for any member of the mob as any member of the mob will do for him, *mutatis mutandis*. Therefore, the community will suffer not only from having one murder committed in it, but from two or more murders due to said Stringweather, and the murderers will be executed by a lot of other murderers in a mob who will go free. With two less murderers in the community (if they get the right nigger), the community will be better off, in spite of the other murderers who go free. Therefore, again, there are reasons for declaring his death a benefit.

"*Fourthly:* Yet it cannot be a good thing for any community to suffer such acts of violence. Hence the whole series of events seems lamentable.

"*Fifthly:* On the other hand, to take only the every-day common sense view of it, the exit of old Stringweather by any road was a good riddance for any community.

"*Finally*, therefore, I say, you may go round and round and you will find yourself at last standing in the same tracks that you stood in when you started. And whether the ways of Providence are justified in politics, who shall say?

"You give it up, do you?"

"Now, Logan, perhaps you'll say why you sent for me. What can I do?"

"We'd better be going now. Come and we'll see — we may be too late"; and I followed him as he unbolted the door and rushed out on the street.

"That nigger, Marshall," he explained as we ran, "he's a friend of yours, or I wouldn't have sent for you. They put him in jail this morning; and, when they raid the jail to-night, they will swing him."

"Can't the raiding be prevented?"

"I've telegraphed the Governor for troops; but everything is done for political effect, and nothing will be done. God in heaven couldn't save the nigger that really killed him, if he is caught. But maybe we can save Marshall."

We were now at the house of a justice of the peace. Without greeting, Captain Bob went on:

"Do you swear, Nicholas Worth, that on October 14, you saw and conversed in the City of Marlborough with John Marshall, coloured, of Edinboro, as late as five o'clock *post meridiem?*"

"Yes," I said, "I swear."

"That'll help, for the body was found at four o'clock."

Somebody had recalled that Colonel String-weather had often spoken with disgust of Marshall's school. When his body was found in one of his fields, his head crushed in by a blow, evidently with an axe, Marshall was not at home and there was no axe at his wood-pile. On that "evidence" he was arrested and lodged in jail.

Captain Logan and I had now come to the hotel in an excited crowd. "Gentlemen," he said, "Professor Worth swears that the Negro, Marshall, was in Marlborough at five o'clock the day of the murder. He could not have got there till ten o'clock that night. Stringweather's body was found at four o'clock. The man, therefore, could not have been the murderer. Do you swear that, Professor Worth?"

"I do."

"Damned if that don't look queer," one of the men said, who had followed us from the street. "The conductor on the night train last night didn't remember seein' him. Why didn't he see him? Nobody seed him git off here."

"No matter, gentlemen, I can produce other witnesses to this Negro's presence in Marlborough till five o'clock."

The crowd talked, grumbled, subsided, aroused itself again, divided into little groups, again assembled, and discussed the conductor and the axe with which the deed was done over and over again.

Captain Bob and I walked to the jail. The jailor was sure there'd be no mob. Yet he said that he was well armed and had two extra policemen inside. Two? Why, if a mob came, Marshall would surely be hanged. Beyond the jail in a vacant lot, a great company of Negroes was gathered. We went there and ordered them home. "You'll cause trouble — go home!"

We walked about the neighbouring streets, talking to whomever we met, explaining what we knew.

"Mighty concerned about a damned nigger," one fellow remarked as he passed on. "Must love 'em."

Well, the mob did not gather at the jail, and toward morning we went to bed.

One of the memorable days of my life had been marred, and from weariness — the day had seemed weeks long — I fell asleep at dawn in the "energetic city" of my humiliation; and old Stringweather lay in his coffin.

All the horrid facts came out in due time, after the campaign was ended. Colonel Stringweather had threatened to strike a newly hired Negro whom he had employed to build a fence. The Negro hit him with an axe. He was caught and tried and hanged a few weeks later, and Marshall was let out of jail.

The campaign became more furiously a discussion of the One Subject than ever; and the people in the towns were afraid to go to bed lest there should be race riots. The political managers were become desperate.

Yet it was not so in the country, especially in that part of the State where the best farms were, the cotton farms. The farmers' organizations were at work there; and many candidates for the Legislature (some on one ticket and some on the other) were "organization" men — men of their own kind. These farmers had become earnest for economic relief. They at least had found another subject. And in some of the rural counties many Democrats responded to our educational appeal. There were many such men who were going to vote for me and for all the Democratic candidates but my opponent. We heard of them every day and by every mail. They spoke to me wherever I went. If they never had bolted before they would bolt now.

But gradually the shock of the riot at Edinboro made men pause and be more careful. It was already plain that the murder had had nothing to do with politics. But it inflamed the race-feeling nevertheless. The Northern newspapers had sent correspondents to Edinboro. The murder was under discussion throughout the Union. The State was receiving a criminal notoriety that caused even Major Thorne to be very careful. The *Globe* published an editorial on "Caution" every day till the election, calling on all good men to see that the fair name of the Commonwealth should not suffer by any violent act of irresponsible men.

A fortnight had now passed since the criminal sensation, and there had been no subsequent disturbance reported from any place in the state. The rebound from recklessness had come; and my winning of the election seemed certain, whether the Republican ticket should be elected or not.

And, wherever I had spoken especially during these two weeks, our programme had been received with enthusiasm. I had large audiences, made up now of more white men than black. At last the idea seemed to be understood — that I was not talking party politics, and that, of all the candidates, I alone spoke of the training of the young — of the bringing of a better chance for the country boy and girl.

It was interesting, it was exhilarating, it was exciting, glorious, to see these people wake up. They were not dead. They knew in a dumb way that they had been misled, cheated, disinherited; that they had believed a lie. They were beginning to see that they were not "the most happy and the most fortunate people on God's green footstool." They wished their children to have better chances than they had had.

There was simply an incalculable volume of power — political power, intellectual power, social power, spiritual power — in them if we could release it and guide it. And the time of its release seemed come at last.

CHAPTER XXI

O NE day before the political campaign came on, I had talked long with Judge Bartholomew about my grandfather and their old-time political creed. When I was gone he said to his daughter:

"Much of my will is an Address to my Country-men; and, at my funeral, after the service is read, I wish young Nicholas Worth to read this Address to those who are assembled. He understands its meaning, and he bears the name of a remark-able man, whom I shall soon follow to the Supreme Court of the Universe."

And now the news came that he was dead. I was summoned to hear his affectionate request, and I was deeply touched.

He was the patriarch of Marlborough — indeed, of the State — perhaps its most venerable and certainly its most distinguished citizen. But he had lived so long in retirement that many persons in the capital had probably never seen him, and the life of the city had gone on for many years without thought of him. But his death caused his great career to be recalled.

It may be that every generation in every country produces great men, and that it is only when occasions bring them into dramatic relations to their fellows that they are recognized. But here was a man whose dramatic relations to his fellows had been forgotten by most of them or was at least become dim. Yet the tradition of his legal learning had survived his days of activity; and it was true that several of his decisions had become famous. He had written at least one legal treatise that scholars still held in respect and constantly made reference to.

He was likely to come into a wide fame just when the Southern States cut themselves off from the current of the world's thought. When the State seceded he resigned from the bench of its highest court and published a solemn and well-reasoned argument to show that secession was contrary to the Constitution. Passages from it were quoted at the time in all parts of the Union; but presently the day of soldiers came; and his reasoning was not long heard above their guns. He had spent the rest of his life at home with his library and his family. The political fury of the time passed him by respectfully. He expressed his opinions without obtruding them on the public. During the discussion of secession, he and my grandfather had talked much together. My grandfather's common sense was fortified by the Judge's learning, and the Judge's learning was fortified by my grandfather's common sense.

"A remarkable man, sir," he would say to me. "If Nicholas Worth had been trained to the law, he would have shown as fine a legal mind as we have in our whole history — a strong grasp on fundamental principles, and most excellent judgment."

All the town and many persons from a distance attended the funeral which was held on Sunday; and the Bishop read the service and spoke briefly of his courageous career. St. Peter's was not yet repaired, and the service was held in the room of the court over which he had presided.

Then I read to the crowded company a document that, if we knew history when we see it, would long ago have become historic. The solemn eloquence of it came like a great voice from the dead:

"As events showed secession to be a great crime against the Nation, followed, as great crimes are wont to be, by reprisals and errors and passionate misjudgments and wrong acts, I abjure my countrymen to keep steadily and patiently at the long labour of thoroughly reëstablishing the national structure of the Fathers. The law must be supreme. There is no other road to an orderly and secure society.

"The war for secession was the last great

struggle of English men against their brothers for the full rights of free men; and those full rights must be kept secure.

"We have had an untrained race thrust into the body of our citizenship. Citizenship must then be so fortified by sound laws and by their sacred observance that it shall withstand this violence, and lawlessness be prevented. For lawlessness has in all times and places begotten lawlessness.

"I would not have had this untrained race thus thrust suddenly into the body of our citizenship and we should not have suffered it if we had refrained from secession. But since it has come we must make our character and our citizenship strong enough to withstand the shock.

"And I charge my countrymen in this, my last will and testament, to make and keep the financial record of our beloved State free even from the technicality of repudiation. Bonds that were issued by adventurers who stole the proceeds still ought to be paid. Men and states must pay the penalty of their misfortunes as well as of their sins.

"May God have for our Commonwealth a great destiny in the proud Union of States now, in spite of the follies of impetuous men, made eternally indestructible — a place of honour hereafter forever through law and the faithful obedience to law. Amen."

Great spirits speak a common language. As I read this solemn deliverance of the dead, I seemed to hear my grandfather's voice; and I sat as in a dream while the choir sang and the great judge was borne from the crowded room.

I felt again the power of those great builders who had made us a Nation — a hovering of their spirits, as I had felt it the day we buried the old man whose name I bear; and the smaller life about me seemed a jarring anachronism.

CHAPTER XXII

THE ELECTION

AND now the day of the election was come. In Millworth the sun rose in a clear sky — a good omen. Early in the day I went into Marlborough to the office of the Club.

Minute instructions had been sent to our lieutenants in every county, and now we telegraphed to many of them a message of cheer and of caution — let them watch the polls carefully. If the Negroes should be permitted to vote, my election seemed certain. Friends of our cause were to go early and to stay late at the polling-places to prevent intimidation and miscounting. Our first fear was that in many counties the Negroes had been so frightened beforehand that they would not go to the polls at all.

There never had been a quieter forenoon at the little capital. Men walked idly up and down the streets with an air of embarrassment, as if they were exceptionally energetic on all other days and found idleness irksome.

"What's the news?" a passerby would ask as he looked in the door of our Club.

"Nothing; too soon yet."

And another would presently repeat the idle question.

At every village and voting place in the State that we had yet heard from there was the same sort of calm. About the ballot-boxes sat the judges of the election, chewing and smoking, and maintaining a grave silence.

As the afternoon wore on, the anxiety at the capital became greater. But there was yet no news. Telegrams came from a few towns that a full vote was being polled; some reported that I was surely winning; and one fellow spent his telegraph tolls on a facetious message of ridicule. "All quiet here," said another.

Presently a message came that told of the lightest vote ever cast in Tacawan County. "No Negroes have come to the polls at all." This was one of the counties where a Red-shirt Club had made parades with pine-torches by night and had fired into the air volley after volley of pistol shots near all Negro settlements. This was as much as to say: "The wise nigger will not vote this year."

The Republican managers had sent word to them all that these demonstrations were meant only to frighten them, and protection was promised to every coloured man who should vote. But, four years before, there had been an election riot in the county and several Negroes had been killed. It turned out that not more than a dozen or two went to the polls there this year — out of nearly a thousand. These were permitted to vote without protest — just to show that there was no intimidation!

Late in the afternoon a telegram came to the Democratic headquarters which read, "Coon hunt successful." It meant that the young Democrats of one "close" town had, the night before, taken, in different parties, as many as fifty Negro men on raccoon hunts, going a considerable distance by train. They gave the Negroes much liquor, lost them in the swamps, and returned by the only trains that reached the town in time to cast their votes. Fifty Republican votes were in the "coon woods," and the Democratic majority there was peacefully saved.

But early in the evening, news did begin to come. "Riot at the polls in Wayland County." When the facts became known, weeks later, it was plain that a riot had been planned. On the outskirts of a crowd of Negroes, some of whom had voted and some had been challenged and rejected, a pistol was fired; and a free fight began. Nobody was killed, and only one man was wounded; but all the Negroes retreated before more could vote. During the excitement, the ballot-box into which many votes had been deposited, was whisked away by a sort of sleight-of-hand, and another was substituted for it that contained only a few regular Democratic ballots. But there was no proof of this trick. A confession was made of it by the man who did it, many years afterwards.

As the night advanced, town after town sent favourable reports. At last came news of large majorities for us in Wayne and Talcott and Worth — all these old Democratic counties. The capital itself and the county about it gave a large majority for me.

At last — by midnight — it was plain that the election was won: there could be no doubt of it, if these returns were all true. And they all came as reports from trustworthy men — won beyond a doubt! For the Republican ticket had received more than its usual share of votes, because of the coalition with the farmers, and a certain number of Democrats surely had voted for me instead of the Reverend Mr. Craybill.

I sent a friend to the Democratic headquarters to hear what gossip he could.

"Oh, yes," said the committeemen, "of course we have won, but the returns come in slowly, and we cannot yet tell by how large a majority."

At the telegraph office many messages were sent in cipher to Democratic leaders especially in the Negro counties. It was now past one o'clock in the morning. The crowd at each headquarters had not diminished. Those who were sleepiest roused themselves at intervals and added long rows of figures.

Presently a great shout went up in the street in front of the Republican headquarters. Someone set fire to a barrel of rosin, then to another, and another. That was the usual bonfire of victory. The illumination drew a crowd. The crowd shouted a howl of victory. Men began to sing and to cry:

"Logan our next Governor!"

It was an ill-advised shout.

Up the street a similar crowd formed in front of the Democratic headquarters. A portrait of Tom Warren was lifted in a transparency. Each crowd grew larger and yelled louder. The Republican mob was the bigger and the noisier, because it was made up of more Negroes than whites. It seemed that every Negro man and boy and even many women in the town came to see and to shout.

"Down with nigger rule," came a cry from a balcony. The cry ran down the street as a wind runs over a prairie. Each crowd surged nearer the other. The police tried to keep them apart. There were only half a dozen policemen and they were soon run over.

"Down with nigger rule!" and somewhere somebody fired a pistol. Instantly a general firing began. Leading citizens of both parties, men held in the highest esteem, came out on the balconies of the two hotels and shouted exhortations to peace and quiet. The large figure of Major Thompson, the mayor of the city, was seen on a horse, trying to make his way into the struggling mass, crying "Disperse!" "Disperse!" and waving his cane in a command to disperse. But the mob seemed to take his waving cane and gesticulating motions for encouragement. The Governor himself shouted "Order!" from a second story window; but few heard him.

Some one yelled, "Turn out the street lamps," with the hope, I imagine, that the mob would disperse in the dark.

One after another the lights went out. In a few minutes, it was very dark — a night without a moon.

Nobody knew what was happening. Now and then a pistol shot was heard, and a dozen more would quickly follow, then a yell would break the silence. The voice of a policeman above the din commanded every man to go home. After a while the street lamps were re-lighted. The foolish mob had dissolved except that little knots of men gathered here and there, asking one another what had happened. The Negroes had all gone — in terror.

"Down with nigger rule!" would come now
and then from a window, out of which a pistol
shot was fired.

Three negroes were found dead, and the report
was that several more had gone home wounded.

By this time it was clear that the whole Republican ticket had won the election — if the counties
that were known to have Republican majorities
voted as usual; for there had been very considerable Republican gains in many Democratic
counties.

But most of the telegrams that came to us
said only, "Returns delayed."

The meaning of this came over me with a
dismal certainty; and we all agreed that we
should have to face the plain fact of being counted
out. We understood the desperation of our
enemies.

Senator Barker all this while had sat at his
headquarters in a quiet mood. To him it was
a game, and not even a game of chance. He
had no doubt of the result and he was not worried.
This was his business and his profession as well
as his sport.

Of course, he had not troubled himself to
think of the Negro as a real menace. Certainly
he was no greater menace than he had always
been. But young men — excitable men — had

taken his words seriously. He had said that the Negro was a menace. They believed that he was — believed it with fanaticism. And, if the Negro was a menace, the sooner we are rid of him the better.

Senator Barker had said also that I was playing into the hands of the Negro and wished to put the black man on top, to subvert white civilization. To him that was professional talk. But to excitable young men it seemed truth. They regarded me as an enemy to the Commonwealth, a menace to social life, an ogre.

There were, therefore, throughout the State, many such men who regarded it as a patriotic and even sacred social duty to see that the Democratic ticket won, at whatever cost. To make false returns, if that were necessary, was a patriotic duty.

I now saw their point of view and their state of mind. It was a state of mind that no reason could reach or touch. Their very courage made them dumb to all that we had said. I saw clearly that I should not be allowed to win.

More telegrams had come. The drift of them all was that in the Democratic counties the Democratic majority was greater than usual, and from the Republican counties the count was for some reason delayed — was very slow in being reported.

Thus the hours wore on. The streets became almost deserted. Now and then some belated drunken fool would call in a thick voice:

"Down with nigger rule!"

Another:

"Licked 'em ag'in."

Another telegram would come — no meaning but the old one — delayed returns.

We talked little more. There was nothing to say; and one by one we went home. Before going to bed I walked out on the balcony of the hotel. In the sky the first red of dawn was creeping up. I saw a dog licking a blot on the sidewalk across the street. It was the spot where a Negro, shot in the riot, had fallen dead.

But I did not go to bed as I had meant to. A telegram came from Captain Bob Logan:

"I propose to demand Federal interference. State must be put under martial law. Is in a virtual insurrection. Expect you to join me in demand. Election a wholesale fraud. Am preparing for fight, continuous fight. Don't surrender."

I went to the Republican headquarters. The door was closed. When I came back to the hotel, I found a morning paper — all screaming headlines of victory and an editorial on "The Saving of Anglo-Saxon Civilization." There was only a humorous allusion to "the foolish little band of deluded reformers."

The riot was described in ten lines. "The names of the unfortunate Negroes," it said, "had not yet been ascertained." And the naïf remark followed, "They would have been wiser if they had stayed at home."

I answered Captain Bob Logan: "Act only after consultation."

It turned out as I had expected. The State was not in insurrection. Breaches of the peace had occurred at several places, but they soon ended. There was no riot or bloodshed except in Marlborough itself. The result had been brought about by the intimidation of Negroes and by false election returns. There was no appeal to the Federal Government. There could be no successful appeal to any authority or tribunal.

Professor Billy took the train as soon as he had read the morning paper, and came to see me.

"It's hard on you, old man; for it's hard always to seem to be whipped. But it's all right for the cause. It may be a real victory yet. A legislature favourable to us may have been elected. We can't yet tell. At any rate, it's a fine, hard first-blow in a knockout fight. We could hardly expect our cause to win everything at once. It's hard on you — that's the worst of it. But, of course, we can't at once work a revolution for education among a people who do not yet care to be educated. It will take a long time."

"A long time — a long time" — that phrase kept ringing in my ears. We had hoped to do at once what could be done only after a weary period of agitation; and the result must come gradually — must come very slowly, if it ever come. Meantime, so far, it seemed to me we had failed.

And Louise Caldwell telegraphed: "I do not believe the first reports. We cannot lose. Keep in good hope."

Nothing came, of course, of Captain Bob Logan's threat to demand Federal interference. When he received my telegram, he cried, "Coward," with an oath; and it was far into the morning when two of his friends, after a long effort, persuaded him to go home; and they went with him, one on either side, to his door.

The report came from Edinboro a few days later that he had ever since been in bed — had wrought himself into such a passion that a severe illness had followed.

In the afternoon, I met Senator Barker on the street. He was in the glow of a victorious humour:

"Worth, I am afraid our boys ran you pretty hard on that nigger business. Don't take it to heart. Now you're beat, come back into the fold. Nobody cares a damn about the nigger except for campaign purposes. But you can't ever buck against the Anglo-Saxon — see? That'll down the Radicals every time. You'd better come back to the party where you belong. This is the advice of an old campaigner.

" The nigger," the Senator went on in his good-natured way, "I'm sorry for him. The Democrats in the South use him to hold on to political power, and the Republicans in the North used him for the same purpose. He is used to fire the heart of the North and to fire the heart of the South, and he never gets paid for being a boogy."

Ah!

I saw still more clearly the ranging of Great Forces, but the force that I stood for, could it ever win?

The deep-seated doubt that ever lurks — the Doubt that was the dragon of all the old fables — came forward again; and I caught myself taking stock of my poor plight and of all my small assets of hope. But that way self-consciousness lies, and I sought counsel of a better philosophy. Rest, said I, brings the normal mind and the right perspective. I went home. I heard the river flow over the dam. The cotton was now white again in the fields. And, before I fell asleep, I made a happy plan, which I should carry out on the morrow, telling no one but my mother.

CHAPTER XXIII

PINE HAVEN lies on the ocean's beach, on the long, sandy slope that bore the great, long-leaf pine forests, a village of rest, so far from all activities that men sought it who wished for a time to forget the world wherein they had become weary. There was a saying that the very dead found Pine Haven more restful than the grave. And there was no pleasanter season there than November. The wind that gave a gentle hint of winter — a gentle hint is all that it ever gave — sang through the pines an answering melody to the roar of the ocean — the lonesomest place on a low, lone shore.

I went there to sleep, to get away from people and letters and telegrams and explanations and regrets and advice and condolences — all the tiresome after-things of a political defeat; and I took Uncle Ephraim with me, who was "feelin' mightly poo'ly."

There was a hotel, and there were huts (called cottages), in rows under the pines. I engaged one of these. On the left and on the right were others, where rested old gentlemen and old ladies from several States, come to get the early winter air, soft and full of the resin and of the sea. Old ladies with shawls that were heirlooms; aged men with long broadcloth coats — these gentle relics of a dying generation, with white hair and feeble steps and benignant faces, stopping at this quiet station before taking the last long journey.

Among them I found, to my delightful surprise, Professor Randall, my dear old friend, the teacher of Greek in my youth — grown prematurely old. I had not seen him since I left college. His hair was white, the fringe of it that was visible around the black skull-cap that he wore. Very white, too, was his imperial; for he wore a Napoleonic beard, which gave him a sort of military appearance.

He did not even know that I had been a candidate for office and a renegade and a traitor to my race. (We were in another State, which meant, in those years, almost another country.)

We began where we had left off. Did I keep up my classics? Oh! too bad! It is a terribly distracting time — yes — yes — men can no more find the old leisure — the old leisure. All life is changed — changed. He had found more time for reading during the active campaigns of the war than any of his practical acquaintances now find in every-day life — more time really in battle. It is battle now — yes, yes, all battle.

He had his classics with him? Yes, of course. I took his Homer, and found, somewhat to my surprise, that I could read it — halting now and then. And we read the Odyssey to one another in Greek, to his infinite delight and to my great gratification.

We had been going through this pleasant pastime several mornings, sitting in front of his cottage, when, while we were reading, Uncle Ephraim came along.

"Professor Randall," said I, "Ulysses approaches us. I will beckon to him."

The old man came up to the porch, and I went on:

"He is stranded here a little while on his journey home. And I fear he'll never see Penelope nor come into his kingdom again."

"Yer 'umble sarvant, suh. (What kin' o' prank's dat what Mars' Littlenick up to now?")

"He has come a long journey since he left the windy plains of Troy, and he is resting here on his way back to his kingdom."

Uncle Ephraim bowed, as an actor in a play. "De kingdom nigh come fur an ol' man lak me."

"At home the faithful dog keeps watch for him."

"Yes, suh, got two on 'em."

"And, if favourable winds and the protection of the shining goddess favour him, he will return to his own."

"Yes, suh, dat's what I hopes."

"In his descent to Hades he spoke with the spirit of mighty Agamemnon."

"Mars' Littlenick, I'se heard o' de speerits of jus' men made parfec', but dat 'Gamemnon — he ain't none o' de prophets, is he? 'Tain't in de Scriptur' what I larnt."

"Sit down, Uncle Ephraim. I was talking Greek to the Professor."

"I thought it mus' be som'in' lak dat. I'se jes' a ol' nigger, boss, his sarvant and his pa's sarvant, and *his* pa's sarvant afore him; an' I ain't none o' dem 'Gamemnons nur nothin' else. Mars' Littlenick, he fetch me here ter wait on 'im, sayin' dat de ocean and de pine trees would do my co'f good. You mus' 'scuse him, suh, when he gits frolicsome lak dis."

A man of imaginative temperament, who once learns the Greek language so as to read it easily, opens the door to as supreme a clear pleasure as can be found in the sweep of knowledge or of art. There is no keener joy than his reading may give him. It remains true, with all the shifting of the currents of knowledge and with all the variations of experience, that no man may be a supremely cultivated man — a gentleman in all his intellectual appreciations — who has not felt for himself the clear-cut, self-restrained mastery of the greatest of all arts, shown best perhaps by a Greek play or a Greek oration.   And thus I pushed aside the world and found forgetfulness even of the long, soft, sweet dream of restful affection that seemed now gone.

How a youth may love and dream, and dream that he loves, and live the love and the dream, not knowing whether it be dream or love and life; and if it pass, or seem to pass, become old with the solemn age of youth, and mourn because he has touched the very limits of human experience!

As I was saying, I forgot even the old tangled skeins of things, when I re-read with Professor Randall the story of Ulysses, and caught the joy of the old man's talk, as we walked under the pines.   The blue Ægean was there, and ever audible its roar.

Once in a while the procession of the aged would be relieved by the appearance of a newly wedded pair.   I pointed to a young couple one day, and said to my old philosopher:

"Why do you suppose they came here, Uncle Ephraim?"

"'Spose? Why, I knows, an' you knows. Dey's jes' married. Time you was doin' dat, Mars' Littlenick. You de haid o' de fam'bly, you know."

"Well, Uncle Ephraim, I'm sometimes afraid to marry. The lady might be too soft."

"Fore God! you don't want er bony one — does yer?"

Well, Uncle Ephraim's cough was better. I had slept and slept; we had finished the Odyssey; in fact, I was becoming somewhat weary of resting.

And I had thought out many things.

The future? The service of my country? That was a grim piece of humour now. Marriage? Oh, my sweet cousin, we had never really known one another.

While I was pondering these grave subjects, one day the old man brought a copy of the *Globe* from the post-office; and surprise overwhelmed me at what I read. Here was a long letter from Pine Haven about me. They had followed me even here. But, thank Heaven! it was not a political letter.

I was discovered after a turbulent and misdirected and fortunately unsuccessful campaign — so the introduction of the letter ran — in this quiet place in the company of my old teacher, the venerable and learned Professor Randall; and Professor Randall and I were spending our time reading the Greek authors.

Then followed half a column of eulogy of the scholarship of the "typical Southern gentleman." He did not go to Saratoga and lead a frivolous life, but sought quiet and communed with the eternal youths of the ancient world.   Then another half column in praise of my own scholarly accomplishments!

I had forgotten the oratorical habit of mind and its insincerity.   This newspaper's opposition to me during the campaign had not been sincere. It was professional.   Everybody knew that I had never thought for a moment of proposing or of practicing "the social equality of the races." Yet men (thousands of men) voted against me, and thousands of women regarded me as a sort of social ogre,   because these oratorical phrases about "social equality," "white supremacy," the "bottom rail on top," and the like, were repeated thousands of times.   As soon as I was defeated, by fair means or foul, I was perhaps not quite forgiven; but my "social equality" was no longer subversive of society.   The *Globe* tacitly confessed that the whole contention had been false.

And now, a casual remark made no doubt by Professor Randall about our reading Homer, provoked an equally insincere eulogy of me for accomplishments that I did not have, and a eulogy of the "typical Southern gentleman," that must have surprised him, if he be capable of surprise in his Walhalla.   A month ago I was a vile enemy of social order.   Now I was a scholarly ornament of society.

And it became plainer and plainer to me that there is nothing real in the oratorical zone. The real things here are these pines and the sea, these two old men, my brother's work and the cotton fields, Professor Billy and his unwearying plan for a college for girls. The rest is a hollow sham, or sheer inertia.

When we were to start home I felt like picking up forgotten threads of old things, and I said to Uncle Ephraim that we would go and see Sam.

"Sam who?"

"Sam who used to belong to us."

"Sam what run away? I thought he done gone or was daid, or som't'in' happen ter him."

"He's teaching."

"Sam a-teachin' school? Whar'd he git his larnin'?"

For Sam was now a teacher in a large school for Negro youth. In the pamphlet of explanation of the school, he appeared as "Samuel Worth, Teacher of Building."

It was Saturday when we arrived. Professor Worth (Is "dat what we got ter call Sam, Mars' Littlenick?") showed us the workshops of the school. Here were young men learning carpentry; here were others learning shoe-making; and others, harness-making; others were laying bricks; others were learning to shoe horses; others to plan and to build houses (this was Professor Worth's own department). The young women were taught to cook, to sew, to do fine laundry work, to care for poultry, to nurse the sick. There was a farm where both sexes worked, and a dairy where women were taught to make butter. And at night they had lessons from books.

And there was not a white man on the premises. All this work was done by coloured men and women.

"Now dat's de way ter larn de young folks ter be some account," Uncle Ephraim said.

Saturday night the custom was for all the students to gather in the great hall, a large auditorium of which Sam was the architect, and to sing the plantation melodies. Professor Worth was the leader of the singing as well as the teacher of building. They insisted that Uncle Ephraim and I should sit on the platform. In they came, six hundred of them, more than half being half-white. After the reading of a chapter from the Bible and a brief prayer, which all recited, the singing of the religious songs and plantation melodies was begun.

That mighty chorus of six hundred voices sent the rolling old refrains up to the rafters.

They sang, "O Lord, What a Mornin'."

I saw tears come to Uncle Ephraim's eyes.

"Let 'em sing dat ag'in, suh, if you please,"

said the old man; and again, even louder and more melodiously, the Heavens were rolled up as a scroll, and the Great Day was come!

Here was a reason, as I had found a reason among the white folk, why we who are born here ever feel the call of the land to serve the people. Here were the fundamental crudities exposed. Here were three hundred half-white faces before me — three hundred tragedies — the white man calling out in every one of them to the life of his kinsmen and the black man holding him to the plane of the African. And here was the African, now through the tutelage of slavery, trying to become an independent, full-grown man — all children in civilization, not yet understanding, nor yet understood, pulling upward against odds that must be endured rather than resented, a patient race, with need of all its patience, a humour-loving people, with need of all their humour, a melodious folk, with need of all their music for consolation — pulling up, pulling up, and here at least rising by the best way, the way of trained industry; and yet their very songs were the songs of slavery. But it was a music such as the master race had not developed. The pathos of it would move even old Stringweather to tears, if he could see and hear it in his long home.

Yet a more pathetic fact was that not one of the Stringweathers or their like or their dupes would ever have such an experience, for not one of them would ever visit such a school, nor even believe the truthful reports that were made of it.

I must make an address to the students, they told me; and the Principal introduced me. I do not know what I said — no matter; for something far more important happened when I sat down.

Without invitation or warning, Uncle Ephraim arose. He was feeble, but he hobbled to the centre of the platform, his white head a fitting crown of his great black stature; and he looked down from his height of ninety years. He turned to the Principal and bowed.

There was a long silence. Something in his motion recalled my grandfather. He said nothing, and the silence became intense.

He bowed again.

Was the old man getting a glimpse at last, before he should go, of the great problem of which he was a part, and of which he had never been aware ?

At last he began to speak:

"I wants ter say, suh, I is er ol' man, done pas' de years er de prophets, an' I'll soon be gwine ter de odder sho'.

"Before I goes, whar I'll see de gret men of dem gret ol' times — Mars' Henry Clay and my ol' Marster and Mars' Lawd Gawd A'mighty hisself — I'se much obleeged ter hear dem gret ol' songs and ter see yer a-fetchin' up dese young fo'ks here ter do deir hones' wuk. Now I bids yer far-well."

I looked at Sam, who sat motionless. But presently he awoke and beckoned to the congregation to rise, and again they all sang, six hundred strong:

"O Lord, What a Mornin'."

CHAPTER XXIV

THE BUILDERS

WHEN I came back to Marlborough, to my surprise few persons mentioned the election or my political adventure. The subject seemed wholly to have passed out of men's minds. Everybody had become weary of the unnatural strain and had been glad to turn to other things.

But almost everybody whom I met spoke of my scholarly habits. You would have thought I was a distinguished Hellenist in a community given to classical scholarship. Yet not a man nor a woman who alluded to my "scholarly diversion" knew even the Greek alphabet, nor had any desire to learn it. But that was no reason why they should not take a pride even in accomplishments that I did not have.

Again, therefore, as always in an insincere and artificial world, the comical aspects of life balanced the despondent moods; and it was hard to make up my mind in such an atmosphere which emotion I ought to yield to — amusement or weariness. Amusing it surely was for a time; but could there be anything real in life there?

Yes, a sectional pride was real — very real. The editor of the *Globe* hated with a very fury of hatred what he called "the North." Major Thorne was in earnest. Unlike Senator Barker, he had convictions. He believed with the bitterness of narrowness that I would subvert society if I could. He believed that to educate "the populace" as he called them, would be to put false ambitions into the minds of simple people; and even to talk of educating a Negro was to brandish a firebrand. He had often quoted the Virginian of Colonial times who said that he thanked God that no free school had been planted in the Old Dominion.

He regarded the educational ideas and the whole civilization of "the North" as the preachers regarded the modern scientists and the doctrine of evolution. They knew nothing about the subject, but they knew, whatever it was, that it was damnable. This very day's copy of the *Globe* contained the following editorial:

"The maudlin craze for 'education' — the planting of restlessness and the sowing of impossible hopes in the minds of the populace, at the public expense — is one of the most plausible attacks of a strong, centralized, paternal government. The irresponsible classes deluded and made dissatisfied, the whole social organization disturbed — such would be the only result; and the responsible class must suffer the damage and pay the bill."

The same paper contained also this editorial paragraph:

"We hope it is true that there is thought of giving an important consulship in Greece to young Nicholas Worth. He has won his political reward — as those in high authority at Washington look at it; and, since this post has for some time been held by a Southern man, we should like to see a Southern scholar continue to hold it, now that the late occupant is dead."

No chance for a "castigation" of Mr. Nicholas Worth, as an individual, was ever neglected by Major Thorne; but, when it happened that my virtues or my faults or my accomplishments or my shortcomings, or anything that was mine, could be used to show the superiority of Southern civilization over "the North's" his larger hatred swallowed his smaller; for, if the supposed accomplishments even of a renegade Southerner put "the North" to shame, so much the better. The effort was continuously made to assure "the North" that we were a cultivated and scholarly people.

In a few days a letter came to me from — of all men in the world — Senator Barker. He had no power of effective recommendation, he explained, with the Republican Administration;

but he had already taken pleasure in speaking to the Secretary of State and to the President himself in my behalf. He was, in fact, a social favourite and successful courtier at the White House — the sly old high-liver and story-teller; and he advised me to make formal application and to come at once to Washington.

"Of course," said Major Thorne, who even came to the hotel to see me, "you are entitled to this reward and more, for goin' over to the Radicals. Worth, you'd better come back into the white man's fold; but, if you're clean gone over to the enemy, you ought to have your reward."

Surely it would be a pleasure to take up my Greek in real earnest, if for no other reason than to put this silly mockery to shame. And why not? A week ago I had been dreaming of the joy of just such a life, and I had almost envied good old Professor Randall his remoteness from the world and the pleasure he had got from his reading during all these distracted years. He had known neither the sorrow nor the joy of living through them. Yes, why should I not seek the appointment? It would take me away — honourably — from this hollow life.

I again took stock of my small store of plans and hopes, and tried to look before and after. A career? There was no career. I was an unskilled pedagogue, once dismissed and now again without a post, a defeated political candidate, and (in spite of all this silly praise of scholarship that I did not deserve) a man without specific training for anything, but living in an intellectual atmosphere where I was not at home — and a disappointed or awakened lover, to boot.

There were not more than half a dozen persons with whom I could be wholly frank on all subjects without offence. The horrible Great Tragedy behind us and the myths that had already grown over it and sanctified it — the shadow of these rested everywhere. The private tragedies that had hit close to my own life had, everyone in some way, leaped out of this shadow. In a land brilliant with sunshine, you must walk in twilight. I could not be wholly frank even with the good women closest to me. Margaret could never have been happy with me, really knowing me; nor I, after I had really come to know her. To my mother I had been willing to be silent, at least on religion; for I owed an affectionate respect to any opinion that she might cherish. We had all life in common but this small section of it. Even an implied untruth — an untruth of silence — to her was hardly a tax on my frankness or honesty of mind. Our affection covered more than all conceivable differences of opinion.

But this could not be so in my relations with anybody else without open falsehood. To my

aunt and to my cousin and to all good women
like them, I must be offensive or I must be silent
on our history, on the real condition of the
Southern people, on the Negro, on the Church —
on almost all subjects of serious concern. I
must suppress myself and live a lie, or I must
offend them.

This in spite of the very considerable freedom
of opinion and of discussion among men only.
In men's society in Marlborough, a freedom
was granted that was never allowed at the fireside
or in public. I could talk in private as I pleased
with Senator Barker himself about Jefferson
Davis or about educating the Negro. He was
tolerant of all private opinions, privately expressed
among men only. But the moment that an
objectionable opinion was put forth publicly or
in the presence of women or to Negroes, that
was another matter. Then it touched our Sacred
Dead, our Hearthstones, etc,. etc. In this fashion,
most men who thought led a sort of double life;
and to most of them there did not seem to be any
contradiction or insincerity in such a life.

But the suppression of one's self, the arrest of
one's growth, the intellectual loneliness and the
personal inconvenience of living under conditions
like these — this was not the worst of it. For
a man, even in the ardour of youthful freedom,
can adjust himself to a false society (and all

society is more or less false) as, for example, one could adjust one's self to society in Russia, and find many pleasures left outside the zone of necessary silence.

But there can be no such thing as a democracy with any zone of silence about it. I could perhaps content myself — to a degree I had done that very thing — and smother my spirit of revolt, as many men of naturally independent temperaments had done, but for a fact of much larger significance than one's own personal intellectual comfort. For these men who ruled by the ghost called Public Opinion held the country and all the people back almost in the same economic and social state in which slavery had left them. There was no hope for the future under their domination. The people who least suspected it were the most completely suppressed.

And the very land suffered, for all our life rested at last on cotton. The soil was becoming poorer under a system of tillage that grew worse. The Negro was the principal labourer, and, without training as a farmer and as a man, he was becoming a less efficient worker. So, too, the white farmer. Training was denied to both. The pitiful short-staple yield of impoverished acres was sold for the starving price of low grades because it was not skilfully nor promptly gathered from the fields; it was wastefully handled; and it went at last to pay mortgages on itself. Life could rise no higher till efficiency and thrift came in. There would be no broadening of thought, because only old thoughts were acceptable; no change in society, because society's chief concern was to tolerate no change. The whole community would stand still, or slip further back.

A change must come. Yes, but I should be dead, my life all lived to little purpose, in this changeless twilight of half silence and smothering atmosphere.

To think of spending my life in Marlborough as it then was or as it seemed ever likely to become! The Old Soldiers, the Daughters, the endless twaddle about fair women and brave men, the prayer-meetings half the week, the bishop — Great Heavens! a man would smother there, or wither up while the long summers shimmered above the sidewalks and curled the shingles on the roofs.

I would answer Senator Barker appreciatively and at least go to Washington and see what all this meant.

The chance to get the appointment seemed greatly helped, too, by the information, which came to me in a roundabout way, that the two managers of the little Republican machine in the State — the postmaster at Marlborough and the collector of internal revenue — favoured my appointment. I had had little to do with these men. They were not held in high esteem. But there seemed no doubt that their advice was sought and valued at Washington.

And consular appointments in those days were frankly considered "spoils." The postmaster and the collector knew of no one else who could be decently even thought of for such a post; and, of course, there was another reason for their unexpected kindness to me — a reason that I, a mere infant in politics, had not yet discerned.

All this out of an accidental absurd newspaper letter about me from Pine Haven! It hardly seemed worth while for a man to try to plan a career if it could be shaped for him in so haphazard a way by such trivial and accidental events. I would, therefore, at least go to Washington. That was the one suggestion now in sight.

Louise Caldwell was visiting my mother the day I went home. She made sad pilgrimages to Marlborough once or twice a year, and she often stopped on the way to spend a day at Millworth. They talked much about flower-culture and she usually carried with her a great sheaf of colour from the garden. But there was still something of the old sad undertone in her talk. I guessed that she and my mother recalled old sorrows, going back to the tragic night of her visit to our house in her childhood.

When we came to supper the whole household fell to talking of the *Globe's* editorial about the consulship to Greece; and I told them of the letter from Senator Barker and of my decision at least to go to Washington. My Aunt Eliza was much impressed. It would be a great honour.

But my mother dissented. To her it meant my absence.

Charles laughed — laughed long and loud. "Of course General Barker and Sam Thorne wish you to go away. They are sorry you ever came. By going you will give up the fight, to their relief, and be under obligations to them when you come back. If they can send you to Greece and get rid of Billy Bain, life will be easier for them."

And when I afterward told Charles of the friendliness of the postmaster and the collector, he became more emphatic still.

"Of course they wish you to commit yourself thus formally and definitely to their machine — to be under obligations to *them*. Their machine and the Democratic machine work together — one has the Federal offices, the other the State offices. They are allies that feign hostility — all playing the same game."

I did not go to Washington at once, as I had meant to do, and in a few days I saw Professor Billy.

"Barker?" said he, "Senator Barker? Yes, yes; I've heard of him, I think. I'll tell you a story about him.

"He had long owed a Hebrew tailor in Washington a bill. (He had long owed most persons bills, who knew him.) The Jew had just taken his son, Isaac, into business with him.

"'Isaac,' said the old man, 'I gannot zometimes fint de disdinguished Zenator always at home. He owes us a larch pill. Go to de Zenate and zee him and gome back wid de moneys. Be sure you geds de moneys, Isaac.'

"Isaac came back and said nothing. 'Did you not ged de moneys, Isaac?'

"'No, fadder.'

"'You vill never sugzeeds, Isaac, till you learns how to gollect pills from chentlemen. I vill haf to go meself.'

"When the old man returned, Isaac asked: 'Fadder, did you ged de moneys from de disdinguished Zenator?'

"'Isaac, he is a great shentleman, de Zenator. He showed me de gommittee room, der Zupreme Gourt, de —— '

"'But, fadder, did you ged de moneys?'

"'No, Isaac, I did not ged de moneys from

de disdinguished Zenator; but he said dat you vas a goot bus'ness man, and he hoped our bus'ness vould now grow wery fast; and he gafe me an orter for two zuits of glothes.'

"De disdinguished Zenator, Nicholas Vorth," Professor Billy went on, "has the warmest interest in your scholastig gareer — he hopes dat it vill brosber."

If my brother and Professor Billy were right, how simple was I! The more I thought about it, the surer I became that they *were* right. My academic habit of mind kept me far behind them in seeing great practical facts and in understanding men. I have ever been slow in developing. Besides, had I not the very qualities of mind that I had often deplored in my countrymen, especially that sort of simplicity that marked an arrested development and a sort of impractical method of thought that was in fact the "oratorical" mind?

But by their help I now saw clearly. I would stay. I would at least not be driven or cajoled away. Had I not been cowardly even to think of going away? Would I not be seeking merely my personal comfort? After all, was any really great cause won in a single battle or won in two battles, or three?

I wrote Senator Barker my thanks and explained

that my plans forbade the consideration of so flattering a suggestion as he had kindly made.

But the question now arose, What should I do? The Professorship of History at the University was filled by another; and, if it had not been, my political enemies would now oppose my re-appointment.

I remained at Millworth for a continuous stay, for the first time for several years; and I found out more definitely what Charles had been doing.

There was not one big mill-town now but a succession of mill villages. The number of mills had increased partly by Charles's own building and partly by Cooley's investments. He and his sister made frequent and sometimes long visits to Millworth, where they had built a little house, near my mother's. The two flower-gardens were adjacent, and Adelaide and my mother kept up a fierce friendly rivalry in their floral work and sport.

I came to know Charles anew, and through him I got a large vision, of which (weary as you are) I must tell you.

Everywhere in the mill-villages were orderliness and cleanliness. Men, women and children worked, but under a system, which others had declared impossible, that required work in the mills to alternate with work at home and at school. The whole community was a school. Everybody at some time learned more or less of every craft required by King Cotton, from the preparation of the soil and the planting of the seed to the making of garments from the cloth. Nor was this all; for the schools were practical and other crafts also were taught there — if there are any crafts that are not needed on a cotton-farm and in a cotton-mill and on the way from one to the other. Many of these activities had not yet reached any considerable development. They were yet in their infancy. But they were all practised, even if some only in an amateur way.

"We can solve all our problems here — right here," Charles would say; "and the aim is to teach the people from their infancy that they can do better work and lead happier lives here than anywhere else — and to make this true."

He had scientific direction for the farm: it was not one big "plantation" but many small farms all worked by a sort of coöperation. The gardens about the mill-cottages were parts of it; and poultry and vegetables were sold from every one of them. Many experiments had been tried and were in progress with different soils and seeds, so that the whole plantation was an "experimental farm"; and Charles's boast was

(I think it was true) that the community grew more products well for the market than any other community in the United States. "We do not yet begin to know," he said, "the variety or the value of the things that our soil and our sunshine and our rains (helped for certain purposes by irrigation) will produce. Nobody has yet put them to a test."

And his mind had wandered to still larger problems. He had an inventor trying to construct a machine that should gather the cotton from the plant — the one machine that must reduce cotton-culture to a really economical and scientific basis.

He had studied markets, too. Many great possible demands for cotton products had not yet even been found; and those markets that the Southern mills supplied, were supplied in an awkward and expensive and indirect way. When the best breeds of cotton are grown on lands properly fed for its culture, and when it is worked and gathered by perfected tools and handled intelligently, and spun and woven cheaply, and when all the mechanism for its world-wide sale and distribution is made smooth and direct — then (such was the plan he had it in mind to prove) the South will become one of the most prosperous workshops in all the world, perhaps the most prosperous. If men of England and of New England had come to the cotton — instead of having slave-grown cotton sent to them — most of the mills in Old England and in New would now be in these States; and the world's great trade routes would lead to Southern ports. The English race would, by this great industry, have by this time developed here better perhaps than it has yet developed anywhere; for nowhere has it such a natural economic advantage.

Pondering on all these things I wrote in my diary, which I kept with the irregularity that is the only precaution a man who keeps a diary may take lest he become an egotistical fool — I wrote in my diary at this time what you may here read, if you are so inclined:

"The plain truth that cannot be blinked is that we must regain our character. We are not honest about the old subjects of controversy — the things that go to make public opinion. The old, false position in the slavery controversy gave political discussion a false position, gave the Church a false position, and our very women became the sentimental victims of this false position.

"About things of every-day life — personal acts as between man and man — we are as honest as other folk, frank, cheerful, helpful, brotherly, with some humour and with infinite good-humour. But the structure of public opinion is yet false; and we are false in dealing with men in the mass.

"And this falseness is kept alive by the wrong kind of training. We do not take up the problems and the tasks of our own lives directly. We 'educate' the young in our own inherited fallacies.

"Such a change in character can come only from within and must be forced upward from the bottom. It must begin on the soil and with our tasks of the soil; and we must do the work ourselves. There is no worse fallacy in a democracy than the academic dogma that reforms proceed from the top downward — that somebody is going to bring us a happy change of method or of thought. In us ourselves lies the power of rebuilding the Commonwealth, and there is no power elsewhere that can do it. A thousand political changes would bring no change unless we ourselves change. What a farce is every political programme till the people are developed! And the men that we call 'educated' — they agree with us that the masses ought to be trained; but they have no strong impulse to do so. Nor do they know how. For they themselves were mistrained — in a view of life that has nothing to do with our life here and now; and they have accepted the ignorance of the masses as a part of the order of nature. The most difficult task of all is the task of arousing the 'educated' people to action."

And on another day:

"I think that Louise Caldwell understands this as no other woman among us."

And then on a night of meditation:

"O my Southern Brothers, you who have silent, deep-calling moods when you catch the ambition of our father's fathers and of their fathers who were among the great builders of the Republic, and their spirit calls to you — we, too, have a chance, a great builders' chance, if we will see it aright. Two great tasks have been done here — the foundation of our liberties has been laid and the wild continent has been subdued. The third task is ours — the right training of these delayed people, for upon this training rest the extension of liberty and the fruitful uses of nature.

"And you men and women who teach, you who make up the great army that drills the children and the youth of our many-million dwellers on the soil, who yet sparsely settle an ill-tilled land, it is not through mediæval methods that you will do builders' work — not by droning the lore of priests of dead centuries, but by work that begins on *this* soil, shaped for *these* children, to train *their* lives for *this* home. This upland cotton-belt is a good home for new constructive work in your high craft, for a new conception and practice of 'education.'

"And, if there be men who are soul-homeless

dwellers or wanderers in the great towns of the world, made life-weary by the practice or by the spectacle of mere money-getting and spending and by the unjust and therefore misused power and arrogance of Privilege, here on this soil, life has the wholesome and simple purpose that they miss and long for — healthful work that helps men and that the worker grows by; for the builders of a civilization have never doubted the value or the aim of life nor ever suffered soul-weariness.

"I suspect, in fact, that the builders of things are the happiest of mortals, and always have been — the builders of things, whether of states and laws or of 'works' and mills or of colleges; for these are the men who satisfy their own longings, who find life good, and to whom we look for guidance."

Thus I was finding myself; and I should yet help to work out, with a larger understanding, the great problem of building up these people — in better ways than by political effort. I felt some satisfaction at the outlook.

It was that very week's issue of *The White Man*, continuing its personal abuse of me, which had been a regular part of its contents during the campaign, that contained a column of which the following are paragraphs:

"Educated with Negroes, studying and living on a social equality with them; returning to his native State and seeking to niggerize the public schools; dismissed in disgrace; sleeping in the house with Negroes at his own grandfather's former home, about which there were unpleasant suppressed rumours during the campaign; promptly on hand to defend a Negro when Colonel Stringweather was murdered; since the campaign travelling with a Negro to visit a Negro school — thus Mr. Worth seems to have abundantly earned a reward at the hands of the Negro-loving party.

"And he has made this nigger-business pay. For he has curried favour with his Northern friends, who have thus been induced to make large investments in cotton-mills in which he is interested.

"Now it is said that there are further rewards in store for this traitor to his people — that he is to have a fat consulship. The further off the better for his State. For his own country has spewed him out as the whale spewed Jonah. This is a white man's country. Let him go."

Paragraphs like these have, I am told, appeared about me in almost every issue of that paper for twenty-five years. But I long ago made it a rule not to read abuse of myself or of anybody else.

CHAPTER XXV

LOUISE CALDWELL wrote: "No, do not go to Greece — except to Acropolis, where you will please come to supper next Wednesday."

Louise and Richard lived in the same little stone house where they were born, which my father had sold for Colonel Caldwell after he had gone to Egypt never to return, and from which their mother had gone, also on an endless absence. It was the most cultivated and attractive household in Acropolis, in spite of a certain loneliness that haunted its gray walls and hovered about their tall oaks in the grove around it. A cheerful earnestness dwelt in that household of two, against a background of sadness. Or perhaps the sadness and the loneliness were inferred by their neighbours, because both Louise and Richard remained unmarried and because of the tragedies that were associated with the house. Richard had built another little square stone house beside the old one, and the two were connected by a covered porch. The new house had only one room which everybody knew as the "big" room — "library, living room, drawing room, state dining room — everything," said Louise.

"Even a room fit for a wedding," Professor Billy had once said to her.

"Certainly. When I marry I shall surely be married here."

"And leave it for a home in Boston?"

"Leave it for Richard and his wife," she answered.

For Cooley spent much of his time at Acropolis, when he came South, and the gossips of the village could think of but one reason for his visits to the Caldwells. It was even frequently remarked that before the winter was gone there would be a wedding.

"We are met to celebrate our victory, even if our standard-bearer did fall," was Louise's greeting to me.

"A winged victory, and a mere torso at that," I replied.

Professor Billy strode in: "A torso, yes — for we lost the head; but it's a victory nevertheless. The enemy's situation is like Uncle Isaac's predicament after his great revival. He had brought scores of sinners to repentance — a rich harvest of souls; and his thought turned to the great addition to his church-membership that would follow and to the increase of

contributions.   'All dese souls snatched frum
de burnin'.' "

Judge Bevan entered the room and Professor
Billy's story was cut short — rather, postponed;
for his stories were like the Confederate army:
they might be overcome by overwhelming numbers but they could never be conquered.

All the company was soon come — a dozen of
us who had worked together and could play
together.

The President of the University had not been
counted as one of us, and there was a look of surprise at his presence when we were to celebrate
the victory, if it were a victory, or at least to con-
sole me.   But as soon as we were seated at supper
the results of his more intimate interest in Professor Billy became apparent. He, of all men,
would a year ago have regarded a general prop-
aganda for universal education as a dangerous
thing — the putting of false hopes in the minds
of the "populace."

"Gladstone has truly said," he began, with
an unusual earnestness, "that no movement for
the upbuilding of the masses ever starts with the
classes. Nor can such a movement ever be
entrusted to the classes. We have gone on too
long, madam, too long" (turning to Louise, as if
for permission to unbosom himself), "far too long
confining our work in this university to the

professional, well-to-do class — the 'gentlemen,' as we call them.   We must bring in the sons of the people.

"The incoming Legislature, composed of raw countrymen, who know little about fiscal problems, may pass ill-considered measures and commit extravagances and embarrass the State treasury. But, if they shake us up to our full duty in educating the whole people, I do not care.   Financial embarrassments can be remedied by good subsequent management; and it will be a cheap price to pay for the waking of the masses from their long lethargy.   The weakness of our whole system is that we have too long considered education as a thing fit only for the favoured few."   And down came his fist on the table.

"I beg your pardon, madam" (with a bow to Louise), "for my earnestness."

I looked across the table at Professor Billy, and he smiled back at me.

"Mr. President," he asked, "how can we open the university wider to 'the sons of the people'?"

"It's an atmosphere, an atmosphere, sir.   It's in the way the people regard the institution.   A lad from any family may come here now.   But it has been understood that it is a place chiefly for the sons of 'gentlemen.'   You can change it. *You*" (turning to me) "can change it.   It will be the work of men of your generation.   This

must be the intellectual centre for *all* the people —
ALL the people.   I beg your pardon again, madam,
for my earnestness."

The victory began to be apparent.   Who had
been declared elected was a little matter in comparison with such a change of thought in such
a man.

Louise clapped her hands, and Professor Billy
went on:

"Uncle Isaac, you see, had brought all these
sinners into the fold of the redeemed; and, after
due notice, he held a meeting to admit them into
church-membership.   But although the last sinner
of 'em had been converted in the Zion Episcopal
Methodist Church, most of them were found to
prefer the Baptist Church.   'Dey needn't go off,'
said the old man in telling me, 'dey needn't go
off 't all; fer I'd er dip de las' one uv 'em in de
pond, if dat's what dey 'ferred.'   But they did
go off; and he didn't get the fruits of his victory.
The old man was very angry at the loss of
an expected increase in the contributions, and the
next Sunday he preached a very plain sermon,
telling how he suffered from such a long walk to
church.

"'It's a fur way ter come on a Sunday atter a
hard week's work, and 'taint cordin' to Scriptur'
dat de sarvant o' de Mos' High shed allers walk,
spacially on de hot days o' summer — not 'cordin'

ter de Scriptur' what speak of Pontius' Pilot (for he went ter cheerch by boat on de Sea o' Galilee), and Judas's Chariot (dat was 'fore he denied de Lord when de cock crow); dey bof had ways ter git dar 'thout walkin' in de hot sun; and, ef you don' fetch in de converts what I preach to 'pentance and fergiveness o' sins, you'se got to enlarge de collection fer a hoss and wagin fer dis sarvant o' de Mos' High.'

"The enemy have the 'victory,' but their Legislature has joined the other church, and how Tom Warren's administration is going to get to church on hot Sunday mornings — remains to be seen. The Legislature holds the contribution-box.

"I have a list of the members of the House," he went on, "with a memorandum about the educational record of every one of them but three or four; and I have letters here from fifty of them. A new day is come for the public schools. All these are with us, as far as they understand our programme."

The company cheered. Louise proposed the health of the "defeated victor," and the old President seemed the best pleased man among us.

"A real victory in defeat, sir. Such a death, I hope, has no sting in the most glorious resurrection that will follow."

"We even won Acropolis," said Richard. "The

village voted for a public school — the first that was ever authorized in the shadow of the University.   Mr. President, we will put you on the local School Board.

"I shall be proud, sir."

Very early after supper the President and Mrs. Bevan went home.

As soon as they were out of hearing, we began to reconstruct the university.   We should have several travelling professors, who should supervise instruction in certain practical studies at various places, and who should, in effect, be educational missionaries.   We should have departments with trained men to direct road-building and country and town sanitation; we should train teachers for the public schools; we should have short courses of study which grown men might attend and learn something about farm-management and high-bred stock, and better fruit-growing.   (The apple-crop of the State will one day be of greater value than the whole agricultural product of every sort now is, and why should this not be a subject of university study and experiment?)

"Yes," said Louise, "and presently we'll have women trained here who by some means, which Professor Bain will devise, shall bring a new dispensation in the country kitchens."

Nothing is so fascinating nor so easy as to sit

by a comfortable wood fire and in a glow of righteousness re-fashion the world.

"And we shall make a state-wide organization
of women to visit and to decorate and encourage
the country schools, and we'll make it fashionable
by electing the young wife of the Governor as the
President.   We'll — we'll ——"

"Will you explain this?" asked Cooley, with a
logical wish to bring us to earth.   "Miss Caldwell
drove ten miles over a wretched road to put a few
pictures and a map in a country school-house.
The ladies of the neighbourhood met her there.
She explained the pictures to the children and
was imprudent enough to remark that I had given
the map.   The school-mistress, thinking to show
her appreciation, wrote a letter to *The Marlborough Globe;* and the *Globe* remarked that it
was all very well for our ladies to take an interest
in the 'free' schools, but that we could procure
all the maps we needed without receiving alms
from Boston.

"Within a week an old lady in New England
gave five thousand dollars to the Negro college
in Marlborough.   Then *The Globe* published a
list of such gifts to Negro schools in the State and
in a blank space in the adjacent column reminded
us that no money given to education by 'Northern philanthropists' had gone to white schools
in our State.   'Thus,' it said, 'New England

keeps the colour-line in evidence but expects us to forget it.'"

"You miss the point, Cooley," Professor Billy explained. "The most pious fisherman will become profane if he catches a very little catfish, for its fins are too sharp for so little meat. But, if the catfish be big enough, it's worth being pricked for. Try us with big aims, and you'll land Major Thorne with docile gratitude."

"Uncle Isaac has anticipated you in his request for a large gift. He heard Senator Barker's speech in which he said: 'Educate niggers, sir? Why, if this wild educational mania continues, our Yankee friends will come down and build a nigger college on every hill — on every hill in the State — a nigger college, to be taught by social-equality white men.' Uncle Isaac remembered that, and the first time he saw me after the election, he said:

"'Boss, ef you'se ready ter begin ter buil' dem colleges, de hill t'er side o' Bethesda is de bes' one in dis neighbourhood.'"

Richard had been putting the burning logs in better shape on the fire, and in his laughter he ran gaily across the floor. Professor Billy followed him and they began to dance. And we all danced. The rugs were removed and an impromptu ball followed our Utopia-building and our Negro stories.

When we ceased, Professor Billy gave a clog-dance till his face was ruddy and streaming. While we were applauding and laughing, the maid came in and said that there were gentlemen in the hall — a number of them, students — who wished to see me.

"Let them come in," said Louise. and she met them and welcomed them. The floor was still vibrating, I dare say, from Professor Billy's dancing and his flushed face showed all its freckles.

"Professor Bain has been somewhat exercised," she remarked. The boys smiled with a wise look, for they had seen the whole performance from the hall.

Then a real gravity came over us. For these young fellows had a spokesman who had prepared a pretty, formal speech to make to me. It was a speech of approval and of regret that I had not been elected. Most of these boys had been in my classes; and this was a brave and beautiful thing for them to do.

Their little ceremony over, they felt more at home, and they became for a time part of our celebrating company. There was much talk about the development of the university by a more liberal policy of instruction; and, when they had gone, someone began to recite the creed that I had made in my campaign speeches, article by article in turn:

"I believe in this land — our land — whose infinite variety of beauty and riches we do not yet know. Wake up, old Land!

"I believe in these people — our people — whose development may be illimitable. Wake up, my People!

"I believe in the continuous improvement of human society, in the immortality of our democracy, in the rightmindedness of the masses. Wake up, old Commonwealth!"

Then we made definite plans (having for a space turned Professor Billy from his buffoonery) for the enlargement of the Club, for judicious instruction of the Legislature (President Bevan will address it on some suitable occasion); the wife of the Governor would be elected President of the Women's School Association; a suitable person should be sent, if possible, by a Legislative committee to report on the best school-practice in other States; perhaps Superintendent Craybill would call a great meeting at the capital of all the county superintendents of schools if a way were found to pay their expenses; Senator Barker must be informed as early as possible of "the wishes of the people"; we should have educational maps made of the State showing all the important facts about the schools; we should ——

"What we call education," said Louise, who led us all in plan-making, "is a petrifying process.

When men wish to perpetuate their stagnation, they organize it into a 'system' and call it 'education,' and endow institutions and engage men who lead easy lives, safe from struggle, to train young men who in turn wish to lead lives safe from struggle, to perpetuate the stagnation of their predecessors.

"We learn, and we can teach only by action. This campaign cost us only one casualty and it moved the whole State further than it had before moved in a life-time. And we find ourselves only by action. That is the way we found one another. That is the way we found the President of the University and enabled him to find himself — noble action."

"And such a direct wrestling with the people," I added, "is the most instructive experience that a man can have in a democracy. I have thrown to the dogs all the social and economic theories that I had before; and I now have a better measure than books had given me to test my knowledge by. I have a fund of experience and a point of view that develops a man's common sense. And, as for an interest in one's fellows — you cannot come thus face to face with thousands of honest, earnest people without knowing that to serve them is the keenest joy and the highest privilege in life."

"And the Negro," said our Lady of Battle, going to the heart of the whole matter, "cannot longer be made an instrument to stifle free speech and free opinion. Even a senator who has been the shadow of a party's obliquity on our political dial will soon learn that."

She was soon showing Cooley (for the rest of us had seen them) five pictures that she had drawn which she called "our history in five chapters." They were pictures of Lowassee Falls in the river nearby at periods of about half a century.

First, in the year 1700. A trapper and an Indian were looking at the river tumbling over the rapids. Man had not touched this virgin world except to seek game.

Second, in 1750. There was a hut by the river and a patch of corn. The white pioneer had settled there.

Third, in 1800. Iron had been discovered nearby and there was a furnace and forges — an iron-working shop where brawny men of English and Scotch stock had built a flourishing industry. Their wares of iron were sold far and wide. And the river now turned a mill.

Fourth, in 1850. Slavery had come. White men had ceased to work with their hands. The iron-works had become a ruin. Only the corn-mill had life in this desolate picture, and slaves were waiting for the grist that their masters had sent to mill. Far down the river endless cotton-fields extended, worked and wasted by slaves.

But the once busy place at the falls was in decay, the mechanical arts neglected.

Fifth and last — the present time. The waters of the falls were turned to use, and white men were excavating the foundations of the old iron-work to build a cotton-mill.

"There," said she, "is the rise of industry, the dignity of labour and their decay and their beginning again. You may trace the changes in Southern fibre and character in these five sketches, and they show us our way."

While she and Cooley were talking over these chapters of our history at one end of the big room, Professor Billy said to me:

"Is Cooley enlisting for life under that banner, eh? Do you suppose so?"

"What do *you* suppose?" I asked.

Then Miss Bevan came up to us, and she surely ought to be an authority on such a subject. We asked her opinion.

"If it were a matter to regret, I should fear it," she said.

Professor Billy seemed anxious not only to find an answer to his question but also, it seemed to me, eager to bring such a match about. But our conversation was presently broken off because Richard came within hearing. The ladies soon put on their wraps and the subject had to be postponed.

Professor Billy strode to the middle of the room and in the manner of the grand oratory bellowed forth:

"Ladies and Gentlemen: The sun in all his majestic course does not shine on a happier company than the chivalry and beauty (the ladies, God bless 'em) here gathered. If Olympus sent its godly denizens to dwell below, they would seek our clime and be content.

"Thus, Ladies and Gentlemen, under these hospitable auspices, have we celebrated our victory in defeat, and buried the dead and raised him again to life. For we are not conquered but only overcome by overwhelming numbers. Sir, the brave cannot suffer defeat in our vocabulary."

And as he bade our Lady of Battle good night, he said in a stage whisper:

"And we are a hospitable people. Lady, be kind to the stranger that is within our gates."

CHAPTER XXVI

THE GOVERNOR'S INAUGURATION

THE night before the Honourable Thomas Carter Warren was to be inaugurated Governor of the Commonwealth, the trains that came into Marlborough were loaded with "delegations" from the four points of the compass. All during the afternoon, brass bands playing patriotic airs were marching up the street from the railway station, some preceding military companies, others white men's clubs, others young men's leagues, and others miscellaneous crowds from different enterprising towns, all come to the inauguration. In addition, for instance, to the white men's club and the young men's league from Edinboro, was a group of "E. E.'s," who combined an advertisement of the town with a patriotic display.

It was a pleasant night with just a touch of winter, such a night as often comes in our land of exquisite temperatures, when it is a joy to walk out. The crowds went, of course, after supper to the big parlours of the hotel, where the retiring Governor, the new Governor, Senator

Barker, and other distinguished men held an informal reception.

During the early hours of the night, you would have seen there, at some time, everybody in the State who was anybody, from the President of the University to old Birdcastle, the librarian. The doors stood open; there was no ceremony; anybody who chose walked in. Surely we have some of the qualities of an ideal American democracy. There were, perhaps, three thousand visitors in the hotel, men who came from the mountain counties, and men who came from the low counties; there were, besides, the members of the General Assembly, which was in session; there were judges from the highest court of the state; there were preachers and teachers and editors and business men — all as dwellers in one neighbourhood. Those of the same age usually addressed one another by their given names. There was the familiarity of neighbourly residence, and yet courtesy.

One group was exchanging reminiscences of the war; another was laughing in great guffaws at some wag's latest story; another was discussing business affairs — it was a neighbourly party; and band after band, from sheer excess of good feeling, took its turn in the street to play.

The next morning, the whole little city was decorated. There were more flags than had ever been seen there before — State flags, a few Confederate flags, and flags of the United States. All these were used in decorating the platform that had been built in the Capitol Square, where the inauguration was to take place.

And during the morning still bigger crowds came — more military companies, more young men's leagues, more white men's clubs, more firemen, more veterans, more organizations of every sort, till the town was packed as nobody had ever before seen it packed.

At the Old Place, Uncle Ephraim knew nothing of all this preparation. They did not receive any newspaper there, for now there were no white folks on the plantation. He had long had a plan to go to see young Mr. Warren and talk to him about Julia; and this purpose had grown stronger since the old man's visit to the great school for coloured people, where they "fotch de young fo'ks up ter hones' wuk."

"I ain' got much longer ter stay here," he'd say to himself, "and 'tain't gwine ter do ter leave dat li'l white nigger gal here a'ter I'm gone. T'others kin take care uv deirselves. But dat li'l white gal, she's diff'ent; and I gwine ter see what kin be done 'bout dat. She don' seem ter 'blong wid de balance on 'em. She stay roun' de house here and call me 'Un' Ephum,' an' ax me ques'tuns jes' lak she b'long ter me. 'Tain't gwine t' do, when I'se gone."

And so the old man had hitched up his mule, and with Lissa and Julia had driven to town.

He went to Jerry, the blacksmith's shop, to leave his wagon and mule, as he always did.

"Big day in town, Unc' Ephum," said Jerry.

"I tho't dere mus' be someth' ne'er gwine on. I heers a ban' a-playin' down de street — ain't dat er brass ban'? And der seems a pow'rful lot er fo'ks come ter town."

"Don't you know de new Guv'nor gwin' ter be 'naugerated ter-day?"

"Dat's it — is it? No, I hadn't heerd it. Jerry, d'you spose' de new Guv'nor kin be seen ter-day?"

"'Couse he kin. Ever'body done come jes' ter see 'im. Dat is, de white fo'ks has. Dat's what de day fur."

"Can't no colo'd fo'ks see him ter-day?"

"I 'spose so — if any ob 'em goes."

Uncle Ephraim kept his own counsel; but he called to Lissa and Julia to come on. They would go down into the city now.

Before they had come near to the Capitol Square, they became part of a great throng which was trying to push its way into the yard. There were military guards everywhere, trying to keep the crowd in proper shape, and to leave space in the middle of the street for the procession. Everybody was in good humour, but everybody was pushing one's neighbour and being pushed by another.

Uncle Ephraim thought he saw more room across the street, and he called to Lissa and Julia to follow him. He escaped the guard, who with a smile looked at the venerable Negro trying to run; but the guard put his gun before Lissa.

"No; you can't cross there."

She pointed to the old man, who was beckoning to her.

"Never mind, he's all right; you can't cross, I tell you," and he pushed her back. Uncle Ephraim tried to re-cross the street, but a guard on that side said:

"I reckon not, old man. This side's good enough for us. Move on, move on, if you want to get up to the Square."

By that time the procession had started from the Governor's Mansion at the other end of the wide avenue. First, there was the chief marshal and his staff; then General Grissell, in the gaudy uniform of the Commander of the State Guards; then a mounted bodyguard of cavalry; then a carriage trimmed in white, and drawn by four white horses, in which sat the retiring Governor and the incoming one. The next carriage was assigned to Mrs. Warren, the new Governor's mother, and Senator Barker sat with her. Her carriage also was trimmed in white and was drawn by two white horses; and then the Governor's Guard, with gorgeous new uniforms, marched behind, in command of Colonel Talcott.

As these moved slowly forward while the band played the State hymn. The vast crowd threw up its hats and cheered — cheer after cheer. The applause rolled up the street far in advance of the procession, and men cried themselves hoarse before they saw any notable person coming.

Behind these came carriages with judges and other state officers and distinguished citizens, and so long a row of militia companies and clubs of various sorts that the Governor had reached the Capitol Square before the end of the procession had started.

Uncle Ephraim had been pushed by the crowd — not clearly knowing where he was going — to a standing place as near as any one "of the general public" could hope to get. And so had Lissa and Julia — on the other side.

An hour passed — or more. The old Governor, the new Governor and his aide, the Chief Justice and the Bishop were now seated on the stand; and the bands were playing all about, while the guards were keeping the way open, the best they could, for every club and organization to find the place reserved for it.

And at last the old Governor arose, and everybody was quiet. He turned to the Bishop, who came forward and offered a prayer, which nobody could hear. The bands played again.

Lissa and Julia had by this time come even nearer to the stand. They were supposed, by the men standing about them, to be white country folk, and they invited them, inch by inch, to move forward.

The Chief Justice, with his gown on, arose and read the oath of office, and the Honourable Thomas Carter Warren took it, and became Governor of the Commonwealth.

The solemn ceremony over, the judge bowed and sat down, and the new Governor stood facing the multitude. No man so young had ever before come to the high office, and a swelling happiness arose in his heart. The vast crowd, extending almost as far as he could see, were shouting and waving hats and handkerchiefs and flags.

"We're here fifty thousand strong," shouted a giant's voice; and

"We'll see you through," answered another.

He turned toward the renewed cheering that was now heard far on the left, and his mother had risen and was standing by him. She kissed him, and the cheering was then begun again; and more bands struck up "Dixie."

Far back on the platform sat his betrothed, and Senator Barker twitted her for not following his mother's example. She blushed, and the company saw her, and a shout went up for her to appear.

"The bride! The bride!" And she was at last obliged to rise and bow.

The Grand Marshal at last came forward and called for silence. From sheer excess of enthusiasm, it pleased the crowd for a while to defy him with renewed applause; and he and the Governor could do nothing but stand and smile.

"Dat's de Gov'nor — see de Gov'nor!" said Lissa to Julia; "de young man dar wid his han' raised and de black co't on and de flower in his co't. Ain' he han'some, Julia?"

Uncle Ephraim did not know where his wards were. But he held his hand to his ear to catch the sounds from the platform. The Governor had at last begun to speak.

"Now he gwine magnify," said Uncle Ephraim to himself, and he listened still more intently.

The Inaugural began on a high note of praise of the old Commonwealth and our people — "the happiest good people under the high arch of heaven."

"There are others richer," he went on, "but none more hospitable. The sun does not shine on a happier land, or on a people with more of the ancient virtues. (Applause.) Now that we shall be forever free from the danger of Negro supremacy our cup of happiness will be full — full to the brim. (Prolonged applause.) We wish our coloured fellow-citizens nothing but peace and happiness among us. We are their best friends. But this is a white man's country — discovered by white men, cleared by white men, settled by white men, owned by white men, and white men must rule it!"

The applause stopped the speaker. Uncle Ephraim seemed surprised at its tumultuousness. "'Cou'se dat's so. Dat's been so all de time — 'bout der white fo'ks. Did dese men 'spec' de niggers gwine git all de lan', somehow or n'er?"

"And this cause, to which, under God, I dedicate myself to-day in your presence, means the safety of our hearths and our homes, and the supremacy of the Anglo-Saxon forever. This is not Africa. This is the United States of America — and our beloved Southland.

"To our coloured friends I say: 'You will prosper under our rule. The Negro will prosper under our rule. You will not be deluded by false friends, who would substitute a book for a plow. And our land has need of you; but it needs you in the place where you belong.'"

The Governor said many other things, of course, but it was hard to hear him, after the standing crowd had begun to be restless.

"A great oration," they all said, when he was done. The cheering and the music now stretched itself down the avenues as the crowd melted away. Many remained near the State House, where the new governor was going at once into his office, and would shake hands with all the people who should come in. "I'm Governor of all the people alike," he had said, "the rich and the poor, the white and the black."

Uncle Ephraim had almost forgotten his errand. But now it occurred to him that he might, after all, speak with the Governor. He had concluded that Lissa and Julia would find their way back to Jerry's shop, where they would eat their dinner from the basket, and feed the mule, and wait for him.

The old man lingered and saw the Governor go into the State House with the Senator and the men in gold lace, and a large crowd pushed in after them. He came nearer the door, waiting his turn.

There were very few coloured men in the crowd, and Uncle Ephraim's large figure and venerable appearance attracted much attention. Now and then someone would say to him: "Goin' in to see the Governor, Uncle — are you? That's right."

"You're the right sort, ol' man. The Governor'll be glad to see you."

"Uncle, did you vote the Democratic ticket?"

By this time he was in the hall. By the Governor's door there stood a man in uniform, who was keeping the line in order so that only one person could go in at a time.

Uncle Ephraim stepped aside. "I'll wait till

dey's all gone." He stood there patiently for an hour or more. Passers by made remarks to him, some of them jocular, but all respectful. Now and then he would hear one man say to another:

"That's an old-timer for you. See that old darkey?"

"Say, Uncle, it's a great day for white folks like you and me — ain't it?"

"Old man, why don' you go in? The Governor'll have a good word for you."

"Now that kin' of an old fellow's all right. No demnition foolishness 'bout him, I bet you."

At last the way seemed clear. A few men were rushing in and out, but the crowd was gone. Now he'd go in. Just as he got to the door, the Governor was coming out.

"Yer sarvant, suh," said Uncle Ephraim, bowing low.

"Glad to see you, old man," and the Governor held out his hand.

"Yes, suh, I come ter town ter see you in partic'lar."

"That was very kind of you. I appreciate that. I wish more of the coloured people had come."

"Yes, suh, but 'twas er partic'lar matter dat I come about."

"What is it, Uncle?"

"A sort er personal confear'nce, if you please, suh."

"Uncle, I can't talk personal matters to-day. You must come and see me some other day."

"I don' believes yer knows me, suh. No? I's Eph'um what lives out at ol' Mars' Nick Worth's place 'fore he died."

"Yes, Uncle Ephraim, I know you now. Come and see me any day."

"Yes, suh — yes, suh; but kin I bring dat li'l gal along what now is growin' up and I'se gittin' mighty ol'?"

The Governor had walked along the hall, and by this time was near the front door.

A messenger opened it for him.

"Come alone, Uncle Ephraim," he called back at the old man as cheerfully as he could; and he remarked to his waiting aide: "An old nigger that I've known all my life."

"Good God! John, I'm tired," he said, with a heavy sigh, as he stepped into his carriage at the street, to be driven home — with little time to eat something and to prepare for the evening.

For the day was to be a Great Day indeed for Tom Warren; and it had seemed fit to crown it with his marriage. St. Peter's was now repaired and decorated as it had not been for many a year. At six o'clock the wedding was to be there; then a supper at the home of the bride. She was the daughter of Chief-Justice Branch, and, next to my cousin Margaret, the most beautiful young woman in Marlborough; and the young couple were, of course, to receive the society of the whole State that evening at the Inaugural Ball at the Governor's Mansion.

His mother met him at the door and embraced him long, and shed happy tears.

"My son, your dear father looks down on you with pride to-day."

Then, presently, after she had gazed at him for a moment: "Tom, you are weary. It has been a great strain. Come, eat something as soon as you can. You seem very tired. Perhaps you'll have time to lie down for a moment."

Uncle Ephraim, in the meantime, had gone to Jerry's blacksmith shop, where he found Lissa and Julia, almost hopeless of his coming, sitting in the wagon eating their dinner.

There sat with them a young, light Negro who wore a long black coat — evidently a preacher; and he was eating his full share out of the basket.

As an introduction of him, Lissa said: "Unc' Eph'um, dis gem'man, who is a preacher, is a-collectin' money fur de heathens."

"Yes, suh," said the preacher, "whare'er I goes I 'members dem dat are in de outer darkness, an' I gits what I can fur de heathens."

The old man's mind was deeply occupied with more immediate things. Besides, he didn't like this yellow, glib man, dressed so finely eating his dinner.

The fellow went on: "You is a ol' man in Israel, suh."

"I'se ol' 'nough," said Uncle Ephraim, "but I'se allers lived in dese parts. I ain't neber been ter Israel, suh. An' ol' Marster lived here afore me."

"Our only master, brother, is our Master in Heaven."

"Yes, dat's whar ol' Marster gone. I knows — 'cose he's in Heaven."

"But I spoke of Our Lord, de Saviour of mankin'. He is our Master."

"Yes, Mars' Jesus you mean. 'Cose I knows Him."

"It is for those who do not know Him — for the heathens in the outer darkness, that I was speakin' ter de lady."

The old man's patience was gone.

"Young man, let de heathens git da'r own money. I ain't got none ter spar'."

"But ter give to them is to give ter de Lord."

"Let de Lawd mek His own money, den."

"Yes, brother, but de Lord — He do not —— "

"He kin mek it, ef He want any. Didn' He mek wine outen water? And, ef He kin do dat, He kin make money outen some'in or ne'r, if He need enny small change. You go 'long 'bout your bus'ness."

As the preacher walked away, Jerry said: "Unc' Eph'um, you don' set much sto' by dese young preachers what comes roun' de ladies, does yer?"

"Yaller, long-coat town nigger," said the old man.

"Or maybe you don' give much ter de church?" said Jerry with a smile; for Ephraim was notoriously careful with his dollars.

"Ain' got long 'nough ter stay here now, ol' as I is, to git no profit on it."

"Well, did yer hear de Guv'nor?"

"Yes, I heerd him."

"Mammy say he a mighty good-lookin' man," said Julia.

"Good-lookin' or no, der ain' no sich Guv'nors now as dey was in de ole days, when dey didn't talk 'bout de col'red man dis, de col'red man dat. Seems ter me dey mighty scar't 'bout de niggers. In de ole days it was de Nunion, de Nunion forever, long 'fore you was born."

"What is der in politics for a col'red man, Unc' Ephum?" asked Jerry.

"Nothin'! Not a hill o' 'taters, nor a year o' corn, nor a stalk o' cotton."

"Dey ain't gwine let de col'red fo'ks vote no mo' — is dey?"

"Dey ain't vote much as 'twas. 'Pears to me dey don' care nothin' sure enough 'bout de col'ed fo'ks dese days."

"Is de anythin' in de talk 'bout puttin' 'em back in slavery — de young 'uns, I mean?"

"How kin dey do dat? Don' I own my lan'? Who's gwine ter take it frum me? Who's gwine ter say I must wuk for him? Ef dey put dese triflin' town niggers in de chain-gang or in slabery — dat's all right."

"But I don' lak," the old man went on in a sort of reverie — "I don' lak so much talk 'bout de nigger and de white man. Godamighty, Jerry, ain't we gittin' 'long wid one er'ner same as we allers is? Nothin' ain' happen. But all of a suddent dey all falls a-talkin' 'bout de white man and de lan' — makin' a mighty 'do 'bout nothin'. An' dey don' give no schools lak dat un I seed, whar de fetch up de young uns to hones' wuk. All mighty quair ter me, Jerry."

As they drove home, the old man said once in a while to himself: "Haf ter come agin. I scared it gwine ter be bad times some o' dese days fur de col'ed people."

There had not been in my day — I dare say there never had been — such a gorgeous wedding in old St. Peter's. Anna Branch was married to the young Governor in the wedding-gown of her great-grandmother; and every family in the Commonwealth that went back to Revolutionary times had its sons and daughters there.

It was a memorable day in the social annals of Marlborough.

That night, while I was dancing at the Inaugural Ball with Margaret, she reminded me that the next big event in St. Peter's would be her wedding.

"May you be the happiest bride ever married there!"

"Wasn't Anna's wedding perfectly grand, though?" she said, and then whispered: "But cousin, honest now, isn't it grander some day to be a Bishop than to be a Governor?"

"Yes," I said; "a Bishop holds his job longer."

As I came away, General Grissell, Commander of the Militia of the Commonwealth, stood in the hall near the door of the stuffy little ballroom, in a uniform more gorgeous than any Field Marshal of any great army wore on the day of his greatest triumph. With rotund and radiant satisfaction, he waved his hand toward the couples that were coming out, and said in his pompous, sonorous, swelling way:

"Such a galaxy of beauty and chivalry, sir, cannot be found in any other capital of the world — here or abroad — not a single one, sir!"

CHAPTER XXVII

THE FORTRESS OF DESPAIR

IN OUR climate we go and come the same
paths, day after day, year after year; and
to go a new road is the thing of all things
that we do seldomest. Although I had walked
and ridden and driven about the capital most
of my life and had come and gone and gone and
come, I had never been on the road that leads
due south from the city. True, the southern
part of the town was unattractive, for the ill-
kept streets dwindled at last into lanes and paths
that ran down to the vegetable gardens of the
Negro women who sold their "truck" in the
market. Just beyond the little stream and its
valley the highest hill in the region rose, crowned
with a great fortress-like building of brick. I
now had a reason to go there.

But it takes us long to make a plan in our
Southern world, longer after it is made to decide
to carry it out, then a good deal of discussion or
consideration when it shall be carried out, and
finally a long time of preparation to carry it out.

As I went along an unfamiliar street near the

very edge of the city, I came to the Roman Catholic chapel. Yes, I knew there was such a chapel. I knew Father Murphy, but he lived and worked in another world than mine. And so here it is, I said to myself, in this obscure street that his altar and his place of labour are. I looked in the door, for it was open, of course. Unlike the other churches, it was always open. A taper was burning on the altar, and I saw several forms bent in prayer.

I went in and sat down on a seat near the door. It was somewhat dark there, and at first I did not see a kneeling figure on the seat just in front of me. It was a woman muttering a prayer.

As she moaned louder, she spoke her words more distinctly and I heard:

"O Merciful Mother of Jesus, I ain't a white 'oman and I ain't a black 'oman. Save my chile in de deep waters, O Merciful Mother of Jesus. She is whiter'n I is. In de deep waters, oh — o — o — om — Merciful Mother of God."

That was the only white man's church in the city into which a heavy-laden black woman would or could go for the unburdening of her sorrow, and here was a soul so exposing its innermost tragedy that I felt ashamed to hear it longer.

O Merciful Mother of God.

In a little while I reached the asylum. About this great fortress of despair, there were large grounds — in front well-kept drives and shrubbery, and on either side and behind fields or gardens where the harmless patients were led to work or for exercise. It was a pleasant winter afternoon, as mild as a Northern May. At a distance I saw women walking and marching, perhaps playing some outdoor game, and still further groups of men were moving a pile of bricks in wheelbarrows with slow, monotonous motions.

When I entered the building and told my errand, one of the young physicians became my guide. We walked down a long hall where women sat with sad, blank faces; and, when we came to a cross-hall, he stopped and said:

"By the way, here's a lady whom I think you know."

There stood by the large window, in a travelling dress, with a travelling bag in her hand and a hat on, a gentle, white-haired woman, gazing down the road.

"Are you going to leave us, Mrs. Caldwell?" asked my companion.

"Yes," she said, in a hopeful, beautiful voice, "the Colonel is coming for me presently"; and she turned to the window again and continued her watch.

"She does that every afternoon of her quiet moods; for every afternoon the Colonel is coming for her — every afternoon all these blank years since the war; and there she stands patiently till an attendant leads her to her room and takes off her hat and gloves and puts her cloak and bag away. Then she says with resignation:

"The Colonel will come to-morrow."

O Merciful Mother of God.

Then we went into the field where the men were at work.

"We'll find him here, I think," said my companion.

We stopped and watched the slow procession of men, each with a wheelbarrow. They would go to the end of the path and empty the bricks on the ground; then back again, in a slow, sad procession, for another load. Workmen, apparently sane, loaded the wheelbarrows for them.

We saw one man coming with his wheelbarrow turned upside down.

"That's he."

"Captain Bob," said my companion, "why don't you turn your wheelbarrow over? That isn't the way to do it."

Captain Logan stopped, put the wheelbarrow down and assumed an oratorical attitude:

"Sir, you must think I'm a lunatic. It's you that's the fool — ha! ha! If I turned it over, don't you know that that ballox-box stuffer there would put bricks in it?

"Hello, Captain," he went on in a moment, bowing to me. "I say, Approach! I will inform you.

"It was thus and so: 'Sambo,' says I. 'Yes, Master,' says he. 'You infernal fool,' says I, 'don't you know you are free and a gentleman?'

"Well, they cheated his damned black head off, his rollin' white eyes out, his flabby wide nose flat — they cheated the very wool off his head.

"'Go to Africa, you cuffy,' then says I; 'you aren't worth saving.'

"And they babbled 'Nigger,' 'Nigger,' 'Nigger,' for fifty years and the nigger came, and the nigger multiplied, and the nigger stayed and the master went nigger-mad. Understand again, sir, saw nothing but nigger, said nothing but nigger — not worth saving; and the nigger got the 'taters and the 'possum and the old gentleman went crazy, got nothin' but a wild brain and a loose tongue."

"Captain Bob —— "

"Sir, you wait till I give you leave to speak. I have the platform now. Don't interrupt me again, and steal the election.

"The black brute then choked the sense out of him, left his mind emaciated, with its tongue hanging out, like a dog's — the mind of the whole people with its red tongue hanging out, slobbering lies. Understand?"

"Captain Bob!" my companion cried again. "Don't you know this gentleman?"

"Yes, that's Captain Hoppergrass. I've met you before, Captain. When I was Governor, what office was it you wanted? Don't recall?

"Well, I now go about my business." And he took his inverted wheelbarrow and went on.

O Merciful Mother of God.

The fortress took its toll of us as the more kindly grave did also.

CHAPTER XXVIII

THE INTERRUPTIONS OF HISTORY

AGAIN months went by, perhaps years for all I know, for I cannot now be sure without looking up dates, and we care little for dates in our climate. Why should we? So far as we know, time is inexhaustible. We are, therefore, not fussy because it passes. This admirable trait of taking the passage of time calmly, as some other traits of ours, has been misunderstood and even construed to our discredit. But I cannot now stop to correct so venerable an error, and our enemies may continue to make the most of it while I go on with this chronicle.

Well, it was after the events already told that I found myself again engaged on that History, which has been as prolific a dam of interruptions as I ever bestrode. My mother in her gentle way made my writing difficult, though it would have given her infinite pain if she had known it. She would come into my writing room just when my narrative had begun to flow, with so welcome an interruption that any task would properly have to wait upon her affection.

She was very happy during these years. Barbara had come home from China, matured and calm after her experience, and she did not care to return. She found exercise for her helpful impulses at home. There were more mill villages now and she seemed to know all the women and the children in them, and she was a minister of joy to them.

A mill population becomes peculiar. Set off from other life about it, all having the same experience, all living under the same conditions — mechanical conditions at that — they become a fixed class. This gave my brother much concern, and at Barbara's suggestion he had worked out a plan of inducing some mill families to go on farms and he brought other families who needed the discipline of mechanical regularity from farms, to take their places.

But, as I was saying, Barbara led a busy life that gave her helpful nature contentment; and my mother was made happy by her coming back to such normal work. And her grandchildren were now her particular joy, for she was come to that beautiful stage of white hair and immaculate caps and gardening joys and freedom from care that becomes early grandmotherhood.

I only was on her mind. I was her first-born. "So very like your father," she remarked, till we fell into the habit of smiling when she said so, and she unsuccessfully tried to leave off the habit. Charles would say to his little boy, when mother fondled him, "So very like your father," and get a slap from her on the cheek for his impudence.

Still she would come in from the garden with a vase of fresh flowers for my desk just when the chapter on "The Handicrafts of the Colonists" was fairly begun; and she would tell me how much she had learned about the care of rose-bushes from Adelaide Cooley. Louise Caldwell, too, had a boundless store of floral knowledge which she had learned as a girl in England. But there were some secrets which neither of them knew as well as her own mother; and (I am glad to recall) it took half the morning to explain these to me, who knew nothing of floriculture.

Another morning she would come in to make sure that the curtains did not obstruct the light or that they kept the glare out "while you are writing." She would have been sure, if you had asked her, that she had not entered my room except a moment now and then to see that I was comfortable. Yet it was in that room on those days that History suffered great delays and that I had the inestimable gain of renewing my childhood and of finding the compass of my life. As I write this narrative, I am conscious as I set down every incident that far more interesting incidents have slipped from my memory, for I have only certain lucid remembrances. But the day has not yet come when my mother's hovering about me those weeks or months or years seemed less clear than yesterday.

"I think you ought to marry, my son. You are already much older than your father or your brother was when they were married; and they were old enough to be good husbands."

Or, on another morning:

"I think that every Worth for five or six generations was married before he reached your age; and you bear your father's and your grandfather's name."

These remarks would fall without connection with what went before or with what came after — while the History waited.

And, in the afternoons when we would drive, she would say, "Your father planted those trees the very year we were married. He was then not as old as you are."

But all things, even affectionate interruptions, come to an end at last; and one day a long discussed plan was carried out — mother and Barbara went to Boston to make a visit to the Cooleys. There was some talk of my going with them, but I made an heroic resolve that nothing on earth should now interrupt me, and I remained at home.

But the long habit of being interrupted could

not be broken suddenly. If nothing else happened, my thoughts proved migratory. I recall that, instead of writing, I fell to wondering one day whether Louise Caldwell would really marry Cooley. Her friends said so. Why did I not find out? I ought to have gone to Boston and forced Cooley to tell me. But Louise herself — had I not known her since our childhood? Would she not tell me? Were we not good friends? Surely she had been the very fire and inspiration of our work. What a glory shone about her when she cheered us! What an extraordinary task she was doing herself in organizing the Women's School League. Had she taken time to think of marriage? And Cooley? Cooley would not see a great chance in marriage unless he had reasoned it out in the most logical way and eliminated every conceivable danger of error. Cooley had talked to me of all things but marriage. I had been in the swing of a great effort and my personal intimacies with him and everybody else had been neglected. Moreover, I was ever slow, I suspect, at discovering facts of this kind.

Yet, whenever my mother had let her suggestive remarks fall, I had seen Louise; and an emotional, clear remembrance stirred within me as I recalled her on horseback that morning in the mountains. Or sometimes I thought of her on the evening of our "winged victory." Or I saw her with my mother in the garden. It was always she that I saw. Again she would come to mind as the mistress of the pleasantest and most hospitable home during my life at the University, where she was one of us, not as a soft and restful mood but as a companion in our most active hours, our Lady of Battle. I had even come to call her "Lady."

I was amazed at my sloth, my foolish omission, my complete absorption in our public task. True (and here lay my difficulty as I now mused on the subject), Louise had not invited tender approaches. Something of an old sadness sat on her, except when she was fired by a great plan. She did not suggest nor provoke confidences and compliments, as my cousin Margaret had through all my boyhood. The man who should win her must buckle on his armour and do a doughty deed.

"The Handicrafts of the Colonies" suffered another delay while I went to Acropolis — to visit Richard. This particular year was going badly, he told me; I was gone from the University and Billy was busy at the Legislature; and he was glad that the year's work was nearly done. He would go to the mountains early. He talked so much about his plans and paid me such continuous attention that (it was plain) he thought I *had* come to visit *him*. And Louise was gone on a visit of a day to somebody — yes, she would come back to-morrow afternoon.

I had never yet gone wooing nor even reconnoitring when the lady seemed to expect me. I was weak enough at that moment to wish that the task could be done, when it were to be done, as any other great business of life — with a certain directness and without tantalizing delays.

While Richard was about his work the next day, I sat in "the great room" as they called it, and wrote Louise a letter. I had no notion of leaving it for her or of giving it to her; but it pleased my mood so to spend the time. I had come first to find out whether she were engaged to Cooley; for I regarded it as important to proceed with proper caution. Yet in that letter I wrote nothing about Cooley. I went to the main matter. And I confess to a most agreeable sensation in writing it. I was adding a postcript to it, which had drawn itself out as long as the letter itself, when a carriage drove up and she got out. I crumpled the letter into my pocket and hurried to open the door for her.

Her greeting was kindly, of course, and (so far as I could make out) unsuspicious. It was not a strange thing for me to be a visitor there, and there was nothing in her manner which showed even surprise, not to say excitement. As we walked into the room she stooped and picked up a piece of paper.

"Oh, that is a letter I was writing!"

When she gave the sheet to me, I betrayed such surprise that she smiled, and I began to talk about — plans for the summer.

"I have not had a chance to tell you," she said, "that I, too, am going to Boston. I simply couldn't get away when your mother and Barbara went, and Adelaide has made plans for my coming."

"Lady Louise," said I, descending like a thunderbolt, "am I rude to ask if Cooley also has not made plans for your coming?"

"I hope so."

"And are you not making plans for his coming here?"

"He is always welcome without plans."

And in a moment she asked: "When do you go to Greece?"

"When you marry Cooley."

"Have you your appointment yet?" she asked laughingly.

"Has Cooley his?"

"O Lady Louise," I cried, "it is I who — I —— "

"But I tell you" (and she ran toward the door) "that I am going to Boston. I have *that* appointment."

Caldwell came in then and she went out of the room.

At supper we talked of old subjects, of course.

The next morning, I had resolved to try no further to get her secret from her — that seemed dangerous for me. But I would go and see Cooley.

When I reached home I received a letter from him saying that he was engaged to be married! That settled it. Logical, straightforward Cooley, *he* had now told me, without my taking a long journey.

But what a pang seized me! If I recall the mood and I am sure to do, there came something very like despair. It was I who had borne the brunt of the battle, as I started to tell her — not Cooley. She was obliged to know what I had almost said; for she ran away before I could say it — mercifully ran away. And she would not tell me because I had bantered her — aroused her pride of fight.

But she was gone. At least she spared me the pain of hearing a refusal.

Then I finished Cooley's letter — the rest could be of no importance I was sure. "Yes, the Boston newspapers are just waking up to your political fight," he wrote — "to its good effects." *The Cotton Boll* had published much about the "Rump" Legislature, about the farmers' victory and the general awakening. The old State was coming to life, and Boston had heard of it. So Cooley wrote, and there was a wish, therefore,

in Boston to hear me explain the "revolution."
Would I not come and make an address to the
Midweek Club — two weeks hence? Besides,
I could then meet his betrothed, about whom he
would tell me more.

I must go — I saw that with painful clearness—
if for no other reason, because my refusal would
be misinterpreted by both Louise and Cooley.
But, after all, I had forced myself to believe, by
saying it over and over again, that I had saved
myself and her from open embarrassment. I
had not declared my love. She might guess.
Yet how could she know? But I must not fail to
congratulate them under the circumstances that
they had themselves prepared. I would bravely
go, therefore, and play the part assigned to me
and come home with mother and Barbara.
Apparently, too, Cooley and Louise were keeping
their engagement a secret from everybody, to
be sprung with some ado. For neither mother
nor Barbara had written of it in their short letters
to me.

I again put aside the History, and gave my
time to making notes of the address that I was
to deliver in Boston; but I wrote Louise this
jaunty little letter, to make sure that she should
know that I knew of her engagement, and with
the hope that she would think that I had known
it when I came near to embarrassing her. For,

if she thought that I then knew it, she would understand my speech as only an effort at innocent banter:

"Dear Lady Louise:

"I've heard from Cooley, you know; or did you not know? And you can guess what he wrote me, about which I shall speak when I may. This is only to tell you that he has written to me.

"Good-bye, till Boston; for I, too, go in a fortnight — to deliver an address on the 'revolution.' So many of us are going that soon the whole population will be 'tainted.' Look out lest you become 'Yankeeized.'"

I put off my journey to Boston a day later than I had meant to start because Uncle Ephraim sent me word that he'd be "mightly obleeged" if I'd meet him in town the day after to-morrow.

The old man told me of his perplexity about a very delicate duty which rested on his mind and which might, he feared, be performed discourteously; and he sought my judgment.

He had lately gone to see the Governor again, and this time he had not been kept waiting, for Tom Warren had again played fair. He received the old man and heard his whole story.

"I ain' tell 'bout me and de Guv'nor's talk ter no man livin', Mars' Littlenick, but you — not even Mars' Charlie, whenever I sees 'im ag'in. Nobody don' know it 'cept you and me an' Marthy.

"When I got done talkin' to de Guv'nor, he got up fum his cheer and walk de floo' and said:

"'Unc' Ephum,' says he, 'how I know dat dis gal is railly my chile? How I gwine ter know dat?' Den I says to him, 'Ef you wuz ter look at her an' den look in de lookin'-glass, you wouldn't ax dat question no mo'.'

"An' den he sez, 'Does you say dat yourse'f?'

"An' I sez, 'Yes, suh, dat's what I sez.'

"An' den he walk de floo' some mo', saying som'in ter hisse'f; an' den he walks right up ter me an' sez:

"'Unc' Ephum, you'se a jus' man. You think it's right dat I should purvide for dis chile? Many men does not.'

"Den I sez ter him, 'Yes, suh, fur who gwine purvide fer her when I'se gone? Her mammy done run off wid a yaller preacher, and Gawd knows what gwine ter 'come er her when I dies and Marthy dies; and we'se bof gittin' uncommon ol' and feeble.'

"An' den I tol' him 'bout dat school; and he'd heerd som'in 'bout dat som'ers befo'; and he set down den an' dar and write a check, an' he wen' out de doo' an' was gone a minit; an', when he comes back wid de money, he say,

'Sen' 'er at onc't an' I'll pay her bills dar —
somehow 'er ne'er.'

"Now what I wants ter know, Mars' Littlenick, is how he gwine ter pay dem bills 'thout
writin' his name dar atter I'm daid an' gone?

"An' would yer ax him 'bout dat? I do' wan'
ter pester 'im. De gal don' gone ter de school.
An' ought I go an' tell him she done gone? I
wants him ter know I done spen' de money right."

"No," said I, "say nothing more. The Governor will attend to it. He's a good deal of a
man, Uncle Ephraim."

"Yes, suh, he's a gem'man."

"Is that all that troubles you, Uncle Ephraim?"

"Yes, suh. So far-well, Mars' Littlenick. I
hopes you and Miss Anne and Mars' Charlie
and all de t'others un yer keeps mighty well.
Tell 'em how-dy fer de ol' man. I'se gittin'
mighty feeble. Mebbe I won' las' long. Far-
well ag'in, Mars' Littlenick. I'se much obleeged
to you, suh."

He was a prophet as well as a patriarch, for I
never saw him alive again.

CHAPTER XXIX

I WENT to Boston to congratulate Cooley, with rather a heavy heart. But I had fortified myself, and I would do it bravely. "That done," I had mused on the way, "I'll try to think out my own future, for it now seems somewhat blank."

The journey was a weary one. My thoughts were not good company. Then, too, there was the address that I had promised to deliver — that also was a bore now; for my campaigning fever had long ago run its course and I was no longer in the oratorical mood.

The way seemed longer even than it had seemed on my first journey to Harvard. How should I feign the surprise that I should be expected to show? Worse yet, how should I feign the pleasure that I should be expected to express? And why this foolish silence? They were mature persons, and to prepare a dramatic surprise was a juvenile performance — possibly out of taste, too. Besides, the news ought to be given out at her home, not his. They had all become very silly.

Yet I could not deny that the main matter had good sense to commend it. Cooley was a noble fellow, and Louise ought to live a wider life than she could ever find in Acropolis. She would adorn Boston and profit by her position there, a position of earnest elegance, with Cooley and Cooley's growing fortune. And surely they had been deliberate about it. I had only myself to pity or to blame — not them. But it would be an awkward business to see them. I wish it were done and over.

At last, of course, the train did arrive. I drove straight to the Cooley house. Mrs. Cooley and mother and Barbara and Adelaide and Cooley — they were all in a gay mood and gave me a hearty welcome.

How should I open the subject? And where was Lady Louise? There was no mention of her. When was the surprise to be sprung on me? And were the others in the secret?

"You've just time to dress for dinner, old man," said Cooley, after our greetings were over.

The mystery deepened. But *I'd* not show impatience, since they either did not feel impatience or were concealing it with remarkable success and unanimity. I'd show calmness, too — great calmness — even if before the evening were over I were obliged to take Barbara into my confidence and ask where Louise was.

When I came down to dinner, there they all were — except Louise. Well, I should not betray my curiosity.

I noticed a look on their faces that showed that something was about to happen.

Then Cooley grasped Barbara by the hand and led her in front of me.

"By your leave, sir ——"

It was Barbara, and not Louise!

When they laughed and mother put her hand on my shoulder, I did not know whether I was more surprised or gratified.

"By your leave, Nicholas," said Cooley again.

And I kissed Barbara and most heartily congratulated them.

But where was Louise? I should not ask abruptly; but I must find out.

Nothing was said about her during the dinner, and it was late in the evening when Barbara made casual mention of something that happened "while Louise was here."

"Where is she?" I asked, in as natural a tone as I could.

"She went home two days ago. Professor Caldwell was very impatient to get ready to go to the mountains ——"

It was the next night that I must deliver the address to the Midweek Club. Could I wait?

The night seemed ages long, and the next day was an eternity.

I made an address on Cotton, telling how a new civilization must and will be built — was already building itself — on it. I showed how Cotton is one of the fittest subjects of craftsmanship and of scholarship and of statesmanship. There is no wonder that it was King in the old controversies. It has shaped the life and so far as we can see it will always shape the life of the people in the Southern States — fortunately for them; for it will become the solvent of social troubles and race-differences.

"We must build our education on Cotton," said I, "and not merely copy and repeat the routine training of people elsewhere. We must study our soil, seeds, plants, varieties — breed better growths. We must bring all soil-science and planting skill to bear on this plant of many-sided values, about which we yet know little."

I pictured a family with a few acres — a comfortable family with profitable acres — lovingly studying the cotton-plant from the playtime of childhood till they became old, ever finding new values, new uses. Other farm products, of course, they grew for man and beast, and the cash that cotton brought was their comfortable profit. I pictured a community of farmers some with big and some with little farms, all skilful and conscientious in their studies and experiments and successes.

I pictured the place that Cotton must take in our school courses. To grow it well must be a part of every school-child's training. Then I told of its coming place in our mechanical and technical schools — how to pick it and to gin it and to bale it and to assort it and to spin it and to weave it; then of its place in our economic studies — it means a world-trade; then of its place in our literary studies as a fashioner of a life on the soil which, though rural, touches many crafts and many lands; then of its place in possible artistic studies.

"We yet have our peculiar problem," I said, "with its pathos and its humour; and we yet have our emotional strain, our quick pulse, our cheerfulness and our closeness to the soil; and here (so we believe) we shall work out a life somewhat different from the life of New England or the life of the prairie. But it may be an even fuller and richer life, being later and of a more leisurely coming; and we shall prove that our democracy is equal even to the strain put on it by the one great error of the Fathers."

The audience — certainly a part of it — was disappointed. They had "the South" in their minds associated only with the Negro; and they had expected me to talk mainly about our race-problem.

"We are deeply interested in the education and welfare of the coloured people," said the well-known Mr. Deemer; "and we know that you, too, are. We hoped that you might discuss that phase of Southern life somewhat."

"Yes; but with this difference from you, perhaps. I care nothing for the Negro merely because he is a Negro. I care for him because he is a man — or a child. I prefer to think of the people in the Southern States as a people — white and black alike — living under certain conditions, which can be made very fortunate and prosperous conditions, rather than about any particular class or race of them. The Negro has brought us much trouble, for which not he but your ancestors and mine are chiefly to blame; and it is too late to punish *them*.

"What you mean by the race-problem is, we hope, a temporary trouble. Cotton will remove it, if we master the arts and the sciences that it presents and suggests. It is all a matter of right training.

"In any proper scheme of education, there are no white men, no black men — only men."

"But," said Mr. Deemer with emphasis, "the black man was oppressed, enslaved, brutalized. Has he not a special claim on our help?"

"No. He was enslaved, but he profited by slavery more than the white man profited. He was oppressed in the sense that some slaves were oppressed wherever slavery has existed. Brutalized? He was a savage to begin with, and we have civilized him.

"You make it harder for us, my dear sir, who are giving our lives to train both black and white men, by the sort of emphasis that you put on the black man.

"You give aid and comfort to our enemies at home, to the men who would neglect and degrade the Negro; for you 'draw the colour line' in all speech and thought and action — the 'colour line' and the sectional line. You give plausibility to the argument which we have to meet constantly — that the good Yankees will take care of the Negro."

"But ——"

"Are you willing to take my word for it that every time you and men like you talk about this 'problem' (there is no 'problem'; it is a state of society) you make it worse?"

"But I was trying to explain," he went on. "Take the matter of the mixture of races, for instance — all illegitimate. Surely you grant that that is a great evil?"

"Granted. The same evil exists here — exists everywhere where women are weak. When you have stopped it here, come and tell us how you did it. If your talk about it in the South made one sin less, I should say 'talk."

"Agitation will ——"

"Merely muddle the mind and give our old politicians a longer lease of life. Let me make a practical suggestion. I will give you the names of two most excellent schools, one for poor white boys, one for coloured youth. They are doing right work. They need help. 'Help' means, money, clothes, books, tools — anything useful. If, whenever you feel the impulse to write or to speak about 'the race problem,' you will resist it and spend the same moral force in collecting money or any other useful things from your neighbours and will send what you collect to either of these schools, you will do a good deed in a world that has been talked to weariness."

Cooley applauded and the audience followed his example. But I fear that Mr. Deemer has ever since regarded me as a disappointment.

Then a bishop took up the subject. His condescension toward "the South" kept many good people from understanding us. The South was one of his "specialties." He went there every year to attend the meeting of the Board of a theological school for coloured youth. His attitude toward the South was very like Colonel Stringweather's attitude toward the North, with the difference that the Colonel was a poor man whom few knew, and the Bishop was a rich man and the companion of richer men; and he was much sought after and he talked unctuously to many 'philanthropists.' The poor old Colonel gloried in the poverty of our people. He used to say that the South was the only country left in the world where men are contented without money, believe in God, read Scott's novels, bake sweet potatoes properly, and vote the Democratic ticket. The Bishop suggested fat bank-checks of absolution — a sort of insurance fund of silence about sins near at hand.

This comparison, like most other comparisons of men, is unfair to both. For the Colonel came to believe his creed while he was preaching it and the Bishop also had repeated his till he probably thought it true. Yet, in God's name, are men not to be censured for believing false things?

In truth, the "professional" Southerner — the man whose capital in life is the fact that he is a Southerner — and your "professional" reformer of the South have many resemblances. Your Southerner shows his intimacy with the Deity by swearing; your reformer shows his intimacy by a condescending familiarity; and you may take your choice of them for bores. They are alike in that neither will learn anything; different only in the angle at which their complacent density misses common sense and a helpful knowledge of mankind.

But, at the Bishop's prodding, I made a confession which (as I recall it) ran thus:

"Is our dream ever to come true," I asked, "of a Southern people again become normal, well-balanced, just to all races, strong in political wisdom? and with their share of influence in our national life? Yes, at some time, but we must first be rid of one heavy drag on our minds and our emotions. I will make a confession to you that every candid Southern man must make — of a shadow that follows him.

"I do not myself, of my own will, carry or feel any sectional consciousness. It is the community that will not let me lose it — the present community, the past, and the shadow of the past, the whole combination of forces that we mean when we speak of 'The South.' For instance, I try to study the large problems of the Republic and I adjust myself to them precisely as I would if I had been born and lived in Boston or in San Francisco. But, while men in Boston and San Francisco may think their thoughts and express their opinions and work out their problems without a sectional consciousness, I may not.

"And the fault is not mine. It is first my community's fault. When I hold an opinion that differs from the dominant formula, I am asked if I have forgotten that I am a 'Southerner.' The sectional self-consciousness all about us — as the atmosphere is about us — has kept us sectionally self-conscious. I must be myself plus a 'Southerner.' Now a Southerner is a proper and proud thing to be, but (here comes the sorrowful paradox) I cannot be the Southerner that I should like to be, because of the presence of this must-be 'Southerner' — this self-conscious 'Southerner' that is thrust upon me. If it were not for this self-conscious 'Southerner' that must become a part of every public Southerner's self, better men would enter public life from these States.

"This shadow 'Southerner' is a dead man which every living man of us has to carry. He is the old defensive man.

"Nor does he cling to us at home only. He follows us wherever we go in the United States. You invited me here because I am a 'Southerner.' If I had been born in Ohio or in Pennsylvania you would not be interested in my experiences and opinions. Wherever we 'of the South' go, we are judged not on our merits. When men judge us they add something for this accidental reason or they subtract something; and they say, 'You were born in the South, were you not?'

"For this false note in our lives I lay blame especially on the attitude that you have toward the South. If you, you who live in New England in particular, would regard us who now live and work in these Southern Commonwealths as citizens of the Republic, your regarding us so would help to make us so. So long as we are regarded as a problem we must play the part of a problem, whether we will or no.

"And thus we carry an unfulfilled ambition that gives a deep seriousness to our lives, an ambition for these States and these people as a part of the Union. The ambition that men felt in the time of Washington, of Jefferson, of Marshall — this is what I mean. They and their fellows, who were our ancestors, wrought out their high wish. Our wish, equally high, we have not wrought out, and you hinder us. In the life, in the thought, in the conduct of the Republic, we have not the share that we should like to have. In our own fathers' house, we are yet disinherited in a certain sense, disinherited because of the shadow 'Southerner,' whom you help to keep alive.

"Do you wonder that we are become weary of being a problem? We do not ask your pity; but we do ask your sympathy and your understanding — we of the post-bellum South who had nothing to do with its old misfortunes, but whose lives must be spent in the struggle out of the shadow of them. We ask that we be regarded in a normal way."

Deemer — old Deemer — for, though he was then less than forty, he seemed as old as Bunker Hill monument, so solemn and impersonal was he and so lacking in perspective and adaptability and humour and imagination, being the product of a long ancestry of pedagogues that had bred down in him to mere precision of speech, and of another line of moralists that had transmitted to him only two formulas, one about Peace, the other about the Coloured Man — poor old Deemer, who had written a pamphlet on "A Better Organization of Human Society" and had never seen the humour of such an effort — for Deemer, these smiles and tears. And he lived with Mrs. Deemer — properly enough — for she also carried in her mind a geometrical plan of civilization by which she could instantly measure any new idea that came along. There are conceivable conditions in life where Colonel Stringweather would have been companionable; for he drank and prayed and swore and sent missionaries to the Congo, and cursed "niggers" at home, but he had the charm of forgetfulness if not the faculty of learning.

It was saying something like this to Cooley as we walked home, and he remarked:

"You know Mrs. Deemer is rich, don't you? Do you know how she got her fortune? One of her ancestors laid the foundation of it in the slave-trade. Another Bristol story. The family has not even yet quite the social stand that it aspires to."

"You know," I reminded him in turn, "that Edwards's father — Edwards, of *The White Man* — was a slave-trader. Allies yet. Truly an abnormal interest in the Negro seems to descend to the second and the third and the fourth generations."

Poor old land! It has not only to bear its inherited misfortunes and its continued follies, but it has also to hear, above the sorrows of its children of two races, the gospels of saviours whom we may not crucify!

Cooley and (worse yet) mother and Barbara expected me to remain in Boston several days — perhaps a week. How I should manage gracefully to go had annoyed me all day. But (thank heaven!) just before we went to the Midweek Club, a telegram came from Charles, saying that he'd be glad if I could come home soon.

I told them, then, that most important business pressed for attention at home; and a good train for the South left at midnight. I must go.

Did ever a man come to such a turn in the road as this when he was breathless on such an errand? The longer I live the more I wonder at the ungeometrical plan of any human life.

I bade them all good-bye (I was sorry I couldn't wait to go with them), and in the sleeping-car before my thoughts would come to the main track that they must now run on, I had time to think again, as I always thought on a visit to Boston, of the orderliness, the thrift, the frankness of the people — a clean land, clean towns, open minds, a frank and unaffected interest in public affairs, men and women who read books, who talk well, who know what other interesting folk are doing in every part of the world, who get pleasure from the arts, who live an intellectual life, who have full freedom of opinion and of expression — no zones of silence. I felt intellectually at home with them, as I felt intellectually at home nowhere else. And yet a man who had only his own personal career to work out, a mere personal success to achieve, a fortune to build, a professional standing to win, or even a larger problem to solve in an orderly and free community where public opinion has its normal action — how small a task that seems! The glorious thing is to do a larger service, and the greater the difficulties the greater the service.

But — now I will soon finish my interrupted conversation with Louise — at last. ."Good night, you wretched, happy, hopefully weary, baffled dog!" I said to myself, and fell asleep, as the train went southward. "May you now hit the right trail at last!"

CHAPTER XXX

THE FRUITS OF VICTORY

I HAVE ever been subject to interruptions, as some dispositions are to malaria; and all my enterprises suffer delays, this orderly narrative among the rest. Thus the rush of other things has now carried me past the real event of the whole story. For it is time you were learning that events do sometimes come to pass even in our dateless, long-summered life. To go back a little, then:

Professor Billy was right, as, upon my soul, I believe he always was. The Legislature turned out to be not only friendly to our programme to train the people but eager for it. The country members who came up to Marlborough, as they became acquainted with one another, discovered that better schools and more of them was what the people wanted. Professor Billy had been very active among them. He knew them all, and they turned to him as their guide. He was a countryman like themselves; he spoke their speech; he told the kind of stories that they liked; and he told them better than any other man.

More than that, he was the boon companion of all his enemies. As soon as a man opposed him, he sought him and won him. Senator Barker's sport was fishing, and Professor Billy was the best fisherman in the Commonwealth, and they talked on long tramps down the river. The Reverend Doctor Suggs had no sports, except argumentation and gluttony; and Professor Billy found it convenient to appear on Sunday mornings at Marlborough and to attend the doctor's church and walk home with him to dinner, which he, too, enjoyed and praised. Note you well — he did not assume these pleasures. He really liked to fish. He really enjoyed Senator Barker's companionship. He really liked to hear old Suggs preach, and he loved a good dinner as well as Suggs loved it. In the meantime, he visited the half-dozen most enterprising towns in the State and suggested to the business men that a great State college for women would be of commercial advantage to the town in which it should be situated; and perhaps the Legislature would establish such a school if proper advances were made. How much would the Board of Trade subscribe? Would it guarantee a proper site and take up a subscription to put up one building?

As soon as the Legislature was organized, therefore, and the committees were appointed, the Committee on Education of the House began to receive bids from different towns for such a college. This was helpful; for, if any town should subscribe a large sum, the appropriation by the Legislature might be, by that much, smaller.

And so it came about, with surprising promptness, that the Committee set a day when these rival towns should be heard. Members of the Boards of Trade from half a dozen of them came. The project had now entered the stage of competition — it appealed to the sporting mood of each group of men. If Marlborough would bid so much, Edinboro would bid more; and thus the excitement ran high. It seemed to be taken for granted that the college would now be established. The only question was, which town shall have it? By a happy chance — Professor Billy was a pastmaster at bringing happy chances about — Senator Barker came from Washington on the day of the Committee's hearing; and he was, of course, invited to be present and to make an address. And it was not the Committee only that would hear him; for there were so many "delegates" from rival towns and so many women present that the meeting had to be held in the hall of the House; and the Legislature adjourned for the day so that all the members might attend the meeting.

Professor Billy and the gods had much merriment that day at the unfolding of events, especially at the progress of Senator Barker's great speech.

The distinguished Senator began by recalling the fact that he had always "favoured" a great college for our women, God bless 'em; and, even when other subjects of the public interest had seemed to press more urgently, he had never opposed it, if done under "proper auspices"; and now he believed that the time was ripe.

Then there issued from his vast caves of speech a honeyed blast of compliments to the fair daughters of our happy land. "To them my thanks, my most grateful and eternal thanks, as an old Confederate, for their loving tribute to the loyal dead of the Lost Cause — their unceasing devotion shown by their completion of the Soldiers' Monument, which will stand forever, whatever wind blow, as a proof of their noble gratitude and appreciation.

"In proposing such a school, therefore, I am not proposing class-legislation, as it has sometimes been feared, but legislation for the nurture of men and women alike. The hand that rocks the cradle rules the world — our fair women, God bless 'em."

Governor Warren, too, most heartily approved the plan "as now presented to a Democratic Legislature, under auspices that will ensure the conduct of such a great school after the approved methods of our own people."

It turned out, too, that the religious press had

no objections to offer — another happy chance. Just at that moment, in fact, their two principal papers were engaged in a bitter theological war about infant baptism; and the reverend editors had all their belligerent vocabulary in use against one another.

Thus the college came into being as the creature of the Senator's gallantry. Was it not his plan from the first, which he had held back till the time should be fully ripe? And you may now read over the door of the main building in stone letters the words "Barker Hall," and see a life-size portrait of the Senator hanging in the hall. The inscription under it recites that he was "one of the distinguished founders of this school."

O History, what a wayward tongue you have, whether you speak in script or stone or paint or legend!

But again Senator Barker and other things have hurried me unduly for the orderly conduct of this narrative. I must tell you that Energetic Edinboro made the highest bid for the college — a beautiful site and enough stone from nearby quarries for all the buildings required. For the young commercial men of Edinboro were not to be outdone.

And Professor Billy was immediately chosen President of the College for Women and instructed to superintend the building and organization of it.

Nor was this all that the newly loosed zeal of the long-neglected people did. "The School of Cotton Crafts" was a phrase that stuck in the memories of men in the cotton counties. We had all spoken of that when we had suitable audiences; and it was an easy thing to explain because Charles and Barbara had planned it and, to an extent, worked it out at Millworth. Having made proof of the popular favour with which the college for women was received, the legislative committee now showed a mood to establish also a school of cotton-crafts. Thus suddenly and unexpectedly the hitherto unnoticed work at Millworth came into great notoriety. There was, in some quarters, a conscientious avoidance of linking my name with it; for, mind you, my educational programme had been "overwhelmingly repudiated"; and all plans that were now brought forward bore the careful label of "after the manner of our own institutions," so that the Senator and the Governor and Mr. Superintendent Craybill could in good faith and with good face support them as the plans of this "educational administration."

Charles found himself famous, as he deserved, and the legislative committee sent a "special educational commissioner" North, even to Massachusetts, to find out and to describe "the best things in modern educational practice." The commissioner was a young fellow who had been a pupil of Professor Billy's, but he had taken no offensive part in public agitation. He had gone to see the Senator and the Governor and Major Thorne at Professor Billy's suggestion.

And someone who will write more freely of my brother Charles than I can write will, I have no doubt, some day tell you the whole story of what he had done and planned and foreshadowed; for it means a new, long step in both our economic and social history, which even yet has not been fully taken nor wholly understood.

The cotton crafts reach from the proper preparation of seed to the best artistic designs for fabrics; and all these were sketched at Millworth. But, of course, the humbler economic steps were first to be taken; and it was chiefly at such tasks that Charles had worked.

I do not know whether you have happened ever to think of it — that a hundred years hence, to say nothing of five hundred or a thousand, every foot of soil that will grow the cotton-plant well will be worth — who shall say what? For there will then be many millions more human creatures to be clad and adorned, but there will be no more acres of earth on which cotton will grow well.

"Therefore, men," my brother said every Christmas to his most skilful workers, when the big Millworth dinner was eaten, to which every worker in the villages sat down — "therefore, men, during the coming year the farmers' coöperative company hopes to see as many as possible of you admitted by the Land Committee to land-ownership. Unimproved land is the cheapest thing we have in our country. A few years' skilful work will make it the most valuable thing in our country. Every man here may have as many acres, up to twenty, as he and his family can cultivate to the required standard — free of charge, to become his as soon as he brings it to that degree of culture which your own committee requires.

"In a word, every man here may become a skilled farmer and the owner of a farm, free, as soon as he prove that he is worthy of owning land."

It was very simple. The unimproved land was cheap. In every direction the mill companies and the coöperative farm company bought it, with a certain small proportion of their profits which were set aside for this purpose. Contrary to prediction, the price of unimproved land had not greatly risen after years of this regular buying. The increase of value was in the price of the improved land.

The standard of cultivation laid down was high. The staple crop must be cotton and the yield required was at least four times as great as the average yield had been by the old methods; and other crops also must be grown — vegetables, fruits, corn and hay enough for the stock; and every farm must yield some such by-products as poultry and cream; and all these things were supervised by the superintendents and experts of the coöperative farms' company, which was made up of those who had already come to own land.

"We have few sick women and children," Barbara boasted, "for, before they become sick, they are sent to do light outdoor work on the farms. A strawberry patch, a poultry yard, a lettuce garden, a cabbage field, to say nothing of the cotton-fields themselves, are the best preventives of illness. And half the small farming in all these places is done by happy women and children, some of whom have become surprisingly skilful. The danger is that the mills will be able to get only the left-over and least intelligent workers — if it be right to call that a danger; and success on the farms has already forced an increase in mill wages."

Charles, not being an academic economist, maintained, against Cooley's opinion, that the private ownership of land, as we have it now, is sure to cease when the pressure for its use becomes strong enough, as it will become; and it was his notion that the farming company should give men land to be held free so long as it should be cultivated to a required standard. "This is the first step," he would say. "The men who use the land best must at last get its fruits, and our system of ownership and control must ultimately shape itself to this primary principle of justice; and, for the present, the cost of the land is so little that it is an economy to give it away if you can give it to productive users of it. Our predecessors seemed to regard land as more valuable than men. The Millworth plan regards land only as one instrument for training men; and land becomes whatever the men on it make it."

It thus came about, as you know, that Millworth became famous. A stream of writing economists and reformers came to see the villages. The country was flooded with much printed misunderstanding of a simple thing. There were men who now saw the way to the millennium, forgetting that the millennium itself will require the best possible leadership and the most careful management.

"Your men of learning know less," said Charles, "about the practical management of men than any other class, I verily believe. Not one has ever come here, I think, but came out of the clouds and went back into the clouds again. They expect some 'system,' some 'trick,' some economic device to work a change in men —

instead of plain, straight skill and work; and they think that 'systems' manage themselves. They always think of the land first — of men afterwards."

But the "hayseed" legislators went straight to the point. We must have a school of cotton crafts, they said; and they fell to discussing the real work that had been done at Millworth. Not only, then, had Professor Billy's plan been carried out, but it looked as if the dream that I had sketched from Charles's work would also come true. In a word, the work that I wished to have done seemed likely to be done without my having the trouble to do it — done by the very men who had "overwhelmingly defeated" me. I have my vanities, I am sure, but they were not so great as to mar my pleasure at this result.

As for Professor Billy, the best way to make sure of his success, it was proved, is to oppose him, to defeat him, to "bury him out of sight"; "for," said he, "if you really believe in the people and serve them till they believe in you, their political masters become your slaves."

The educational commissioner reported to the legislative committee that most of the States made far larger appropriations to the public schools than our State, and the Legislature forthwith doubled the former sums granted, and passed an act permitting local school taxation to be greatly increased.

You may say that all the facts that this young man discovered were well known and had been repeatedly published and explained by us all. True; but do you, too, not forget the difficult art of managing men for their own upbuilding?

There is knowledge enough now in the world to construct a millennium (and that is what your dreamer does and expects the perfect day to dawn); but it cannot come until men have used this knowledge to their own upbuilding. For, when a better social and economic order does come, it will not come by any "system" of economics or other doctrine, but by the definite personal work of a long succession of great leaders of the people and by the slow tuition of experience; and the new order, which is ever brought nearer when a great leader arises, will be only a slowly evolved society of human beings most of whom are willing to work more skilfully, to live scientifically, and to act toward one another more justly than we are willing to do.

When, therefore, you and I build our dream of the City of our Hope (as, praise God, all men must), we will remember that its wide arches rest on the long-forgotten, joyful labour of men like Charles Worth and William Malcolm Bain;

for they loved their fellows and found life sweet in toiling for them.

And now, by your leave, back to my own immediate dream; and, if I have thus far done you the slightest pleasure by this poor tale, you will now pray with me that it may come true.

CHAPTER XXXI

TO THIS HIGH MOMENT

I TOOK the precaution this time to inform Louise that I was coming. On the train I wrote her a note saying what an infamous joke it was that Barbara and Cooley had played on me.

"I did not approve of such indirection. Still, a man can not rise higher than his companions and surroundings, and I laughed with them at myself. To get the laughing done with, I shall go to Acropolis to-morrow, to hear your ridicule and to have it over."

I wrote that and other such light matter in a note that was sent as courier to what I meant should be the most momentous visit of my life.

That night I had some dull talk with Charles — it seemed dull to me, and he remarked that the journey had tired me — about Barbara and mother and about my little speech in Boston and old Deemer. "I'd like to see him," said Charles. "He must be a sort of rarified and refined Babb, since he knows God and His purposes so well."

But he was glad — very glad indeed — that I

had hurried home, bringing him the news. For Barbara had written to nobody about her engagement to Cooley. A committee of the Legislature was coming to Millworth the next day to see the farm and the mills and the farm school. They seemed very earnest about the establishment of the School of Cotton Crafts; and I could help him entertain them and explain the farm and the mills and what they meant. He was very glad I had come. The news about this committee's visit had reached him the day I left home for Boston, and he had telegraphed me on that account.

"May I pay attention to the committee when they first come and show them the farm, and then leave them to you and the mills in the afternoon, and may I go to Acropolis where I have an engagement to-morrow with Caldwell?"

"Oh, yes."

And I wondered what else could happen to delay me.

I reached Acropolis just as everybody was finishing supper. The Caldwells, I was sure, had waited for me and I drove straight to their squatty stone house. The doors were shut, the windows were closed; I saw no light.

"Dey done gone, suh, ter de mount'ins. Day b'fore yisterday de perfessur and Miss Call'well shet up and went off," said the driver, who might have told me sooner.

To-morrow was Sunday, and no train ran toward the mountains on the Sabbath — not so long as the firm of Suggs & Babb did business for the Lord.

I am impatient now at the mere remembrance of these dilatory incidents. Why a man who had known and admired a woman for a long time should hit upon one certain day or week rather than another when he becomes suddenly determined to win her — that I leave you to decide for yourself, while I hurry on with these eager memories. But, when he has hit upon such a day, Good Lord give him decent speed!

At last I reached the railway station at the foothills, and there was a long drive up the mountains. Caldwell had built his summer hut on the outskirts of our highest mountain village — of course, as far away as possible.

It was in the afternoon when the stage began the drive of thirty miles up the mountain. We went half the distance beside a river which plunged down, turning here and there for mere practice of its strength, a toy-like mill. Now and then we passed a comfortable mountaineer's house. But the cabins of the left-over people were as barren as the pathetic little churches. We saw but one school-house. Barefoot children with meager clothing ran out of the huts to gaze at us.   These fertile valleys were cultivated only here and there, all badly.

We reached a terrace on the steep slope where the road turned to a gentler grade.   Over the declivity I saw the winding valley miles away below, infrequent huts dotting the long landscape, and the river stretching like a ribbon till the lowlands were lost in the mist.

At the next turn the sky had become red with the approach of the sunset.   The air was cooler. An orange and crimson panorama spread toward infinity before us.

We had driven through the richest imaginable forests, dense and odorous, and an incalculable carpet of undergrowth gave bloom and perfume, fold on fold; and now the road was fringed with mountain laurel, and the great rhododendron would soon open its gorgeous and endless show of splendour — the very garden of the gods and a play place left yet for half a continent.

We passed, in this land of enchantment, a hovel by the road from which five half-clad children rushed, followed by a lean and noisy cur; and a slatternly woman stood in the door. A little patch of corn and a little patch of cabbages were visible at one side.   And we overtook a man a little farther on with whom I had conversation.

"Do'ant know this here country none too well.

I lives on t'other road yan side o' Ochawatchie.
But my bus'ness takes me ever'whares — sellin'
sewin' machines an' organs. Is yer frum New
York?"

"No; but I came through New York the
other day."

"Is bus'ness purty peart thar now?"

"I suppose so."

"When you wuz thar did you happen to see
the sewin' machine men, Johnson and Thomas?
They mus' be mighty peart in bus'ness."

This, within that scarlet and blue horizon, and
under that dome — changing splendour following
changing splendour — and in the reverent shadows
of the most incalculable and multitudinous growth
and bloom and perfume, the gay riot of sun and
rain for ten thousand years; and I turned from our
fellow-traveller in silence, for pity and for shame.

The delicious night came on before we reached
the village. It was too late to go up the mountain
to Caldwell's — at least I so decided.

But I was still debating that question while
I ate supper at the village hotel. I was with
alternate smiles and vexation recounting my
delays and repeating to myself the errand I was
come on. "And the end of it?" I must have
said aloud, for the Negro waiter answered.

"What yer say, boss?"

"Bring me more waffles."

"Yes, suh, right off' er de griddle."

Is this a thing ordained by nature, planned by the very gods from the beginning, as all lovers fondly persuade themselves their happy matings are ? Or is it only a plan that I had carefully reasoned out as I had accused Cooley of reasoning all things out ?

It was both. True it might have come gently and naturally some day while we were talking of other things. But it didn't happen so to be ordained. It must be a matter of hot pursuit and of fierce combat.

And the result ? If it had been so meant in the fitness of all beautiful things, there could be no doubt. And with this comfortable reflection I fell asleep in the hotel, to the sound of a mountain stream tumbling over the rocks in the yard.

The next afternoon Louise and I were walking on the table-land where I had seen her that memorable morning on horseback. We had talked during the day of many things — of all deep things of life; for there was a solemnity in the joy that I had come to seek. All life's plans — the miserable waste of time that had passed — it takes any life so long, so very long, to find itself and precious years are gone before we begin to live. And the future — one must, when the adjustment is found — make sure that the road ahead leads straight.

Go to Greece? Oh, no! I should go nowhere. Everything had been made plain by the one effort of our lives. Action and only action clears the vision. Work, work here, noble, constructive work here — it seemed a high privilege.

With the vanity of a lover I had directed all the talk about myself.

"But you?" I asked. "You may live where you will. There is Boston, where the arts find expression — there is music, there are men and women who read and think and talk, intellectual companionship and growth, men of wit and women of refinement, the flash and radiance of trained minds. Here the battle to be won is a rough one — man's work rather than woman's."

"I will recite the old creed," she said, and we walked toward the precipice where there was the far view of the valley.

"*I believe in this land — our land — whose infinite variety of beauty and riches we do not yet know. Wake up, old Land!*

"*I believe in these people — our people — whose development may be illimitable. Wake up, my People!*

"*I believe in the continuous improvement of human society, in the immortality of our democracy, in the rightmindedness of the masses. Wake up, old Commonwealth!*"

We had now reached the summit. The sinking

sun was making such a show of colour over Flower Mountain that the whole universe seemed bathed in brilliancy — one infinite canvas of ever-changing gorgeousness.   We stood for a moment in silence, and the whole drift of the day's talk, the whole force of our lives and the convergence of all our hopes pushed toward one great utterance — pushed with all the force of the inevitable; and the silence became heavy between us.

Then she said, "Shall we go?"

"No, Louise, I have come to stay with this vision.   I have found the fulness of life at last."

She looked at the great mountain across the valley.

"Life," I said "has climbed to this high moment, through errors and uncertainties climbed — to this high moment when the way seems clear and I am here — to stay?"

I clasped both her hands.

"I think it was meant to be so," she said simply.

I drew her to me.

"When we were at Acropolis I wished you to come here," she whispered, "because I love these mountains.   They bring the heroic mood. And my lover must be a man of the heroic mood."

"You make him so."

"There are men that are led by thought; there are men that are led by dreams; but the dreamer who thinks is the leader of them all. Great men tell great dreams here, Nicholas," and she pointed again toward the blazing horizon.

"And the dream is come true," I said.

"Forever true."

"True forever."

There was a noise on the path leading to the bungalow. I turned and saw a boy with a telegram in his hand.

"This is for Mr. Worth."

It was from Charles.

"Professor Bain was killed instantly this morning by a blast at the Edinboro quarry."

We were silent for a time, 'till I found my voice:

"Oh, Love, the master-spirit of our little world is gone."

We stood on the cliff and saw the enfolding darkness creep up the vast slope; and, forth into the uncharted silence, O Brother, we spoke our unheard good night.

Then we walked home, too happy and too sad for speech.

CHAPTER XXXII

MY BROTHER and I have kept the Old Place, to which another generation learned to make pilgrimages of childhood. We often went there with our children in pleasant weather for a night of story-telling; and we did not forget to tell them about the two old men who lie near each other beyond the garden. Their great-grandfather and Uncle Ephraim thus took places in their minds (as I was glad to see) among their heroes. Sometimes they kept company, in their young memories, with Agamemnon, sometimes with George Washington — no matter: they were safely placed in those galleries of the great down which we may look all our lives because we looked down them first in childhood.

When Nicholas Worth IV. ("he will be the haid o' de fam'bly") became old enough to go to college, I said to him what my grandfather had said to me. He had been about the world somewhat, as I had not while I was a lad; and I wished his horizon to be as wide as possible. He took the cue. I was a Harvard man — so would he be. And now the time had come for his graduation.

He knew something of our problems, for, though sanitation has begun to clear them up, they were with us yet, in milder forms. He, too, had perhaps felt some repression in the atmosphere, but he had know a freedom of opinion that I had won only after many a hard battle. I had made plain to him my own struggles, and I had told him, as well as I could, what he might expect. He might live where he would. He need not inherit our misfortunes. I wished him to be free.

What would he do and where would he live?

His mother and I were talking with him on these subjects on his day of bloom at his college. He was now become a man, and he seemed well balanced and quiet in spirit. Ah! how that wild night of my oratorical triumph came back to me with a surging remembrance! Had this boy emotions, or was the stock breeding down to calmness?

That night, when I came in from a dinner with some old friends, he was sitting in his mother's room at our hotel.

"Nicholas tells me," said she in tears (I think they were tears of joy, but you cannot always be sure of the cause of a woman's tears) — "Nicholas tells me that he wishes to live in the South; for he wishes to serve his own country."

" *To serve his own country* " — the very phrase over again! I fell into a dream, and went far back into a previous era of existence, and travelled over thirty years. I was just returning from this journey when I heard his next sentence:

"Yes, sir, there is nothing so noble as the work you have done to build up our people — you and Uncle Charles. It is the great task of our time. I should not do my duty to seek a career elsewhere."

Patience — a long patience even yet; but he, too, believes, with the fine instinct of youth, that the democratic idea has gradual healing in it for all social evils and misfortunes. And it seemed to me proof of a high quality that he should hear and heed when a hard, long task calls him. How long, how hard, no one could tell him.

It is sometimes difficult to recall the long journey that we have travelled since the days of Senator Barker and Colonel Stringweather and Captain Bob Logan and the rest. They now seem centuries behind us.

And yet I see some of the same shadows that fell across the paths of men now long dead — the same shadows across the same paths; and, although the men that now go these ways are not the same, yet so nearly like their forerunners are they that you cannot put your finger on the calendar at any one day or year or decade (or century ?) and say: "Here men change from what they were." But on any day or year or decade you may say: "Men are to-day much like their fellows of yesterday, except that they have a little wider sympathy and a little better knowledge of one another." Therefore, every day brings its joy to him who does not expect too much.

And in truth the mill villages this very autumn with the fields about them white with cotton, in this soft air that invites to easy labour, is a place that much-travelled men might envy us; and I hear the falling water in the river. These are fundamental forces and for us they mean home; and, however far a man may wander, I suspect that his home is where his highest task calls.

And this very autumn, too, when quail were thick on the Old Place, I went there with my son, my nephews, and a group of their friends for a few days' sport. One day it was dark — I was sure it would rain. The weather did not deter the young fellows, but I decided to remain indoors. Besides, I might get a quiet morning on the History. I had some time before found a copy of "Cotton is King and pro-Slavery Arguments," which I had brought to the house as I might bring back an old piece of furniture that belonged there; and, instead of writing, I was sitting by the fire reading for my amusement the argument of a once-great bishop to show that slavery was divinely ordained. The coloured boy came in and told me that a lady had driven to the gate and was coming toward the house.

I went to the door and met her.

"If I am not intruding" — she began, in some confusion, "is — is this place for sale?"

"No, madam."

"Perhaps — I must have been misinformed." She was evidently merely finding an excuse to talk. "It is the old home, is it not, of Mr. Worth?"

"Yes, I am Mr. Worth."

She had not yet told me who she was. She wore a heavy veil. I confess that I was puzzled. It had, I dare say, been many a year since any strange lady had come here.

"Mr. Nicholas Worth?" she asked. "Yes? I am Mrs. Wheelwright, of Pittsburgh. You do not know me?"

Then, with a sad smile, she lifted her veil and said, "I am Julia — Lissa's child, and I was a baby here."

She had come, she said, to see her childhood's home and Uncle Ephraim's grave.

Then she told me her history.

Tom Warren had again "fought fair." He had sent money to complete her education. She had lived through her whole girlhood at a school in Nashville, Tenn. There she was graduated and then went to Oberlin College, in Ohio — still as a "coloured" girl; but her "colour" would never be detected outside the South. From Oberlin she had gone to one of the smaller cities of Illinois, where she "passed as white," and there she became a teacher in the public schools. The only person who knew her whole career was a good woman in the faculty at Nashville.

"I tell you," she said, "what nobody else knows."

She had married a mechanical engineer many years older than she, who by an invention had become a man of considerable fortune; and they now lived in Pittsburgh. She had come South for a few weeks "for her health" — with no idea that she would reveal her identity to anyone. After this pilgrimage to the Old Place, she would start home the next day.

We talked long. We went through the garden to see the graves of the two old men. Often her eyes became moist as she recalled this or that incident of her childhood; and so did mine.

When she drove away, I sank into as deep a reverie as ever overwhelmed a man. This had been her home, and there was no human being but me to whom she could tell so simple a fact without risk of wrecking her own life and her husband's life. She had stolen away and made a long journey to see it once more. Even to her father she dared not reveal herself for her own sake as well as his. He had other daughters now — very like her, I noticed.

The young men came in from the hunt. I told them that a strange thing had happened. A "Yankee" woman had called to ask if the place was for sale, and she looked over it, and I had a long and interesting talk with her. "Shall we sell the Old Place, boys?"

They looked up with wonder at so absurd a question, and we passed from the subject with a laugh — as we pass by many dark tragedies that lurk just behind the hedges of our lives.

We all hope, indeed, that the Old Place will be kept by Nicholas Worths yet unborn; for we have made its large hall a library and a sort of abbey of the great of our little world; and we have put there mementoes and memorials of them for our children to see. In one book — a little biography and volume of addresses which we have had beautifully bound — you may, if you care to, read this inscription that Lady Louise and I wrote:

This to his Inspiring Memory — his Unquenchable Gayety of Spirit, the Boundless Sweep of his Sympathy, and his Conquering Confidence in all the People of this Commonwealth, who Owe him a Joyful Immortality of Gratitude.

Therefore to you who read this, if you believe (as I do) that our American ideal is invincible and immortal and that men may in truth govern themselves and give fair play and abolish privilege and keep the doors of opportunity open — even here where fell the Shadow of the one Great Error of the Fathers — we who have toiled where doubt was heaviest now send good cheer.

THE END